PRAISE FOR ROBERT WHITLOW

"Robert Whitlow has pulled back the curtain on a dilemma of the heart. What are the ramifications of Jon's desire to help someone else? The story is a mirror for the reader—will we choose to love and serve others even at great personal cost?"

—CHRIS FABRY, CHRISTY HALL OF FAME AUTHOR, FOR *WITNESS PROTECTION*

"*Double Indemnity* is another winner from Robert Whitlow, one of my favorite authors. The taut suspense builds until the likable pastor is falsely accused of murder, and his new girlfriend, an attorney, has to solve the case. Highly recommended!"

—COLLEEN COBLE, *USA TODAY* BESTSELLING AUTHOR OF *THE VIEW FROM RAINSHADOW BAY* AND THE ANNIE PEDERSON SERIES

"A rich and compelling story of family, faith, and friendship with just the right dose of legal thriller, *Relative Justice* is a winner."

—*SOUTHERN LITERARY REVIEW*

"Robert Whitlow's legal expertise shines in *Relative Justice*, a story of patent infringement and illegal gains, but it's his characters who will steal the readers' hearts. Katelyn Martin-Cobb, her husband, Robbie, and his family face trials that allow them to heal old wounds and forge new bonds. Whitlow's fans are sure to enjoy going along for a memorable roller-coaster ride."

—KELLY IRVIN, AUTHOR OF *TRUST ME*

"*Promised Land* is a book about coming home. Of becoming settled in your spirit and your relationships. With layers of intensity, thanks to international intrigue, moments of legal wrangling, and pages of sweet relationships, this book is rich and complex. A wonderful read."

—CARA PUTMAN, AUTHOR OF *LETHAL INTENT*

"This tense legal thriller from Whitlow boasts intriguing characters . . . One gripping chapter leads to the next . . . Readers will have a hard time putting this one down."

—*PUBLISHERS WEEKLY* ON *CHOSEN PEOPLE*

"If you're looking for a book with unexpected twists and turns that delves into the cultures of Palestine, Israel, and their peoples, you must check out this engaging novel."

—BOOKREPORTER.COM ON *CHOSEN PEOPLE*

"A legal thriller written from a contemporary evangelical Christian worldview, *Chosen People* presents intriguing, well-rounded characters, thought-provoking moral dilemmas, tense drama, and several surprising plot twists."

—*MYSTERY SCENE*

"My verdict for Robert Whitlow's *Chosen People*: compelling, realistic, and inspiring. Robert combines the intensity of a legal battle against terrorists with a poignant depiction of Israel, with all of its tensions and grandeur. As a lawyer who handles cases for terrorism victims, I loved the realism of the novel and felt deeply the joys, disappointments, and triumphs of its characters. But the matters of the law were eclipsed by matters of the heart—faith, love, and hope in the midst of despair—this is where Whitlow truly shines."

—RANDY SINGER, BESTSELLING AUTHOR OF *RULE OF LAW*

"Whitlow writes a fast-paced legal suspense with amazing characters. There are twists and turns throughout, and a number of unexpected surprises to heighten the suspense. Whitlow is an amazing writer and he touches upon delicate topics with grit and respect."

—*RT BOOK REVIEWS*, 4 STARS, ON *A TIME TO STAND*

"Whitlow's timely story shines a spotlight on prejudice, race, and the pursuit of justice in a world bent on blind revenge. Fans of Greg Iles's *Natchez Burning* will find this just as compelling if not more so."

—*LIBRARY JOURNAL*, STARRED REVIEW, ON *A TIME TO STAND*

"Part mystery and part legal thriller . . . Definitely a must-read!"

—*RT BOOK REVIEWS*, 4 STARS, ON *THE WITNESSES*

"Whitlow's characters continuously prove that God loves the broken and that faith is a lot more than just showing up to church. [This] contemplative novel is a fine rumination on ethics, morality, and free will."

—*PUBLISHERS WEEKLY* ON *THE WITNESSES*

"Attorney and Christy Award–winning author Whitlow pens a character-driven story once again showcasing his legal expertise . . . Corbin is highly relatable, leaving readers rooting for his redemption even after family and friends have written him off."

—*PUBLISHERS WEEKLY* ON *A HOUSE DIVIDED*

"Christy Award winner Whitlow's experience in the law is apparent in this well-crafted legal thriller. Holt's spiritual growth as he discovers his faith and questions his motives for hiding his secret is inspiring. Fans of John Grisham will find much to like here."

—*LIBRARY JOURNAL* ON *THE CONFESSION*

WITNESS PROTECTION

ALSO BY ROBERT WHITLOW

Guilty Until Innocent
Double Indemnity
Relative Justice
Trial and Error
A Time to Stand
The Witnesses
A House Divided
The Confession
The Living Room
The Choice
Water's Edge
Mountain Top
Jimmy
The Sacrifice
The Trial
The List

THE CHOSEN PEOPLE NOVELS

Chosen People
Promised Land

THE TIDES OF TRUTH NOVELS

Deeper Water
Higher Hope
Greater Love

THE ALEXIA LINDALE NOVELS

Life Support
Life Everlasting

WITNESS PROTECTION

ROBERT WHITLOW

THOMAS NELSON
Since 1798

Witness Protection

Published in Nashville, Tennessee, by Thomas Nelson. Thomas Nelson is a registered trademark of HarperCollins Christian Publishing, Inc.

Thomas Nelson titles may be purchased in bulk for educational, business, fundraising, or sales promotional use. For information, please email SpecialMarkets@ThomasNelson.com.

Library of Congress Cataloging-in-Publication Data

Names: Whitlow, Robert, 1954- author
Title: Witness protection / Robert Whitlow.
Description: Nashville, Tennessee : Thomas Nelson, [2026] | Summary: "Jon Tremaine has lived in hiding for years—will coming out of the shadows to help a friend be too great a risk?"—Provided by publisher.
Identifiers: LCCN 2025042250 (print) | LCCN 2025042251 (ebook) | ISBN 9781400352081 paperback | ISBN 9781400352098 hardcover | ISBN 9781400352104 epub | ISBN 9781400352111
Subjects: LCSH: Witnesses—Protection—Fiction | LCGFT: Legal fiction (Literature) | Thrillers (Fiction) | Novels
Classification: LCC PS3573.H49837 W57 2026 (print) | LCC PS3573.H49837 (ebook)
LC record available at https://lccn.loc.gov/2025042250
LC ebook record available at https://lccn.loc.gov/2025042251

Printed in the United States of America

26 27 28 29 30 LBC 5 4 3 2 1

To those who persevere through pain
for the purposes of the Lord.

For our light and momentary troubles are achieving for us an eternal glory that far outweighs them all.

—2 CORINTHIANS 4:17

CHAPTER 1

Jon Tremaine drove his dusty red pickup along the dirt road that separated two large tracts of pencil-straight pine trees. At forty-two years old, he had dark hair that had recently started showing streaks of gray. Sitting in the passenger seat of the truck was Betsy, a three-year-old Catahoula leopard dog. Ever since growing up in Louisiana, Jon had always wanted one of the dogs bred by early settlers to herd wild cattle and hunt feral pigs. Reaching over with his right hand, he scratched the energetic dog behind her floppy ears.

Tree farming wasn't a six-month process. Pine trees took fifteen to twenty years to reach the right size to be harvested as pulpwood. The trees to Jon's left were eighteen years old. It was hard for him to believe it had been that long since he planted the seedlings. At the time, he had just relocated as part of the Federal Witness Protection Program, also known as the Witness Security Program or WITSEC. Federal agents with the U.S. Marshals Service moved Jon from a Houston safe house to southeast Georgia following his testimony before a federal grand jury and in two criminal trials. Fourteen members of an organized crime syndicate known as the Los Reyes cartel were sentenced to prison based in part on Jon's testimony. As incentive for his testimony, Jon was granted total immunity from prosecution and a new identity.

Two years earlier, Jon was promoted and placed in charge of the entire southeastern Georgia operation of Granger Forestry LLC, the company that owned and operated fourteen thousand acres of timberland in Glynn and Brantley Counties. In addition to running the farm, Jon was responsible for communicating with the company's major European investors in Spain and France. The fact that Jon spoke both Spanish and French, the latter with a Cajun accent, was one of the reasons for the promotion. Visiting investors liked interacting with someone who spoke their native language. Jon was also good with accounting and knew how to manage the immigrant workforce that performed the day-to-day labor on the tree farm. Upper management had no idea about Jon's criminal history.

Jon reached a bumpy section of the road and firmly gripped the steering wheel. He squinted as the sun caught an opening in the trees and shone directly into his brown eyes. His phone, which was locked into a cradle on the dashboard, signaled an incoming call from his wife, Sarah.

Other than the federal agent assigned to his case, no one in Jon's current life knew his real name except his wife. Jon met Sarah, the assistant director of the local battered women's shelter, shortly after his promotion to a position that evolved into his becoming manager. They dated for a year before marrying seven years ago. Her work at the shelter turned out to be good preparation for marrying a man who needed to live a secret life because of a dangerous past.

Sarah, at thirty-two, was seven and a half months pregnant with a baby boy. As her due date crept closer, she'd cut her hours at the women's shelter to two days a week.

"I'm on my way and should be there in ten minutes," Jon said before Sarah spoke. "I had to make sure the men cleared the fire damage from last month. The trees that remain look better than I expected. The fire didn't destroy as many—"

"You need to head to Cesar Mendez's trailer," Sarah said, speaking rapidly. "His wife called and said something about him being arrested."

"Arrested? Why?"

"Maria was hysterical, and I couldn't make sense of what she said. I told her you'd be there as soon as you could."

It was several miles to the trailer park maintained by the company to house some of the workers. Jon checked his watch. On the dirt and gravel roads, it would take around ten minutes to get there.

"I'm on my way," he said.

"Do what you need to do, and don't worry about getting home for supper. I'll keep a plate warm for you."

Kelli Quinn stopped for a red light on the outskirts of town and rubbed her tired eyes. There had been so many last-minute details to take care of that she hadn't left Atlanta until 1:30 p.m. for the five-hour drive to Brunswick. The moving van would be arriving at her aunt Carly's house in the morning. Kelli's aunt lived in the New Town neighborhood, a misnomer since many of the houses in the upwardly transitional neighborhood were more than a hundred years old. Carly Withers, a retired schoolteacher, had inherited the house from her parents. Over the past few years, it had tripled in value.

The last hour of the drive had been blissfully quiet. Both seven-year-old Emma and eleven-year-old Max had fallen asleep. Kelli glanced in the rearview mirror at the children. Emma, with her reddish-brown hair, green eyes, strong chin, and confident personality, was a copy of her mother. Max, much quieter and more reserved than his sister, had the dark hair, brown eyes, and lanky frame of his father. Brad Quinn, a software engineer, had abandoned the marriage and the family nine months earlier. Kelli knew that she and Brad had grown apart but didn't think he was prepared to call it quits. As soon as the divorce was final, Brad moved with his new girlfriend and her children to California.

The divorce had hit Max harder than Emma. The boy couldn't accept why his dad had chosen to leave him and move to Los Angeles with another woman and her two sons. Kelli was trying to be emotionally present for the children while struggling with her own feelings of betrayal and rejection.

"Mom, are we there yet?" Emma asked in a sleepy voice.

"Almost," Kelli replied.

"I'm hungry. Let's stop."

"Aunt Carly is fixing supper."

"What is it? I may not like it."

"Fried chicken. Do you remember our visit two months ago? You liked it then."

"It's not nuggets."

"I liked her fried chicken," Max interjected. "And that other thing she made with smashed-up crackers on top."

"Squash casserole with the yellow and pattypan squash she grew in her little garden," Kelli replied. "It may be too late in the year for fresh squash."

Kelli reached the center of town. Not only were her eyes tired and her heart broken; her soul was weary. The strain of her forced decision to resign after six years with a well-respected law firm in Atlanta had taken a toll. Before the marital breakup, Brad had worked remotely and could watch the kids when they were at home. Kelli flourished at the Peachtree Street law firm where she landed after spending two years with the U.S. Attorney's Office. She had been on the verge of becoming a partner when Brad abruptly left. She thought she could navigate her home and work responsibilities. But as a litigator with an active caseload and constantly changing demands on her time, Kelli found it impossible to balance her responsibility to her children with the requirements of a career. Three nannies failed. When Kelli was passed over for partner, she met with the managing attorney. He suggested reassignment to a different team with a significant cut in pay and permanent associate status. Kelli read the description for the new job and realized she'd be working just as hard as before but for less money. A request for additional modification in her job duties was rejected, and she concluded there was no future for her at the firm. The severance package was a huge disappointment.

The streetlights flickered on as they turned onto Union Street. Carly lived in a rambling wooden home on a corner lot. Built shortly after the Civil War, the original house was narrow with two stories. Decades later additional wings were added to the right and the left. The wing on the right was devoted to a large kitchen and a much smaller dining area. The wing on the left contained two bedrooms, a living room, and a spacious bathroom. There were two bedrooms upstairs. Aunt Carly had invited Kelli and the children to stay with her until they found a place of their own. The movers would drop off a few items at the house on Union Street in the morning and then take everything else to a storage unit.

Kelli pulled her blue SUV into her aunt's driveway. The lights were turned on in the open-air porch that stretched across the front of the original house. There were two wooden rockers and the same porch swing Kelli had enjoyed as a child. She checked her appearance in the rearview mirror. Her reddish-brown hair touched her shoulders. The green eyes she shared with Emma looked fatigued.

"Leave everything in the car," she said. "We'll unpack later."

"Except my tablet," Emma responded. "I need it in case I get bored."

Carrying the tablet in its pink protective case, Emma ran ahead toward the front door. Max stayed beside Kelli as they left the vehicle.

"Do you think we can be happy here?" he asked.

"That's a big question," Kelli replied, looking down at her son. "I wouldn't lie to you and say yes because I don't really know. I'm going to take it one day at a time."

"That's hard to do."

Kelli put her arm around his shoulders. "I'm here for you no matter what," she said.

"Dad said the same thing."

Kelli winced before taking Max's hand in hers as they walked slowly toward the house. He was still young enough not to pull away. Kelli stopped at the bottom of the steps.

"The main reason we're here in Brunswick is so I can keep that promise," she said. "Do you believe me?"

Max looked up at her. Kelli wasn't an emotional person, but the expression on her son's face caused a lump to form in her throat.

"I want to believe you," he said hopefully.

Kelli leaned over and planted a kiss on the top of his head. "Let's go inside and eat some fried chicken and squash casserole," she said.

"Mom, come on!" Emma called out from beside the swing. "I want you to ring the doorbell."

The door opened before Kelli reached it. Wearing a faded summer dress with an apron around her waist, Aunt Carly opened her arms as wide as she could. Her dark eyes were alive, even though her joints were becoming increasingly misshapen as a result of the rheumatoid arthritis that had forced her to retire from teaching.

"Welcome!" announced the slender woman with a short mix of gray and brown hair. Half-frame reading glasses sat perched on the end of her nose. "I'm glad you ran late. I just took the squash casserole out of the oven. I remembered how much Max enjoyed it the last time you came, and I harvested the last of it from my garden this afternoon."

Carly took a deep breath as she closed the door. She had five nieces and nephews, but she'd nurtured a special affection for Kelli ever since her niece was a little girl. Opening her home to Kelli and the children wasn't a hard choice.

When she planned the welcoming meal, Carly hadn't been sure she could pull it off, but the infusion she'd received the previous week from her rheumatologist was still providing relief. Not that the pain was gone. Mornings were the worst, evenings after a day of activity a close second. But today Carly felt better than she expected. Shortly before Kelli arrived, Carly had slipped into the long room where Max was going to stay. A ceiling fan stirred the air. On the nightstand beside the bed was a small vial of fragrant oil.

Carly had gone through the entire house, anointing the doors and rooms by touching them with oil placed on the tip of her permanently bent right index finger. She could have used ordinary vegetable oil from the pantry; faith was the key ingredient to the process. But Carly liked the scent of the oil from the land where Jesus's feet were anointed during his earthly ministry. The fragrant liquid came from a supplier in Tiberias, Israel. Hebrew letters she couldn't read were printed on the label. Just as the fragrance lingered, she hoped the healing effect of her prayers would touch the family she knew was hurting.

The vial was in the pocket of Carly's apron as she followed Kelli and the children into the kitchen.

CHAPTER 2

Jon's truck bounced up and down on the bumpy roads. Cesar had been employed at the tree farm for almost eight years. Originally from Mexico, the thirty-year-old first-generation immigrant had obtained employment authorization with Jon's help from U.S. Citizenship and Immigration Services. He and Maria had two little boys. Six months earlier, Jon had sold his older model red pickup to Cesar, who was making payments on the vehicle.

The trailer park came into view. The purchase of ten double-wide units placed in two rows of five had been Jon's idea. The location of homes on the farm meant the men were quickly available when needed for emergencies. The rent was reasonable and the accommodations stabler than what was usually available for immigrant workers in the area. Over half of the workforce lived in the trailers, and there was a waiting list to get in.

Jon pulled onto the gravel-covered parking space beside the Mendez home. At the sound of his truck, Maria dashed out the door and down the steps. Jon could see through the open door of the trailer that several other women were inside. He was barely out of his truck when Maria began speaking in a torrent of Spanish heavily influenced by her mixed Mexican–Native American background.

"Mr. Jon," she said, "Cesar is in the jail, and they won't let him out! He went to pick up a crate of chocolate, and they arrested him!"

Cesar had a side business buying cocoa from relatives who lived in the Oaxaca region of Mexico and selling the gourmet chocolate to a restaurant distributor in Atlanta. The intense bitter chocolate was used in expensive restaurant dishes.

"Was there something wrong with the documents from the shipping company?" Jon asked. "All the forms have to be filled out correctly. The business office on the ship should have given him what he needed."

"I don't know!" Marie replied. "But Cesar is in the jail in Brunswick, and they're not going to let him out! Please, will you go?"

Jon pressed his lips together tightly. He could call the police but knew that wouldn't satisfy Maria.

"Okay," he said. "But I can't promise anything tonight."

"Thank you, thank you," Maria said. "With the money from the chocolate, we were going to help Cesar's grandmother pay for a surgery she needs. But if we have to, we can use it to get him out of jail."

"How much do you have?"

"Ten thousand dollars."

Jon knew Cesar was frugal but was still impressed with the amount he'd saved.

"Hold off on that," Jon replied. "I'll let you know what I find out."

Jon left the trailer park. The drive to Brunswick would take forty minutes. He called Sarah to let her know his supper would have to go from the oven to the refrigerator. The main highway was mostly deserted on a Thursday evening. Jon accelerated to five miles over the speed limit. He'd not even received a traffic ticket since relocating to Georgia.

"Betsy, you've never been to the jail," he said to the dog as they sped through the darkening evening. "Trust me, it's not a place you want to stay."

Emma skipped past Aunt Carly into the house. Kelli received the obligatory hug and kiss on the right cheek. Her aunt's bony arms didn't completely wrap around Kelli, who was careful not to squeeze too hard. Max received a pat on the head.

"How was the drive?" Carly asked as they entered the small, high-ceilinged foyer of the original house.

"Tiring when you tie it together with all the last-minute things I had to get done. I'm sure I left some loose ends."

"You'll get it worked out. I'm so glad you're here."

Kelli knew her aunt's words were sincere. Carly had insisted that Kelli and the children stay with her free of charge while getting settled in Brunswick. She also placed no time limit on her hospitality.

"Since there's just the four of us, I thought we'd eat in the kitchen," Carly said.

The smell of crisp fried chicken greeted Kelli. The refrigerator, stove, oven, sink, and most of the counters and cabinets were against one wall, leaving an open space for a large, round antique oak table. The table could seat six. To the right of the table was a bank of three windows that provided light for a wide variety of indoor plants positioned on wooden racks. Carly was a knowledgeable horticulturalist.

"Look at all these tiny white flowers!" Emma exclaimed, reaching out toward a lower plant.

"Don't touch—" Kelli started.

"It's okay," Carly said. "Fall blooms on an oxalis are a bonus to be celebrated and enjoyed. Let's eat while the food is warm."

They served themselves buffet-style. To Kelli's relief, Emma didn't complain about the chicken and selected a drumstick. The little girl rejected the squash casserole but loaded up on sliced carrots sautéed in butter and brown sugar. Max selected two pieces of chicken, a small portion of carrots, and a generous serving of the casserole. There were hot yeast rolls and butter on the table.

"I didn't brew any tea," Carly said. "I hope water is okay."

"Perfect," Kelli replied as she fixed her plate. "I starved myself all day because I knew we'd have a feast when we arrived."

Emma, who was already at the table, lifted a roll to her mouth.

"Don't eat until we pray," Kelli said. "That's the rule here."

Emma slowly lowered the roll. Once the four of them were seated, Carly spoke to Emma: "Emma, praying isn't so much a rule as it is an opportunity. I'm thankful you're here and told you that first thing. It's the same with a meal. Being thankful in little things helps us be grateful for bigger things."

Emma didn't respond. Carly and Max closed their eyes. Kelli motioned for Emma to do the same but then kept her eyes open as Carly's gnarled fingers came together in a misshapen clasp.

"Lord, thank you for bringing Kelli, Max, and Emma here this evening and for this food. Amen." Carly opened her eyes and smiled. "It's best not to pray too long when the food is hot and waiting to be eaten."

Kelli bit into a chicken thigh. "Aunt Carly, this chicken is delicious," she said, savoring the flavors.

"I found a farmer who raises his own hens. They're organic without tasting gamy."

"What does that mean?" Emma asked, a partially eaten drumstick in her hand.

Carly gave an explanation that revealed the teacher she'd always be. At sixty-two, she was seven years older than Kelli's mother, Valerie, who lived with her third husband in St. Petersburg, Florida. The two women couldn't be more different. Valerie inhabited a world with herself at the center, yet quickly dismissed Brad as a narcissistic loser and suggested her only daughter should move on to a new relationship as soon as possible. Kelli wasn't in the market for romance. Relocating to Florida hadn't been an option for Kelli and the kids. And not just because Kelli wasn't licensed to practice law in the Sunshine State. A long weekend was the maximum time she could endure a visit with her mother.

Max remained quiet as he shoveled casserole into his mouth.

"Eat some chicken too," Kelli said. "There's more casserole on the stove."

Max picked up a breast and took a bite. His eyes lit up. "This is good. Better than the other time."

"I'm glad to hear that," Carly said with a chuckle. "A cook always wants to improve and appreciates an honest critic."

"I wasn't criticizing you," Max quickly responded.

"That's not the way the word is used," Carly responded.

Another teaching moment about the nuances of *criticism* and *critique* followed. Kelli could remember similar conversations from her childhood. Carly loved words.

"So it's not a judgment," Carly said. "It's an analysis. Does that make sense?"

"Yeah," Max replied. "It's like the review of a product on Amazon."

"An honest review," Carly replied.

They ate in silence for a few moments. Seeing the children around her aunt's table brought a measure of peace to Kelli's soul. They finished the meal, including a second large serving of casserole for Max. Carly was good at not pestering the children with questions but responding to what they brought up. When they were silent, she let that happen as well. At one point, she glanced at Kelli. "We'll talk later, if that's okay?"

Kelli nodded.

"What's for dessert?" Emma asked.

"Don't ask," Kelli responded. "It's impolite."

Carly picked up her phone, which was beside her plate. "That reminds me to place our dessert order."

"What do you mean?" Emma questioned.

"Do you like homemade ice cream with fresh strawberries?" Carly asked.

"I'm not sure I've ever had it. Mom, is that what we had at the beach?"

"That was good ice cream but not homemade."

Carly slowly touched the letters on her phone.

"There," she said. "They should be here in about ten minutes."

"Who's coming?" Emma asked.

"They want to surprise you," Carly replied.

Jon turned off the Norwich Street Extension onto Sulphur Springs and then into the parking lot at the Glynn County Detention Center. With its brown brick and white roof, the headquarters for the local sheriff's department and jail looked like a high school. Jon parked in a visitor's place near the front door. There wasn't much activity on a Thursday evening. He cracked open the passenger-side window so Betsy could get fresh air and went inside to the reception area. A middle-aged female deputy was seated behind a glass partition. She slid it open as he approached.

"Can I help you?" she asked.

"I'm Jon Tremaine. One of my employees, Cesar Mendez, was arrested earlier today. I'd like to find out the charges against him."

The woman eyed Jon for a moment, then turned to her computer monitor and typed on her keyboard.

"It's a drug charge," she said after a few seconds passed. "Cocaine and fentanyl trafficking with intent to distribute. He's set for arraignment Tuesday morning at ten thirty in Glynn County Superior Court."

Jon swallowed. This was a lot worse than he'd imagined. Nothing about Cesar had given him a clue that the earnest hard worker might be involved in something like this. Jon hesitated.

"Would it be possible to talk to one of the detectives?" he asked.

"That's up to them."

"Could you check?"

"What's your name again and your connection to Mr. Mendez?"

Jon explained in detail who he was and how he knew Cesar.

"Have a seat. I'll check with Detective Briscoe," the woman said.

Jon sat in a beige chair with a thin cushion on the seat. Being in a correctional facility, even one as outwardly benign as Glynn County, was like revisiting the scene of a nightmare. Jon nervously tapped his fingers against the armrest of the chair. He saw the woman talk on the phone and lower the receiver without any signal to him. She could have simply been answering a phone call. Ten minutes passed.

Jon decided to wait two more minutes before leaving. Then a door opened, and a large, muscular Black man in his forties, wearing a dark suit with the tie loosened, entered.

"Mr. Tremaine?" he asked.

Jon stood and stepped forward. "That's me."

The detective extended his hand. "Noah Briscoe," he said. "Mendez asked for you earlier when we explained his right to contact an attorney."

"I'm not a lawyer—"

"I understand. Come to my office."

Jon followed the detective through a metal door that clicked shut when it closed behind him. The heightened confinement was ten times worse than the reception area. Jon had spent several months in jail after his arrest. His heart beat faster. The detective entered a small office.

"I'll leave the door open," he said.

"I prefer that," Jon quickly responded.

"Place your cell phone on the desk. No recordings of our conversation allowed."

"Yes, sir."

Jon placed his phone on the desk, the screen saver photo of Sarah in one of her maternity dresses now in view.

"The receptionist confirmed what the accused told us about your relationship with him," the detective said.

Uneasy in the presence of the detective, Jon tried to keep his voice steady. "I'm his boss, that's all. He and his family live in housing provided by the company on our property in Brantley County. His wife called and said he'd been arrested and asked me to find out what I could."

The detective stared at him for a few seconds without speaking.

Jon knew it was standard police practice to gauge a person's level of nervousness when under investigation. Jon tried to make his breathing calm and regular. To do that he chose not to speak. The detective cleared his throat. "What do you know about Mendez importing chocolate from Mexico?"

"He has family connections in the Oaxaca region. They send him a crate of raw product every so often. Cesar sells it to a restaurant distributor in Atlanta. It's been a way to supplement his income from the tree farm."

"Have you ever assisted with any of the deliveries?"

Suddenly, Jon realized that he was under investigation. He quickly debated whether to end the conversation until he could consult with a lawyer. He decided that would only increase the detective's suspicion.

"I arranged help through a local lawyer to set up the paperwork for him to be an importer and traveled with Cesar to Atlanta for his first meeting with the distributor. I didn't participate in their discussion. The man spoke fluent Spanish, and it was a simple transaction. Cesar gave him an invoice; he inspected the chocolate and paid."

"With cash?"

"Yes."

"Do you remember the man's name who bought the chocolate?"

"No."

"You speak Spanish?"

"Yes, and French."

"And Cajun?" the detective asked.

Jon didn't respond.

Briscoe leaned back in his chair. "I played two years of football at LSU before I blew out my knee. I ate my weight several times over in red beans and rice. If you ever hear about a place around here that serves good beans and rice, I'd like to know about it. I even got to liking crawfish."

As the detective talked, Jon relaxed. He replied in a more normal tone of voice: "The best local beans, rice, and crawfish come from the kitchen at my house," he said. "My wife grew up around here, but she's a quick learner."

"If you ever have leftovers, consider giving me a ring," the detective responded, then paused for a moment. "Tell Ms. Mendez that her husband isn't getting out of jail anytime soon and that the FBI is opening a federal investigation as well."

"No bond?"

"Not yet. That will be handled at his arraignment on Tuesday. It's going to be high. Not sure what the feds will do."

"What about visiting hours?"

"Monday and Thursday for two hours from 4:00 p.m. to 6:00 p.m. and Sunday afternoon from 2:00 p.m. to 6:00 p.m. That's when kids can come too. Most likely he'll stay here even if the feds file their own charges."

Briscoe led the way back to the reception area. They stopped in the waiting area.

"I know you're just trying to look out for one of your employees," Briscoe said. "I appreciate that, but people make mistakes that have more serious consequences than they imagined."

"Yeah," Jon said, nodding. "That's true."

CHAPTER 3

Kelli suggested to Carly that she take the children into the living room while she cleaned up in the kitchen.

"Show them your collection of board games," Kelli said. "What was the one we played the last time we came?"

"It was Sorry!" Emma replied. "Only there was nothing to be sorry about when I sent Max's pieces back to the beginning."

"We may not have time to finish a game before dessert arrives," Carly said.

"Go," Kelli said, shooing them out of the kitchen.

Kelli put the leftovers in the refrigerator. There was only one piece of chicken, a thigh. Kelli didn't mind eating cold fried chicken. She might even make it part of her breakfast in the morning. She carefully rinsed everything before putting the dishes in the washer. Her aunt had a particular way of doing things that Kelli had memorized on previous visits. She was wiping the counters when the doorbell rang. Carly and the children were already standing at the door when Kelli entered the foyer. It was Ann Carter and her husband, Roy.

Kelli's law school friend had a container of strawberries in her right hand. Roy cradled a metal cylinder from an ice-cream maker. A tall woman, Ann was as slender as she had been when she and Kelli sat next to each other in torts class during their first year in law school. She was wearing shorts, a cotton top, and sandals with her blond hair in a ponytail. After going prematurely bald, Roy had elected to keep his head shaved, which made his dark eyes more striking. Ann gave Kelli a quick hug.

"Where do you want to serve dessert?" Ann asked Carly.

"We're right here; let's eat on the porch."

"I'll grab some extra chairs," Kelli said. "And bowls and spoons."

"You'll need help with that," Roy said.

Roy worked as a veterinary technician specializing in large animal care. He had a four-year college degree and an advanced degree with an emphasis in bovine and horse care. Roy was about the same height as Ann but with a well-developed muscular physique.

"I'll get the chairs," he said, grabbing two with each arm. "How was the trip?"

"Tiring, but it was nice to arrive to a home-cooked dinner, and now this surprise from you and Ann."

"This is Ann's doing. It was an excuse for me to put away my old hand-cranked ice-cream maker and get one with an electric motor."

They returned to the front porch. Positioned next to Ann, Emma dangled her legs from the porch swing. Kelli sat beside them.

"Is it true that you're going to be Mom's boss?" Emma asked Ann as they gently swung back and forth.

"Is that what she said?" Ann replied with a glance at Kelli.

Kelli didn't respond.

Ann patted Emma on the leg. "Your mom and I have been friends for a long time and thought it would be fun for us to work together."

"I don't think being a lawyer is fun," Emma responded.

Ann motioned to Kelli. "You take over this conversation. She's your daughter."

"I'll defer," Kelli laughed. "Time for ice cream and strawberries."

The dessert kept Emma's mouth occupied. It was a warm evening but late enough in September that insects weren't a bother. Emma left the swing and sat on the steps near Carly.

"Moving the kids after less than two months of school may not have been the best timing," Kelli said to Ann. "But I appreciate you making a quick decision."

"It wasn't quick. I've thought about being part of the same firm with you for years. It just seemed you were settled on your career track in Atlanta while I slowly built my practice here in Brunswick."

"And you're sure I won't be a drain? I'm not bringing a book of business."

"Remember what I told you when we first talked. I can keep you busy so long as you're not looking for complex litigation. And it will be nice not having to refer out simple lawsuits that keep coming up for my regular clients."

"You could be a litigator—"

"Maybe, but I don't want to. And a big benefit to running your own practice is the freedom to do what you want. For me, that's spending time with Roy and being involved in activities at our church. For you, that's spending time with your kids."

Kelli appreciated the contrast between her friend and the Atlanta firm where she was under pressure to bill two thousand hours a year.

"And if you're satisfied earning less," Ann continued.

"Brad is on the hook for increased payments under the order issued by the judge at the supplemental child support hearing held after my job ended. I'm fine with him helping to fund my new lifestyle."

"When do the children start school?"

"Monday. We'll take the long weekend to settle in with Carly," Kelli said. "If it's okay, I might bring the kids to the office tomorrow so they can see where I'll be working."

"Of course. Maybe around lunchtime so we can grab a bite together."

"Not a salad delivered to my desk so I can keep billing my time while I eat?"

Ann smiled. "No. There's a nice place close by that lets you build your own salad and has a healthy kids' menu."

"Great."

The homemade ice cream was a hit, especially with Max, who asked Roy a bunch of questions about the process. After Ann and Roy left, Kelli, Carly, and the children returned to the living room. Emma yawned broadly.

"Maybe you should finish the Sorry! game tomorrow," Kelli suggested.

To her surprise, Emma nodded.

"Showers for both of you," Kelli said. "Emma first. I'll get your suitcase from the car."

Max went with Kelli to help her. There was a lightness in his step as he grabbed both Emma's suitcase and his own.

"This feels like being on vacation," he said.

"Good," Kelli replied with a smile.

After both children were in bed, Kelli returned to the living room to talk with Carly. She found her aunt fast asleep in a slender leather recliner with her eyes closed and her mouth slightly open. Kelli tiptoed out of the room and upstairs to her bedroom.

Jon snapped a leash on Betsy and took her for a short walk in the grass near the sheriff's department. Back in the truck, he drove more slowly on the return trip to the trailer park. He thought about calling Maria to break the bad news but decided he should talk to her in person. She had recently been laid off from her job, and the rent would soon be due for the trailer. Cesar's truck payment to him could be postponed, but company housing was available only for current employees of Granger Forestry. Jon could protect an employee's job for a while but not indefinitely. And the valuable worker would have to be replaced.

Cesar would also need legal representation. He would likely qualify for a court-appointed lawyer, but Jon remembered the court-appointed lawyer assigned to his case. If he'd taken the lazy attorney's advice to quickly plead guilty, Jon would still be sweating out the final years of a twenty-year sentence in a federal prison in South Texas.

He reached the trailer park. The lights were still on in Cesar's trailer, but he didn't hear any noise from other people as he stood on the small stoop in front of the door and knocked. Maria opened it.

"I talked to Cesar," she said morosely in Spanish. "There were drugs in with the chocolate."

"Did he admit to smuggling drugs?" Jon asked in shock.

"No! No!" Maria replied emphatically. "The police used a dog to find the drugs in the bottom of the crate. Cesar didn't know anything about it. He said it was cocaine bricks wrapped in foil and some kind of pills. There was a second floor to the crate, a secret place. It was damaged, and some white powder spilled out. Cesar pointed it out to one of the men on the dock, and the man's supervisor called the police."

Jon frowned at the description of the shipping method for the cocaine and fentanyl. It was one of the techniques used by his old criminal gang. The cocaine would be enclosed in airtight plastic bags with cayenne pepper or other strong spices or chemicals used to disguise the scent of the drug and defeat the use of dogs trained in narcotics detection. Unwitting third parties used to transport drugs were called "blind mules." There could easily be forty to fifty kilos hidden in a crate like the one used to transport the chocolate.

"The fact that Cesar pointed it out should count for something with the police," Jon replied. "He wasn't trying to hide anything."

"The police said they'd been watching him and think he brought in drugs before."

"Ugh," Jon grunted. "I met with one of the detectives. He didn't tell me much but says the FBI is getting involved, and the bond to get Cesar out of jail will be very high."

"What is bond?"

Jon explained the process.

Maria shook her head sadly. "What are we going to do?" she asked as tears began to stream down her face.

"You look after your sons. I'll try to find out more information."

Jon left without saying anything about the trailer rent or Cesar's job. Arriving home, he parked his truck in the open carport attached to their single-story ranch-style house. Jon opened the gate to the fenced-in backyard where Betsy stayed. Sarah was waiting for him at the front door, wearing a nightgown with a light robe wrapped around her. Jon took off his work boots and left them beside the door.

"What did you find out?" she asked.

"I'll go over it while I eat."

Jon placed his plate in the microwave. The long, narrow kitchen was at the rear of the house. There wasn't another residence in over a mile. When all the electric lights were off at night, the sky exploded with stars. Jon sat at a small table covered by a red-checked vinyl tablecloth. Sarah poured a glass of ice water and sat across from him while he told her what he'd learned about Cesar's arrest and his conversation with Detective Briscoe.

"Do you think the detective suspects you're involved in whatever happened?" she asked in alarm.

"That thought crossed my mind, but he didn't ask any follow-up questions about my interaction with Cesar and his chocolate business." Jon took a drink of water. "Let me jump ahead. Maria talked to Cesar, and the police claim they've been watching him for a while related to other shipments."

"You went with him to deliver chocolate in Atlanta."

"That was just the first time," Jon said, keeping his voice calm. "Surely Cesar wasn't on their radar at that point."

As soon as the words were out of his mouth, Jon knew they weren't true. Cesar could be caught up in an investigation that had been ongoing for months or even years. He finished telling Sarah what he'd learned from Maria but left out the method of concealment for the drugs and the similarity to what he'd seen in the past.

Sarah sighed. "I feel sorry for Maria and their little boys."

"Yeah. She won't be able to stay in the trailer once Cesar is off the company payroll. I'll stall as long as I can."

"Maria and Cesar go to a little Spanish-speaking church near Blackshear," Sarah said. "Maybe someone at the church can help them find a place."

Sarah ran her fingers through her hair. "What if there's a news report or something online about the arrest that mentions Cesar working for Granger?" she asked.

"I still want to wait. That will give Maria time to figure out what she's going to do."

Sarah frowned. "It's not the kind of housing emergency I'm used to dealing with, but it's still a crisis. We should help them if we can. After all, Cesar saved your life last year when that damaged tree was going to crush you."

"I thought about that earlier," Jon said as he nodded. "And he spent six months recovering from shoulder surgery."

Shortly after 3:00 a.m. a sharp pain in Carly's lower back jarred her awake. She shifted position in an attempt to get comfortable, but it was futile. Going into the adjoining bathroom, she took a long, hot shower. The water had a soothing effect on her joints. The next step involved sitting in a chair and strategically placing heating pads over the most tender joints. Tonight that included her lower back and right ankle. Once the heating pads were properly positioned, Carly opened her Bible. In the night, she lived in Psalms. The honesty of David's thoughts and feelings about his circumstances and God's response often mirrored her own soul. She turned to a familiar passage in Psalm 69 in the New Living Translation:

"I am suffering and in pain. Rescue me, O God, by your saving power. Then I will praise God's name with singing, and I will honor him with thanksgiving . . . For the LORD hears the cries of the needy; he does not despise his imprisoned people."

Carly knew there were many sources of pain and distress, and multiple origins of captivity and need. Carly lifted up the psalmist's words for herself but also turned them outward for others. This step had been a key to her mental and emotional survival in the midst of disease. She took what the Lord provided her and prayed it for others. She'd felt Kelli's pain during the visit weeks earlier, and it was stronger this evening when her niece stood on the front porch. The children were also caught in upheaval and turmoil. Trauma didn't respect age. There was much to pray about for Kelli and her family. Carly read and prayed for almost an hour. Before closing her Bible, she included a few moments of praise in advance of an answer.

An early riser, Kelli rarely relied on an alarm clock. While it was still dark, she put on exercise clothes and went out for a walk. The streets of Carly's neighborhood were empty. Without a destination in mind, Kelli simply started walking rapidly. In college she'd been a jogger, but by the time she entered law school, she'd realized that she preferred walking because it required less concentration and exertion. She'd come to a corner and either proceed in a straight line or take a random turn. If she lost her way, the GPS feature on her watch would guide her to Carly's house.

Unlike her neighborhood in Atlanta, the streets of Brunswick were pancake-flat. Just as her feet were allowed to move forward without conscious direction toward a destination, Kelli didn't try to dictate the thoughts in her mind. She let herself inhale air tinged with a hint of the ocean, feel the comfortable temperature against her skin, and listen to the birds that, like her, were awake to greet the day. Dawn brought amber light as she returned to Union Street. At the house, Kelli peeked into the kids' bedrooms. They were sprawled out, still deep in sleep. Carly had not yet appeared. It looked like her aunt was also sleeping in on Friday.

Kelli was sitting in a rocker on the front porch finishing a cup of black coffee when the truck arrived. The eight boxes Kelli wanted delivered to her aunt's house were stacked at the rear of the truck. The movers quickly placed them in the foyer. Max came out of his bedroom rubbing his eyes.

"Go back to bed," Kelli said to him. "I'm going with the movers to the storage unit. We'll unpack this stuff later. It's mostly clothes and personal items."

"I want to go with you."

"There's nothing for you to do at the storage unit," Kelli said, but then she relented. "You have two minutes to get dressed."

Max sat in the passenger seat of Kelli's SUV. It was a fifteen-minute drive to the storage facility in a less prosperous part of town. The driver backed up to the unit. Kelli raised the sliding door. Using hand trucks, the men rapidly carried the remaining boxes and items of furniture down a ramp.

"Can I put that table in my bedroom?" Max asked when it appeared. "That's where I like to build things and do my homework."

The narrow wooden table was an antique. Years earlier it had been in one of the rooms at Carly's house. Recently, a LEGO set under construction had often sat on the dark, shiny surface. Max and Brad used to spend hours sitting beside each other at the table while putting together specialty kits. Kelli had put the table on the list to be stored because she was concerned it would trigger bad memories for Max. The table would barely fit in the back of the SUV.

"Are you sure?" Kelli asked.

"Yes."

"Okay, but we probably need to find something that Emma cares about too."

"Her horse lamp," Max replied quickly. "Unless it's in one of the boxes at the house."

"I don't think so. It should be labeled."

Kelli and Max went into the unit. Within a few seconds, Max called out, "Here it is! The box says 'bedroom lamp.'"

Kelli had bought the lamp, which was an old piece but not an antique, on a whim at a yard sale when she and Brad were first married. There were three hand-painted wooden horses surrounding a wooden spindle. It had been a fixture in Emma's room since she was a baby. When she was four years old, Emma named the horses Sprint, Happy, and Frisky. Recently, she'd expressed an interest in riding. It was something Kelli promised they would discuss with Roy once they were in Brunswick. Roy was familiar with the horse facilities in the area.

They put the table and the lamp in the SUV. After the movers finished, Kelli took one last look at the pile of stuff and wondered what she should have given away or sent to the dump. There were items in the storage unit that, like Max's table, held memories for her, once good, now bad, but she hadn't wanted to expend the emotional energy in Atlanta needed to undertake a purge before the movers arrived.

At the house on Union Street, Emma squealed with excitement when she saw the lamp. "Thank you, Mom!"

"Thank your brother," Kelli replied. "He's the one who suggested you'd like to have it here and not wait until we move into our own place."

Kelli went into the kitchen and joined Carly.

"Good morning," Kelli said to her aunt. "I'll get the boxes out of the foyer in a bit."

"No rush. I gave Emma cereal for breakfast with a banana cut up on top."

One of Kelli's self-identified failings as a mother involved the inadequate breakfasts she provided to her children. Emma was used to scrounging for something to eat from the pantry. The most common breakfast for the children was a cup of yogurt. Max joined them.

"Mom, would you make scrambled eggs with cheese in them?" he asked. "And some crispy bacon?"

"I have bacon," Carly said. "I'd be glad to—"

"No, I'll do it," Kelli said.

Emma entered. "Aunt Carly, I want to show you some of the outfits I brought with me. I found the box they're in."

"Go," Kelli said to Carly.

Kelli took the eggs from the refrigerator. Max joined her.

"Why are the eggs brown and in a little bag?" he asked.

"Aunt Carly buys eggs from a man who has his own chickens. Some are layers, and some are fryers. Stay and help. It's time you learned how to do this."

Cooking breakfast together had been a common practice for Brad and Kelli during the early years of their marriage. Brad made the best spinach-and-mushroom omelet on the planet. While Max and Kelli worked, she explained the difference between the types of chickens.

"You sound like a farmer," he said.

"That's the limit of my knowledge."

Max used a whisk to combine the eggs, salt, and two tablespoons of whole milk. Kelli started frying the bacon in a cast-iron skillet.

"Mom, I want us to do more things together here than we did in Atlanta," Max said. "I was thinking about that last night before I went to sleep."

Watching the boy who increasingly looked more like his father, Kelli let out a sigh.

"Yes," she replied. "That's one of the reasons we're here."

CHAPTER 4

Sarah nudged Jon with her foot.

"Don't you have to wake up and get ready for work?" she asked in a sleepy voice. "Last night you mentioned something about a survey of some old-growth trees before Monday morning."

"Uh, yes," Jon said, glancing at the clock. "I had a restless night with crazy dreams."

Sarah turned over so that her back was to him and didn't respond. Jon went into the kitchen. He dreamed a lot but rarely remembered anything except jumbled snippets. Not a coffee drinker, Jon preferred to begin his day with a large glass of fresh-squeezed orange juice. Even though it was a few weeks until the Florida orange season kicked in, one of the local membership shopping clubs had fruit available from South America. After he squeezed the juice, Jon toasted a bagel and spread on cream cheese. His phone on the counter vibrated before he took a bite. It was an unknown number.

He swiped to accept the call. "Hello?"

"It's Cesar. Did you talk to Maria last night?"

"Yes."

"Jon, I didn't know anything about the drugs. I need someone to believe me. Do you believe me?"

Jon spoke out of hope, not conviction. "Yes," he said.

"Thank you," Cesar said gratefully. "Can you help me get out of jail? I need to be with Maria and my boys, and I don't want to lose my job."

Jon told Cesar what he'd learned from Detective Briscoe. The young man was silent for a moment.

"That's not right. I don't know anything about any of this. Can I talk to the judge?"

"No, you need a lawyer who will speak for you in court."

"I have some money saved from the chocolate business."

"Maria told me, but I don't believe that would be enough to hire a private attorney for this kind of case."

"What about the lady who helped with the paperwork for the business?"

Jon's lawyer, Ann Carter, had helped Cesar complete the necessary documents to import the exotic chocolate that had been processed into powder and nibs.

"Ms. Carter? She's not a criminal defense lawyer. Even with the money you've saved, I think the government will provide a free lawyer."

"But can I trust someone the government is paying for? I don't think so. The government police are the ones saying these wrong things about me."

"It's not like that," Jon explained. "The lawyer works for you even though he or she is paid by the government."

Cesar was silent.

Jon had an idea. "Perhaps Ms. Carter could come to the jail and explain it to you. Would that help?"

"Maybe."

Jon hated the unavoidable sense of helplessness when facing the power of the government. He knew how Cesar felt. After his initial arrest in New Orleans, Jon sat in a jail cell staring at the bars and wondering when, or if, he'd ever experience freedom. Input from someone outside the system would have been welcome.

"I'll contact her and find out."

"What about Maria and the boys? Are they going to be kicked out of the trailer?"

"You know the rules, but I'll delay everything as long as possible. If she has to leave, I'll help her get settled someplace else."

Jon blurted out the last comment, but as soon as it left his lips, he knew it was the right thing to say.

"Thank you. People in the church will help."

"Sarah mentioned that as a possibility."

"What about my truck? You gave me a good deal, and I still want to pay you."

"Don't worry about the truck. Are you being treated okay in the jail?"

"Yeah. I'm in a cell by myself, but I was with the other men for dinner last night. The big detective named Briscoe came by early this morning to talk to me. He's the one who let me call you."

"What did he want to talk about?"

"Mostly questions about you. Where you came from and how I know you."

Jon sat up straighter in his chair. "What did you say?"

"I don't know much about you except that you're a good boss who cares about his workers. I told him you helped me get my green card. He asked about the trip we took to Atlanta to sell the first shipment of chocolate. I gave him the name and address for the man I sell to."

Jon paused. "Is anyone listening to this conversation?"

"I don't think so. I'm on the phone in a hallway near the place where they take your picture and fingerprints."

"Anything else from the detective?"

"That's about it. The guard is telling me I have to hang up now. Bye."

The call ended. Jon stared at the bagel on his plate. Usually he ate every crumb. Today he didn't want a single bite.

At 11:30 a.m. Kelli and the kids prepared to leave for the office. They'd unpacked the boxes and found homes for their clothes and personal items. Carly allowed them an extra closet in the upstairs hallway of the original house. Kelli was surprised when she saw that it was empty.

"What did you have in here?" she asked her aunt.

"Leftover items from your grandmother that needed to be culled. I saved the bits of embroidery but got rid of boxes of old recipes, articles from magazines, and letters from political candidates she supported, all of whom are probably dead."

Kelli smiled. Her grandmother, a home economics teacher, was part scientist. The slender woman with sparkling dark eyes rarely left a recipe unmodified and even stipulated things like the brand of flour needed for best results. She was also interested in politics and never missed a presidential debate.

"I hope you kept some of her cookie recipes," Kelli said. "I loved those crispy ones with bits of pecan, chocolate chips, and rice cereal."

"I use margarine—that's what makes them so flat and crispy. Would you like me to make a batch?"

"Only if you have time."

By the time Kelli closed the door of the closet, it was full of winter clothes and shoes. There wasn't a dress code at Ann's office, but Kelli intended to wear nice outfits. Meeting a potential client in jeans wasn't in her professional DNA.

"Come on!" she called out to Max, who was in his bedroom with a pile of LEGO pieces in front of him on the wooden table.

Emma came out of her room at the sound of her mom's voice.

"Max is always the last one ready to go," Emma said with frustration.

"He gets focused on things and loses track of time."

It was a seven-minute drive to the law office. That alone was going to have a positive impact on Kelli's day-to-day life. They passed the old Glynn County Courthouse that now housed the probate court. The two-story structure was built in an Edwardian style popular in the early 1900s and had an elaborate cupola on top that housed a clock. Ann had a wills and estate practice and frequently went to the building. The newer courthouse on H Street was also an attractive building with large columns and Palladian windows on the front. The more mundane federal courthouse sat nearby.

Ann's office was in a small single-story brick building on a side street. Formerly the location of an accounting firm, the building wasn't impressive from the street view, but the rent was right for an attorney keeping her overhead low. Kelli parked behind the building. There was already a parking space reserved with her name on a small sign in front of it.

"Mom, there's your name!" Emma exclaimed. "Does that mean no one else can park here?"

"Supposedly, but if a client does, I'm not going to have the car towed."

They went through the rear entrance. To the right was the break room. Emma looked in and saw a bowl filled with individually wrapped candies. She took a quick right. Seeing what her daughter had in mind, Kelli reached out and grabbed the back of Emma's shirt.

"Not until after you eat a good lunch, and then you can only have one," she said.

"I promise to eat—"

"No," Kelli said. "Here's my office. You'll be spending time here."

The office was small but cheery. There was an abundance of natural light through two long windows. A table with a dock for a laptop served as the workstation. Two chairs sat in front of the desk. Emma plopped down in the swivel chair behind the desk and did a quick spin. Max sat in one of the chairs facing the desk.

"This chair is faster than the one in your other office," the little girl announced.

"I'll put photos in here," Kelli said, touching a tall étagère between the two windows.

"Welcome!" announced Ann from the doorway. "I heard Emma promising to eat a good lunch."

Ann was wearing stylish slacks, a fashionable top, and heels that made her even taller.

"I want the children to meet Lauren," she said.

On the way to the reception area, they passed Ann's office. It was twice the size of Kelli's space. Across the hall was a compact conference room that contained a table with eight chairs. Emma poked her head into Ann's office.

"Why is your office so big?" Emma asked her.

"Because she's the one who started the law firm," Kelli replied. "She deserves it."

"When we move into our new house, I get to pick my bedroom before you do," Max said to Emma.

"That's not fair!" Emma protested. "Girls care about stuff like that more than boys."

"Enough," Kelli said, holding up her hand.

"And the reception area is through here," Ann continued.

The waiting room was small, with seating for no more than six people. Against one wall was the desk for Lauren Brannen, the receptionist, bookkeeper, and part-time legal assistant. Ann had assured Kelli that the petite young woman with blond hair and blue eyes had extra capacity to help. Kelli, who was used to a skilled support staff at both the U.S. Attorney's Office and the private law firm, wasn't looking forward to training someone who'd recently turned twenty.

"Good morning, Ms. Quinn," Lauren said when they appeared.

Kelli introduced Max and Emma. The little girl stared intently at the young woman's desk.

"Is that your boyfriend?" Emma asked, pointing at a photo on the corner of the desk.

In the picture, Lauren and a young man who towered over her were standing together on the beach. Lauren was wearing a long, light green dress, and the wind was blowing her dress and her hair.

"Yes, that's Curt and me this past summer. He comes by the office several times during the week to take me to lunch. I'm sure you'll meet him."

"He's cute," Emma said.

Lauren smiled. "I think so."

"We're going to grab a bite to eat and should be back around one," Ann told the receptionist.

"Okay. I just put a call in your voicemail from Jon Tremaine," Lauren said. "He'd like an in-office appointment this afternoon if possible. Says it's urgent."

"The kids and I can wait if you need to call him immediately," Kelli said.

Ann paused. "He's the manager of a big tree farm. I've represented him individually and done a bit of corporate work, but I'd love for us to handle more of their general business. Lauren, call him back. I think I'm clear at one thirty. We won't stay too long at lunch."

CHAPTER 5

Jon scrubbed the sawdust and grime from his arms in the mudroom sink. He didn't eat lunch at home every day, but it had been a tough morning.

The crew was using a motorized cutter to harvest a stand of mature trees Jon had identified before the men arrived with the equipment. The cutter could grasp a tree with hooks and cut it off close to the ground. After separating the tree from the ground, the machine stripped the limbs from the trunk and hoisted the logs onto the back of a hauler that took the timber to a pulpwood processing plant near Brunswick. Once the most labor-intensive part of tree farming, harvesting was mostly mechanized except in places like the gulley where Jon was almost killed. Today he got dirty because the equipment malfunctioned. He had to adjust the saw and the steel rollers that removed the spindly limbs from the tall pines. He opened the refrigerator just as Sarah came into the kitchen.

"Why are you home?" she asked.

"We had a two-hour delay due to an equipment breakdown, which meant all three haulers are on their way to the mill at the same time. I didn't want to simply pile logs in the woods while they were gone. Also, I couldn't wait to see you."

Sarah patted him lightly on the arm. Jon didn't expect a kiss. He finished fixing his sandwich and sat at the little table in the kitchen. Sarah took out a salad topped with a generous portion of grilled chicken and joined him. Jon ate a couple of bites.

"I'm going to talk to Ann Carter and see if she's willing to go to the jail and talk to Cesar," he said.

"Does she handle criminal cases? I thought her office just prepared wills and business contracts."

"You're right, but it's bothered me all morning that Cesar might end up with an appointed lawyer who doesn't fight for him. He called early this morning and told me again that he's innocent. I want to believe him, and it doesn't feel right to abandon him without at least trying to help him obtain good legal representation."

Jon told her about his conversation with the worker. Sarah reached out and took his right hand. "The detective asking you even a couple of questions scares me. Do you think you should keep a low profile?"

"I will, but I know how momentum can build against a man like Cesar in a criminal investigation. It's like a freight train. Charges were filed against me that had no basis in fact. If someone had spoken up earlier or offered better advice, I would have really appreciated it."

Sarah didn't respond. They sat in silence for a few moments before she spoke: "Jon, I don't want you to relive what you went through before we met or have someone accusing you of doing something wrong. That's what I care about more than anything."

"Thanks, and believe me, I totally agree. Even thinking about this makes me sick to my stomach."

Jon forced himself to take a bite of his sandwich.

"I thought about calling Chris Polter and moving up our meeting," he said. After his final guilty plea, Jon had met monthly with an FBI agent who monitored his status. His case was later transferred to a U.S. marshal named Chris Polter. Inspector Polter was now near the end of his career and looking forward to spending more time on his sailboat and with his daughter's family in Biloxi. They met for coffee every six months or so. For the past year, the biggest item on their agenda had been discussing Chris's progress in restoring a twenty-eight-foot sailboat.

"Didn't you talk with him last month?"

"Yes, but I should make the feds aware that the name of one of my employees might show up in an FBI investigative report."

Sarah had never been present for Jon's meetings with Chris. He and Jon used burner phones that had no purpose other than their limited communication.

"That's up to you," she said.

"Are you okay with me talking to Ann Carter?"

Sarah stabbed her fork into the salad. "Yes. I can tell when you've made up your mind about something. But please be careful. And no secrets between us."

"I promise."

While they ate, Jon shared with Sarah additional details about the first real lawyer who came to see him in Texas and how helpful and life-changing that meeting turned out to be.

"That helps me understand why you want Cesar to talk to a private lawyer," she said. "I haven't tried to pry into details about your past, but you know I'm here to listen if you ever need to talk."

"My focus is on the future, our future, not my past."

Kelli liked the restaurant. It was bright and airy. The ingredients available at the salad bar were fresh and the dressings homemade.

Both Max and Emma were satisfied with their meals. Ann insisted on paying.

"I'm not going to let you do that on a regular basis," Kelli said.

"Today is special."

"I like it here," Emma said from the rear seat of the vehicle as they drove back to the office.

"That's what I want to hear," Kelli replied with a happy glance at Ann.

When they entered the reception area, a deeply tanned, physically fit man in his forties was sitting in one of the waiting room chairs.

"Hi, Jon," Ann said. "I'll be with you shortly."

"Thanks again for lunch," Kelli said. "I look forward to coming to work on Monday."

Emma gave Ann a hug. Max hung back.

"You should meet Jon Tremaine before you go," Ann said to Kelli.

Ann turned to the man, who stood as Kelli introduced herself and the kids.

"Jon and his wife are about to have their first child," Ann said. "It's a boy, isn't it?"

"Yes."

"Kelli was a law school classmate who is joining the firm. She's worked in Atlanta for the U.S. Attorney's Office, followed by several years with a private litigation firm. She's also familiar with corporate law. Because of her trial experience, we'll be able to handle more types of cases."

"I try to stay out of the courtroom," Jon said with an accent that revealed his Cajun roots.

"That's the goal, but it's not always possible," Kelli replied. "It's nice meeting you."

Kelli was about to turn away, but Jon's voice stopped her.

"You worked in the U.S. Attorney's Office?" he asked.

"In Atlanta."

"Civil or criminal?"

"Mostly criminal. My boss ran the white-collar crime section."

Jon looked at Ann. "Would it be possible for her to sit in with us?"

"Her kids—" Ann started.

"I can entertain them," Lauren offered.

Kelli looked at Max and Emma. Her daughter seemed excited about spending time with the attractive young receptionist. Max less so.

"Do you have a computer Max can use?" Kelli asked.

"Yes," Lauren replied. "And I have photos of places where Curt and I like to go that might interest Emma."

"How long will it take?" Kelli asked Jon.

"I'll be as quick as possible. It's urgent."

Ann led the way to her office. Kelli could tell the client was anxious. Ann sat behind her desk as Kelli and Jon sat beside each other across from her.

"What's going on?" Ann asked.

"It has to do with one of my best employees. He's in jail and facing state and possibly federal drug charges, most likely for possession and distribution of cocaine and fentanyl."

Ann took notes while Kelli listened. Her experience in drug cases was mostly limited to money laundering. The largest case involved a sting operation entailing several million dollars. There had been enormous tension in the office while the transaction was up in the air, because the government advanced the money utilized in the transfer. All the defendants, including a bank officer and a CPA, pleaded guilty. Kelli's boss received a commendation from his superiors in Washington.

"I know Cesar will probably qualify for a court-appointed lawyer," Jon said. "But I'd like someone to meet with him now to explain what he can expect. I'll pay the consultation fee, of course."

Ann looked at Kelli. "You're much more qualified to do this than I am."

"Does your employee speak English?" Kelli asked.

"You spent a summer abroad in Spain," Ann said. "Didn't you study in Madrid?"

"Barcelona."

"Cesar's Spanish is quite a bit different from what you spoke in Spain," Jon said. "His English is decent enough. He's one of the men I send out on jobs or deliveries when it's necessary for an employee to speak English."

"Even if Cesar and I can carry on a conversation, going to the jail for an hour or so isn't going to accomplish much."

"It would let him know we care about him. I believe he's innocent, and I can't stand the thought of him getting into major trouble."

"He's already in major trouble," Kelli corrected.

"True, and intervention by a competent lawyer as soon as possible can have an impact on what takes place down the road."

"That sort of assistance takes a much higher level of involvement," Kelli said, shaking her head. "And sounds like representation."

Kelli started to let Jon know she couldn't help, but the look of desperation on his face stopped her.

"Is there something else you're worried about?" she asked.

Jon glanced down at the floor for a moment before responding. "I probably shouldn't be concerned, but yes. I was with Cesar when he delivered the first shipment of chocolate to Atlanta. The detective I talked to indicated they'd been watching Cesar for a while. That made me wonder if drugs were hidden in every shipment, which raises the potential I might be dragged into the situation."

"Okay," Kelli said slowly. "Even if that's a possibility, I'm not sure what you can do about it at this point."

"Try to quickly establish Cesar's innocence. Concern about myself exists but isn't the main reason I'm here."

"Nothing the government does happens fast, except when they're collecting taxes," Kelli replied.

Neither Ann nor Jon responded to Kelli's attempt at humor. She thought for a moment. Jon Tremaine seemed like a very decent man.

"Sorry about the tax comment," she said. "I'll go to the jail and talk to Mr. Mendez, but I can't report back to you what we discuss."

"Unless he waives the attorney-client privilege, correct?" Jon asked.

"Do you want me to ask him to do that?"

"Yes."

"A conflict can still surface that makes the waiver invalid, such as your interests becoming adverse."

"I don't think that's going to happen."

"Anything else I should know?"

"No," Jon quickly answered, rising from his chair. "Thanks for agreeing to do this."

"I'll show you out," Ann said.

Kelli remained in Ann's office until she returned.

"That was unexpected," Ann said. "Do you think Jon might be implicated?"

"It's possible. The feds cast the widest net possible and have the resources to do so." Kelli paused. "Your client seems fairly knowledgeable about legal matters. I mean, how many clients would suggest waiving the attorney-client privilege in this sort of situation?"

"He has a responsible position at the company. I think he worked his way up from the bottom and is now in charge of their whole operation in this part of the state. In addition to Spanish, he speaks French or German or both."

"Interesting."

Ann tilted her head slightly. "How did you know to ask him if there was something else on his mind? I had no clue."

"A litigator develops a sense of when a witness is holding something back. And he seemed nervous. More so than would seem justified for an employee who's in trouble."

Kelli stood. "I'll gather up the kids and ask Carly to watch them while I visit the jail later this afternoon. Have you ever been there?"

"No," Ann replied with a smile. "And I hope I never have to."

Before leaving the law office parking lot, Jon took out the burner phone and sent Chris Polter a text asking for a meeting. Usually it took the inspector a day or so to get back to him. Driving home, he rested his hand on Betsy, who'd waited in the truck while he met with the lawyers. The dog licked his hand.

"Are you going to be my therapy dog?" Jon asked.

At the worksite the equipment was operating properly and they were able to almost meet the goals for the day. Before dismissing the men, Jon gave them an update on Cesar. They stood in a semicircle and listened soberly. The crew supervisor, a man named Diego, spoke up.

"What about Maria and his boys? Where are they going to live?"

"I'm working on that."

CHAPTER 6

Carly and Emma pulled the Yahtzee box from a stack of games in the living room. Max eyed the dice game skeptically as his mother came into the room.

"Can I go to the jail with you instead of playing a game?" he asked Kelli. "I've never seen a real jail."

Carly started to speak but shut her mouth.

"No," Kelli replied. "This isn't the time for a tour. After I'm more familiar with the facility, I'll find out when certain areas are open to the public."

"Will you go into a room with bars where they lock you up?" Emma asked.

"No, they'll have a special room where a lawyer can talk to one of the prisoners."

"I'm going to be a lawyer someday," Emma said to Carly.

"I don't doubt you can be anything you want to be," Carly replied before turning to Kelli. "Do you think you'll be home for supper?"

"Definitely. And tonight I'm going to cook for you."

Kelli left. Carly had been experiencing more pain than usual, likely a result of her extra activity the previous day. She opened the Yahtzee box and explained the rules of the game to the children. It took only a few rolls of the dice for them to understand the object of play. Emma was more competitive than Max, but the boy's cool head was suited to formulating strategy.

"Could we have some popcorn to celebrate?" Emma asked after she finally won a game.

"Sure, come on into the kitchen and help."

"I'm going to my room," Max said. "I don't want any popcorn."

Carly had an old-fashioned popper that sat on the stovetop. A handle was used to rotate the stirrer inside. Carly let Emma operate the mechanism. Nothing seemed to be happening.

"Do I have to keep turning the crank?" Emma asked with a frown on her face.

"Yes, and eventually it will start popping."

As if on cue, a kernel popped. When the popcorn was ready, Carly added a dash of salt and some melted butter. They sat at the kitchen table. Emma ate a couple of bites.

"This is the best popcorn of my life," she said. "It's a lot better than what Mom fixes in the microwave."

Every day provided additional evidence that Emma was Kelli's daughter. As a child, Kelli helped Carly prepare popcorn in a device identical to the one they'd just used. Carly told Emma about it.

"Mom says you're nice, but I have to be careful what I say around you because you don't watch much TV."

"I don't watch a lot of TV. I'd rather read or do something else."

"Like play a game or make popcorn?"

"Or talk to you."

Emma ate several more bites of popcorn. "Did you like my dad?"

For years Carly had prayed for Kelli and Brad. Brad was quiet and reserved. Carly couldn't recall a significant conversation with him. In their limited interaction, she didn't pick up on any warning signs that he might abruptly jettison his wife and children. He had seemed devoted to Kelli and the kids. His sudden departure with another woman was a shock.

"Yes, I liked your dad."

"I miss him. He's not coming to visit for over two months! Can you believe that?"

Not sure how to help a precocious seven-year-old girl navigate these murky waters, Carly stayed silent.

"It's okay if you just listen and don't tell me what I should think," Emma continued.

Startled by the complexity of the little girl's thoughts, Carly reached out and patted Emma on the hand.

Emma looked at her with soulful eyes. "But can you help my mom? I've seen her crying when she didn't know I was watching."

"Yes, I want to help all three of you."

Kelli parked in front of the jail. She'd phoned ahead to confirm access to Cesar Mendez. The woman on duty asked to see Kelli's driver's license and her bar association card.

"Have a seat," she said. "I'll let you know when the prisoner is available."

As a prosecutor, Kelli rarely visited a jail. The defendants in white-collar matters were almost always out on bond while their cases moved through the system. Fifteen minutes passed. During that time, a man who was clearly intoxicated and a woman who was screaming at the arresting officer entered. Kelli returned to the woman at the window.

"Any idea when I'll be able to see Mr. Mendez?" she asked.

"We're short-staffed on Friday afternoons."

Ten minutes later, the woman signaled for her to come forward. As she did, a door buzzed and opened. A young male deputy in his twenties appeared.

"Ms. Quinn?" he asked.

"Yes."

"Follow me."

Kelli entered a hallway. They passed through another electric door. The deputy stopped.

"Do you want the door open or closed while you meet with the prisoner?" he asked.

"Uh, closed."

He used a key to unlock the door. Inside the small room was a slender Latino man with short dark hair and a wispy mustache. He was sitting in a chair on the other side of a small table. He gave Kelli a puzzled look. The door closed behind her before Kelli introduced herself.

"I work with Ann Carter, the attorney who helped you when you first started importing chocolate. Jon Tremaine asked me to come see you."

At the mention of Jon's name, the man nodded.

"Is it okay that we speak English?" Kelli continued. "Do you understand what I said?"

"Yes," the man replied. "My English is okay."

Kelli sat down across from him. "I'm not agreeing to represent you," she said, "but I'm willing to listen if you want to tell me what happened."

As Cesar's story unfolded, Kelli could see why his boss thought the sincere young man might be telling the truth. But there was also the possibility Cesar was a willing participant in a drug-smuggling scheme.

"Will you tell me about your family members in Mexico who ship the chocolate?" she asked.

"It's my uncle and my cousin. They pick the beans and sell them to Philippe, a man in our village who turns them into chocolate. Philippe agreed to let my family send chocolate to me because I could get a much better price than at the local market."

"How do you communicate with your uncle and cousin?"

"Email or phone."

"Do you have copies of the emails?"

"Yes. I save them in a folder on my computer. Everything about the business is in one place. I use a spreadsheet."

"Okay," Kelli said, impressed. "What was Mr. Tremaine's role?"

"He is my boss."

"I mean with the chocolate."

"Jon took me to see Ms. Carter so I would have the right paperwork, and he drove me to Atlanta the first time to meet with the man who bought the chocolate."

Kelli realized that Cesar and Jon Tremaine were on a first-name basis.

"You went to Atlanta in Jon's truck?" she asked.

"Yes, and he sold me his old truck. I'm paying him two hundred dollars a month for it."

"Did you pay Jon anything for helping you with the chocolate business?"

"Uh, I filled his truck up with gas when we went to Atlanta." Cesar thought for a moment. "And I gave Sarah some chocolate so she could make mole."

"Who is Sarah?"

"His wife."

"Did the police ask you questions about Jon?"

"Yes. I told the detective that he went with me to Atlanta but not about giving his wife chocolate as a gift."

Kelli leaned back in her chair. Jon Tremaine seemed to be in the clear. And the more she talked to Cesar, the less convinced she was that he might be guilty.

"Do you have any idea why the police found drugs in the shipment of chocolate from your family?"

Cesar leaned forward. "I've thought about that a lot since I've been locked up. I believe someone put the drugs there after my uncle packed the pallet."

"Why do you say that?"

"Because it didn't look right to me when it came off the ship."

"Why not?"

"It was wrapped in plastic that looked different from the other times I received it."

"How was it different?"

"My uncle and cousin wrap green plastic over brown cloth. I'm not sure what you call it."

"Burlap?"

"I think so. This time the crate was only wrapped in green plastic, very tight like it was done with a machine. And the cloth was gone."

"Did you ask your uncle about it?"

"I couldn't because I was arrested and brought to the jail from the place where they unload the ship."

"Do you have photos of other shipments?"

"Yes, I always take a picture with my phone and send it to my uncle or cousin to let them know it arrived."

"Did you take a picture of this shipment?"

"Yes, and I sent it to my cousin and Philippe."

"Where is your phone?"

"The police have it."

The information wasn't proof of innocence, but it raised the possibility of tampering.

"What's your cousin's name?" she asked.

"Manuel Mendez. And my uncle is Christo Sotero. Can you get my phone from the police?"

"The lawyer who represents you can get access to it at some point. You'll need to ask the judge to appoint a free lawyer for you when you're taken to the courthouse on Tuesday for your arraignment."

"Arrangement? What's that?"

"Arraignment. You'll be brought before a judge who will ask if you're guilty or innocent and then set bond. You should say, 'Not guilty,' and ask for an appointed lawyer."

"Will you help me?" Cesar asked. "If Jon trusts you, then I trust you."

"He doesn't really know me. We just met earlier today for a few minutes."

"That's good enough for me," Cesar said, speaking rapidly. "I don't have much money, but I'll pay you what I have. We were saving the money from the chocolate so my grandmother could have a surgery."

"How much money have you saved?"

"Around ten thousand dollars."

Kelli raised her eyebrows. "And how much do you earn working at the tree farm?"

"Last year I made around forty-eight thousand dollars. We work a lot of overtime."

"How many children do you have?"

"Two boys, Sancho and Emmanuel."

Kelli thought for a moment. "The money you've saved and earn may have an impact on whether you qualify for a court-appointed attorney. Do you have a lot of bills?"

"No, we don't spend more money than we need for food and clothes and rent."

"Credit cards or loans?"

"No, except what I owe Jon for my truck."

Kelli pushed her chair away from the table. "Is it okay if I talk to Jon about what you told me today? Because I'm a lawyer, our conversation can be just between us."

"You can speak to him."

Kelli took a waiver of attorney-client privilege from her purse and explained it to Cesar. He signed it without asking any questions.

"Thank you for coming to see me," Cesar said. "It is very lonely sitting in the jail cell where all I have are my thoughts and worries."

Jon was on the jobsite when he received a phone call. He stepped over to his truck to get away from the noise of the equipment and saw it was the lawyer who'd agreed to visit Cesar in the jail.

"Hello," he said as he got inside the vehicle.

"It's Kelli Quinn. I'm on my way home after meeting with Cesar."

"How did it go?"

Jon listened as the lawyer relayed the conversation.

"There's a chance he's telling the truth," Kelli said. "And the difference in the appearance of the most recent shipment creates the possibility of tampering after it was prepared by his family. The fact that you were involved in taking the first shipment to Atlanta is a minor issue."

"Where does that leave us?"

"In the same place where you were before I went to the jail. The criminal process is going to have to unfold. Cesar is set for arraignment on Tuesday. Based on the amount of money he has in the bank and what he earns in wages, I'm not sure he's going to qualify for an appointed attorney. It's a multistep evaluation that includes a financial affidavit. The superior court judge will make the final determination of eligibility. There will be a similar process if Cesar is charged in federal court."

"He isn't going to earn anything while he's locked up."

"But they'll still consider his wages prior to arrest and the money he saved to pay for a family member's surgery."

Jon paused for a moment. "His wife is going to need any money they've saved to survive. How much would a private attorney charge to take on a case like this?"

"That could vary a lot. Don't worry about a bill from me for going by to see him. It only took an hour and a half. Cesar is a nice man, and I'm sorry he's going through this."

"I intend to pay you."

"No, it's fine."

The call ended, and Jon remained in his truck. Some of his codefendants paid hundreds of thousands of dollars for legal representation in the Texas cases. The Porsche 911 Jon was driving at the time of his arrest was seized by the FBI and subjected to forfeiture. Within a month of his arrest, he was penniless. One of his great-uncles sold two cars and cashed in a bag of gold coins he kept at the bottom of a well so that Jon could hire the private attorney who successfully negotiated the plea deal. Jon promised to pay his uncle back, but Uncle Nate, who had no children of his own, died from a heart attack while the case was still pending. Jon moved to Georgia with little more than the clothes on his back and a truck that required a quart of oil every five hundred miles. No one could claim that for Jon, crime paid.

As he was about to get out of the truck, his burner phone vibrated. It was Chris Polter.

Tomorrow at 10:00 a.m. The usual place.

At home, Jon took a shower and joined Sarah in the kitchen. She was stirring a pot of chili. Standing behind her, Jon put his arms around her expanding waist.

"Your chili is the best on the planet," he said.

"You always say that," Sarah replied, resting her head against his shoulder for a moment.

"Because it's true."

"How did it go with the lawyer?"

"Good. I'll tell you while we eat."

Jon sprinkled cheddar cheese and corn chips on top of his chili. While they ate, he told Sarah about the meeting with Ann and the new lawyer named Kelli Quinn.

"It's good that Ms. Quinn has experience in criminal cases," Sarah said. "Do you think there's a chance she'd represent Cesar?"

"Not without being paid. I thought about asking her if she'd put her name on the appointed list for the local federal court. If so, the case could be assigned to her, but she just arrived in town and may not be interested in doing that." Jon ate a bite of chili before adding, "I sent a text to Chris asking for a meeting. Also, something strange happened to me while I was talking to the lawyers. I got all nervous and shaky on the inside. My palms even got sweaty."

Sarah raised her eyebrows. "You've always been the one who's calm in the midst of a storm, whether at home or at work."

"I know. Driving home, I wondered if I might have a touch of PTSD. Maybe this situation with Cesar has triggered what I went through years ago."

Sarah was unaware that after Jon agreed to testify against the members of the cartel, he had received two death threats and was placed in protective custody. One morning while being transported to court, Jon was almost killed. A sniper fired at the vehicle in which Jon was riding. The bullet shattered a window and missed Jon's head by less than a foot.

Pushing away her bowl of chili, Sarah moved close to him and wrapped her arms around his neck. She held him for several seconds. Jon shifted slightly, but Sarah didn't loosen her grip. When she finally let go, he saw that her eyes were wet with tears. She leaned over and kissed him on the lips and then on his forehead.

"Jon Tremaine," she said. "Whatever you've been through in the past and whatever you face in the future, I want you to remember that I love you with my whole heart for my whole life."

CHAPTER 7

Saturday morning, Kelli took the children to Oceanview Beach Park at Jekyll Island. Before they left the house, Kelli and Carly fixed a picnic lunch of sandwiches and fruit. When they finished, Carly handed her a plastic bag filled with cookies. "These are the cookies you asked me to bake."

Kelli opened the bag and sampled one. They were flat and extra crispy.

"Perfect," Kelli said.

"I bought some margarine and have plenty left over," Carly said with a smile. "That means I'm going to have to make more cookies."

"If that's the case, I may share these with the kids instead of hiding them and eating all of them myself."

It was a thirty-minute drive from Carly's home to Jekyll Island. Emma kept up a constant banter sprinkled with questions about what they would do.

"I want to do more than play on the beach," she said. "Is this the place that has putt-putt golf?"

"It's not far away, at Great Dunes Park."

"I want to go."

They paid an access fee and crossed onto the island via a causeway. In the back of the vehicle were chairs, an umbrella, the picnic lunch, the bag of cookies, and a box of beach toys that had been unloaded from the moving truck. As soon as they parked, Emma jumped out and ran toward the water. Max stayed to help Kelli.

"I think we can do it in one trip," he said, loading up both arms.

Seeing him assume manly duties touched Kelli. "Only because you're amazing," she said.

They made their way to an open spot on the beach. Emma returned from splashing in the surf.

"The water is warm!" she exclaimed.

"It's had all summer to heat up," Kelli said. "Stay and help us with this stuff."

They spread out a beach blanket, positioned the chairs, and secured the umbrella in the sand. A breeze was blowing but not enough to tip the umbrella. Kelli opened the box of sand toys. Emma grabbed a plastic shovel and pail and ran off. She wanted to dig a hole and fill it with water. Max laid out his tools on the blanket.

"I'm missing my little shovel," he said. "The one that I use to shape the towers."

"We'll get another one."

Max gathered everything and trotted toward the water. Kelli sat in the sun and watched. Her son would find a place with access to wet sand, make a pile, and shape a castle worthy of being photographed by beach walkers. When Brad was on the scene, the pile of damp sand could be much bigger. Today Max would have to settle for less.

Kelli enjoyed watching the waves. The consistent rhythm of the ocean spoke of continuity in the midst of change. That's why a trip to the ocean was at the top of her to-do list upon arriving in Brunswick.

She and Brad had been to Jekyll Island and other beaches many times. They'd visited this same beach two years earlier. Remembering that day, Kelli glanced to the right to the spot where the four of them had set up their umbrella in front of a solitary palmetto tree growing amid the dunes. Instead of wallowing in regret over what she'd lost, Kelli wanted to press into the reality of a new life. Looking back to the beach, she saw a couple in their mid- to late thirties walking along the surf and holding hands. From a distance, the man looked so much like Brad that Kelli did a double take. She quickly glanced away. Any hope of settling into a new life evaporated. Getting up from her chair, she walked over to Max, who was working steadily.

"Do you have a bigger shovel I can use to help you collect a mound of sand?" she asked.

He looked up at her and pointed. "Over there."

Max's sandcastle turned out great. Several people stopped to take pictures. Most posed with Max. Meanwhile, Emma saw a jellyfish but avoided getting stung.

Shortly after they finished their picnic lunch, Emma asked, "Can we play golf now?"

"Are you already tired of the beach?"

"Kind of," Emma replied. "But now that we live here, we can come back anytime we want."

Max reached into the cookie bag.

"How about you?" Kelli asked her son. "Are you ready to leave?"

"I don't care so long as we can bring the cookies."

They loaded the car and drove to the putt-putt golf course. Arriving at the course, they stood in line behind two large families, one white, the other Latino. Kelli looked at the young fathers, thought about Cesar, and wondered if he ever brought his children to the beach.

"I want a pink ball," Emma piped up.

Max selected green and Kelli settled on blue. Max had significantly improved since the last time they'd played. He played par through the first eight holes, including a hole in one. Kelli and Emma both knocked balls off the carpeted course into the vegetation.

"How did you get to be so good?" Kelli asked.

"I've been practicing at home."

"Where?"

"A golf game on my tablet."

Kelli wasn't sure how a video skill transferred to real life. They stopped to wait for one of the families to finish the next hole. The father was carrying a little boy who was too small to participate. The man would set the boy down, play his ball, and pick him up. The little boy rested his head on his father's shoulder. Emma pointed at them.

"That little boy is cute," she said.

They finished the game. Next door to the golf course was an ice-cream parlor. Kelli and the kids entered the air-conditioned space. One of the families followed them in. There were ten in their group, including what appeared to be grandparents. It was obvious they came from a lower economic status. Kelli and her children ordered ice cream. She leaned over the counter and spoke to the young woman serving them.

"Whatever that family orders, tell them it's on the house," Kelli said in a soft voice. "I'll pay for it."

Kelli sat between Max and Emma and watched. Some members of the family weren't ordering. The young server looked at Kelli, who nodded her head.

"You all can have something!" the server announced in a loud voice. "It's free today!"

Watching the group eat was more enjoyable for Kelli than the scoop of rich butter pecan in her own waffle cone. As soon as she could do so without being obvious, she returned to the counter and paid the bill. Then she and the kids left.

"Did you buy ice cream for that family?" Max asked as they walked to the car.

"Yes."

"I thought so." Max nodded as he continued, "That was cool."

Driving home, Kelli knew part of the motivation for her generosity had to do with meeting Cesar Mendez. The man sitting in jail couldn't be with his family to play putt-putt golf or eat ice cream.

Jon parked in front of the coffee shop on River Street in Savannah at 9:58 a.m. He knew Chris Polter was already in the area, but the U.S. marshal always let Jon arrive first to the designated location. Even after all these years, Chris liked to make sure no one seemed interested in Jon's presence. Five minutes later the beefy inspector with thinning blond hair walked through the door and up to the counter. He brought a hot tea to the table and placed it in front of Jon.

"Taxpayer dollars at work," said the former Marine Corps MP, who had an upstate New York accent. "The barista drizzled in a few drops of honey."

"Thanks," Jon replied. "I appreciate you scheduling a meeting off the books."

Chris had piercing blue eyes and forearms that would make Popeye envious.

"You wouldn't want to see me if it wasn't important. What's going on?"

Jon laid out the sequence of events surrounding Cesar's arrest.

"Were you anywhere near the docks on the day he was picked up?" Chris asked.

"No."

"Alibis for your presence?"

"I was with a crew at the tree farm. Cesar had the day off to take delivery of the load of chocolate."

"And your concern is that the local detective or the FBI may dig into your background?"

"Yeah, it's hard for me to trust anyone in law enforcement—"

"Except me," Chris interrupted with a grin.

Jon nodded. "Right. Also, I didn't want my name surfacing in a report that came across your desk without you knowing what was really going on."

"Do you know what's really going on?"

Jon didn't answer. The inspector took a drink of coffee, then lowered his cup to the table.

"What do you think?" Jon asked.

"Everyone knows that a jury is supposed to operate under the presumption of innocence, but we aren't in front of a jury. I think Cesar is probably guilty. He may not be a bad guy, but it's not uncommon for people you'd invite over to the house for hamburgers on the grill to make terrible decisions and end up in a lot of trouble."

"I fall in that category," Jon said.

"I didn't know you then, but I'll let you believe that if you want to. One item in your employee's situation that stuck out to me was the means of concealment for the contraband. You said it reminded you of the way your cartel operated."

"Yes. Los Reyes had many streams of entry for product but routinely operated in a similar manner. We occasionally used blind mules for transport."

"Makes you sound less innocent to me," Chris said. "Anyway, it doesn't take a brilliant detective to conclude this isn't a small-time local operation but part of something bigger than piggybacking on a single shipment of chocolate. If that's true, the FBI probably has a file that contains a lot of information."

"Could you obtain access?"

Chris raised his eyebrows. "I'm your handler, not a private investigator for your employee."

"Of course, I just—"

"Want to help your worker. But I'm interested in you, not an unrelated drug investigation. I'm going to include what you've told me in my report of your status but won't reach out to anyone with the FBI about a local investigation. It goes without saying that you need to keep your distance from anyone potentially linked to criminal activity."

"I don't believe Cesar is guilty."

"Make sure any help you give him doesn't bite you. If I hear about anything you need to know, I'll contact you and set up a meeting."

"Sounds good."

The inspector leaned back in his chair. "Have I shown you what I've done to my boat?" he asked.

"Not the latest. You were replacing some of the deck boards."

Chris took out his regular phone. "That's complete, and I've done a lot since then."

Returning home, Jon gave Sarah a report and spent the afternoon working on her list of chores. At 5:00 p.m. he sat on the back step with Betsy beside him. As he wiped his forehead with a rag from his back pocket, Sarah appeared with a glass of ice water.

"I'm going to work on resetting those pavers that have come loose," Jon said as he stretched out his legs in front of him.

"Would you rather go to dinner in Brunswick? I'm paying."

For a split second, Jon thought he'd overlooked the significance of the date on the calendar. It wasn't their anniversary, but Sarah had a list of other special days, and he could have forgotten one.

"What day is it?" he asked cautiously. "The anniversary of our first date?"

"No, that's next month. This is just a day for me to do something nice for my husband, so long as it's not too expensive for a woman on a part-time salary."

"I'm a cheap date."

Sarah leaned against the railing. Jon took a long drink of water.

"How did you feel today?" she asked. "You know, about talking to Chris Polter and everything else that's going on."

"Chris didn't really say or do anything special, but he made me feel more normal. I don't like the fact that I'm lurking in the darkness trying not to be discovered."

Sarah rested her hand on his shoulder. "Do you remember what I told you the other day?"

"About loving me more than life itself?"

"Not my exact words, but you can remember it however you want. Go inside and get ready. I'll give directions to our specific destination when we're close to town."

Going to dinner didn't include Betsy tagging along in the rear seat of the truck. Jon and Sarah were quiet during the drive into Brunswick. He glanced over at her. Sarah was wearing a yellow maternity dress and sandals.

"You look great," he said.

"I'm great with child," she replied. "Turn right at the next light."

Their route took them by the local sheriff's department and jail.

"Slow down," Sarah said when they were close to the law enforcement complex. "Where is Cesar in those buildings?"

Jon pointed to a single-story structure on the far right. "If you look closely, you can see the razor wire. That's where they let the prisoners exercise. I don't know how they separate the prisoners inside. Initially, they placed Cesar in a single cell except for meals. That will likely change."

"Will he be in danger?"

Jon had experienced many anxious nights behind bars. Young and strong, he wasn't an easy target for harassment, and his known connection to the Mexican gang caused other prisoners to steer clear of him. But when he agreed to testify for the government, he was placed in solitary confinement. From that point forward, Jon ate in his cell and wasn't allowed in the exercise yard with anyone else. One day, he was in a hallway accompanied by a guard when a member of the gang saw him and cursed at him. Jon stared straight ahead and tried to ignore him. Three days later the shot was fired at the car in which Jon was riding.

"They usually keep things under control in a local jail," he said. "When there are a lot of violent criminals in a state or federal facility, it can be much rougher."

"Cesar needs to get out. He's a gentle soul."

"True, but his bond is likely going to be very high. And the fact that he and Maria are so frugal with the money they've saved to help Cesar's grandmother with her medical treatment may disqualify him for an appointed lawyer."

"It's terrible to have to make that sort of choice."

"Yes."

"Turn left and drive three blocks," Sarah said.

Jon made the turn.

"I know where we're going," he said, nodding. "It's the place with Bahamian dishes. We can eat outside. I love it."

Carly woke up early on Sunday morning and felt well enough to go to church. She'd taken it easy the previous day while Kelli and the children were at the beach. Coffee was brewing in the kitchen when Kelli appeared, rubbed her eyes, and yawned.

"Did I wake you?" Carly asked. "I tried to be quiet."

"No, I was up several times during the night and didn't wake up for my morning walk."

"I'm sorry."

Kelli tapped the side of her head. "Even when my body is exhausted, my brain sometimes refuses to stay turned off."

"What kept you up?"

As soon as she asked the question, Carly wished she could pull it back. Kelli gave her a wry look.

"Different things. Tormented by the past, worrying about the future."

The machine signaled the end of the brewing cycle.

"Is that regular coffee?" Kelli asked.

"Yes. A special blend that a friend grinds. My doctor says it's okay in moderation."

"Moderation isn't in my vocabulary when it comes to coffee. Is there enough for me to have a couple of cups?"

"Sure."

Carly poured the coffee. "Still drink it black?"

"Yes. I don't want to hide the flavor."

Carly added cream and sugar. The two women sat at the kitchen table.

"I didn't expect one thing that woke me up last night," Kelli said after a few sips. "I met with a man yesterday at the jail. Some of what he told me is confidential, but I can give you the basic story."

Carly listened as Kelli told her about the man who worked for one of Ann Carter's clients.

"Sometimes I feel sorry for myself, you know, being forced into a single-parent role. But this man is locked up and can't be with his wife and children."

"Are you thinking you should help him?"

"Not really," Kelli said, hesitating. "But he may not qualify for an appointed lawyer, which will put him in a tough spot. I'm not going to be very busy for a while, so I could probably take it on. But not pro bono. It would be way too complicated to accept without payment."

"Talk to Ann about it."

"Yeah," Kelli replied. "I'll tell her what I found out and see what she says without suggesting anything." She leaned back in her chair. "Are you going to church this morning?"

"Yes, the early service. Would you like to bring the kids and join me?"

"No." Kelli shook her head. "Just because I had a restless night doesn't mean they can't sleep in. They'll have to be up early for school tomorrow."

The children were eating breakfast when Carly left the house. It was a ten-minute drive to the church she'd attended since she was a child. Attendance had been declining in recent years, and parts of the historic structure were never used. Carly knew everyone in the pews. Going through the familiar routine, she tried to imagine Max and Emma beside her. There was no one in the sanctuary under the age of fifty.

The 9:30 a.m. service, called the geriatric meeting by some members of the congregation, had started twenty-five years earlier due to overcrowding at the 11:00 a.m. service. Now the sanctuary wasn't full at either service. But inertia is a powerful institutional force, and most of those who attended the early service didn't want to give it up. During the responsive reading, Carly was touched by the Scriptures from Romans. It was one of her favorite chapters in the Bible. The text for the sermon, read by an older gentleman with a distinguished voice, was Romans 5:1–5:

> "Therefore, since we have been justified through faith, we have peace with God through our Lord Jesus Christ, through whom we have gained access by faith into this grace in which we now stand. And we boast in the hope of the glory of God. Not only so, but we also glory in our sufferings, because we know that suffering produces perseverance; perseverance, character; and character, hope. And hope does not put us to shame, because God's love has been poured out into our hearts through the Holy Spirit, who has been given to us."

The rhythmic, unwavering majesty of the words touched Carly. Alan, the minister serving as an associate to the senior pastor, delivered an excellent sermon. He was about the same age as Kelli and might be a good person to talk to her about matters of faith. Her niece had certainly experienced a recent heavy dose of suffering. Discovering hope would be new to her.

CHAPTER 8

Sunday afternoon Jon and Sarah packed a full meal in the truck and took it to Maria. She answered the door wearing a nice dress.

"Thank you so much," she said with a big smile when she saw the food. "I just got home from church, and the boys are hungry."

"It's three o'clock," Jon replied. "What time did it start?"

"About ten o'clock, but you know how people are. They come when they're ready."

Punctuality was a challenge on the tree farm. Jon used modest incentives that encouraged adaptation to American work culture.

"It was a good service," Maria continued in Spanish. "The church prayed a long time for Cesar. It gave me hope."

"That's good," Jon replied, then translated for Sarah.

"Prayer works," Sarah commented.

"Come in," Maria said, stepping to the side.

Accepting hospitality was one of the cultural lessons Jon had learned to follow. They entered the double-wide mobile home that seemed more like a regular house on the inside. The boys were watching an animated show on TV. Jon and Sarah placed the containers of food on the kitchen table.

"Is that a good show?" Maria asked Jon. "They are learning English, but I don't know what they're saying."

Jon turned to Sarah and repeated the question.

"Yes," Sarah said. "My nieces and nephews watch that show."

Jon and Maria talked while the three of them unpacked the food. At the smell of dinner, the boys left the TV and came into the kitchen. Dark-haired and slender like their father, Sancho was seven and Emmanuel was four.

"Did you go see my daddy?" Sancho asked Jon in English.

"Yes."

"Are you going to help him come home?" the little boy continued.

"I want to."

"Don't bother Mr. Jon with questions," Maria said in Spanish.

"It's okay," Jon replied.

"Let's pray and eat. Mr. Jon, will you say a prayer?" Maria asked him in English.

Jon looked at Sarah. He had no church background. Sarah attended church as a child and a few years earlier had experienced a renaissance of faith through her contacts at the women's shelter. She occasionally listened to online church services. Jon had an open invitation to join her but didn't. There was always plenty to be done around the house.

"Go ahead, honey," Sarah said with a smile. "She asked you, not me."

Jon scowled at Sarah, then folded his hands together in front of him. Both of the boys stared at Jon for a moment before copying him. Jon squeezed his eyes shut.

"God, we thank you for this food," he said, then paused. "And please get Cesar out of jail."

Jon opened his eyes.

"You forgot to say, 'Amen,'" Sancho said with one eye open and one shut. "That lets God know you're finished."

"Amen," Jon quickly added.

The boys didn't turn their noses up at any of the food Sarah had prepared and ate with gusto. Emmanuel especially liked the mashed potatoes with melted butter on top. He ate two servings.

"He has not had potatoes like that to eat," Maria said in halting English to Sarah. "How do you cook?"

"Can you explain?" Sarah asked Jon.

Jon tried to remember the steps and communicate them in Spanish. Twice he had to stop and ask for clarification from Sarah. Maria nodded.

"I will cook mashed potatoes for Cesar when God answers our prayers," Maria said.

Jon told her about asking Kelli Quinn to visit Cesar at the jail and what the lawyer told him. Maria listened intently.

"I know it made Cesar feel better. Our pastor called the chaplain at the jail. I hope to visit Cesar at the jail this week."

"I want to go," Sancho said in Spanish. "I've drawn some pictures to give Papa. He can put them on the wall of his room."

"No," Maria said, shaking her head. "Not the first time."

They had apple cobbler for dessert. Once again, Maria wanted to know how to prepare it.

"I'll talk to Sarah and write down the recipe for you," Jon replied.

Sarah helped Maria clear the table while Jon went outside with the boys. There was a soccer ball beside the front door. Sancho was adept with his feet and Emmanuel showed more coordination than Jon expected. Cesar had always been one of the more athletic employees and could rapidly ascend a tree with climbing boots and spurs. Sancho easily dribbled the ball around Jon.

"Try to stop me," he said with a laugh.

"I am."

The boys played happily. Jon marveled at their resilience. Back inside the house, Sancho ran to a bedroom and returned with a stack of papers in his hand. He laid them on the table.

"Here are some of my pictures," he said to Jon. "Tell me the ones you like best. I want to give Papa good ones."

There was a diverse selection, including their house, the family, a soccer ball, a pickup truck, and several others. Jon chose the ones of the family and their house. The family drawing had enough detail to immediately distinguish between the two boys, and the child had done a nice job with Maria's long hair. The house drawing was equally accurate.

"I believe he'd like these," Jon said. "It will remind him of the things he loves."

"Okay." Sancho nodded seriously.

The boys returned to the TV. After thanking them again, Maria walked Jon and Sarah to the front door. Jon stopped.

"Would you be willing to pay the money you've saved selling chocolate to hire a lawyer to represent Cesar?" he asked.

"Yes," Maria said without hesitation.

"I'm not sure it would be enough, but it's worth a try. Do you think Cesar would agree?"

"He'll have to," Maria replied emphatically.

When Kelli returned from her walk on Monday morning, Max was already stirring. Emma had her eyes closed. Kelli touched her daughter on the shoulder and shook her gently. It was a ten-minute drive to the children's school.

"Time to wake up and get ready for school," Kelli said.

"Can I start school next week?" Emma asked groggily. "No one knows I'm here, and I could do fun things with Aunt Carly."

"The school knows you're coming, and there will be plenty of time to hang out with Aunt Carly."

Emma turned over and faced the wall. Kelli didn't force the issue. She'd learned that Emma liked to wake up on her own terms. Kelli paused at the bedroom door and peeked through the crack next to one of the hinges. Sure enough, Emma slipped out of bed. Kelli went into the kitchen. Carly, dressed for the day, was already there.

"What are you doing up so early?" Kelli asked.

"I didn't beat you out of bed. How was your walk?"

"Uneventful."

"I have a friend who walks and prays in her neighborhood."

Kelli didn't respond. Carly continued, "The teacher in me knows that the first day of school at any age is a big deal. I thought I'd help by fixing breakfast."

"Nothing fancy. I don't want the kids to get spoiled."

"It'll be simple," Carly said with a wave of her hand. "Take care of yourself."

When Kelli returned dressed for the day, the children were eating scrambled eggs and toast with jelly. Carly wasn't there.

"Why don't your eggs taste like this?" Emma asked Kelli. "They're so light and fluffy."

"Nobody fixes better eggs than Aunt Carly," Kelli replied. "Where is she?"

"I think she went someplace to lie down," Max replied.

Kelli found her aunt in the living room with her head on a cushion and her legs stretched out in front of her on the sofa.

"I had a bad twinge in my back and had to get off my feet," Carly said.

"Don't overdo."

"I know, I know. It's just because it's the first day. I'll take it easy after you leave. Are you fixing lunch for the children?"

"No, they'll eat in the school cafeteria."

Kelli sat at the table. Max had already finished and gone to brush his teeth.

"May I have a second helping of eggs?" Emma asked in her most polite tone of voice.

"Not if we're going to make it to school on time."

"That's okay. Good nutrition is a reason to be late."

Kelli reached over and took Emma's plate. "Why are you trying to get out of going to school?" she asked.

Emma sniffled and looked at Kelli with sad eyes. "Because it's a new place, and I don't have any friends."

Kelli pulled the little girl to her feet and held her close in her arms. Kelli ran her fingers through Emma's hair. "You're going to begin new friendships with at least one or two girls before you get home this afternoon."

"Are you sure?" Emma asked, her head still pressed close to Kelli.

"Because you know how to be a friend, you're going to have friends. Remember your first day at your old school? You came home talking about Laura, Brittany, and Amber."

"Yes," Emma said as she turned away. "But what if I can't find the right bus to ride home?"

"Max is going to help you. Just look for him when they let you out of school."

"Okay," Emma sighed. "I guess I'll go."

Emma was cheerful and chatty during the ride. Max didn't say much but acknowledged Kelli's last-minute instructions about looking out for his sister. After dropping them off, Kelli faced her own case of nervousness.

She parked in her designated spot and checked her appearance in the rearview mirror. As she'd gotten older, Kelli's hair had lost more of the reddish tint that still flashed in Emma's locks. Kelli's green eyes retained their fire, but the fire was now tinged with sadness. She took a deep breath and opened the car door. Entering through the rear of the building, she went directly to her office. There was a large arrangement of flowers on her desk along with a kind note of welcome, written by Ann and signed by her and Lauren. Flowers had never been part of the law firm culture in Atlanta. Kelli stepped over to Ann's office. Ann was staring at her computer monitor.

"Good morning," Kelli said. "Thanks for the beautiful flowers."

Ann turned away from the monitor and smiled. "You're welcome. How are the kids?"

Kelli sat across from Ann and told her about the children.

"Emma will be fine," Kelli said. "She makes friends easily. Max isolates himself."

"How do you feel about your first day at work?"

"Positive. I'm ready to be productive."

"Making that happen is what I'm working on," Ann replied. "I'm putting together a list of files for you to review. I'll send it over in an hour or so."

"Anything with an impending deadline?"

"Nothing urgent," Ann replied and shook her head. "I hate last-minute rushes."

"Just like law school. You never crammed for an exam."

"But that didn't put me in the top ten percent of the class like you."

"That stuff means nothing now that we're in practice." Kelli paused. "Tell me the truth. How do you feel about me being here this morning?"

Ann smiled. "Excited. The thought of working with you makes me happy."

"I'm glad," Kelli said, standing up. "Oh, I went to the jail on Friday afternoon and met with Jon Tremaine's employee."

"I forgot about that. How did it go?"

Kelli summarized the visit. "I called Jon and filled him in. And waived any consultation fee. I hope that's okay."

"Of course," Ann said. She scrunched up her nose. Kelli recognized it as a sign that her friend was thinking.

"Would you consider representing Cesar?" Ann said. She quickly added, "Not that I'm telling or even suggesting you do so."

"Drug trafficking isn't my area of expertise, and a criminal case can be a huge time commitment."

"Yeah, I can imagine," Ann acknowledged. "And any fee would have to come from the money they saved for the sick relative. Anyway, thanks for doing that. I want to develop a business relationship with Jon. Like I said the other day, he could be a good source of work down the road."

CHAPTER 9

Jon was squeezing orange juice at 5:45 a.m. when Sarah came into the kitchen. He glanced over his shoulder.

"You're up early," he said. "Are you okay?"

"Yes." Sarah plopped down in one of the kitchen chairs.

"Should I start brewing the coffee?"

"Yes," she repeated.

Sarah always measured out the coffee the previous evening so that all she had to do was press the button in the morning. She didn't program it for the same time because her arrival in the kitchen varied. Jon pushed the button.

"I'm going to toast a bagel," he continued. "Do you want one?"

"No."

Jon was used to Sarah's lack of communication until she was fully awake, but he had no clue why she'd shown up in the kitchen.

"It's going to be a nice day with enough clouds to make it cooler," Jon said, looking out the window over the sink. "That's good because one crew needs to be on the ground clearing out volunteer plants. The other group is going to be spraying for bark beetles."

Volunteer seedlings had to be removed like weeds from a garden. It was hard work performed by hand at a fast pace. Sarah didn't respond. While the coffee dripped, Jon spread cream cheese on his bagel. He added cream and sugar to the coffee and brought a mug over to Sarah.

"Thanks," she said but didn't take a sip.

Jon sat across from her. He took a bite of bagel and looked at her expectantly.

"What's on your mind this morning?" he asked. "Aren't you going to the shelter today?"

"Yes. I have several meetings on the calendar this morning." Sarah took a deep breath and sighed. "I didn't sleep well last night. At first I tried to ignore what was running through my head. You know how sometimes a person tries to process what's going on in life through dreams?"

"Yes," Jon said, then waited.

Sarah sipped her coffee. Jon heard Betsy bark at the back door. The dog knew when he was stirring in the house. Usually he let her in immediately.

"Is it okay if I let Betsy inside and feed her?" he asked.

"Sure."

Jon opened the door, and Betsy pattered inside. She stood beside Sarah, who scratched the dog's head while Jon poured a generous portion of dry dog food into a metal bowl. Betsy would eat cheap kibble, but Jon made sure the pet received a quality breakfast. The dog buried her nose in the dish. Jon returned to the table.

"I think we're supposed to help Cesar hire a lawyer," Sarah blurted out.

Jon, who was about to take another bite of bagel, lowered it to his plate.

Speaking rapidly, Sarah continued, "I kept thinking and dreaming about Cesar's boys and how sad it is that he's not with them. I know he might still go to prison even if he gets a private attorney, but I feel like we need to do whatever we can to help him. He risked his life for you, and I don't feel right about not considering how we can help him. Maria seems so strong, even though I'm sure she's frantic with worry."

Sarah stopped as tears came into her eyes. She grabbed a napkin from the plastic container in the center of the table.

"You mean help pay for an attorney?" Jon asked.

"If it was you instead of Cesar, I'd want someone to step in and help," Sarah explained. "You're the one bringing in most of the money now, but we have money in that mutual fund we opened when you got the big raise. I checked the balance in the middle of the night, and it's been doing pretty good. How much do you think it would take to hire a lawyer? Do you want to talk with the woman who went to see Cesar at the jail? If we're going to do this, I want him to have a good attorney. What do you think? That's it."

Sarah stopped and leaned back in her chair. One of the things Jon loved most about his wife was her compassion for people in need. He remembered how he felt when his great-uncle came to his rescue. Jon reached out and took Sarah's right hand in his.

"I think you're more amazing than I ever imagined," he said. "How much should we offer to pay a lawyer to represent Cesar?"

"I have no idea," Sarah replied. "All I know is what I feel in my heart about him and his family."

After her conversation with Ann, Kelli returned to her office. She logged on to her computer and began familiarizing herself with the firm software. It wasn't as sophisticated as the product she used in Atlanta but looked to be adequate. She entered a final password as her phone buzzed. It was her first phone call. Concerned it might be the school regarding a problem with one of the kids, she quickly picked up the receiver.

"Yes," she said.

"Jon Tremaine is calling," Lauren said. "Do you want to take it?"

Kelli hung up the phone after talking to Jon Tremaine and returned to Ann's office. Ann was on the phone and motioned for Kelli to take a seat while she finished the call. Ann lowered the receiver.

"What's up?" she asked.

"I just got off the phone with Jon Tremaine. He must have overheard your comment earlier about me representing Cesar Mendez. He talked to Mr. Mendez's wife, and they want to hire me. Ms. Mendez has access to ten thousand dollars, and Jon is willing to add twenty thousand to it."

Ann's eyes widened.

"Is thirty thousand enough for a drug trafficking case?" she asked.

"Only if you say it is," Kelli replied.

"I have no idea."

"Typically, the fee could easily be two or three times that much. There will be charges filed by the local DA, and the feds will likely step in and claim the drugs crossed state or national boundaries due to arrival on a ship. Of course, Cesar can be prosecuted in both jurisdictions, but the federal charges usually take precedence because they have greater resources and stiffer sentences. The same lawyer should probably handle both cases."

"All that makes sense," Ann said. "But do you want to do it for a reduced fee? I mean, you've not been here half a day and this pops up. Do you want to get more settled before taking on significant litigation?"

"If I'm ever going to handle a case like this, now would be the time," Kelli said and shrugged. "Once I'm busy with other matters, it'll be harder to squeeze in a matter that's not in the normal flow of my work. Mr. Mendez may not qualify for an appointed lawyer, which puts him in a tough spot. Even though the amount Jon Tremaine mentioned is low, it isn't unreasonable given the circumstances. Collecting a fee like that would also jump-start my first month of revenue. That's tempting."

"I told you there's not going to be the same kind of pressure to produce that you faced in Atlanta. Your kids are your first priority. If you're as diligent as I know you can be, the money will come."

Kelli had heard this speech from Ann when they discussed the move to Brunswick. It touched her then and meant even more now that it wasn't a theoretical conversation. Kelli thought for a moment before speaking.

"I liked Mr. Mendez and heard enough for me to question whether he's guilty. It's a plus to believe justice is on my side," Kelli said, then paused. "But if it turns out differently, I can deal with it."

"I support you whatever you decide. Jon must really think a lot of Mr. Mendez."

"Yeah. Apparently, Cesar saved his life at the farm when a tree fell. Jon also said something about 'paying it forward' in our conversation. I'm not sure exactly what he meant by that and didn't ask him."

"Now that you've decided to take on the case, would you collect the entire fee up front?"

"Yes, once I file notice of representation in the case, I'm committed and don't want to have to worry about the money."

"You have my blessing," Ann said.

"Blessing?" Kelli responded with a smile. "That's a word I never heard at any of my previous jobs."

Kelli returned to her office and called Jon. It went to voicemail, and she simply asked him to call her back. In the meantime, she prepared a contract of representation and reviewed the local court rules. Federal court procedure was the same, but state court practice had a few wrinkles she hadn't foreseen. She didn't recognize the name of the U.S. attorney for the Southern District of Georgia. The woman had moved to Savannah from Mississippi. The local DA was a man in his late thirties who'd been a third-year student at the University of Georgia School of Law when Kelli and Ann were first-year students. Kelli buzzed Ann.

"Did you know Matt Davis, the DA, when we were in law school?" Kelli asked. "He was a couple of years ahead of us."

"No, but he acted like he knew me when he was raising money for his campaign last year."

"Did you make a donation?"

"No, I didn't, though Roy and I voted for him."

"What about Gretchen Smith, the U.S. attorney in Savannah?"

"Never heard of her," Ann replied. "You're on your own in this case. I'd like to help but doubt that I can. Did you talk to Jon?"

"Still waiting on a call back."

"I do know one of the local public defenders," Ann said. "He goes to church with Roy and me. His name is Owen Perkins. He'll talk to you if you mention my name. He owes Roy a favor."

"What kind of favor?"

"It has to do with a horse. Owen has a mare and a gelding that he inherited from his parents. His kids ride them and he boards them at a local stable. A few weeks ago, Roy did a farm call late one Saturday night for a problem with the mare and only charged for a regular visit."

"I may check with Owen."

"Oh, and I won't be able to join you for lunch," Ann said. "I have a client meeting out of the office."

Five minutes later, Jon Tremaine called.

"What did you decide?" he asked Kelli.

"I talked it over with Ann, and I'm willing to represent Mr. Mendez for thirty thousand dollars."

"And if he's indicted by a federal grand jury?"

"Yes, I'll represent him in both state and federal criminal cases. We'd need the entire fee paid up front."

"Okay, it will take me a day or so to get the money. To be clear, this will cover all the way to trial?"

"Yes, but no appeals."

"I guess the feds will take the lead."

"That's usually how it works."

"Can you meet with Cesar at the jail and let him know?" Jon asked.

"Yes. Does he know that you're going to pay part of the attorney fees?"

"No, because I needed to confirm everything with you. But it's not a secret. Like I said earlier, I've talked to his wife."

"Once Mr. Mendez signs a contract of representation, I won't be able to communicate with you unless he signs another consent form," Kelli advised.

"Understood. What about hiring a private investigator? I realize that would be an extra expense, but it could be worth it."

Kelli was impressed by the tree farm manager's commitment to helping his employee.

"Since I'm new to town, I don't have any idea who to contact. I thought I'd rely on court-ordered discovery and my own investigation."

"I'll check out investigators." Jon paused. "I can also be a resource."

"What do you mean?"

"Just my familiarity with shipping. All of our lumber isn't processed locally. We export premium logs that aren't going to end up as a cardboard box."

"Okay," Kelli replied.

Jon was quiet for a moment.

"Are you going to immediately talk to the DA and try to negotiate a plea bargain?" he asked.

"I understand the reason for your question," Kelli replied, "but we can't decide the best way to help Cesar until we know as much as we can about the government's case. Federal prosecutors have a ninety-five percent conviction rate. It's lower in state courts. When I worked for the U.S. Attorney's Office in Atlanta, we won every case during a two-year period except one. Defendants enter pleas when it makes sense given all the circumstances. But I promise that I'll be committed to representing Cesar, not trying to process him through the system."

"Thanks; that's what I wanted to hear."

Feeling better, Carly put on a floppy white hat and pink work gloves. She then spent almost an hour outside in her garden. Carly grew everything from seeds she planted in early spring inside the house under grow lights. If she couldn't start a plant or flower from a seed, she didn't include it. There was something satisfying about nurturing a plant from its tiniest form all the way to mature production of a vegetable, fruit, or flower. The growing season was long in coastal Georgia, but it was time to pull up dying plants. Usually it wasn't frost that killed the plants. They simply wore out. Carly bent over to pull up some squash that was producing only anemic blossoms and whose leaves were turning brown.

"Carly!" a female voice called out.

Carly straightened up. It was Lois Gautier, her next-door neighbor. In her late forties, Lois and her husband, Vince, were recent empty nesters who'd moved to the neighborhood about six months ago. They'd married out of high school and their youngest child was now in college. Lois, a petite woman with short blond hair, worked at the county courthouse. Vince was a financial adviser. They'd downsized to the house next to Carly, a one-hundred-year-old residence that had been fully restored by the previous owner. Carly walked over to the low fence that ran along the property line. She removed one of her gloves and rubbed a sore knuckle.

"I saw a blue SUV in your driveway over the weekend," Lois said. "Do you have company staying with you?"

"Yes, my niece Kelli and her children arrived on Thursday evening. They're going to stay with me until they find a permanent place to stay."

"That's right," Lois replied. "You told me about them a few weeks ago. Is she the lawyer who went through the divorce?"

"Yes, she's working with Ann Carter. She and Kelli were close friends in law school."

"We don't see Ann very much at the main courthouse," Lois said. "I think she handles a lot of wills and estates. Is that what Kelli is going to do?"

"She went to court often when she worked in Atlanta. I think most of the cases were for big companies. It will probably be different in Brunswick."

"Make sure she knows I'm here to help. Maybe you can introduce us. I'd love having her and her kids over for dessert one evening. Vince reads annual reports, and I'm left with the TV or a book."

"Why aren't you working today?"

"I took a personal day off for a dental appointment early this morning."

"Is everything okay?"

Lois touched the right side of her face. "Still numb from the shot. I had to have a root canal. It took forever for my dentist to dig out the root. Have you had one?"

"Thank goodness, no."

Lois turned to leave. "Don't forget about dessert. The sooner the better. My root may be gone, but I still have a sweet tooth."

CHAPTER 10

Jon left Maria, who'd been overcome with emotion at the offer to pay the majority of the fees for Cesar's lawyer. In a bag on the seat between him and Betsy were eight homemade tamales.

"We'll pay you back," Maria said, a wad of tissues still in her hand as they stood at the front door. "Cesar is a hard worker."

"I'm not looking for repayment. But let's keep this between us."

"I understand."

"Great. I'm not going to report to the company anything about Cesar for at least a couple of weeks."

"Yes, sir. I know we can't stay here unless he's working for the company. That will give me time to find another place to live. I mentioned it at church on Sunday. One of the deacons knows about a little house that may be available soon."

As Jon and Betsy bounced along a dirt road, the dog had her head on the seat and her nose pointed at the bag of tamales. Jon scratched the dog's ears.

"I know that smells interesting, but it might give you an upset stomach," he said.

Betsy shifted her head to the side so that another area was open for scratching. Jon obliged. By the time he reached the jobsite, it was close to noon. Six men were spread out among the trees spraying insecticide to ward off an outbreak of bark beetles. The biggest threat to the tree farm wasn't fire. It was the multiple types of pests and blight that included weevils, brown spot needle blight, and webworms, among others. Monitoring the health of thousands of acres and responding to problems was a never-ending task. Jon and the men spent a lot of time simply walking through the woods. When a problem was identified, the solution could be chemical treatment, pruning, or removal.

Jon had a large container of ice water in the bed of his truck. When the men saw him, they gathered for a drink. Jon took out the bag of tamales and passed them out.

"Who made them?" a man named Diego asked.

"Maria Mendez."

"I thought so," the man said and nodded. "What's going on with Cesar? Anything new?"

The conversation was entirely in Spanish.

Diego held up the half-eaten tamale in his hand. "I believe a drug gang used Cesar as a mule without him knowing it. I've heard this happened last year to a guy importing fruit from Mexico. He was arrested at the docks in Savannah."

"Any details?" Jon asked.

"He was from Michoacán, you know, the place where they grow avocados all year round. There were drugs hidden in some crates of avocados his family sent him. I think he's still in jail."

Sarah was at the kitchen table when Jon came into the room. He had saved the final tamale for her, putting it on ice in the cooler for the ride home. He'd decided to surprise her with the fresh tamale for lunch.

"How was work this morning?" he asked.

"Good. A woman we've been helping for six months has a new place to live with her kids in North Carolina. And I was happy when you texted the news about the lawyer for Cesar."

"No regrets about the money?"

"I told you how I felt."

Jon handed the tamale to Sarah.

"Maria gave me some of these," he said. "I shared them with the work crew but saved one for you."

"This is authentic, isn't it?" Sarah said as she placed the tamale in the microwave to heat it up.

"No doubt."

Jon mentioned what he'd learned from Diego on the work crew.

"You should tell Cesar's lawyer," she said.

"I will," Jon said before adding, "It makes sense for the cartels to target ports of entry like Savannah and Brunswick where security might not be as tight as places closer to the border."

"Jon," Sarah started.

"I'm just thinking out loud."

"Let the lawyer do the investigation."

"Speaking of investigation, it may be necessary for the lawyer to hire a private investigator," he said. "That would be extra."

"Whatever it takes," Sarah said resolutely.

"You're sure?"

"One hundred percent."

At 3:00 p.m. Kelli was waiting in the interview room at the jail for Cesar to arrive. She'd spent the rest of the morning and her allotted lunchtime getting organized at the office. The only work environments she'd previously known included strict supervision of every detail. At Ann's office Kelli would be much more autonomous. She checked the time again on her phone. Max and Emma should be home from school soon. Kelli regretted not being there to greet them, but Carly would provide a good welcome.

The door opened and Cesar entered. As soon as he sat down, Kelli leaned closer to him.

"Is that a black eye?" she asked.

Cesar gingerly touched the area around his right eye socket. It was clearly swollen and discolored.

"Yes," he said.

"What happened?"

"I slipped in the dining hall and hit the edge of a table."

Kelli looked at him skeptically. "Are you sure someone didn't hit you? Did they place you in the general jail population?"

Cesar shrugged.

"Are you in a cell with other men?" Kelli persisted.

"Yes."

"I'm going to report this to whoever is in charge of—"

"No," Cesar said as he held up one hand. "That will make it worse. It's better to let things go. I'll work it out myself."

"How are you going to do that?"

"The Latinos look out for one another. I kept to myself at first, but that was a mistake. It will be okay."

Though unsatisfied, Kelli dropped the issue. "I'm here because your wife and Jon Tremaine hired me to represent you; they're going to pay the attorney fee. That is, if you want me to be your lawyer."

"My wife and Jon?"

"She's paying ten thousand dollars from the money you earned selling chocolate, and Mr. Tremaine is paying twenty thousand."

Kelli watched the conflict roll across Cesar's face.

"That's the money we were saving for my grandmother's surgery," he said, then stopped for a moment. "But she would tell us to use it because God will provide in another way. But Jon paying money? I don't understand."

"He mentioned something about you saving his life."

Cesar shook his head. "I just did what I thought I should. There was no time to think. The tree was going to hit him, probably in the head."

"Now he wants to help you. Do you want me to represent you?"

"Yes." Cesar nodded.

"You need to sign this contract of representation. I'll read it to you. Stop me if you have any questions."

Cesar sat silently while Kelli read the document, and then he signed it.

"There's also an agreement authorizing me to talk to Jon about your case. It's like the paper you signed the other day. You don't have to sign it for me to represent you."

"I don't have anything to hide from him. He's smart and can help more if he knows what is going on."

After Cesar signed the authorization, Kelli leaned back in her chair. "I'll be there with you in court. Have they delivered any documents to your cell?"

"One of the guards brought me some papers, but I left them in my cell. They were from the court."

"I can check with the courthouse. You'll be brought over for an arraignment, and the judge will set bond for your release."

"I don't understand everything you are saying. I should have asked more questions the other day, but everything is happening so fast."

Kelli explained the process again.

"Because it's a high-volume drug trafficking case, the judge has to set the bond. A magistrate can't do it," she said. "The bond could be anywhere from twenty-five thousand to over one hundred thousand. A professional bondsman usually charges fifteen percent of that amount."

Kelli did the math on her tablet and showed Cesar, who nodded.

"The problem is that you could post a bond in state court, then be arrested and charged in federal court. The bond wouldn't carry over."

Cesar's puzzled expression required another, longer explanation. The client's face revealed his disappointment.

"I hate you being locked up one second longer than possible," Kelli said sympathetically. "But it could be financially risky to post bond until we know what's going to happen with any federal charges. Federal court is where these types of cases usually end up, and it's where I have more experience."

Cesar sighed.

"Is your wife coming to the arraignment?" Kelli asked.

"No, she needs to look after the boys."

"Is there anything you want me to tell her?"

"Don't tell her about my eye," Cesar quickly said.

"Okay."

"And explain what you told me about the charges and the bond. Her English isn't very good." Cesar paused. "If you like, Jon can do it."

"That's fine."

"Thank you," Cesar said. "I'll be praying for you every day. Maria will do the same."

Carly and Emma were in the living room playing Parcheesi when Kelli arrived home. Emma hopped up from the chair as soon as she heard the front door open. When she did, she knocked some of the animal pieces from the board onto the floor. She stopped to pick them up.

"Go," Carly said with a wave of her hand. "See your mother and give her a hug."

A few seconds later, Kelli and Emma returned to the living room.

"Where's Max?" Kelli asked.

"In his room doing homework," Carly replied.

Kelli plopped down in a chair near the game table. Emma snuggled in beside her. Kelli gently scratched the little girl's back.

"Did you make any friends today?" Kelli asked.

Emma leaned back against her mother. "Mom, you can't make a friend in one day. It takes time to know who you can trust."

"Some adults should remember that," Kelli replied with a glance at Carly.

Max entered. He'd changed from the clothes he wore to school into shorts and a T-shirt.

"Tell me about your day," Kelli said.

"The coach for the middle school track team was in charge of PE. After he saw me run, he said I might be a good runner for the team. If I'm interested, he said he can give me a workout routine."

"That's great," Kelli replied. "Your aunt Carly was a runner in high school. Didn't you win some races?"

Max gave Carly a puzzled look.

Carly smiled. "It's true. I loved to run."

"Do you have ribbons?" Emma asked.

"I doubt it," Carly answered. "If I do, they're faded by now."

"I'd like to see them," Emma said.

Carly turned to Kelli. "Tell me about your first day. Do you have homework?"

"No, and I don't want to start bringing work home. That's one of the things that will be different in Brunswick. Still, I was busier than I expected. We'll talk over supper."

Carly forced herself up from the chair. "I'd better get started—"

"No, finish your game," Kelli said. "I stopped by the store and bought what I need to make beef stroganoff. I skipped lunch, and I'm starving."

"I love that!" Emma exclaimed. "Especially the noodles."

"Is there any more squash casserole?" Max asked.

"Yes, and we can warm it up," Carly said.

Carly and Emma stayed in the living room. Max returned to his bedroom to finish his homework. Carly decided to revisit the friend issue with Emma.

"Did you meet any girls who could become friends after you get to know them?"

"Maybe," Emma replied thoughtfully. "There's Sasha, Polly, Jenny, Larissa, and another girl named Emma. Would it be weird to have a friend with the same name? She doesn't look like me. Her hair is dark as night."

"Dark as night?"

"Yes, that means it's black. Did you know Mom gets her hair dyed when she goes to the hair place?"

"A lot of women do that."

"Do you?"

"No," Carly chuckled. "The gray is taking over the brown without a fight from me."

"I think your hair looks interesting," Emma replied.

Emma continued to chatter while they played. Max finished his homework and joined them for a game until Kelli announced that supper was ready. They sat down at the kitchen table.

"Smells wonderful," Carly said, admiring the appearance of the dish.

"And I heated up the last of the squash casserole for Max."

Carly said a blessing, and they began to eat.

"Emma needs to tell you more about her day," Carly said.

"Not now," Emma replied. "I want to eat."

"How about you, Max?" Carly asked. "What else happened besides the conversation with the track coach?"

"Nothing I want to talk about," Max answered while looking down at his plate.

Carly glanced at Kelli, who raised her eyebrows.

"Can we talk about it later?" Kelli asked.

"Yeah, I guess so," the boy replied.

They ate in silence for a moment.

"I signed up my first client," Kelli said. "It's a criminal case. Not what I was expecting. The defendant works on a tree farm for a man Ann represents."

"A tree farm?" Emma asked. "Trees just grow on their own."

"Not all trees," Kelli answered. She explained what little she knew about the process.

"I know the wife of a man who works at a tree farm," Carly said. "She's the assistant director at the battered women's shelter. I volunteered there a few years ago. Her name is Sarah Tremaine."

Kelli raised her eyebrows. "I'm sure she's the wife of the man I talked to. I can't provide details, but he's doing a lot to help his employee."

"I'm not surprised. Sarah has a big heart."

They ate in silence for a few moments before Carly spoke: "Oh,

Lois Gautier, my new neighbor, works in the criminal division at the courthouse. She saw me this afternoon and wants you and the children to come over for dessert one evening."

"What kind of dessert?" Emma asked.

"Whatever she wants to offer," Kelli replied, then turned to Carly. "I'd like to meet her. It would be good to know someone who works in that department."

"I'll text and ask about a good evening. She was out of work today because she had a root canal on a tooth."

"What's that?" Emma asked.

Carly motioned to Kelli. "I'll let you handle that one."

CHAPTER 11

The rear deck of Jon and Sarah's house faced south. When the weather was cooperative, they ate supper outside. There was a hint of fall in the air, and before leaving the jobsite after he'd returned in the afternoon, Jon called Sarah and asked her to take a couple of steaks from the freezer to thaw. Twice a year they bought half a steer from a local famer who raised Angus cattle. It provided plenty of meat and enough for an occasional larger gathering. Jon used an old-fashioned kettle grill and natural lump charcoal. He sat in a wooden rocker and stared across the yard while he waited for the coals to turn sufficiently gray to start cooking. Betsy lay on the deck beside the rocker. Sarah was inside the house.

"Keep that tail out of the way," Jon said to the dog when she flapped her tail perilously close to the spot where the rocker met the deck.

As if she understood the sentence, Betsy moved a few inches away from the chair.

"Smart dog," Jon muttered.

Sarah joined them and sat in a matching rocker. She handed him a glass of unsweetened tea.

"Thanks," he said. "The fire will be ready in a few minutes."

"Medium, please," she said. "No rare meat until our son can decide for himself how he likes his steak cooked."

They rocked in silence for a minute.

"The money to pay for Cesar's lawyer hit our account late this afternoon," Jon said. "I'll take a check to the arraignment in the morning and give it to the lawyer. Maria gave me the cash when I stopped by to see her this morning."

"Ten thousand dollars?"

"Yes."

"Where did you put it?"

"In my sock drawer."

"Jon!"

"No," he said with a smile. "It's in the company safe."

They rocked in silence again.

"So you're going to the courthouse?" Sarah asked.

"Maria isn't going to be there, and I want Cesar to see a friendly face. What are you doing tomorrow?"

"Lisa Roberts is coming over for a couple of hours. She has some things to give me."

Sarah and Lisa Roberts had been friends for years.

"Baby clothes?"

"No, with four little boys, the clothes for her kids were worn out by the time the youngest got a chance to wear them. I suspect it's toys and something she made. I don't know how she finds the time, but Lisa is a great crafter. We should get together some night with her and Mark."

"Set it up."

Jon went into the kitchen and brought out the steaks. They were thick rib eyes. He lifted the top of the cooker and put them on the grill. The grill was so hot the steaks instantly sizzled.

"I've been thinking about Cesar," Sarah said. "Did I push too hard for us to help him?"

"No," Jon replied. "I was all in."

"It does make me a bit nervous."

"We won't miss a meal, and our son will have new shoes."

"Not about the money. I can't keep from worrying about you being around whoever is smuggling the drugs."

"I won't be around them."

"Okay." Sarah sighed and laid one hand on her abdomen. "I'm feeling extra protective."

The timer went off, and Jon flipped the steaks. The grill marks were nice. He lowered the top, reset the timer, and looked to the west. The sun was below the tops of the trees, which cast long shadows across the yard. The sun would set but, in his new life, would rise again with potential for tomorrow. When it was time to take the steaks from the grill, he put them on a platter.

"We'll let them rest for a few minutes," he said.

Sarah didn't move from her chair.

"Were you ever in danger when you worked for the bad guys?" she asked.

"Yes."

"How much danger?"

"It was very dangerous. Do you want details?"

Sarah was silent for a few moments. Jon had spared her a lot of specific information. The incident in which he was almost shot was the worst, but there had been several times when guns were drawn in his presence.

"No, I'd rather focus on the fact that you're safe now," she said.

"I agree," Jon replied. "And my immediate focus is on cutting into this steak."

After supper, Kelli maneuvered to get some alone time with Max by asking him to help her clean up the kitchen. Carly and Emma returned to the living room so Carly could read the little girl a book.

"It's tough going to a new school," Kelli said as they stood beside each other at the sink and rinsed the dinner dishes.

"Yeah."

"Did you meet any boys who might be friends with you?"

"What's the use?" Max shrugged. "You can't count on people."

Max's words stung. Determined, Kelli pressed on: "Was there anything specific that made it a tough day?"

Max didn't immediately reply. He put a plate into the dishwasher. "There were some boys who said some things to me during PE."

"What kind of things?"

"About what they were going to do to me."

Kelli knew bullying was real, especially for adolescent boys. Max had never faced any serious harassment at his school in Atlanta.

"I'm sorry," she said. "Did they threaten to hurt you?"

"Yeah."

Kelli bit her lip and experienced a moment when she desperately wished Brad was still available to help.

"What can I do?" she asked.

"Nothing."

They finished loading the dishwasher. Kelli cast about in her mind for a possible strategy.

"Do you have other classes with any of these boys?" she asked.

"I don't think so, just PE."

"What about talking to the track coach?"

Max quickly shook his head. "No."

Kelli had a sudden thought.

"Maybe he could start you on a training program during PE that will keep you from having to be around them," she suggested.

Max's eyes brightened a little.

"That's not a bad idea," he said. "There are kids who do other things during PE because they're on a sports team."

"What's the coach's name? I'll get in touch with him tomorrow."

"Coach Matthews, but I can do it if you want me to."

"Promise me that you will."

"Maybe," he replied.

After the children were in bed, Kelli told Carly about her conversation with Max. Her aunt's face clouded at the mention of bullying.

"I know the principal of his school," Carly said resolutely. "He was in my classroom years ago to observe when he was a student teacher. A call from me will get action."

"Let's see if Max can handle it on his own."

"You want to put a stop to this before Max gets labeled as a target."

Carly's warning concerned Kelli.

"It will help when he develops a friend group," Carly continued.

Kelli nodded. "That's not as easy for him as it is for Emma. He's so much more private and reserved."

"Max is deep waters," Carly agreed. "I'm going to be praying for him."

The following morning during her early morning walk, Kelli's thoughts centered on Max. She didn't pray, but she channeled a lot of internal energy toward her son in the hope he would have a better day. She and the kids were a few minutes late getting into the car for the drive to school. As usual, Emma was talkative and Max quiet.

Because she had to appear in court with Cesar, Kelli was wearing a dark suit with a white blouse. For the moment, however, she was focused on the children.

"I'm going to sit with Sasha and Larissa at lunch today and with Polly, Emma, and Jenny tomorrow," Emma said.

"What if they have something to say about it?" Kelli asked.

"It'll work out," Emma replied confidently. "They're not used to planning ahead like me."

Kelli didn't doubt the truth of Emma's claim.

"What about you?" Kelli asked Max. "Who will you eat lunch with?"

"I don't know. I'll look for an empty seat."

"What period is PE?"

"Third."

"Are you going to talk to Coach Matthews?"

"Who's Coach Matthews?" Emma asked.

"The middle school track coach," Kelli answered. "Max, are you going to talk to him about a training program during PE?"

"Probably."

It was the closest thing to commitment Kelli could pry out of him. When the kids got out of the car, she pulled forward out of the traffic line and watched them walk up to the school. Emma was immediately joined by another girl. Max trudged forward alone.

At the law office, Lauren greeted her.

"Good morning!" the receptionist said enthusiastically. "Welcome to day two!"

"Good morning," Kelli replied matter-of-factly. "Ann sent a text that she's out of the office this morning for client meetings. I have to be in court at ten thirty for an arraignment."

"Yes, I saw that on your calendar. We're not used to having things like that on the schedule."

Lauren lifted her hands from the keyboard and flexed her fingers.

"Are your hands okay?" Kelli asked. "An administrative assistant at my last job got carpal tunnel syndrome."

"No, I'm fine. Actually, great."

Kelli saw something glitter on Lauren's left hand. It was a diamond.

"Are you engaged?" Kelli asked.

"Yes!" Lauren clapped her hands together. "Who does that on a Monday night? Curt totally surprised me. He took me to the restaurant where we had our first date. No one was there when we walked in, and I thought it was closed. Turns out, he'd rented it for the evening! That's why he did it on Monday. It was one thing after another. He got down on one knee and asked me to marry him. A photographer was secretly filming the whole thing. After I said yes, our friends and family came out of hiding for a big dinner. When I get the video, I'll send it to you."

"Were you expecting him to ask you?"

"I was hoping, but we hadn't picked out the ring. He used my mom for info about that." Lauren held out her finger. "Don't you think it's perfect?"

To Kelli it looked like thousands of other engagement rings, but she didn't want to pour water on Lauren's joy.

"It's beautiful," she said.

"Thanks. Oh, please tell your little girl about it. She seemed so interested in Curt. Do you think she would like to see the video?"

"Absolutely."

Lauren looked down at her desk. "Jon Tremaine called early this morning. He's going to meet you at the courthouse and pay the attorney fee."

"That's not necessary."

"Should I call him?"

Kelli hesitated. "No, it's fine. If he's helping to pay for the representation, there's no reason he can't be there."

Kelli continued to her office. Brad's marriage proposal included no surprises. Kelli picked the location—a park bench where they first professed their love—and the two of them selected the ring after multiple trips to the jewelry store. Brad didn't get down on one knee but simply placed the ring on her finger and kissed her. At that time, Kelli's confidence was high that she'd never take it off. The ring was now in the bottom drawer of her jewelry box.

She logged on to her computer and prepared the notice of representation for Cesar's case. Seeing the heading, "In the Superior Court for the County of Glynn, State of Georgia," made her involvement seem real. Often a lawyer would waive formal arraignment on behalf of a client, but as a new attorney in the local circuit, Kelli wanted to meet the presiding judge and give him a chance to put a face to her name.

She left the office with plenty of time to find a parking space and arrive in the courtroom prior to 10:30 a.m. She'd accompanied Ann to the courthouse during one of her earlier trips to Brunswick. Kelli took a deep breath before entering the building. There was no reason to be nervous about an arraignment, but this was the first time she would appear in a courtroom with which she expected to become familiar in the coming months and years. She went into the clerk's office to file her representation notice. A short, middle-aged woman came forward to help. Her name tag read "Lois Gautier."

"My aunt Carly told me about you," Kelli said with a smile on her face. "I'm Kelli Quinn, her niece."

"Nice to meet you," Lois replied, extending her hand. "I hope you and your children can come over soon for a snack or dessert."

"We'd love that."

Kelli handed Lois the notice of representation in Cesar's case.

"I've been hired to represent Mr. Mendez," Kelli said. "He's being arraigned this morning."

Lois glanced down at the pleading and nodded. "I saw his name on the calendar. I'll enter this electronically so the judge and DA will see it on their screens when the case is called."

Lois glanced past Kelli and pointed. "There's Matt Davis, the DA."

Kelli turned around.

"Mr. Davis! Please come here for a moment!" Lois called out.

As soon as she saw the DA, Kelli remembered him from law school. He'd gotten older but still had a full head of chestnut-colored hair. Wearing a light gray suit, he was over six feet tall with a lean build.

"Lois, I need to be upstairs in a couple of minutes," he said.

"I wanted you to meet Kelli Quinn. She's just moved to town and is working with Ann Carter."

The DA faced Kelli. Recognition appeared in his eyes.

"Kelli Laughlan," he said, remembering Kelli's maiden name. "I was one of the judges for the moot court competition during your first year in law school. You won that round. Didn't you come in first place when you argued in front of the visiting judges from the court of appeals?"

"No, second."

"You were outstanding." The DA looked at his watch before adding, "I'd love to hear what you've been up to, but I have to go."

"I'll see you upstairs," Kelli replied. "I have a case on the calendar for arraignment."

"You could have filed a waiver."

"Thanks, but I wanted to introduce myself to the judge."

"Oh, I'll take care of that for you."

The DA hurried off. Kelli faced Lois, who had a big smile on her face.

"You made quite an impression on Matt when you were in law school," Lois said. "How many years ago was that?"

"Too many. He has a good memory."

"Men remember things when they want to."

Kelli shook her head. The assistant clerk was obviously a romantic, even if there was no romance to be found.

CHAPTER 12

After circling the courthouse twice, Jon found a parking place big enough for his truck. Inside the building, a sign directed him upstairs to the main courtroom. Before climbing the stairs, he had to pass through a metal detector and submit to a deputy lackadaisically waving a wand in front of him. When Jon had been in jail, he considered the metal detector his friend. Fewer metal items in the cellblocks increased the chance of survival for the inmates. Out of habit, Jon quickly glanced around at the other people preparing to move forward. Hypervigilance at a metal detector was a reflex. Nobody looked like an immediate threat.

Jon climbed the stairs. In a manila envelope he had ten thousand dollars in cash and a twenty-thousand-dollar check. His heart started beating faster when he reached the second floor.

Jon's courthouse appearances in Texas had taken place with tight security. Part of the time, Jon was numb and reeling from the attempted murder. Even though Jon had given extensive statements to the FBI, in court, testimony was necessary to seal the fate of the higher-ranking members of the cartel. Jon had connected the financial dots that created an evidentiary noose around their necks.

At twenty-three years old, Jon was usually on the periphery of the inner workings of the criminal enterprise, but he had one item that made him invaluable to the prosecution: a flash drive from a computer that contained extensive information about the members of the group, their roles, and the sources of revenue.

Jon's first job after graduating from college with an accounting degree was in the auditing department of what he thought was a legitimate business importing raw materials from Mexico and Central America for American companies. Before he landed the job, all of Jon's previous employment had required the use of his back, not his brain. He didn't love being stuck indoors all day in front of a computer monitor, but the pay was good. When, after nine months, the opportunity came to help conduct an inventory of raw cotton bales being imported from Mexico, Jon jumped at the invitation. He went to the Port of Houston, one of the busiest in the country. Late in the afternoon, they were finishing up when a steel band securing one of the bales caught on the door of a metal shipping container and broke. The bale fell off a forklift and cracked open, revealing several plastic bags inside.

Jon turned to the man working with him and pointed to the bags. "Is that a special kind of cotton packed inside the bales?"

The man didn't respond. Several men quickly came forward, righted the bale, and hauled it off on a hand truck.

"You could say that," the man said, glancing over his shoulder. "But I wouldn't ask any questions about it. It's all part of the inventory."

Jon looked toward the area where the men in charge were standing and, for the first time, noticed an armed security guard. Back at the accounting office, he started to mention the incident to his boss, a man named Jack Nix, but the warning at the jobsite stopped him. Two days later, Nix, an alcoholic who regularly left the office early and dumped extra work on Jon, called him into his office and shut the door.

"I understand you were paying close attention during the cotton inventory the other day," Nix said.

"I was doing my job," Jon replied, his eyes questioning. "Did everything add up correctly?"

"It did," Nix said and then paused for a moment. "Have you kept your work here confidential? As I explained when you were hired, we don't want any details of our business leaking out to competitors or anyone else. That's why you had to sign a confidentiality agreement."

Jon recalled a stack of documents that he didn't read closely because he was excited about the job offer. "I don't talk to anyone about the details of my work."

"Not even your girlfriend? What's her name? Diana?"

"Danielle. She's not interested in accounting stuff."

"Do you talk with any other members of your family about your work?"

"My mom died of cancer when I was a kid, and my father and his girlfriend live in Spokane."

"So it's just you and your girlfriend?"

"Pretty much."

Nix leaned back in his chair. "How would you like to increase your responsibilities and double your salary?"

Startled, Jon sat up straighter in the chair. "What would I be doing?"

"Increasing your inventory work. It would involve a bit of travel, mostly here in Texas, but also to Mexico and Honduras. Everything would be confidential. You'd still report to me."

If he doubled his salary, Jon could make steady progress on repaying his student loans and start saving money for an engagement ring to give Danielle, who was starting to pressure him for a higher level of commitment.

"What kind of material would be subject to inventory?" he asked.

"Anything we import. I need someone I can trust on the ground. The locals often try to cheat us."

Jon remembered the armed guard at the Port of Houston. "Would I have to confront someone—"

"No, no. We have other people who handle that. Your job would be to make sure the numbers match."

Earning extra money and getting out of the office appealed to Jon.

"Sounds good," he replied. "I got a passport a few months ago so Danielle and I could go to Cancún."

"You won't be going to Cancún," Nix said with a smile. "But you'll stay in first-class accommodations and get to see parts of countries that most tourists don't visit."

Within a year, Jon had received bonuses that enabled him to pay off all his debts and put money down on the yellow Porsche. He and Danielle moved into a luxury townhome. Jon explained his sudden wealth to Danielle as being the result of his skill and value as an employee. He knew he was working for a criminal enterprise but couldn't resist the lure of so much money. Internally, he justified his participation as doing a job that had to be taken care of by someone. Why not him? And he wasn't involved in actually selling or distributing drugs. Only later, after his involvement deepened, did he start to see the violent side of the business.

Entering the courtroom, Jon saw Kelli Quinn. She was talking to Cesar, who was wearing an orange jumpsuit with the words "Glynn County Inmate" printed on the back. Jailhouse garb was dehumanizing. In

Texas Jon had been forced to wear a lime-green jumpsuit. He pressed his lips together tightly and walked down the aisle toward them.

Kelli looked up as Jon Tremaine approached. He held his hand out to Cesar, who vigorously shook it.

"What happened to your eye?" Jon asked with concern in his voice.

Cesar shrugged. "Nothing much."

"Did you get into a fight?"

"I worked it out."

A deputy appeared and escorted Cesar back to the holding area.

Jon handed an envelope to Kelli.

"Inside is a cashier's check for twenty thousand dollars and ten thousand in cash," he said.

"Ten thousand in cash?"

"Yes, I brought it straight from Maria Mendez."

Kelli handed the envelope back to Jon. "Keep it until we're finished here. Hopefully, the judge will set a reasonable bond and we can coordinate his release with the federal authorities."

Before Kelli could continue, a bailiff standing beside the elevated bench where the judge would preside called out, "All rise! The Superior Court for the County of Glynn is now in session, the Honorable Clarence Godfrey presiding."

Kelli and Jon stood beside each other. Jon leaned over to her.

"Should you mention to the judge that Cesar is in danger at the jail?" he asked.

"We'll see."

Judge Godfrey, a short man in his fifties with gray hair and wearing half-frame reading glasses, took his seat behind the bench.

"Have you ever been to a criminal arraignment?" Kelli whispered to Jon after they were seated.

It took Jon a moment to answer.

"Not here in Brunswick," he said. "But I've seen it on TV."

"Real court is a lot more boring than what you read in books or see in the movies."

Kelli watched how the judge and Matt Davis interacted with each other. The judge allowed the DA to run the criminal docket without any interference. That wasn't surprising, given the routine matters coming before the court. It wasn't until there was a motion to suppress evidence that things became livelier. Matt moved the cursor on his laptop.

"Your Honor, we'd like you to hear the motion to suppress in *State v. Tadwalter*," the DA said.

"Why now?" the judge responded. "Move it to the end of the calendar."

An older lawyer with flowing white hair and wearing a blue seersucker suit and a yellow bow tie rose from his chair. Beside him was a young man in his thirties wearing a dark blue suit.

"Judge, I have to be in federal court in Savannah at one o'clock," the older lawyer said. "Your indulgence in allowing us to proceed out of turn this morning would be greatly appreciated."

"Mr. Christopher, I didn't know you were representing the defendant," the judge said.

"The family hired us on Friday," the older lawyer replied. "The motion was filed by previous counsel, but I'm ready to proceed so long as you'll allow an additional five days for filing a supplemental brief on the law."

"Mr. Tadwalter's previous counsel continued the matter three times," the DA said to the judge. "Given the importance of the issue, the State would like to have the motion heard and resolved."

"Very well. Proceed."

Kelli was impressed with the presentation of evidence by both Matt Davis and Lynwood Christopher. The police officer who conducted the search and seizure of the defendant's limited-edition BMW sports car found ten stolen bearer bonds worth ten thousand dollars apiece.

Kelli leaned over to Jon and whispered, "The defense lawyer is very smooth. He may get the search and seizure thrown out under the Fourth Amendment."

"Is mere possession of the bonds, even if they're stolen, a crime?"

"Not necessarily. That's what the trial on the merits would determine."

Both lawyers offered a brief argument. Matt's succinct points were persuasive and made Kelli doubt whether the motion would be successful.

"The DA is good too," she whispered to Jon, who didn't reply.

The judge took the motion under advisement. Matt Davis returned to his laptop. "*State v. Mendez*, arraignment."

Kelli stepped through the gap in the railing while a deputy brought over Cesar. Matt spoke: "Your Honor, I'm pleased to introduce you to Ms. Kelli Quinn. Ms. Quinn recently moved to Brunswick from Atlanta and is working with the law office of Ann Carter. She's representing Mr. Mendez."

"It's nice to meet you, Your Honor," Kelli said.

The judge barely glanced at her and didn't extend his hand over the bench.

"Do I need to read the charges?" the judge asked.

"No, sir," Kelli replied. "We'll waive reading of the accusation."

"How does the defendant plea?" the judge asked.

"Not guilty."

"Very well. Bond is set at two hundred fifty thousand dollars."

Kelli cleared her throat. "Your Honor, we would like to be heard on the bond issue."

"You won't be heard this morning," the judge replied gruffly. "File a motion. Mr. Davis, call your next case."

Matt gave Kelli a sympathetic look and leaned close to her.

"Call me," the DA said in a low voice. "I saw your client's right eye."

Kelli stepped to the side and stood beside Cesar, who was obviously discouraged.

"The bond was higher than I estimated, but the DA is willing to talk to me about it," Kelli said in a soft voice. "I can try to get it lowered, but there's still the issue of separate charges in federal court. You remember when we talked about that?"

"Yeah," Cesar said with a slight nod.

A deputy took Cesar by the arm and led him away. Kelli and Jon left the courtroom together. As soon as they were in the hallway, Jon faced her.

"Why didn't you mention that Cesar was attacked in the jail?" he demanded.

"This was an arraignment. We don't know exactly what happened at the jail, and the judge wasn't going to get into that sort of issue this morning."

Jon spoke softly but intensely: "When a man like Cesar is supposedly linked to a cartel, he's at tremendous risk of being attacked by members of any competing groups and needs someone to get him out as soon as possible."

In that instant, Kelli felt attacked, but she also knew there was truth in what Jon said. As a younger lawyer, she would have been defensive. Now she knew that wasn't usually productive. Staying calm was part of professionalism.

"I understand," she replied. "And I'm going to keep that in mind.

I promise to follow up with the DA about Cesar's safety and file anything that might help get him out on bond."

Jon stepped back. He moved the envelope containing the attorney fee back and forth between his hands a few times.

"Anything else?" Kelli asked.

"I guess not."

Jon handed her the envelope.

"Keep me informed," he said.

CHAPTER 13

On Tuesday mornings, Carly participated in a women's group at her church. Between ten and twelve older women attended. The initial focus of the gathering was on pouring a cup of fresh coffee from a silver coffee server owned by the church. After that, the women sat in a circle, and each one gave a summary of what was going on in her life and mentioned a prayer request. It took quite a while for everyone to share. After that, one of the women was asked to pray. Half the time, the prayer responsibility fell on Carly. If Carly didn't pray, a woman named Jan Baldwin was asked to do so. Carly frequently requested prayer for her health. Today, when it was her turn to share, she repositioned herself in her seat. She was hurting but didn't want to mention it.

"Some of you know that my niece and her two children are going to stay with me for a while until they find a house to rent or buy," she said.

"Prices are sky-high," offered Betty, a woman who still worked part-time as a real estate agent. "But I'll be glad to help her. Will you give her one of my cards?"

Without waiting for an answer, Betty reached into her purse and handed Carly a business card.

"I'll pass it along to her," Carly replied, keeping the card in her hand. "But she may have a contact through the law firm where she's working."

"We should certainly pray she'll find the right house," another woman named Laura added. "And soon. Guests are okay for a few nights. It goes downhill when they feel like they live there. When my grandson stayed with me for two months last summer, it felt more like two years. His girlfriend camped out at my place while trying to keep him interested and made it worse."

"It's not about that," Carly said before the conversation could veer off in an even worse direction. "I'm concerned for Max, her son. He's eleven years old and experienced some bullying the first day of school."

"Is he the sort of boy who might attract bullying?" Laura asked.

Laura occasionally got on Carly's nerves. Her question about Max pushed Carly as close to an explosion of anger as she'd been in years. She managed to calm her thoughts.

"That's not the point," said Jan, who, like Carly, was a former teacher at one of the local elementary schools. "School should be a safe environment for every child. We should pray that Max will find a friend group that can be there for him. Is he interested in any extracurricular activities? That can be a way to accumulate friends quickly."

"Yes, the middle school track coach saw Max run during PE and talked to him."

"Ben Matthews?" Jan asked.

"That sounds right."

"I know Ben and his wife," Jan said. "Would it be okay if I put in a word for Max with Ben?"

"Sure. His full name is Max Quinn."

"Is that the niece whose husband left her for another woman last year?" asked a woman named Harriet.

"Yes. Kelli is a lawyer who's started work this week with Ann Carter's firm. They were law school classmates."

"Ann did wills for Charlie and me," Laura said. "She came to the house to meet with us, just like an old-time doctor. Who does that these days?"

The conversation moved around the circle. When it was time to pray, a woman named Kathy who was leading the meeting turned to Carly.

"Will you lead us in prayer?" she asked, holding up a notebook and extending her hand to Carly. "I made notes about the requests."

"I'd like to pray," Jan said before Carly answered.

Kathy handed the notebook to Jan. The women bowed their heads and closed their eyes. A few of them folded their hands.

Carly loved Jan's communication with the Lord. When the slim woman with silvery-gray hair prayed for Max, the words touched Carly deeply. On their way out of the church building, Carly and Jan walked beside each other.

"That was a beautiful prayer," Carly said. "I especially appreciated what you prayed for Max."

"His situation felt personal. One of my grandsons had a tough time in middle school a couple of years ago."

"How did it work out?"

"His parents pulled him out of public school and put him in a Christian school."

Carly shook her head. "That wouldn't be something Kelli would consider. Let's continue to pray that things improve soon."

Jon left the courthouse. He sat in his truck for a moment before starting the engine. His emotional identification with Cesar's plight forced its way to the surface during the court hearing. Because Cesar was innocent, his situation was much worse than what Jon faced. Jon had been guilty of multiple crimes. And the casual way in which Kelli Quinn approached the case got under Jon's skin. He'd seen how lawyers divorced themselves from their clients and treated them more like objects than people. Jon took a couple of deep breaths. He'd come close to refusing to pay Kelli Quinn, but he didn't have another option for legal representation.

He turned on the engine and cued up some music to listen to while he drove back to the farm. Today his taste ran toward the blues. He started with "Why I Sing the Blues" by B. B. King. There was nothing like a soulful guitar riff to mimic the struggles of life in an unjust world.

Instead of going directly to the worksite, Jon stopped by Maria's house to give her a report in person of what happened in court. He pulled into the front yard.

"Hello," Maria said in Spanish when she opened the door. "Please come inside."

Emmanuel was playing with a toy tractor on the floor of the living room.

"When does Sancho get home from school?" Jon asked.

"I leave around three o'clock to meet the bus."

All the women who lived in the development shared carpool duty to the bus stop that was about a mile away. Jon had tried to convince the school system to bring the children directly home, but the access road was private, and he'd not been successful. They sat at the kitchen table.

"I came straight from the courthouse," Jon said.

"How did Cesar look? Did you get to talk to him?"

"He's doing the best he can," Jon replied evasively. "His lawyer talked to him for a minute or two while entering a plea of not guilty to the charges."

"Did Cesar have to speak? He doesn't like to say anything in public."

"No, Ms. Quinn did the talking." Jon hesitated. "The judge set bond at two hundred fifty thousand dollars, but she's going to try to get that lowered."

Maria ran her fingers through her hair. "I'm going to leave the boys with Victoria and visit Cesar at the jail soon."

Jon hoped Cesar's eye would be better by then. Maria suddenly got up from the table and disappeared into the rear of the house. Puzzled, Jon waited. She returned and laid a thick brown envelope, the kind used in the past to send interoffice documents within a company, on the table. It was closed with a thin red string at the top.

"Look inside," she said.

Jon unwound the string and opened the envelope. It was filled with crisp hundred-dollar bills. The stack was over five inches tall. From his days in the cartel, Jon could roughly estimate the amount of money by the height of the stack but didn't want to say it out loud.

"Is this money Cesar earned selling chocolate?" he asked, knowing it likely wasn't true.

Maria shook her head. "No. I gave you every penny of that. I found this a couple of hours ago under the front seat of his truck when I went to look for a pair of sunglasses. I don't know where this money came from."

"Did you count it?"

"Yes. I think there is around one hundred thousand dollars."

Jon nodded. That was the amount he would have guessed. The workers on the tree farm could be remarkably frugal, especially when they had a goal in mind, but this far exceeded anything Cesar could have set aside from his day job. Jon's mind was racing. It quickly went to the dark place that it was a payout to Cesar from the drug gang.

"Maybe he was saving for something and didn't tell you about it or won the lottery," Jon said quickly, knowing that was more than unlikely. "Did he ever mention buying your own place and moving off—"

"No," Maria interrupted. "That's not the way we do things in our marriage. We always talk about our bills and how much money we have."

Jon was silent for a moment.

"There's nothing to do but ask Cesar for an explanation," he said. "Maybe you can ask him about it when you visit him."

"Won't the guards be listening to what we say?"

"That's always possible."

Maria wrung her hands together as she spoke: "Ever since I found the money, I've worried that Cesar took money from someone without realizing what was going on. He would never help smuggle drugs because he wouldn't want a child or young person to get hooked on drugs or die of an overdose. He loves our sons too much to think about that happening to another person's child. But I can't come up with a reason why he would have this much money and not tell me about it. I helped him clean his truck a few days before he was arrested. I'm sure it wasn't there then."

Maria stopped, took a breath, and then buried her face in her hands. Jon didn't know what to say.

"I don't want to believe Cesar did anything illegal," he said. "I know it's hard, but don't let your imagination go wild. Do you want me to mention this to his lawyer so she can ask Cesar about it? Her conversations with him are always private."

Maria looked up. She wasn't crying, but her eyes were red. "If the lawyer thinks he's guilty of doing something wrong because of the money, will she stop trying to get him out of jail?"

"Lawyers are supposed to represent people regardless of what the person did. It's part of the job."

Jon didn't completely believe that what he said applied to Kelli Quinn, but he knew it was supposed to be the case.

Maria looked down again for a moment. "You spent your own money to hire a lawyer when Cesar had this money in his truck. How could he let you do that? We should have paid all the fee for the lawyer."

That thought had crossed Jon's mind, but he hoped there was another explanation.

"I guess that's another reason we need to know the truth," he said.

Maria sighed. "Ask the lawyer to talk to Cesar about it before I go to see him. Right now, I couldn't look him in the eyes when I visit him."

Kelli logged on to her computer and started working on the files Ann had forwarded to her. Some of them involved the organization of financial records so they could be analyzed. Kelli wasn't afraid to work with numbers. To her, it was like solving a puzzle. The challenge was the haphazard way the clients provided the information.

Ann's clientele was less sophisticated than that of the big corporations Kelli worked with in Atlanta. A lot of cross-checking was required and extra effort was needed to verify the accuracy of the information.

The list of questions Kelli generated for the clients grew longer and longer. She was totally focused when Lauren buzzed her. Kelli picked up the phone.

"It's Matt Davis," the receptionist said.

Kelli accepted the call. "Hello," she said.

"It was good to see you this morning," the DA replied. "I know it's late notice, but I just finished the calendar call and wondered if you had time to grab lunch and catch up."

Startled, Kelli's reflex reaction was to turn him down. She hesitated for a moment.

"Uh, sure," she said. "It's my first week on the job, and I'm mostly doing prep work."

"You jumped into the deep end of the pool when you agreed to represent a man accused of participating in a major drug trafficking operation. How did you get involved in the case?"

The question bordered on impropriety, but there was a vague way to answer.

"He's employed by an existing client of the firm."

"Jon Tremaine?"

"Yes, do you know him?"

"Just by reputation. I know a local man who's an investor in the tree-growing operation that Tremaine manages. He spoke highly of him. I assume Tremaine was the man sitting with you in the courtroom."

"Yes," Kelli said, determined not to provide any more background information.

"Can you meet me at Gordon's Grill?" Matt asked. "It's close to the Brunswick Landing Marina. I'll text you the address."

"Okay."

Kelli gave him her cell phone number.

"Twenty minutes?" Matt asked. "The restaurant isn't far from your office, and I need to put out a couple of fires before I leave."

"Sure."

As soon as the call ended, Kelli began exiting the file she'd been working on. Her phone buzzed again, and she picked it up.

"It's Jon Tremaine," the receptionist said.

Kelli hesitated. She'd already spent as much time with Cesar and his employer as she wanted to for the day. And it was too soon for him to follow up on his request regarding the lowering of Cesar's bond. However, it could be a topic for discussion with Matt Davis over lunch. She determined to keep the conversation with Jon brief.

"Are you there?" Lauren asked.

"Yes, put him through."

"I learned something new when I stopped by to see Cesar's wife that I need to pass along," Jon said.

"Make it quick."

As Jon told her about Maria Mendez finding more than one hundred thousand dollars under the driver's seat of her husband's truck, Kelli forgot about the time limit she'd intended to impose on the call. She asked Jon several questions for which he had no answers.

"Maria would like you to ask Cesar about the money," he said. "Preferably before she visits him later in the week."

Kelli looked at the stack of files on her desk. None of them were urgent.

"I'll go today," she said. "Should I call you or Maria?"

"Me—if it's okay with Cesar."

"Of course. He can invoke attorney-client privilege at any time." Kelli hesitated a moment. "Did you believe Maria when she told you that she and Cesar have no monetary secrets between them?"

"I have no reason to doubt her, but it's not unusual for my workers to have large sums of cash. Most of them are frugal and don't trust banks. They'd rather keep their money in a place where they can see it. But a hundred thousand dollars . . ." Jon stopped.

Kelli had an idea.

"He could use this money toward a bond," she said. "I'm leaving in a couple of minutes to meet with the DA and will bring up the bond issue. I'll call you later."

CHAPTER 14

Before leaving for lunch, Kelli stepped into Ann's office. Her friend had just returned from meetings with clients out of the office.

"How did it go in court this morning?" Ann asked as she placed a stack of papers on her desk.

"Not bad. I reconnected with Matt Davis, who introduced me to Judge Godfrey."

"I've heard Judge Godfrey can be a bear," Ann commented, glancing up.

"He showed his claws but didn't do any damage. I'm going to file a motion to lower my client's bond."

"I don't have time for lunch," Ann said, checking her watch. "I need to work on some of these matters while the details are fresh in my mind."

"That's okay. I'm having lunch with Matt at Gordon's Grill near the marina."

Ann, who was slightly bent over rearranging files, straightened up in her chair. "He asked you to lunch?"

"Yes. Any suggestions about the menu?"

"Best oysters in town. They have them on the half shell and

cook them all kinds of ways. I can't take Roy unless I've had a good month financially at the firm. He's an expensive date. His stomach is bottomless when it comes to oysters."

"Should I let Matt pay?"

"He invited you and will probably turn it in on his expense account. They will be taxpayer-funded oysters. While you're there, think about me eating a pack of crackers in the break room."

Gordon's Grill was close enough to the marina that Kelli could see rows and rows of boats, ranging from twenty-one-foot daysailers to oceangoing yachts. There were even some three-masted sailboats. Inside the café, she didn't see Matt, so she sat down near the hostess station. He rushed in a minute later.

"Sorry," he said when he saw her. "There's always someone wanting to talk to me."

The hostess led them to a table for two in front of a large window with a view of the marina.

"This is nice," Kelli said.

"I called ahead and reserved this table."

Kelli was impressed. She picked up the menu. The options for oysters were extensive.

"Ann said I should order oysters," she said.

"You can't go wrong with any of the seafood. If you're into oysters, we can get a variety and share."

"Sounds good," Kelli replied, placing the menu on the table. "You select and we'll split the bill."

The DA didn't respond to her comment about paying but remained focused on the menu. When their waiter arrived, Matt ordered raw oysters on the half shell along with others either grilled or baked.

"Any other recommendations?" he asked the waiter.

"You might want the oyster chowder. That's what I ate for lunch."

"Done," Matt replied, closing the menu. "Two cups of chowder."

After the waiter left, Matt glanced out the window for a moment before facing Kelli.

"Thanks for agreeing to come on short notice," he said.

"Thanks for inviting me," Kelli said with a smile.

"I have a good reason for us to talk sooner rather than later," Matt continued, speaking rapidly. "I'm sure you're not surprised that the feds are also interested in Mr. Mendez."

Kelli took a quick sip of water. "That's to be expected."

"I've been talking to Gretchen Smith, the U.S. attorney for this district. Did you meet her when you were working in the Atlanta division?"

"No."

"She's not one of those federal prosecutors who think they're ten times smarter than a local DA. She called me shortly after your client's arrest and suggested we keep the case in state court for the time being."

"Why would she want to do that?"

"Something about the nature of their investigation of the entire criminal enterprise. I got the impression from Gretchen that your client was a small cog in a much bigger machine."

"I don't believe my client is a cog at all."

"You have to say that," Matt replied with a dismissive wave of his hand. "But off the record, I want you to know the situation. Gretchen didn't seem concerned about your client getting out on bond. I wasn't going to say anything in front of Judge Godfrey this morning, but we could agree to a much lower bond amount."

"How low?"

"Possibly fifty thousand, which would be great for your client. I saw the bruising on his face near his right eye. Did that come from a jailhouse attack? We've had an uptick in Latino gang activity over the past two years. The rivalries and turf wars can be fierce and spill over into the jail. The situation is one of the bigger challenges I face as DA."

"I'm not sure about the bruising, but Mr. Mendez isn't a cog or a member of a gang. Why would the U.S. attorney be willing for Mr. Mendez to make bond?"

"I'm not sure and wouldn't tell you if I knew. Perhaps it's because he has a wife and two small children, and the feds don't see him as a major flight risk."

"Maybe," Kelli replied doubtfully.

"Actually, I don't believe that's the case," Matt said. "Oh, here comes the chowder."

After they finished eating and split the bill, Matt hurried off to his car while Kelli entered the restroom. She stopped to stare at herself in the mirror. She hadn't been interested in the DA on a personal level but couldn't help evaluating her appearance. As a woman in her mid-thirties, she'd bounced back from two pregnancies and wasn't carrying much extra weight as a result. Leaning closer to the mirror, she had to admit that a few fine lines and wrinkles were creeping into places where she'd prefer smooth skin. And as soon as she found a salon in Brunswick, Kelli needed to talk about extra color in her hair. Age was a relentless adversary. Kelli reapplied her lipstick and walked resolutely out of the building.

After the children got off the school bus, Carly welcomed them into the house with a bowl of fresh fruit. They sat at the round table in the kitchen. Carly wanted to ask Max about his day at school, but it was Emma who dominated the conversation.

"I'm going to like this school better than the one we went to in Atlanta," Emma announced. "The girls in my group share their snacks. Polly brought some homemade fudge that melted in my mouth. I didn't know anything could taste that good."

Emma put a fresh strawberry in her mouth and picked up a green grape.

"This is good," she continued. "And I know it's healthy, but a person needs to experience homemade fudge at least one time in her life."

Carly chuckled. "Would you like me to fix a treat you can share with the other girls?"

"What would it be?" Emma asked. "It has to be extra special."

"I'm up to the challenge if you're willing to help me pick out the ingredients and prepare the treat."

Emma was silent for a moment. She selected a perfectly shaped strawberry from the bowl.

"What about chocolate-covered strawberries?" she asked. "We would have to use the chocolate that's darker than a candy bar. Mom bought some chocolate strawberries last Christmas from a fancy store but only let me taste a tiny bite."

"You had at least ten," Max spoke up. "You kept sneaking them from the refrigerator after Mom left the room."

"Are you going to tell her?" Emma asked, sticking out her chin defiantly.

"Maybe."

"We can use dark chocolate," Carly said. "But you don't want the chocolate to be too bitter. You have to balance the sweetness of the strawberry with the right kind of chocolate."

"Will I be able to try the different kinds of chocolate?" Emma asked.

Carly held up her index finger and thumb so that they almost touched.

"This much," she said. "I'll buy some tomorrow at a local confectionary."

"What's that?"

"A store that only sells sweets," Carly replied.

Emma's eyes widened. "I want to go there."

"One day. I'll stop by while you're in school and also get more strawberries."

"Big fat ones," Emma said as she grabbed some grapes and a final strawberry before leaving the kitchen.

Max remained at the table. He had all the different fruits in a smaller bowl and was eating them with a fork. Carly waited for him to speak, but he didn't.

"Which kind of fruit do you like the most?" she asked.

"Pineapple," he said without changing expression. "That isn't from a can. I like this."

"I cut up the pineapple myself."

Max continued to eat in silence.

"Did you talk any more with Coach Matthews?" she asked.

"Yeah, he came over to me at the beginning of PE. He asked me some questions, and I told him about my dad. After that, he made me his assistant for the day."

"What did that involve?"

"To follow him around and do whatever he told me to do."

"Did you like it?"

"It was okay."

"I guess nobody bothered you."

Max tilted his head to the side for a moment and avoided eye contact. "Only when we were changing into our regular clothes."

Carly tried to keep her voice calm.

"Would you like to tell me what happened?" she asked.

"Not really."

Max finished and left the kitchen. Carly put the remaining fruit in the fridge and went into the backyard to check on the few surviving tomato plants. Lois Gautier was watering a pair of hanging baskets suspended above the rear deck they'd built. She lowered her watering can, waved at Carly, and walked briskly over to the fence. Carly picked a couple of small tomatoes and joined her.

"I saw your niece at the courthouse this morning," Lois said. "Did you know she's representing a drug smuggler with one of those Mexican gangs? What do they call them? Cartels? And the judge didn't appoint her to the case. The defendant hired her. Everyone has the right to a lawyer, and the man might be innocent, but I would have expected her to start out handling traffic tickets with a DUI or two thrown in."

In the short time they'd known each other, Carly had never seen her neighbor so animated.

"Kelli never has talked to me very much about her work," Carly said. "I guess it's because of the confidentiality rules."

"Of course, and it's impressive that she brought in a client like that. I've heard they pay well. And she got off to a good start with Matt Davis, the district attorney. He can be moody, but he had good memories of her from law school and obviously likes her."

"Kelli has a good personality."

"And she's got such a classic look, just like you. I can definitely see similar family features in the two of you."

"You can?" Carly asked in surprise.

"Oh yeah. Were you ever married? I don't think I ever asked."

"No," Carly answered. "I was engaged to a man in the army. He was in a special forces unit and was killed in some kind of secret operation in the Middle East."

Lois's eyes widened. "How sad! How old were you?"

"Young, barely twenty-two and just out of college. He was a few years older. It was a long time ago." Carly held out a tomato. "Here's a tomato. The season is almost over."

Lois accepted the tomato. Carly, who was ready for the conversation to end, turned toward the house.

CHAPTER 15

Jon checked on a crew that was planting seedlings by hand to fill in gaps left by the farm's planting machine. The average number of seedlings per acre needed to be between five hundred and seven hundred. The machine was good for open areas, but there was no substitute for personal attention to each little plant. The gangly seedlings had to be carefully positioned in the soil to increase the chance of survival. The men on the crew were inspecting seedlings that had been planted by machine in a forty-three-acre tract. An experienced eye could quickly sec if the fibrous roots were properly attached to the soil.

Jon and Betsy got out of the truck. The dog ran off about twenty feet away and sniffed the air.

"Whatever you smell, you're not going to run it down," Jon said as he leaned into the bed of the truck and grabbed the narrow spade used to plant the seedlings.

Betsy came over to his side. "Good girl."

As they walked across the ground, Jon instinctively avoided stepping on the new plants. He stopped whenever he saw one out of position and fixed the problem with his gloved hands or the spade. The crew of three men was about two hundred yards away at the edge of the open field. As he drew closer, Jon greeted them in Spanish, which was the most common way they communicated.

"We're almost finished," said Diego. "We have this corner and one more to fill in."

"Good. There's rain in the forecast for the day after tomorrow. The seedlings need a good soaking. Once you're finished here, go to the shop and make sure all the fittings are greased and the blades sharp on the big equipment. We're cutting trees in Section R in the morning."

"Yes, Boss," Diego said. "How's Cesar? Were you with him in court this morning?"

"Yes, it's a tough situation. He entered a not guilty plea, and the judge set his bond at two hundred fifty thousand."

Diego gave a low whistle. "Looks like he'll be sitting in jail," he said, then reached in his pocket and took out a crumpled piece of paper. "Here's my cousin Mateo's number. He told me about the man who was arrested in Savannah. You know, the guy who was importing avocados. Mateo said he'd like to talk to you."

Jon could barely make out Diego's scratchy letters and numbers.

"Why does your cousin want to talk to me?"

"He thinks he can save the farm money on the chemicals we use to kill the bugs. Mateo is a smart guy."

"I may give him a call."

Ninety minutes later, the men had finished planting the seedlings and left for the building where all the big pieces of machinery were kept. Sitting in his truck, Jon called Mateo and introduced himself.

"Thanks so much for calling," Mateo said in barely accented English. "Diego speaks very highly of you."

"I think well of Diego."

"I know you're busy, so I'll get to the point. I understand you export lumber from the Mayor's Point Terminal."

"That's true," Jon replied.

"Do you import as well? Diego told me he drives a truck to the docks every month or so to pick stuff up."

"We occasionally buy chemicals that are manufactured in Costa Rica. Mostly we use organic compounds or controlled cutting, but sometimes stronger chemicals are required, especially for pine beetles."

"If you give me the name of the chemicals, I'd like a chance to see if I can find a cheaper supplier. I'm the representative for a Mexican manufacturer that is trying to break into the American market. After I talked to Diego, I checked, and they have products to treat different types of beetles."

Jon rattled off the names of various chemical products they used. Mateo immediately identified two compounds he could provide. Jon was impressed; Mateo had done his homework. Jon would welcome working with a Latino sales agent.

"I'd be willing to cut my commission to convince you to try our product," Mateo concluded.

"I'm satisfied with my current arrangement," Jon said. "But if you want to send a pricing sheet, I'll look it over. I'll text you my company email address."

"Thanks. I really appreciate you giving me a chance. I know it's a long shot, but if I don't ask, I'll never see if this is going to work out or not."

Jon prepared to end the call but stopped. "One other thing. Diego mentioned you knew about a man in Savannah who was arrested when illegal drugs were found in a shipment of avocados. Do you have any details?"

"Not really. It's a shame people think they can get away with stuff like that."

Kelli was in her office when Ann entered.

"How did it go with Matt Davis?" Ann asked.

"Fine."

Kelli told her about the DA's willingness to lower Cesar's bond.

"That's good news," Ann said.

"But Jon Tremaine called me right before I left for lunch with a troubling piece of information."

Kelli told Ann about the envelope of money.

"Wow."

"I'm going to the jail later this afternoon, and I'll ask Cesar about it. Hopefully, it's not drug money."

"If it is, do you think he'll admit it?"

"Probably not, but I'm pretty good at reading people when they're clearly lying."

"That's a skill I don't have."

"You haven't played as much poker as I have."

Ann chuckled. "I forgot you did that in law school. Didn't you make money?"

"Both in person and online."

Ann stood. "Let me know how it goes with Cesar. What are you going to work on until then?"

The two women briefly discussed a couple of other cases.

"Since the problem in the Davidson matter may result in litigation, will you explain that to the client?" Ann asked.

"Yes. Better for him to know what he's facing now rather than after he's spent a bunch of money fighting a lawsuit that he's not likely to win."

It was 4:05 p.m. when Kelli left the office. She stopped by the reception area to let Lauren know she would be out the rest of the day.

"Ann is letting me leave a few minutes early to get ready for a date with Curt. He surprised me by inviting me to dinner at a fancy seafood restaurant. I've been wanting to eat there for months. It's pricey. Sometimes we each pay for our meal, but tonight he's going to pay for both of us. It's called Gordon's Grill. He told me I could order anything on the menu."

"I'm familiar with it. Do you eat oysters?"

"I usually order shrimp," Lauren replied.

"Tonight would be the time to find out if you like oysters. You can get them raw on the half shell or cooked a bunch of different ways."

"I think I'd prefer cooked."

Kelli told her about the ones she'd liked at lunch. Lauren nodded and scribbled notes. "This helps so much. I don't want to look stupid when it's time to order."

"You'll be beautiful and smart."

"Thanks," Lauren said, beaming.

While she drove to the jail, Kelli thought about Lauren. The receptionist's sweet innocence was refreshing. Kelli hoped Curt was a good man.

At the jail, Kelli parked near the entrance. The same woman was on duty behind the plexiglass shield when she entered.

"I'd like to see Cesar Mendez," Kelli said as she signed in.

"I'll have him brought up."

Five minutes later, a deputy ushered Kelli into an interview room where Cesar waited. There were no signs on his face of additional fights or attacks.

"I know I saw you earlier this morning in court, but there are new developments in your case."

When she told him about the possibility of a significant reduction in his bond, Cesar perked up.

"If the judge approves lowering your bond to fifty thousand, it would cost around seventy-five hundred dollars for you to get out, or someone could post a property bond."

"Property bond?"

"A person who owns land could use the value of the property to guarantee your appearance in court."

"I still don't understand."

Kelli backtracked and tried again. This time Cesar nodded.

"We rent our house," he said, then held up one finger. "But Jon owns his house. He bought it from the company. Do you think he would do the property bond?"

"I don't know. We didn't discuss it."

"Will you ask him?"

"I can," Kelli replied. "But there's something else I need to mention. When Jon stopped by and spoke with Maria about what happened in court this morning, she showed him an envelope of money she found under the front seat of your truck."

"Money? I keep a few dollars in the ashtray."

"There was around one hundred thousand dollars in hundred-dollar bills," Kelli said, closely watching Cesar's face. "Is that your money?"

Cesar's eyes widened. "No!"

"Why was it hidden under the front seat of your truck?" Kelli pressed.

"I don't know," Cesar said, obviously alarmed. "I've never seen that much money in my life. The only cash money Maria and I have left is a few hundred dollars in an empty spinach bag in the freezer."

Kelli leaned back in her chair. If Cesar Mendez was sitting across the table from her in a game of Texas Hold'em, she wouldn't know if he was bluffing or held winning cards.

"Well, the next step is to request that the judge lower your bond," she continued. "You could use some of the money your wife found in the truck to pay a bondsman's fee. That way you wouldn't be putting Jon's property on the line."

"How can I do that?" Cesar replied with a puzzled look on his face. "The money doesn't belong to me."

Kelli nodded. "Good answer."

Carly was in the kitchen checking the status of beef stew in a cooking pot. She hadn't been sure Max and Emma would eat the stew, but both children assured her they liked it, especially if accompanied by corn bread. Made from scratch, corn bread cooked in a cast-iron skillet had been a staple in Carly's family since she was a little girl. The simple recipe handed down from her grandmother would melt butter instantly and tasted great with a drizzle of local honey on top.

Carly heard Kelli enter the house. It was several minutes before her niece appeared.

"Corn bread?" Kelli asked, sniffing the air.

"Yes, and beef stew in the pot. The children said they like it."

"That's true. Max was the first to try it, and it's one of the few times Emma chose to copy her older brother."

Kelli plopped down in one of the kitchen chairs.

"Did you get an update from the kids about school?" she asked.

"Mostly Emma," Carly replied and then relayed what she could remember from the flood of information. "I'm going to need a chart to keep up with her friends."

"Have her do it," Kelli said. "She can decorate it."

"And Max opened up a window of communication to me."

Carly told Kelli what she knew about Max's conversation with Coach Matthews and his invitation to be his assistant for the day.

"Maybe the coach is willing to be a bit of a father figure to Max," Carly said.

"That could be good," Kelli responded. "I've felt like everything was falling on me. I'm supposed to be his mom, not his dad."

Carly then told Kelli about bringing up the issue at her women's meeting, and Jan's connection with Coach Matthews and his wife.

"I hope it's okay that I asked Jan to put in a good word for Max with the coach."

Kelli didn't immediately respond. Carly couldn't tell what her niece was thinking by the expression on her face.

"Should I call Jan and ask her not to do it?" she asked.

"I don't want to be a helicopter mom, but I guess it's okay. It sounds like the coach is a decent man."

Carly slowly leaned over and took the corn bread from the oven. She lifted the lid from the cooking pot. The stew was ready.

CHAPTER 16

It was 2:05 a.m. when the phone on Jon's nightstand rang. He was on call twenty-four hours a day and always kept his cell phone close in case there was an emergency. He grabbed it, hoping it wouldn't wake Sarah. The call was from Maria Mendez. Jon slipped out of bed, went into the hallway, and shut the bedroom door.

"Hello," he said in Spanish.

Maria spoke rapidly. "Someone just broke into Cesar's truck! Catalina's dog was barking, and I looked out the window. I saw a man running away from the truck."

Catalina was Diego's wife. Their house was the closest to the Mendez residence.

"Did you see him?"

"He was dressed all in black. He got on a motorcycle and rode away. It happened so fast, and it was too far away for me to see the license plate number. I went out to the truck, and it was unlocked."

"Did he break a window to get inside?"

"No, but everything was tossed all over the place. I think he was looking for the money in the envelope."

Jon walked into the kitchen and sat at the table in the dark. His mind was churning.

"I got a text after supper from Cesar's lawyer," he said. "She went to the jail this afternoon and asked him about the money. He said he didn't know anything about it. It looks like the money may be connected to the people who were smuggling the drugs."

"What do you mean?"

"Maybe someone stashed the money in the truck when the police arrested Cesar and planned on retrieving it later. Did anyone try to break into the house?"

"No," Maria said and then added in a shaky voice, "I'm scared. If the man comes back, he could hurt me or the boys."

"Where is the envelope?"

"In the refrigerator freezer."

Jon ran the fingers of one hand through his hair.

"Maria, get out of the house," he said. "Take the boys next door and stay with Catalina and Diego."

"What about the money? I'm so scared!"

Hearing the desperation in her voice caused rage to well up inside Jon. The devastating impact the drug cartels had on innocent people was beyond words.

"Go to Catalina and Diego's house," Jon repeated. "Leave the money where it is until I can retrieve it with you."

Jon returned to the bedroom. Sarah spoke before he said anything: "What's going on?"

He told her about the call from Maria. Sarah sat up in bed and leaned against the headboard. Jon sat on the edge of the bed.

"Shouldn't you call the police and let them handle it?"

"No, they would terrify Maria," Jon reasoned. "And the presence of the money might cause them to arrest her and charge her with being part of a criminal conspiracy with Cesar."

Sarah raised her hand to her mouth. "That would be horrible!"

"That's why I believe I should go."

"Whoever broke into the truck could be watching from the woods and—"

"I doubt it," Jon said and shook his head. "If he's connected to the cartel, he'll likely give a report and then receive instructions."

"Oh, Jon, this is a nightmare!"

Jon pressed his lips together firmly for a moment.

"The sooner I get going, the quicker I'll be back," he said.

"Are you going to take a gun?" Sarah asked. "I think you should."

Ten years into the witness protection program, Jon had received permission to purchase a firearm using his new name. The reason he gave for the request was the need to shoot wild animals on the farm. He now owned a pistol, two rifles, and a shotgun. Sarah had grown up around guns in her family.

"Yeah, I'll put my handgun in the truck. And I'll take Betsy. She's good about warning me."

Sarah reached out and touched him on the arm. "Call as soon as you're headed home."

Jon retrieved his 9mm pistol from the lockbox in their closet. Hearing the commotion in the house, Betsy was waiting for him. The dog quictly followed him to the truck and hopped into the passenger seat. It was as if she knew something serious was going on. The dog's confident presence caused Jon's fast-beating heart to slow down.

He drove rapidly along the gravel-and-dirt roads that connected his house to the rental units. Usually it took about ten minutes to reach the houses. Tonight he did it in eight minutes. He slowed only when he was a few hundred yards from the houses. The high-beams on the truck illuminated the woods. He saw nothing except pine trees and the shadows they cast.

As soon as Jon reached Cesar's truck, Maria came out of Catalina's house. Having obviously ignored Jon's request to leave the money where it was, she had a plastic grocery bag in her right hand and walked rapidly toward him. Jon lowered the window.

"Here," Maria said, almost throwing the bag into the truck. "Take it. It's the cash I found in Cesar's truck."

Jon placed the bag on the floorboard of the truck below Betsy.

"Don't go home," he said. "Stay with Catalina."

For a split second, Jon considered giving his gun to Diego but quickly decided against it. The gun was registered to Jon.

"Lock the doors and try to get some rest. We'll report the break-in of the truck to the sheriff's department in the morning and ask them to make sure it's made public."

"Why?"

"So that whoever broke into the truck knows the police have been notified. I'm also going to install motion cameras that trigger a bright light if activated," Jon said. "And heavy-duty locks on the doors for every house, not just your place."

"Thank you," Maria said, noticeably relieved. "That makes me feel better."

Jon was glad he could comfort Maria, even though he knew the precautions he mentioned couldn't prevent determined action by men who worked for a criminal organization.

"I'll check with you in the morning," he said.

"Okay."

"And don't tell anyone about the money or that you gave it to me."

"Catalina and Diego know."

"Tell them to keep quiet about it."

Jon called Sarah.

"I'm on my way," he said. "I didn't see any evidence that the man on the motorcycle stayed nearby after leaving."

"But it's dark. What are you going to do with the money?"

"Put it in the company safe."

During the return trip, Jon tried to think of other things he could do to protect Maria. But in his heart, he knew nothing except a new identity could guarantee safety from a cartel.

When Kelli awoke, she turned on her cell phone. One of the first things she saw was a middle-of-the-night text message from Jon Tremaine asking her to contact him as soon as possible. Kelli would return the call but wasn't going to be ordered around by any client. That sort of interaction was too close to the tyranny she'd endured working for the law firm in Atlanta. She'd considered it normal professionalism at the time but no longer.

During her predawn walk, Kelli found herself thinking about work. Even in Brunswick, the practice of law had a way of creeping into the crevices of every waking moment. The high stakes of a major criminal case increased the demand for her attention. Kelli ran over different strategies for investigation during much of her time spent walking rapidly down the increasingly familiar sidewalks. Only when she was getting close to Carly's house did she give mental attention to the kids. She especially hoped Max would have a good day.

Inside the house, Carly had fixed oatmeal for breakfast. The children's previous experiences with oatmeal were instant packets at a hotel breakfast buffet.

"This should be interesting," Kelli said to her aunt.

Emma made her appearance as Kelli poured a cup of coffee.

"What's that?" she asked, peering into the pan on the stove. "It looks like the paste we use in art class to make papier-mâché."

"Oatmeal," Carly replied. "And just like paste, it will stick to your ribs."

Emma turned to Kelli.

"I want cereal," the little girl pleaded.

"Not today. Keep an open mind about the oatmeal. You don't know what Aunt Carly and I are going to add to it."

Emma plopped down at the round table.

"One spoonful," she said, pouting. "And then I want cereal."

"Two, and we have a deal."

"And they don't have to be big."

"Regular size," Kelli replied.

Carly lowered a ladle into the oatmeal.

"It's been years since I thought about papier-mâché," she said to Kelli. "Do they still use that in school?"

"Emma had a wonderful art teacher at her school in Atlanta. They used mâché to make self-portrait masks. Emma's turned out great. It's somewhere in the storage unit."

Max came into the kitchen and made a quick stop at the stove.

"What can we add to the oatmeal?" he asked. "I ate some at Robbie's house when I spent the night with him."

"I have plenty of options," Carly said.

Carly opened the refrigerator and took out a plate of fruit that included strawberries, blueberries, raisins, and sliced bananas. She placed the fruit on the table and added two small containers of brown sugar and cinnamon with tiny spoons for serving. Kelli set the pan of oatmeal on a trivet.

"I like brown sugar and blueberries," Emma said. "Can I eat them by themselves?"

"No," Kelli replied.

They were gathered around the table. Kelli was about to serve the oatmeal when Carly started praying in a louder-than-normal voice.

"Lord, thank you for this day and this oatmeal. I pray in Jesus' name that Max and Emma will have good days at school and that your holy angels will be with them every second while they're away from this house. Amen."

No one spoke while Kelli served the oatmeal and let the children add what they wanted. Max included everything. Emma stuck to brown sugar and blueberries. She was on her fourth bite before she lowered her spoon.

"Okay, it doesn't taste like paste," she said.

"I'm glad you like it," Carly said with a smile.

Max was halfway through his bowl and hadn't said anything.

"Do you like the oatmeal?" Kelli asked him, even though she knew the answer.

Instead of responding to her, the boy turned to Carly. "Aunt Carly, do you really believe God will send angels to be with us at school?"

"Yes."

"With big white wings?" Emma asked, her eyes wide.

"Maybe," Carly replied. "That's not up to me."

"I want to see one," Emma said. "So I can draw a picture of it."

Kelli had no personal frame of reference for the conversation, but she was concerned how Max might interpret what his aunt believed. Was he going to expect an angel to protect him from being bullied?

Carly spoke: "Max, I believe there is an angel who has looked out for you since you were a baby."

"But we have to take care of ourselves too," Kelli quickly added.

Emma said something about one of the girls at her school, and there was no more discussion on the topic of angels.

"I'll clean up," Carly said when they finished eating, and the children left to brush their teeth.

Kelli remained where she was standing in the middle of the kitchen.

"I respect what you think," Kelli said, "but please don't confuse Max and Emma with your beliefs."

Carly faced her with her gnarled hands on her hips. "I felt compelled to pray like that for the children this morning. If I'd kept my mouth shut, it would have bothered me all day."

"But can we discuss things like that in advance? I don't want Max to be disappointed if he has a rough day."

"I get it," Carly said. "It was a spur-of-the-moment thing. But there's one more topic I should have prayed about."

"What's that?"

"I should have asked God to send an angel with you to the law office."

Kelli managed a slight smile. "I'm not sure angels would welcome hanging out all day with a lawyer."

"There would be a lot to keep them busy," Carly replied.

Kelli thought about her conversation with her aunt while driving the children to school. There were certainly more serious influences to be concerned about in Max's and Emma's lives than Carly's devout faith. But that didn't mean her aunt should be able to say whatever she wanted. Kelli glanced in the rearview mirror at Max, who was looking out the window.

"Max, what did you think about Aunt Carly's comment about angels this morning?" she asked.

"It wasn't a comment; it was a prayer," he corrected her.

Kelli opened her mouth and shut it.

"I'm going to draw a picture of an angel in art class," Emma said. "This is the day when we can draw whatever we like. We're using watercolors."

CHAPTER 17

After a fitful night, Jon got ready to call the sheriff's department and report the break-in of Cesar's truck. Sarah was in the kitchen.

"Do you want to listen?" he asked her.

"Will it be more interesting than scrambling eggs? And do you think a police report will make a difference?"

"I'm not sure. But I promised Maria I would file a report, and I need to follow through."

Jon pressed the speaker button. A woman answered, and Jon provided basic information about himself, Maria, and the reason for the call.

"As far as you know, was anything stolen?" asked the woman.

"No."

"Was there any damage to the vehicle?"

"Not that Ms. Mendez noticed in the dark."

"Does the victim know what someone might have been looking for?"

Jon had rehearsed his answer to that question. He kept it brief.

"Probably money," he replied, glancing over at Sarah, who was standing at the stove with her back to him.

"What makes you think that?"

"There has been money in the truck in the past but not last night."

"Any idea who might have done this?"

"Just the man in black riding a motorcycle."

The woman was silent for a moment.

"What about drugs in the truck, either legal or illegal?" she asked.

"No."

"What's the victim's name and who owns the truck? I didn't get that down earlier."

"Cesar Mendez. He wasn't at home at the time."

Jon held his breath and hoped the woman at the sheriff's department wouldn't ask for Cesar's whereabouts.

"And this occurred on private property owned by your employer?"

"Correct. The company rents dwellings to some of the workers."

"My grandparents used to live in a mill village," the woman said. "I hope the company isn't gouging them by charging excessive rent."

"No, it's below market price."

"That's all I need for now. If the woman or her husband wants to provide additional information, we have Spanish-speaking employees."

"Will this report be recorded and filed on the criminal incident docket?"

"Uh, that's not what we call it, but it will be included in our daily report of thefts or attempted thefts."

"Who has access to that information?"

"Anyone. We publicize the report of a crime in case a member of the public has information and wants to come forward."

"Thanks."

The call ended. Sarah placed a plate of scrambled eggs and link sausage in front of Jon.

"Hopefully, that will put whoever tried to break into the truck on notice that the police are aware of the situation."

"Partly aware," Sarah corrected. "You left out the most important part of the story—the amount of money."

"I don't want that going public. But I did text Cesar's lawyer about it last night."

"In the middle of the night?"

"Yeah."

"Jon, I doubt she's as interested in helping Cesar as you are."

They ate in silence for a few moments.

"And I'm not thrilled with the money being in the house," Sarah said. "Don't you think there's a chance whoever is after it might consider that possibility and come here?"

"You and I are the only ones who know it's in the safe. I told Maria not to mention giving me the money and to pass along to Diego and Catalina the need for secrecy."

"It still makes me uneasy."

On the way to the jobsite, Jon called Maria and told her what he'd done.

"Remember to keep everything quiet," he said.

"I understand. But both Catalina and Diego know about you taking the money. They were watching through the window and saw me give it to you."

The greater the number of open eyes and ears, the harder it was to keep something secret.

"I'll try to talk to Cesar's lawyer about it today," he said.

Carly felt agitated. She knew she'd stepped over the boundary of Southern manners in her prayer and the follow-up conversation at breakfast. In the Withers family, the subjects of religion and politics were usually off-limits. A discussion about politics was occasionally allowed after dinner when the adults assembled in the living room, but matters of faith were private, personal matters not to be brought into public view. For Carly, that changed when she was thirteen years old and encountered the Lord one afternoon at a friend's house. A girl named Samantha asked her to watch a video. It was the testimony of a girl about their age who'd come to saving faith in Jesus. Although she attended church every Sunday, Carly had never heard the gospel explained in such a personal way. A deep longing rose up inside her as she listened. When the girl asked the viewers to repeat a prayer, Carly did so. Samantha remained silent. When Carly said, "Amen," her friend turned toward her.

"Was that the first time you've done that?" she asked.

"Yes."

"I've done it a bunch," the girl replied. "How do you feel?"

"Good."

"Do you feel saved?" Samantha asked.

"I'm not sure how that should feel, but I want to know Jesus the same way that girl does."

Samantha got excited.

"Would you like to come to church with me on Sunday?" she asked.

"I'll have to ask my parents."

Samantha wrote down the name of her church on a scrap of paper. Later, Carly told her parents about the video and asked them if she could visit the church with Samantha's family.

"No, that's not the church for you," her mother said firmly as she placed the slip of paper in the trash.

"Why not?"

"You have our church where we go as a family. It's a good place for you."

Samantha moved away shortly thereafter, but what took place in the girl's home was a tiny plant that grew. Carly began reading the Bible and spent fifteen minutes before going to sleep kneeling beside her bed in prayer. In high school, she joined a fellowship group. She expanded her Christian involvement in college. Returning to Brunswick to teach school, she reconnected with her home church but visited other places of worship as well.

Sitting at the kitchen table, she opened the journal file on her laptop and dictated a prayer for Max, Emma, and Kelli. The appearance of the words in purple ink on the screen made it seem more solid. She stopped to listen for a few moments and dictated in blue the impression she had from the Lord.

Kelli and the children aren't here by accident. You know this, but it's important to remind yourself of the truth. This means your influence goes beyond a roof over their heads and food in their stomachs. Be obedient and see what I do.

Carly opened her Bible to Hebrews 1:14, the Scripture that had flashed across her mind earlier when she bowed her head to pray at breakfast. She added the verse to the journal.

Are not all angels ministering spirits sent to serve those who will inherit salvation?

The ache Carly often felt when praying for Kelli returned. The past year had brought so much pain to her favorite niece. But today Carly's confidence increased that divine help was on the way for both Kelli and her children. She added two words in blue to what she'd previously spoken.

Yes, Lord!

When Kelli didn't call him back by 10:00 a.m., Jon left the worksite and drove into Brunswick. He scratched Betsy's ears as she sat beside him in the passenger seat.

"You always respond when I call," he said.

Betsy tilted her head to the side and licked his fingers.

Arriving at the law office, the young receptionist told him to take a seat. Jon fidgeted while he waited half an hour for Kelli to appear.

"You were the next item on my to-do list," she said.

"Can we talk? I need to tell you what happened at Maria Mendez's house last night."

"Was someone hurt?" Kelli asked.

"No, at least not yet."

Jon followed Kelli into the conference room. He told her about the truck break-in. Kelli made notes on her laptop.

"Based on what happened last night, I think someone stashed the money under the front seat of Cesar's truck and came back to retrieve it," Jon said.

"Unless Cesar put it there and an accomplice came to get it since he's in jail."

Jon frowned. Kelli continued, "I brought up the issue of the money with Cesar at the jail. He claimed to know nothing about it."

"Do you believe him?"

"I can't say," Kelli said and shrugged. "But it's obvious that the presence of the money creates a potentially dangerous situation for his wife and family."

"I already thought about that. I put the money in the company safe at my house. I also filed a report of the incident early this morning with the sheriff's department so that whoever came after the money will be put on notice."

"Notice?"

"That the police are aware of the truck break-in. I'm also going to increase security around the trailers where the workers live."

Kelli made an entry into the laptop and was silent for a moment.

"I'd like to have the envelope dusted for fingerprints without revealing that it was filled with cash," she said. "Who touched it that you know about?"

"Maria and I," Jon said, grimacing. "I didn't consider that possibility."

"If Cesar or someone else used gloves, there won't be any other fingerprints, but it's worth a try. However, if it was handled by an individual or multiple persons with a criminal record, it could identify who's involved. That would be powerful evidence."

"Yeah," Jon replied, then suddenly stopped. "But like I said, my fingerprints are on the envelope."

Kelli glanced up. "Do you have a criminal record?"

"Uh, not really," Jon said after a few seconds passed. "I got into a bit of trouble when I was younger."

"Any felony convictions?"

"No."

"Then it shouldn't be a big deal."

Jon swallowed. Kelli returned her focus to the laptop.

"The only way to access the FBI fingerprint database is through law enforcement agencies," she said. "I think there's a decent chance the local DA will cooperate with me."

Jon felt a bead of sweat roll down the inside of his shirt.

Kelli continued, "Do I have your permission to mention to the DA that you might be in the database?"

"No." Jon shook his head. "Better leave it off the record."

"Okay," Kelli said, looking up at Jon. "I'll make sure he's willing to cooperate. If so, when do you want to bring in the envelope?"

"Let me think about it," Jon replied. "The fingerprint suggestion caught me off guard."

"Okay."

Jon took a breath, then added, "One of my workers heard about a man in Savannah who was arrested when the police found illegal drugs in a shipment of avocados. It sounds similar to what happened to Cesar."

"Do you know the man's name?"

"No, but I'm sure you can find out. Or if you're too busy, I can research it."

"I'll check," Kelli responded.

After Jon Tremaine left, Kelli went to Ann's office and told her about the conversation with the tree farm manager.

"I could tell he was holding out on me about his past," Kelli said. "He was very nervous when the subject of prior scrapes with the police came up."

"Let's check him on our database," Ann said. "If he has a prior arrest or conviction, it will turn up."

Like most law firms, the office had a subscription to a software program that provided a trove of public record information about almost every person in the United States. Lawyers could access the data not out of curiosity, but for business purposes only.

"Jon Tremaine," Ann said as she typed. "I'll enter his current home address from his estate planning file."

Ann opened another screen.

"Here we go," she said, pressing a button.

Her eyes scanned the monitor. A couple of minutes passed.

"No arrests or convictions," she said. "Not even a speeding ticket. But check this out."

Kelli stepped over behind Ann's desk. Ann slowly scrolled through three screens of data. Included were bank records, loans on vehicles, employment history with Granger Forestry LLC, date of marriage to Sarah Huggins, and credit card information.

"He didn't exist before moving to this area," Kelli said.

"At least that's what the database says," Ann replied. "I know he's from Louisiana. It's possible his family raised him off the grid. There are people whose kids are born at home, don't receive Social Security cards, and are homeschooled."

"Any indication that's his background?"

"No, but it wouldn't have been relevant in preparing a will for him and his wife."

"I'll see if he brings in the envelope for fingerprint testing."

In her office, Kelli repeated the search to make sure Ann didn't miss anything. It yielded identical data. She checked social media. There was nothing for Jon or his wife, Sarah. She then tried to find out about the man arrested in Savannah. There was a brief police report that confirmed what Jon told her but nothing else. Kelli made a note of the man's name: Miguel Garcia.

Arriving home half an hour early, Kelli entered a quiet house. She peeked in the living room. Carly was sitting in a recliner with her eyes shut, sleeping peacefully. Kelli tiptoed past the door and into Emma's room. Her daughter was lying on her bed, wearing headphones and looking at her tablet. Kelli took off the headphones.

"You're home early," Emma said.

"Yes, and you'd better get used to it," Kelli replied with a smile. "How was school?"

"No problems," Emma said, then paused. "Except for Larissa and Jenny getting mad at each other. I steered clear of all the drama. It should go away in a couple of days. Both of them ride horses at the same stable. Can you ask Roy to see if there's a place where I can ride?"

"Sure."

Emma reached for her headphones. Kelli continued to Max's room. Her son was sitting at the LEGO table with his back to her.

"Knock knock," she said.

He turned in his chair.

"Hi, Mom," he said cheerfully.

"Good day?" she asked.

"Yes. During PE Coach Matthews put me in a group with some of the boys who are part of the middle school track team. I raced against some of them and did pretty good. After he saw me run, Coach Matthews told me I could train with the team during PE."

"That's great."

"Yeah. They want to have as many fast runners as they can. In some events several runners can score points for the team. Anyway, when we were in the locker room, a few of the boys on the team told the ones who've been bothering me to leave me alone."

"Is that going to work?"

"I think so. Simeon, who's one of the biggest kids in the grade, is the one who talked to them. They looked scared of him. After that, they stayed away from me."

"That's wonderful," Kelli replied with relief.

"And Coach Matthews is really nice to me." Max swiveled back toward his LEGO project. "I think I'm going to like this school."

CHAPTER 18

Jon used his burner phone to contact Chris Polter. Instead of sending a text, he called the inspector. The phone rang several times.

"Why are you calling instead of texting?" the inspector asked in a gruff voice when he picked up.

"Sorry, but I have an emergency and want to talk instead of meet."

"Let me get to a different location."

Jon waited.

"Okay," Chris said. "What's going on?"

Jon told him about the envelope discovered in Cesar's truck that Kelli Quinn wanted the local DA to analyze for fingerprints.

"I didn't think about the possibility of it being dusted for fingerprints when I handled it earlier."

"What was in the envelope?"

Jon licked his lips. He'd never lied to Chris and decided not to start now.

"Around one hundred thousand dollars," he said, then quickly continued: "My theory is that whoever was working for the cartel at the docks stashed it in Cesar's truck when the police showed up. The guy on the motorcycle was sent to retrieve it."

"Nice theory, but this doesn't look good for your worker," Chris said. "Does the DA know about the money?"

"No, and Cesar's lawyer isn't going to tell him what was in the envelope."

"Do you think that will fly?" the inspector asked.

"Not after hearing your reaction."

Chris was silent for a few seconds.

"And you're wondering if your fingerprint history is still in the FBI database?" he asked.

"Yes."

"Yes and no. If they lift good prints from the envelope, the report isn't going to identify you or list your real name. Your fingerprints are no longer accessible via the regular database. They're only identifiable for someone who has authorization to view the witness protection program records. That wouldn't include a local DA."

"That's good," Jon said with relief.

"Not so fast. Most likely, the report will simply indicate that information about some of the prints is not available without proper clearance and authorization."

"Which will lead to questions about why that's the case," Jon replied. "What do you think I should do? Turn over the envelope or refuse?"

"I'm not answering that question. My job is to tell you to stay out of trouble and not do anything foolish that will jeopardize your status in the protection program. I'm not going to give you legal advice." Polter paused. "But you've built a good life, much better than most of the people who get a fresh start. You're about to be a father. Be careful."

"I understand." Jon sighed.

That evening at supper Jon was quieter than usual. Sarah, who had spent the afternoon with her mother and younger sister, chatted about her visit with her family.

"My mom is so glad we're going to have a son. After three granddaughters, she was wondering if a little boy would ever join the tribe."

"Good," Jon replied.

Sarah was silent for a moment.

"Are you thinking about Cesar's case?" she asked.

"In a way," he replied, taking a deep breath.

"Out with it. What's going on?"

Jon told her about the fingerprint issue and his conversations with Kelli and Chris.

"This is getting out of control," Sarah said with a frown on her face.

"I don't want our imaginations to run wild—"

"What are you going to do with the envelope?"

"I thought about that a lot this afternoon. If Kelli can convince the DA to have the envelope tested, I should give it to her along with a fingerprint card from Maria but nothing from me. If she asks why I won't provide a sample, I'll tell her my fingerprints are irrelevant. Then, if the report comes back the way Chris suspects, it will simply mention unknown prints that could be from anyone who's not in the FBI database."

"And you think she'll go along with this?"

"I won't give her a choice."

"And the money? I'm still worried about keeping it here. Even when I was with my family, it was like a shadow following me around all day."

"I haven't come up with a solution for that."

"Give it to the lawyer to look after," Sarah suggested.

"Why?"

"Because it gets the hundred thousand dollars out of our house."

"Okay. I'll take it to her tomorrow."

Jon took out his phone and sent Kelli both an email and a text message but didn't tell why he wanted to meet with her.

The pizzas came out of the oven and were set on racks to cool. Emma ran to her room and returned with the picture she'd drawn of an angel and placed it in the center of the table. Kelli and Max were pouring drinks.

"This is the third one," Emma said. "I threw the other two away, but I'm still not satisfied with it. The wings are too big for the body."

Carly picked up the picture. Emma had done a pencil sketch before filling it in with watercolors. The vibrant red, green, yellow, and purple really popped.

"It's way better than anything I could ever do," Carly said. "Can we put it on the refrigerator?"

"Is that what angels really look like?" Emma insisted.

"I can't say for sure," Carly answered. "The only time I actually saw an angel was years ago at the grocery store."

Kelli and Max brought over the drinks. They all sat down.

"I want to say the blessing," Max said.

Carly looked at Kelli.

"Go ahead," Kelli said, covering her surprise.

Max bowed his head. Carly glanced at Emma, who was sitting with her hands folded in front of her. Kelli had her eyes open. Carly kept her eyes open too.

"God, I know Simeon isn't an angel, but maybe an angel made

him and the other boys come over to me today. Thank you for this pizza. Amen."

Emma reached for a slice with Italian sausage and black olives on top and slid it onto her plate.

Kelli turned to Max. "Whether any angels were involved or not, tell Aunt Carly what happened at school."

Carly listened to Max's account of PE class.

"That doesn't sound like an angel to me," Emma said when Max finished. "The other boys saw what a good runner you are and wanted you to be on their team. It's the same for me with math problems. When we break up in teams for a math contest, everyone wants me to be on their team."

"I still like Max's prayer," Carly said.

"And I felt different today," Max continued. "Less worried about stuff."

"That's good," Kelli said.

Max turned to Carly. "Please, tell us what happened at the grocery store."

Carly was about to eat a bite of pizza but returned the slice to her plate. "Years ago, I was in the cereal aisle when an older man collapsed on the floor. I rushed over to him. A young woman who looked to be in her early twenties joined me. The older man wasn't breathing, and his face was gray. The woman put her hand on his chest and told me to get the manager so he could call 911. This was before most people had cell phones."

"No cell phones?" Emma asked.

"Well, there were a few, but only businessmen, doctors, and lawyers had them."

"The best ones were BlackBerry phones," Kelli added.

"Anyway, I ran to the end of the aisle. I saw the manager, a man named Mr. Fletchall, and yelled for him to call 911. When I turned around, the woman was gone. The man was lying on the floor and breathing. The color had come back into his face. It had only been a few seconds. Even if the woman had tried to run down the aisle, I would have seen her leave. An ambulance came and took the man to the hospital. When Mr. Fletchall told me the next week that the man was going to be okay, I asked him about the young woman. He hadn't seen her."

"Did she look anything like the picture I made?" Emma asked.

"Not exactly. She looked like a regular person. It was summertime, and I think she was wearing shorts and a short-sleeved shirt."

"What color was her hair?"

Carly pointed to Emma's picture. "Yellow, just like the angel you drew."

For Carly, eating a cold piece of pizza was a small sacrifice for the opportunity to share the angel story. After supper, the children left to do homework. Carly and Kelli cleared the table.

"A few months later, I saw the man who collapsed at the store," Carly said. "He remembered me and asked me about the young woman who prayed for him."

"She prayed for him?"

"That's what he said," Carly said, then paused. "By name. She knew his name even though they'd never met."

"Carly . . ." Kelli started.

"I know, I know," Carly said. "It's hard to believe. I wasn't sure whether to tell that part to the children or not."

Kelli was quiet for a moment.

"You probably could have," Kelli said. "Max is already a believer."

Later, while sitting alone on the porch, Kelli read a text message from Jon Tremaine requesting another appointment. For someone who wasn't even the client, Jon was incredibly demanding. Kelli realized he probably thought payment of the majority of the attorney fee bought him access, but there had to be limits. She'd also received a text message from Matt Davis.

> Gretchen Smith confirmed her support for releasing your client at a reduced bond for the figure I mentioned at lunch. File the request and get it on the next calendar.

Kelli immediately replied.

> Will do. Thanks.

The door opened and Emma poked her head outside. "I'm finished. Can I take my shower in the morning? I'm tired, and my stomach is so full of pizza that I need to lie down and let it digest."

It was one of the more creative requests Kelli had heard from either of the children for postponing a shower.

"Will you be able to wake up earlier in the morning?"

"Yes, so long as I don't have to wash my hair. It doesn't need to be cleaned until tomorrow night."

"Let me smell," Kelli said.

Emma came outside. Kelli pulled the girl's head close and sniffed. "You're fine, but this isn't going to change the usual routine. This is only allowed when you overload with pizza. Is that clear?"

"Yeah."

"I'll tuck you in shortly."

"I asked Aunt Carly to do it tonight. Is that okay?"

"Yes, I'll come in after she finishes."

CHAPTER 19

Before going to bed, Jon researched the circumstances under which an attorney could take custody of physical evidence in a criminal case. When he checked his emails in the morning, the first one that popped up was from Mateo Torres with additional information about the chemicals he could provide. The low price for one insecticide caught Jon's attention. There was also a selfie of Mateo standing in front of a cargo bay at the port in Brunswick. A thick, muscular man, Mateo was wearing an orange-and-green cap with the words "Bartlett Construction" on it. Jon thanked him for the email and promised to call him later in the day about the one insecticide. It might be worth giving Mateo's company a chance to supply that specific product.

After breakfast the next day, Jon put on gloves and removed the envelope and cash from the company safe. He stopped by the kitchen to show Sarah what he'd done. She was watering plants in pots placed on a narrow shelf in front of a sunny window.

"Thanks," she said. "I'll feel better as soon as you walk out the door."

"You want to get rid of me?" Jon asked, raising his eyebrows.

"You know what I mean."

"I'm going to meet Diego and install cameras at the trailer park, then take the envelope and money to town around lunchtime and leave it at the lawyer's office."

"What if she doesn't want it?"

"I'm going to leave it anyway."

Jon put a box of surveillance cameras in the bed of his truck. The heavy-duty locks for the trailers were scheduled to arrive later in the week. Jon placed the envelope and money in the glove box. He didn't intend to be out of sight of his truck until the money was delivered to the lawyer.

Diego was outside his trailer running a weed trimmer when Jon arrived. They divided up the cameras. Betsy lay on the ground while Jon climbed a ladder to attach a camera to a slender tree. Diego worked from the opposite end of the park. They met in the middle. The units were solar-powered, but there was enough initial charge for Jon to link them to his and Diego's phones. They leaned against the hood of Jon's truck and checked the placement of the cameras. There was considerable coverage and overlap.

"Looks good to me," Jon said. "What do you think?"

"I think it's also a good way to keep track of the kids," Diego said. "I'm not so sure about anything else."

"They're set up to record for twenty-four hours on a loop. After that the footage will be erased. Either one of us can watch it."

"Okay."

Jon checked the time on his phone. "I'm going to check on the men who are planting new trees and then go into Brunswick. You head over to the tract where they're fighting the weevils."

"Yes, Boss."

On the way to the jobsite, Jon called Mateo. Another man answered in Spanish.

"Is Mateo available?"

"No," the man replied. "He's at the jail."

"The jail?" Jon asked in surprise.

"The police came and got him last night."

"Do you know why?"

"No."

After the call ended, Jon tried to call Diego, but he didn't answer.

Kelli arrived at the office and found Ann with papers strewn haphazardly across her desk.

"Good morning," Kelli said. "What are you working on?"

"I've been here since early this morning trying to sort through the financial records for a new client. They run a hospitality company that provides chairs, tables, tents, and accessories for events like weddings and corporate gatherings. The father started it years ago in their garage. The sons now work for the company, which has several million dollars a year in revenue. They want to buy their father out in a friendly transfer and need to establish a fair valuation without hiring a business broker. I've handled a few matters for them, and they asked for my opinion. Their accounting procedures are archaic, and it's hard for me to get comfortable with the numbers."

"Would you like me to take a look?"

"Only after I take a stab at it. I won't share my conclusions, and then we'll see how close we come."

"Sure."

Ann turned toward her computer monitor, then swiveled back so she could face Kelli.

"One more thing," Ann said. "Did you think any more about Jon Tremaine? I was lying in bed last night trying to figure out the reason for a total absence of personal history prior to him moving to Brunswick."

"Don't lose sleep over it," Kelli replied. "It's not relevant to the case, but I have some potentially valuable information."

She told Ann about Miguel Garcia. "He's been charged with using food shipments as a cover to smuggle drugs."

"Chocolate?"

"No, avocados, which I prefer to chocolate," Kelli said. "It may not be important to my case since there's no connection to our client, but we'll see. At the top of my to-do list is filing a motion to reduce Cesar's bond."

Kelli went to her office and typed up the motion. She filed it electronically with the clerk's office and followed up with a phone call to Lois Gautier.

"I just filed a motion to reduce bond in the Mendez case," Kelli said to the assistant clerk after providing the docket number. "How soon can you put it on a calendar?"

"Tomorrow, if the DA's office doesn't have an objection. And I'm sure Matt Davis isn't going to oppose it. Tomorrow morning is wide open."

Grateful for having inside help at the clerk's office, Kelli was working on another project when Ann brought in an armful of documents related to the hospitality company. She dropped them on Kelli's desk.

"I give up," Ann said. "I know you're used to dealing with big corporations that have everything buttoned up neatly—"

"Except when they're not organized or trying to hide something," Kelli said. "Don't apologize for a client's sloppiness. I like solving puzzles."

"Okay. Can you get back to me by early in the afternoon?"

"Yes."

By noon, Kelli began to question whether she could provide Ann a timely answer. She had a page and a half of questions for the client regarding information that couldn't be answered through what Ann had given her. She went to Ann's office to discuss the situation, but Ann wasn't there. Kelli learned from Lauren that Ann wouldn't be back until 2:00 p.m.

"Are you going to lunch?" the receptionist asked.

"I'm hungry but probably not. I have too much to do."

"I can bring something back for you. I'm going to get a take-out salad from the place Ann took you to the other day."

"That would be great," Kelli said, then told her what she wanted. "I'll reimburse you."

Kelli glanced out one of the front windows of the office.

"That's Jon Tremaine," she said.

Lauren raised her hand to her mouth.

"Oops," she said. "I forgot to tell you that he wanted to come by and drop something off. I was about to send you an email to make sure it was okay when another call came in. It slipped my mind."

"It's fine," Kelli said.

Jon entered the reception area. He had a leather bag over his shoulder. He greeted Kelli.

"Do you have a few minutes?" he asked.

"A few," Kelli replied.

Kelli led the way to the conference room. Before sitting down, Jon placed the bag on the table and opened the flap. Taking a leather glove from his coat pocket, he took out a thick brown envelope tied with a red string at the top.

"Here's the envelope I mentioned," he said. "I don't want to touch it again before it's sent off for fingerprint analysis. I think you should have custody of the envelope and the money."

"Wait a minute," Kelli said, holding her hands up in a stop motion. "I haven't obtained an agreement from Cesar, you, or the DA to run a fingerprint test. There's no reason to bring the envelope and money here."

"Maria Mendez can't keep this in her freezer, and I'm not going to use the company safe."

"Why not?"

"My wife wants it out of the house."

"I have to discuss this with Ann," Kelli replied.

"You can discuss it, but I'm not leaving here with the envelope or the money."

Kelli felt her face flush. She bristled. "You can't give me an ultimatum—"

"It's not an ultimatum. This is possibly connected to Cesar's case. It's my understanding under the ethics rules that in the absence of a court order or other obligation to disclose or deliver an item of physical evidence, a defense lawyer can keep potential evidence in his or her possession for the purpose of testing, examination, and analysis."

"Did you read that on the internet?"

"Yes, at ten thirty last night. Am I right? There's nothing inherently illegal about the envelope or the money. It's not like you're keeping stolen goods or contraband in your office."

"We don't know how or if they're connected," Kelli said without answering Jon's question.

"Look," he said. "I realize I sprang this on you suddenly, but can you understand why I'm doing this?"

"Not really."

"Does the law firm have a safe-deposit box?"

"I'm not sure. Ann and I haven't discussed it. Do you?"

"No."

Kelli used a legal pad to push the envelope and the money toward Jon.

"Then I suggest you get one," she said. "I'm not accepting custody. If you want to force the issue, I'll withdraw from Cesar's case and refund the attorney fee."

Kelli saw Jon's jaw clench. He lowered his eyes for a few seconds. "Okay. I'll leave it here until I can go to the bank."

"No, you'll take it with you now."

"You don't believe I'll do what I say?" Jon asked, his voice getting louder.

"You didn't help by dictating what I have to do." Kelli paused. "And I was also troubled about the absence of information when I ran a background check on you. There's nothing in the public records about you prior to you moving to this area."

Jon's eyes narrowed. "Why did you run a background check on me?"

"Because of your comment about your fingerprints possibly being in the FBI database."

"Why is my background relevant to Cesar's case?"

"It's not, but do you want to tell me why nothing shows up?"

"Did you include my first name?"

"What's your first name?"

"Harold, but I never liked it. I left it behind when I moved from Louisiana and started going by Jon."

"No, we didn't search for Harold Jon Tremaine."

"Who did the search?"

"Ann and I."

Jon shook his head. "Run it again for Harold J. Tremaine. I'll wait."

Kelli went into her office, logged on to her computer, and entered "Harold J. Tremaine." Sure enough, there were entries for Harold J. Tremaine from Baton Rouge, Louisiana. The full middle name, Jon, didn't appear.

She printed off the information and returned to the conference room.

"There's nothing about Jon, but there's information about a man with your date of birth named Harold J. Tremaine. He lived in Baton Rouge."

"He?" Jon asked.

"You," Kelli corrected herself.

She continued to read.

"You lived at two addresses," she said.

Jon quoted the two addresses.

"And worked at a couple of fast-food restaurants and attended a local community college," Kelli continued.

"Where I received an associate's degree in accounting."

"There's not much else," Kelli said. "No bank loans. No marriages. No criminal record."

"Looks like I've lived a boring life."

Jon used his gloved hand to return the envelope to his leather bag. He turned to leave, then stopped.

"You should be more careful in your investigation procedures," he said. "My trust in your competency as an attorney took a hit this morning."

CHAPTER 20

After Kelli and the children left for school, Carly sat at the kitchen table and opened her laptop. Her time the previous evening with Emma had been precious. In the relaxed moments before sleep, the little girl's spunkiness retreated, and she wholeheartedly received what Carly prayed for her. Stroking Emma's hair before planting a kiss on the little girl's forehead was a memory Carly etched into her brain. She hadn't spent any time with Max but had heard enough from him earlier to encourage her. Now, Carly was eager to follow up in prayer for the children.

She stared at her computer monitor and sat quietly for a few moments. Nothing came. This was rare, but the silence didn't upset her. She'd learned how to be still in the presence of the Lord like a child looking up with expectation at her mother. Rest was one of the most active things a child of God could do. Carly took a deep breath and exhaled. Her spirit was a blank slate. Then she realized there was a swirl of interference in the deep recesses of her mind.

"That's not good," Carly said out loud.

A reply came immediately within her heart: *No, it's not.*

Carly pondered the three words. She'd always found the Lord

to be precise. He didn't ramble or needlessly elaborate. Even a simple statement or brief question was rich with meaning. Carly mulled over what might be going on. If there was a block to communication, she knew it had to be on her end.

"What's wrong?" she asked, then waited.

Nothing surfaced. Carly frowned. She wasn't going to fake anything. She continued to stare at her monitor. The blinking cursor was poised to repeat a word. After a couple of minutes of internal silence, she shut down the machine and slowly lowered the screen.

Jon pulled into the parking lot at the local bank that served him and Granger Forestry. Inside, he recognized a middle-aged woman sitting in a small cubicle adjacent to the lobby. He knocked on the doorframe. Ms. Broadway was wearing designer glasses that looked out of place with the rest of her outfit.

"Mr. Tremaine," she said. "How may I help you?"

"I need to rent a safe-deposit box."

The woman swiveled in her chair and faced her computer. "For yourself or the business?"

"Personal."

Fifteen minutes later, Jon exited the bank. He'd made sure the bank employee wasn't watching him as he put on a glove before placing the cash-filled envelope in the box. Betsy waited in his truck. Jon let the dog out on a leash into a green area adjacent to the bank. The phone in his pocket vibrated. It was Diego.

"Mr. Jon, I got your message about Mateo getting arrested," Diego said, speaking rapidly. "I talked to another of our relatives. He says the police claim Mateo got in a fight at a local bar and broke another man's nose. My cousin says it was self-defense. Mateo is going to need a lawyer. Do you think Cesar's lawyer could help him?"

While he listened, Jon returned to his truck. He opened the door so Betsy could jump inside.

"I don't know if Cesar's lawyer would be willing to represent Mateo or not," he said. "It can cost a lot of money."

"Mateo has money. He's very generous. Whenever we go somewhere to eat as a family, he pays for the food and drinks."

Jon closed the passenger door of the truck. He simply couldn't give Kelli Quinn a positive recommendation. "If he wants to talk to Cesar's lawyer, he's going to have to do it directly or through someone else. I'm not going to be his go-between."

Diego was silent for a few seconds.

"Okay," he said.

The call ended. Jon left Brunswick and headed toward the farm. On the way, he called Sarah to let her know what he'd done with the envelope and the money.

"The safe-deposit box can be the place to store your big diamonds and the gold bars we're going to buy," he said.

"A bigger diamond might be nice someday, but I'm more interested in baby clothes than gold bars. I'm really feeling pregnant today. Thanks again for getting that stuff out of the house. And don't be late for supper. I'm planning something you like."

As soon as he hung up with Sarah, Jon called and left a message for Chris Polter. Turning onto the farm property, he stopped to send Kelli a text message.

> Envelope and cash in safe-deposit box. Your call to discuss with Cesar and agree to have the envelope dusted for other fingerprints. I won't object.

Jon couldn't let remote personal concerns or frustration with Kelli interfere with possible help for Cesar's case.

"I hope this is right," Lauren said to Kelli. "They were slammed at the deli, and I wasn't sure the girl who took the order understood everything I said."

"I'm sure it's fine. I'm not a picky eater."

"Me either. Curt likes everything just so. He admits he's a perfectionist. That's why he's so good at his job."

"What does he do?"

"He works in the quality control department of a factory in Savannah. They make something for the military. It's all top secret."

Kelli went to her office to eat. She opened the container and took a bite. The salad had a different dressing than what she'd requested, but it was better than the kind she'd ordered the first time. While she ate, she reviewed again the two sheets of information about Harold J. Tremaine. She debated whether she owed Jon an apology for making the accusatory comment about his background and losing her temper when he asked her to assume custody of the envelope and the cash. Kelli hated losing her cool, but Jon had brusquely pushed her too far with his demand. She finished eating.

Lauren buzzed her phone. "How was your salad?"

"Good."

"Matt Davis is calling," Lauren said.

"I'll take it."

"Good afternoon," Matt said. "I just reviewed tomorrow morning's calendar and saw that you filed a motion to reduce your client's bond."

"Yes. Are you still willing to go along with a significant lowering of the amount?"

"I am, but Judge Godfrey has discretion."

"You won't object to fifty thousand, though?"

"That's correct, Counsel."

Kelli was itching to ask again why Gretchen Smith seemed willing to allow Cesar to get out of jail.

"But that's not the only reason I called," Matt continued. "What are the chances your client might voluntarily answer some questions about his chocolate importing business and his Mexican and local contacts?"

Kelli shifted in her chair. "I can't see that happening without some kind of benefit to him."

"I expected you to say that. Any benefit would depend on his answers. Let's approach it another way. You're a former federal prosecutor. What if I provide you with questions that you can ask him and then you make the decision whether his knowledge might justify a different prosecutorial approach to his case? If so, you and I could talk about the information he reveals without your client incriminating himself."

Put that way, the proposal took Kelli only a second to consider.

"I can do that," she said.

"Good," Matt replied. "I'll put something together and give it to you in the morning."

"Okay," Kelli responded.

She hesitated as she thought about the brief text message that she'd received from Jon Tremaine about having the envelope tested for fingerprints.

"There's one other thing," she said. "Someone tried to break into my client's truck the other night. I believe the person may have been trying to retrieve an envelope. Would you be willing to see if there are fingerprints on the envelope that might lead to identification of a person or persons actually linked to the drugs seized?"

"What if your client's fingerprints are on the envelope?"

"I don't believe they will be. The only people I know who've handled it are my client's wife and his boss, Jon Tremaine. The wife found the envelope and turned it over to Mr. Tremaine."

"What was in the envelope?"

"Some money."

"How much?"

"I'd rather not say."

"Where are the envelope and money now?"

"In a safe-deposit box."

Matt was silent for a moment. "I assume we're not talking about an insignificant amount of money."

"No comment."

"Okay. Your client is the one taking the risk. We'd want to use one of our detectives to establish chain of custody."

"Just the envelope, not the cash. We don't know for sure that either is connected to the case. If my client's fingerprints aren't on the envelope, its contents wouldn't be admissible in court against him."

"Probably not, but I can't promise not to try."

"And if a known criminal is identified, it might provide information as to who set up Mr. Mendez."

"That's a stretch."

"But it would be significant evidence to support reasonable doubt."

"Do you really believe that would justify an acquittal?" Matt replied skeptically. "There's no question the shipment was sent to Mr. Mendez from Mexico, and the contraband was found in his pallet.

It's an open-and-shut case. Maybe I shouldn't be so willing to run the test."

Kelli swallowed.

"But I will," the DA continued. "I'll have one of the detectives get in touch with you. He'll need sample prints from anyone that we know has touched it."

"First I need to confirm everything with my client."

"You don't have his permission?"

Kelli winced. "I wanted to find out your position before talking to him."

"See you in the morning," the DA said curtly.

After the call ended, Kelli typed an email to Jon Tremaine summarizing the call with the DA about lowering Cesar's bond but didn't mention the fingerprint discussion.

> If the bond is lowered to $50K, would you be willing to post a property bond so Cesar can be released from jail?

She sent the email without including an apology.

The unsettledness Carly felt during her morning time with the Lord lingered throughout the day. She made a trip to the grocery store and threw herself into preparing a nice supper. When the kids arrived home, Carly greeted them but didn't ask for details about their day at school. She was standing at the stove putting potatoes in water to boil when Max entered the room.

"What are you making?" he asked.

"Mashed potatoes."

"I like yours a lot more than the ones from a box."

"I'm glad."

Max leaned against the kitchen counter.

"Does my mom believe in God the same way you do?" he asked.

Carly dropped in the last potato and faced him.

"That's a big question," she replied. "I think it would be better if we had that conversation when the three of us are together."

"Why?"

"So she can speak for herself and we can hear each other directly."

Max nodded. "Okay. Should we talk during or after supper?"

"After. It's hard to talk about God or anything else when your mouth is full of mashed potatoes."

"Are you making gravy?" Max asked.

"Yes."

There was a pot roast with vegetables in the slow cooker next to the toaster. Max left the kitchen. Walking in obedience to the Lord could be a subtle process. Carly wanted to prod the children toward understanding and faith, but it would be a mistake to do the right thing at the wrong time. The children were precious fruit that could be plucked with an open hand. Helping their mother, with the accumulated traumas of life wrapped around her heart, required the skill of a surgeon.

"Lord, you're the Great Physician," Carly said.

Yes, I am.

"And I believe Kelli's family is supposed to take the journey with you together," Carly added.

Immediately the heaviness that had been Carly's companion all day lifted. She had her answer. She needed to focus first on Kelli. Tears of tender compassion for her niece appeared in the corners of her eyes. The tears were a gift, the overflow of her heart's desire for

Kelli's good. It was a longing Carly knew she shared with the Lord himself. A verse from Jeremiah came to her mind:

Oh, that my head were a spring of water and my eyes a fountain of tears! I would weep day and night for the slain of my people.

The tears rolled down her cheeks. Carly grabbed a napkin from a container next to the fridge and wiped them away. Weeping like this rarely came over her. Her feelings rose from the depths of her soul, each tear as powerful as a prayer.

"Whew," Carly said after a few minutes had passed and the tears slowed to a trickle. "Thank you."

When Ann returned to the office, Kelli gave her an update on the Mendez case and Jon Tremaine. Ann shook her head when Kelli described Jon's demand that the law firm take possession of the envelope and the cash.

"I wouldn't have predicted that sort of behavior," Ann said. "Jon always seemed very low-key and mild-mannered to me. But it's good to have clarity about his background. It just proves those data programs are only as good as the input we provide."

"Which made me look unprofessional to Jon. He made a snide comment about my ability on his way out the door."

Ann frowned for a moment before she spoke: "One of my cardinal rules of law practice is that if a client loses trust or confidence in me, I'm no longer interested in being that person's attorney. Holding on to representation under those circumstances rarely works out for the best."

"The problem is more with Jon than Cesar, so I'm not there yet," Kelli said. "Also, Matt Davis agreed to send the envelope to the FBI for fingerprint analysis. I'm going to clear it with Cesar, and then a detective is going to contact me about it."

Ann took out her phone and looked at the screen. "While I'm thinking about it, Roy says this Saturday would be a good time for him to take Emma to a stable. Do you have anything on your calendar?"

"No, and I don't need to look," Kelli replied. "Tell Roy that Emma will be thrilled."

Kelli left the office and drove to the jail. Meeting with Cesar, she carefully explained the possibility of having the envelope tested for fingerprints.

"Yes," the client quickly responded. "Anything to prove I'm innocent."

"This would be indirect, not direct proof," Kelli replied, then explained what she meant.

"But you think it's a good idea?"

"Yes," she answered.

"Go ahead."

While sitting in her car in the jail parking lot, Kelli called Matt Davis. She expected to leave a message, but the DA answered.

"My client agrees to the fingerprint testing on the envelope," she said.

"I was expecting your call. I reached out to a local detective who will handle the chain of custody, and I also spoke with Gretchen Smith. She referred me to FBI Agent Perez, who's in charge of the investigation. Agent Perez insists that any money in the envelope also be subject to fingerprint analysis."

Stunned, Kelli wasn't sure how to respond.

"I'm going to have to think about that," she managed.

"Suit yourself. If you decide to move forward, everything must be delivered to the sheriff's department so it can be inventoried and placed in a secure evidence locker. Let me know by tomorrow."

"Tomorrow?" Kelli questioned. "I'll have to contact my client and the person who has the envelope."

"Who's that?"

"Jon Tremaine. Remember, both he and my client's wife handled the envelope."

"They will need to provide fingerprint samples."

Kelli suddenly realized she'd not included that requirement in the email she sent Jon. It was another careless oversight.

"Uh, I'll have to make sure that Mr. Tremaine is agreeable."

"Why wouldn't he be? Does he have something to hide?"

"No."

"Like I said, I'll expect to hear from you by end of day tomorrow."

After the call ended, Kelli returned to the office and told Ann about the new developments.

"When they find out there was a hundred thousand dollars in the envelope, Detective Briscoe and the FBI will immediately assume it's drug money," Kelli said.

"They already knew the envelope contained money, just not how much," Ann replied.

"Yeah," Kelli said forlornly. "This may have been a huge tactical mistake. I was so focused on how this might help Cesar, I didn't consider how it might hurt him. And Jon can say no."

The two women sat in silence for a moment.

"Look," Ann said. "Trying to defend Cesar against the charges with the evidence you know exists is almost impossible, correct?"

When Kelli nodded, Ann continued, "This fingerprint analysis is a long shot, but at least it's a chance to create a basis for doubt."

"I guess so. I need to run it by Cesar and make sure he's good with the new proposal. But what am I going to say to Jon?"

"The truth. Will both of them be present at the bond hearing?"

"I hope so. Cesar would like Jon to post a property bond if the judge lowers it to fifty thousand."

"Will he do that?" Ann asked, her eyes wide.

"I think so."

"Then he's all in," Ann said.

"And he thinks that gives him the right to dictate what I do in the case."

"Calm down about—"

"I'm only venting with you," Kelli said.

Ann was silent for a moment. "One other thing. I suggest you swing by the jail again this afternoon and talk to Cesar. Don't delay. If he has a problem revealing the information about the money, it will make me wonder about his innocence."

There was no rule limiting the number of visits a lawyer could have with a client, but the woman deputy gave Kelli a puzzled look when she again asked to see Cesar. Thirty minutes later, Kelli left the jail more convinced than before that Cesar Mendez wasn't a drug smuggler. He didn't react negatively about informing the FBI and sheriff's department of the amount of money in the envelope or turning it over to the authorities for testing. He insisted that it wasn't his money and he had no right to it.

When Kelli arrived home, Max and Emma had finished supper and were in their rooms on their tablets. Carly was in the kitchen. She came over and gave Kelli a hug.

"What did I do to deserve that?" Kelli asked.

"Oh, I've been feeling a lot of love for you this afternoon and wanted to show you."

"Thanks."

Kelli looked past Carly at the stove.

"What did I miss?" she asked.

"I saved you a plate."

Carly sat at the table while Kelli ate.

"I need to apologize for cutting you out of my conversations with the children about the Lord," Carly said.

"You didn't cut me out," Kelli said. "You're the expert about that sort of thing, not me. If they have questions, I'd rather they ask you than anyone else."

"You were upset with me the other day—" Carly started.

"Oh, that was because the talk about angels and stuff caught me off guard. Thinking about it now, I should probably apologize to you. I've always considered matters of faith and belief to be individual choices, but how are the kids going to decide what they believe without input from adults who love them? Don't hold back in talking to the kids. I trust you. Anything that makes them happier and better adjusted is fine with me. Just keep me in the loop of what they're saying and thinking."

"Absolutely."

Later, after the women finished putting the dishes in the washer, Carly gave Kelli another hug.

CHAPTER 21

Jon and Sarah finished a pork chop dinner. Sarah had dusted the boneless chops in flour and a dry rub, then seared and covered them in a cast-iron skillet to cook. Finally, she topped them with a pan sauce. Jon ate two.

"Is there another one?" he asked.

"Yes, but do you need to leave room for dessert?"

"Maybe. What is it?"

"An experiment. It's not very heavy."

Jon waited. Sarah pointed to the oven.

"Pig's ears," she said.

"What?" Jon asked in surprise.

"I mean the pastry," Sarah continued. "What's the other word for it?"

"*Palmiers* or *les oreilles de cochon*," Jon replied. "I've never told you how much I like them."

"Translate that last part."

Jon laughed. "The ears of pigs."

"I followed a popular recipe. I'm not sure they'll measure up to what you ate growing up."

Jon pushed away his dinner plate. "I'm ready. I just lost my appetite for another pork chop."

Sarah took the cinnamon-sugar pastries from the oven, where they had been kept warm, and placed the pan in front of Jon. He held up one of the pieces that looked like two ears curled close together. He took a bite.

"This is good," he said. "You could sell these at any bakery in New Orleans."

Sarah joined him at the table. After they ate their fill of the pastries, Jon put away the leftovers and placed a teapot filled with water on the stove.

"How does it feel spending more time at home?" he asked as they waited for the water to boil.

"It's going to take getting used to. There is so much stress and tension involved in serving the women at the shelter that sitting here in the middle of the woods feels tame."

"We could have kept the money from Cesar's truck in the safe. You said that was stressful."

"That was different. For some reason, it made me feel connected to what you went through in the past. And I didn't like it."

Jon took out a pair of cups and selected a variety of tea he knew Sarah liked. The teapot emitted a low whistle.

"How did it go with the lawyer when you gave her the envelope and the money?" Sarah asked.

"She didn't want to take it. That's why I went to the bank and rented a safe-deposit box. A couple of hours later, she sent me an email saying that the DA is willing to dust the envelope for fingerprints to see if something turns up."

Sarah sat up straighter in her chair.

"What about your fingerprints?" she asked.

Jon told her what he'd learned from Chris Polter and about his decision not to provide a fingerprint card. He poured the boiling water over a tea bag and brought the cup to the table.

"Chris has my back on this, which makes me feel a lot better," he said. "Also, the lawyer ran a background check on me through some system. At first nothing showed up before I moved to Georgia, but she hadn't checked Harold J. Tremaine."

"I'm so glad you decided not to use that name," Sarah said, making a face. "I'd hate to name our son Harold Jr."

"Based on what the witness program planted in the record, I'm boring enough to be a Harold. Also, it looks like the DA won't oppose reducing Cesar's bond to fifty thousand dollars. There's a hearing set in the morning to find out if the judge will go along with it."

"That sounds good," Sarah said. "But unless you include the money in the envelope, Cesar doesn't have fifty thousand dollars."

Jon kept his back to her as he put away the leftovers. "If it's lowered, we could provide a property bond. It wouldn't cost us anything."

As he turned back toward her, Sarah said, "Unless he skips out."

"If you don't think we should—"

"No," Sarah sighed. "We're in so deep that the possibility of this becoming like a second mortgage on the house isn't that big a step. Cesar needs to be with Maria and his boys."

"And out of the violent environment at the jail."

"Did he get hurt?" Sarah asked.

"Not too bad, but any injury is scary."

Jon sat down across from Sarah, who took his hand in hers before saying, "Let's not talk about Cesar and the case for the rest of the evening."

"Agreed."

After the late supper, they sat in rocking chairs on the back deck. It rarely got cold in southeast Georgia before December, but there was enough chill in the air that Sarah put on a sweater. A full moon rose in the sky as Jon and Sarah continued to rock on the deck. Thirty minutes later, his phone vibrated in the front pocket of his shirt. It was a call from Diego. Not wanting to violate Sarah's request, he let it go to voicemail. After Sarah went inside to get ready for bed, Jon listened to the message. Diego spoke in English: "I checked the recordings for the cameras and saw someone I didn't know come out of the woods after the sun went down. He went to Cesar's trailer and tried to open the door. Maria and the kids are still at our house. The man left when the bright lights for one of the cameras turned on."

Jon sent Diego a text requesting the time of the event. Diego immediately replied:

7:45. Cameras 2 and 4.

Jon pulled up the video feed for camera 2 on his phone, ran it forward to 7:30 p.m., and started watching. At 7:42 p.m. a man came into the frame. He was dressed in all black and wearing a ball cap pulled down low. Jon couldn't be sure, but it was possibly the man on the motorcycle who had broken into Cesar's truck. He was wearing gloves and his face couldn't be seen. The man ran toward Cesar's trailer and out of the frame.

Jon switched to camera 4. At 7:46 p.m., the man's presence triggered the camera. He jerked his head to the side. Jon couldn't get an unobstructed view of the man's face, but one thing was clear. The intruder was wearing an orange-and-green hat with the words "Southside Plumbing" on the front. Jon held the phone closer. The man took a small tool from the pocket of his pants and spent a few seconds trying to unlock the door. He dropped the tool onto the wooden stoop for the trailer and looked toward another trailer. He then jumped off the stoop and ran toward the woods. Thinking about the danger to Maria and the boys if they'd been inside the trailer made Jon shiver involuntarily. He called Diego.

"I watched it," Jon said.

"I looked at the video from the other cameras and didn't see anything more," Diego said.

"Did Maria watch it?"

"Yes, she's really scared."

"Tell her I'm going to save the video and turn it over to the sheriff's department."

"Okay."

Jon was silent for a moment. "Did you see the hat the man was wearing? The one that had 'Southside Plumbing' written on the front?"

"Yes."

"In one of the photos Mateo sent, he was wearing the same color hat with the words 'Bartlett Construction' on it. Do you know if Mateo ever worked for Bartlett Construction?"

"Maybe. He's had a lot of different jobs, or he could have gotten the hat from someplace just to wear it."

"That's possible," Jon said before pausing. "I'm glad the lock on the trailer was good enough to keep the man from breaking in this evening. Hopefully the better locks will come in soon and we can install them on all the trailers."

"Yes, Boss."

The call ended. Jon downloaded the video feed so he could edit it for delivery to the sheriff's department. He stared across the yard, which was illuminated by the moon. Betsy had left the deck when Sarah went inside the house and was patrolling the fence line for their property. It wasn't unusual for the dog to do so, but tonight it took on special meaning. Increased vigilance was justified. As he sat in the chair, Jon thought of the image of the orange-and-green cap. One way the Los Reyes cartel used to identify members and their jobs was through colored caps. The names of the companies on the front of the caps varied according to the person's job with the criminal group, but the color scheme was the same. When he started working at shipment locations, Jon wore a blue-and-gold cap with the name "Stevens Electrical" on the front. That meant he was part of the financial oversight group. Taking out his phone, he looked up Bartlett Construction and Southside Plumbing. There were multiple companies with those names but none within two hundred miles of Brunswick. A feeling of dread rose up in Jon. He closed his eyes. But he couldn't unsee what he'd seen.

CHAPTER 22

Jon left the house before Sarah was stirring. In a thin folder were the papers needed to post the property bond. Kelli hadn't told him what was required, so Jon researched the issue himself. He checked in with the work crew before driving into Brunswick.

"Mateo got out on bond," Diego told him. "I think he's already found a lawyer to represent him."

Jon had no interest in getting involved in another man's criminal case, especially someone he didn't know.

"Good," he said.

During the ride into town, Jon longed for the days before Cesar's arrest, when his biggest worries had to do with invasive insects or a lightning strike that caused a fire. He arrived early at the courthouse. Sitting in his truck, he reviewed the earlier video from the trailer park along with the photograph of Mateo from the dock in Savannah. He strongly suspected that Mateo might deserve more serious criminal charges than breaking a man's nose in a barroom brawl.

Thinking about the hats, Jon remembered the first time he put on his blue-and-gold hat. At that point, he didn't fully realize the significance of what he was doing for the cartel, and putting on the hat seemed like joining a juvenile secret society. Later, every time he saw one of the hats, he became nervous. After he testified in court for the last time, Jon burned his hat in a charcoal grill.

Jon saw Kelli walking up the steps to the courthouse. His uncertainty about the lawyer's skill had grown into a persistent doubt. Cesar had trusted him to select an attorney, and Sarah had agreed for the two of them to pay Kelli Quinn a lot of money. Now, Jon was about to put their house at risk.

Getting out of the truck, he saw two men crossing the street on a corner to his left. One of them was wearing an orange-and-green cap. Jon jerked his head sideways to get a better look. A truck passed through the intersection. When it was gone, the men were hidden in a group of people on the sidewalk. As he walked up to the courthouse, Jon kept looking for the man in the orange-and-green cap but didn't see him.

Kelli entered the back of the courtroom. The seating area was already filling up with people. She walked to the front of the room and sat behind the table reserved for Matt Davis and his assistants. There was no sign of Cesar or the other prisoners who would be brought over from the jail. Some of the defendants were wearing regular clothes and sitting in the rows around her. Kelli felt a tap on her shoulder and turned her head. It was Jon.

"Good morning," she said. "I wasn't sure you'd come."

"What are the odds that the judge lowers the bond?" he asked.

"Very good with the DA's recommendation but not guaranteed. Are you here to post a property bond?"

"Yes."

"Do you have everything you need?" she asked.

Jon held out documents in his hand. "Copy of the warranty deed, current tax statement, and mortgage statement showing that it's current."

Kelli hadn't told him what he'd need to bring. It was another oversight on her part.

"Let me see the deed," she said.

Jon handed the copy to her. The deed was solely in Jon's name.

"Okay," Kelli said. "If your wife's name had appeared on the deed, she'd have to be present."

"I know. I bought the house a year before we married."

Dressed in jailhouse-orange jumpsuits, Cesar and a line of other prisoners entered the courtroom.

"Do I have your permission to tell the judge that you're willing to post a property bond if it comes up?" Kelli asked Jon.

"Yes, but I didn't think he'd handle that aspect of the process."

"Correct. We'll go to the clerk of court's office after the hearing."

Matt Davis and a male assistant entered the courtroom through a door at the front of the room behind the bench. Judge Godfrey followed. Everyone stood. Matt didn't make eye contact with Kelli as he and his assistant opened their laptops.

"Proceed, Mr. Davis," the judge said.

Not knowing when Cesar's case might be called, Kelli settled in to listen and observe. It quickly became apparent that this was a general calendar call with everything from arraignments to bond revocation, entry of guilty pleas, and sentencing. When she was a prosecutor, Kelli had developed a detached attitude toward the people paraded before a judge. Federal court calendars were much shorter. A state superior court calendar was a cattle call. As she listened, Kelli was confronted by the humanity of the people in trouble, especially those from a lower economic level. The system was a steamroller. However, Kelli's sympathy was limited to nonviolent offenders. For several cases the victims were present. In one felony matter, a man was sentenced to twenty years in prison for punching his landlady in the face and knocking her down a flight of stairs. The middle-aged woman was seated in the courtroom in a wheelchair as she recovered from a broken leg.

Three hours passed. The judge denied a bond reduction motion, then spoke into the microphone before him: "Court will be in recess until one o'clock."

Kelli turned around to speak to Jon, but without her knowledge he'd left. Cesar and the remaining inmates were escorted from the courtroom. Kelli stood. Matt Davis glanced over his shoulder and saw her.

"Ms. Quinn," he said. "Come forward."

Kelli stepped through the gate of the railing that divided the courtroom.

"You sound like a judge," she said.

"Sorry," Matt said with a smile. "It may happen someday, but I'm not going to rush it. Your case was the next one on the calendar before the judge decided to take a lunch break. You'll be first up at one o'clock."

The DA opened a leather briefcase, took out a thin folder, and handed it to her. "Here are the questions for your client. Put on your prosecutorial hat and tell me what you think."

"Will do. Based on what I heard in court this morning, Judge Godfrey doesn't like bond reduction motions."

"Don't let that worry you. See you in an hour."

Matt turned away, and Kelli headed to the rear door of the courtroom. Outside in the hallway, she saw Jon typing on his phone. He put the phone in his pocket and came over to her.

"Did they call Cesar's case?" he asked.

"No, the judge broke for lunch, but the DA says we're up first at one o'clock. Are you going to stay?"

"I assume there's no other option if I'm going to post the property bond."

"That's right." Kelli hesitated a moment before saying, "Would you like to grab lunch? There's a deli close by. It's within walking distance."

"Okay."

Jon considered Kelli's failure to let him know what he needed to bring to court in order to post a property bond additional evidence of her carelessness. He remembered her comment about working in the U.S. Attorney's Office in Atlanta. While they'd waited for Cesar's case to be called, Jon checked Kelli's background and saw no mention of work as a defense lawyer. Except for a couple of pro bono cases, all her experience had been as a prosecutor.

Slipping into the hallway, Jon had sent the edited surveillance video from the previous night to the hotline site for the sheriff's office along with an email and a request that a detective review it. He hoped it wouldn't end up on Detective Briscoe's desk.

Jon had then used his phone to find the names of two local attorneys, one male and one female, who specialized in criminal defense law and had good reviews. He'd been ready to call the office of one of the attorneys to arrange an appointment when Kelli exited the courtroom. Instead, he'd quickly saved the information on his phone.

He and Kelli left the courthouse together. It was a clear day with a touch of humidity common to coastal Georgia, even in the fall. Jon blinked his eyes against the bright sunshine.

"I guess watching the calendar call was educational for you," Kelli said. "Did you have any questions about what happened?"

"Not really."

Kelli held up a slim folder in her right hand. "The DA gave me a list of questions he'd like me to ask Cesar. The U.S. Attorney's Office probably prepared them. If Cesar answers, it may benefit how his case is viewed by the prosecutors."

"In what way?"

"That hasn't been clarified."

Jon gave her a skeptical look.

Kelli quickly spoke: "I haven't read the questions, but I suspect they want to know if Cesar has enough knowledge about the criminal activities of the drug smugglers to be of value as a government witness."

As they reached the top of the stairs, Jon looked down and saw two men leaving the courthouse. One of them was wearing an orange-and-green cap.

"Gotta go!" he said to Kelli and rapidly descended the stairs.

"What?" Kelli's voice called out behind him.

Outside the building, Jon looked both ways. The two men were crossing the street toward a parking deck. Jon followed and entered the deck. He ran up and down four rows of cars on the first level without seeing anyone. There were four levels to the deck. Jon stood in front of an elevator and debated where to go next. Beside the elevator was the entrance to a stairwell. He opened the stairwell door and ran up to the second level. Two cars were heading toward a ramp to the exit. Neither of them contained the two men. Stopping to catch his breath, Jon decided the best thing to do would be to return to the first level and wait at the exit. The only problem was that he'd seen two exits when he was on the first floor.

Quickly descending the stairs, Jon positioned himself near the exit that faced the main street in front of the courthouse. He leaned against a wall just outside the opening. Several vehicles passed by. A newer-model brown pickup with large tires and heavily tinted windows approached. The truck was set up for heavy hauling. There were two people in the vehicle. As the truck came closer, the person in the passenger seat lowered the window. He was a middle-aged Latino man with a thick dark mustache and dark sunglasses. On his head was an orange-and-green hat with the words "Bartlett Construction" on the front.

"Hey! Mr. Bartlett!" Jon called out.

The man spun his head toward Jon as the truck slowly continued forward. "No," he said.

"I need to talk to him," Jon said as he walked toward the truck, which was about to turn into the street.

The vehicle stopped. The driver was a young Caucasian man also wearing dark sunglasses but no cap.

"Why do you need to talk to Mr. Bartlett?" the man wearing the cap asked in accented English.

"To discuss a commercial building project. I heard your company did good work and saw your cap when you were entering the parking garage. I tried to catch up to you but missed you."

"What's your name?" the man replied.

"Ben Jones," Jon replied. "I run a landscaping company and need a contractor to build a large storage building."

"You need to call the office. I'm a construction supervisor and don't handle bids for new work."

"Is that the Savannah office?" Jon asked.

"Yeah."

The man motioned for the driver to continue. As he did so, Jon slipped his phone from his pocket. The truck was registered in Georgia. Jon managed to take a photo of the license plate, then recorded a voice memo with the license plate number in case the photo was blurry. Leaving the parking garage, he walked rapidly toward Katz's Deli.

Puzzled by Jon Tremaine's strange behavior, Kelli ordered a Reuben sandwich and sat at a small table for two. She opened the folder to read the questions Matt Davis gave her. Over half the questions sought information that Cesar could answer about his chocolate importing business. There was nothing incriminating about the requests. But then the questions shifted and implied that he had knowledge about the criminal group behind the drug shipment. The only way Cesar could answer the questions would be if he'd withheld information from Kelli during their previous meetings. The DA promised that fully answering the questions would open the door for discussions about immunity from prosecution. Kelli sighed. She could take the folder to the jail and go over everything with Cesar but doubted that would be productive. She'd eaten two bites of her sandwich when the door to the deli opened and Jon entered. She waved, and he came over to the table.

"Why did you run off?" she asked when he sat down.

She listened as Jon told her about seeing a man wearing the same hat that was in a photo sent by a man named Mateo and then seeing two men in a brown truck near the Brunswick County Courthouse. It was a bit confusing.

"I suspect the man I encountered today may have been in the courtroom to see what happened with Cesar," Jon said as he finished.

"I'm not following why you believe two men wearing caps for the same company is significant to Cesar's case."

"It might be connected," Jon replied. "I looked up Bartlett Construction, and there's no company with that name in Savannah. I suggest you run the name through the same database you used to investigate my background."

"I'm still not seeing the relevance."

Jon glanced around the restaurant.

"That's not all," he said.

Taking out his phone, Jon showed Kelli the surveillance video. He suddenly stopped it.

"See," he said. "Same color hat."

"But different company. Maybe that's a popular color."

Jon sat back. "Let's see if either of the men in the truck shows up in the courtroom after lunch. If so, they may be working for the cartel responsible for smuggling the drugs."

"Okay," Kelli said doubtfully. "I'm not even sure there's a link between Cesar's case and a cartel."

"It's a cartel," Jon replied with conviction.

Kelli took a sip of water and slid the folder across the table. "These are the questions the DA wants Cesar to answer. There's no harm in you looking over them. Let me know what you think."

While Jon read, Kelli used a fork to capture some sauerkraut that had escaped from the sandwich.

"Cesar doesn't know anything about the organization," Jon said, closing the folder. "Immunity is great, but it has to be based on intel that will put the primary leaders of the organization in prison."

"Just like on TV."

"Yeah."

"Are you going to order lunch?" Kelli asked. "We have to be back at the courthouse in twenty minutes."

"No, and I'm going to avoid the courtroom until the judge is on the bench. That way I can look over the crowd from the rear without being noticed."

Kelli suppressed a smile at Jon's clandestine comment.

"There will be fewer people because of all the cases taken care of this morning," she said.

"If I notice the two men from the truck, I'll send you a text telling you where they're sitting so you can see if they show any interest in Cesar."

"That's kind of cloak-and-dagger, isn't it?"

"No," Jon replied. "It's not."

Kelli repositioned herself in the courtroom. With fewer people present, she quickly spotted several Latino males. The assistant DA who worked for Matt Davis returned. The DA wasn't with him. Cesar and four other prisoners were brought in. Judge Godfrey took his seat on the bench. The junior DA, a tall, slender man with close-cut brown hair, stood. "Your Honor, we call *State v. Mendez*, Motion to Reduce Bond."

Kelli stepped around the railing and took her position in front of the bench. A guard brought Cesar up to stand beside her. The judge looked at his laptop screen. He didn't speak to Kelli. Instead, he looked over his glasses at the assistant DA.

"What is the State's position on reduction of the bond?" he asked.

"We don't oppose it, Judge."

"In light of the serious charges against the defendant, why are you willing to consent to such a significant reduction?"

The young lawyer glanced at Kelli.

"May we approach the bench?" he asked.

The judge motioned them forward. The assistant DA spoke in a soft voice barely above a whisper. "Your Honor, this case is part of a broader federal investigation. The U.S. Attorney's Office suggested we agree to a reduced bond so that Mr. Mendez can be released."

"Very well," the judge replied, placing his hand over the microphone in front of him. "Prepare an order."

"Already done," the young man replied. "It should be part of the electronic record."

The judge looked at his computer and hit a couple of keys. "It's signed and dated effective immediately."

"Thank you, sir," Kelli said.

The judge didn't respond. The assistant DA called the next case. Kelli pulled Cesar aside.

CHAPTER 23

Heating pads positioned on her neck and back, Carly lay on the couch in the den. She shifted every few seconds in an effort to find a position that lessened the severe pain she'd been experiencing all morning. Carly had managed to hide her discomfort until Kelli and the children left for school and work but then immediately took an extra pain pill and grabbed two heating pads. Using the timer on her phone, she prepared to switch to cold compresses. Alternating between heat and cold helped to lessen the acute pain.

Her phone vibrated. It was an unknown number. Normally, Carly wouldn't have answered, but she decided to respond.

"Hello," she said, trying to make her voice sound normal.

"Ms. Withers, it's Sarah Tremaine from the women's shelter. It's been a while since we talked."

"Hey, Sarah, it's good to hear from you. My niece mentioned your husband the other day."

"Yes, she's representing a man who works at the tree farm. Jon and I don't believe he's guilty."

Carly shifted positions.

"I'm sure Kelli is doing everything she can to help him," she said.

"I hope so, but I'm calling to ask for your help. I still have my notes from one of your talks to the women about dealing with fear and anxiety. Usually that's not a big problem for me, but this criminal case has me tied up in knots. I've tried to put on a strong face for Jon, but inside I'm crumbling. Part of it may be that I'm going to have a baby boy in a few weeks. The thought of our family being in danger sounds silly, but—" Sarah stopped as her voice became very shaky.

Compassion welled up in Carly.

"I'm so sorry," she said. "It's natural for you to be concerned at a time like this."

"It's more than that. There are things I can't tell you that make this situation much worse than it would be for a normal couple. We want to help Cesar because we believe it's the right thing to do, but it's not smart for Jon to be closely involved."

Puzzled but wanting to help, Carly replied, "I'll certainly pray for you and Jon. Is there anything else I can do?"

"Could you tell your niece not to drag him into the situation? Jon is having to be a constant go-between, even though Cesar speaks decent English."

"I'm not sure how to do that," Carly said slowly.

"I understand," Sarah sighed. "Listening to myself ask the question shows me how out of line it is. Maybe all you can do is pray for us."

"That I will do, starting right now. Okay?"

"Yes."

Most of Carly's interaction with God was by faith without the confirmation of feelings. She rarely sensed a palpable presence of the Lord. But this was one of those moments when faith became sight. Within seconds, she was riding the river of God's will. Words poured out of her for Sarah and Jon Tremaine. Snippets of Scripture verses found their way into her intercession. She requested, declared, rebuked, and thanked. All the weakness and pain in her body were thrown into the garbage bin as a result of the Spirit's presence. Nothing was going to hinder her ability to do what God called her to do. When she finally said, "Amen," she took a deep breath and exhaled.

"Amen," Sarah responded in a soft voice. "I've never heard anyone pray like that before."

"It doesn't happen very often for me, but it lets me know how much the Lord loves you and wants to be there for you, Jon, and your baby during this time."

"Yes, I felt that. Thank you."

The call ended. Exhausted, Carly closed her eyes for a few minutes. A sharp pain jarred her, and she rotated the heat and cold packs to different areas of her body.

Jon didn't follow Kelli into the courthouse. He found an out-of-the-way spot where he could watch people approach the main entrance to the building. There was no sign of the two men from the brown truck. When it was 1:05 p.m., he entered the courthouse, passed through security, and climbed the steps to the courtroom. Jon was standing at the back when Kelli and an assistant DA approached the bench to talk to the judge about Cesar. There was no sign of either of the men on the benches. Jon now began to doubt their connection to Cesar, and he felt foolish for being so emphatic in his opinion at the deli. He watched as Kelli talked with Cesar. Leaving the courtroom, he waited in the hallway. Several lawyers were meeting with clients and their families. A few people were in tears. The scene brought back the intense pressure Jon felt when he was in the crosshairs of a criminal prosecution.

Kelli exited the courtroom and saw Jon in the hallway. He looked tense as she approached him.

"The judge lowered Cesar's bond to fifty thousand dollars," she said. "He's signed the order electronically. We can check with the clerk's office about the process for release. There should be a cashier or other person who can handle it."

They walked down the hall together.

"Did the guys you were looking for show up?" Kelli asked.

"No, I didn't see them."

Kelli didn't respond. The more she was around Jon Tremaine, the stranger he seemed. When they entered, the clerk's office was bustling with activity. Lois Gautier came over to them.

"Good afternoon," she said brightly. "What can I do for you?"

"The judge lowered the bond for the defendant in my criminal case."

"I know."

"You know?" Kelli asked.

"Yeah, two men asked about the case right before you came in, and I checked the electronic record. You may have passed them in the hallway."

Kelli looked at Jon, who shook his head.

"I didn't see them," he said.

"What did they look like?" Kelli asked the clerk.

"Stocky middle-aged Latino man with a big mustache and a younger white man."

"Was either of them wearing a cap?" Kelli asked.

"Uh, I don't think so, but I can't be certain. Is the Latino man a relative of your client?"

"No," Kelli replied. "Or at least I don't think so."

"What did they want to know?" Jon asked.

"Whether the bond for Mr. Mendez had been lowered. I checked the record and saw that Judge Godfrey signed the order. When I told them what the judge did, they thanked me and left."

Kelli looked at Jon as he spoke.

"There's nothing to do about them now," he said. "Let's get the bond posted."

"Lois, my client is employed by this gentleman's company, and Mr. Tremaine is willing to post a property bond. Could you point us in the right direction?"

The clerk motioned to the right. There was a long line of people standing in front of a window.

"The assistant clerk who processes bonds, accepts payment for fines, and takes care of payments is over there," Lois said. "But I don't want you to have to wait for an hour. As a supervisor, I can take care of it for you. Mr. Tremaine, do you have the warranty deed showing you own the property?"

"Yes, along with the other documents I think you might need."

Jon laid everything on the counter. Lois glanced through the paperwork.

"I'll be back in a few minutes," she said.

Kelli tapped her fingers against the counter.

"Whatever hunch you had about the man in the green-and-orange cap being interested in Cesar turned out to be correct," she said. "And it makes me reconsider the relevance of the man wearing a similar hat in the surveillance video you showed me."

"Actually, it was an orange-and-green cap, with orange being the predominant color."

"Okay, but why do you think they showed up in court today?"

Jon faced her. "I believe one or both of these men work for the cartel that attempted to smuggle the drugs. The situation with Cesar went sideways at the docks, and someone is trying to fix it. The cartel lost the contraband contained in the pallet of chocolate and one hundred thousand dollars in cash. That amount of money probably isn't a huge deal to an organization like this, but it's important to the man who put it in Cesar's truck and lost it. If he's a lower-level member of the group, his life may be at risk. In the bigger picture, the organization doesn't know what Cesar saw or heard about their operation, if anything. They want to keep tabs on him. They'll also have an interest in whether he cooperates with either the local sheriff's department or the FBI."

Kelli tilted her head to the side and stared at Jon for a moment. "How do you come up with all these theories? And a cartel?"

Jon shrugged. "I'm analyzing it from the perspective of a businessman who wants to earn a profit and protect his ongoing activities. I think what happened today makes it even more likely that a cartel or other large-scale drug trafficking operation is involved."

"I partly agree," Kelli replied. "But mainly because of the interest of the FBI and U.S. Attorney's Office in Cesar's case. The more important question for me as Cesar's lawyer is how to make the charges against him go away. If he's been telling me the truth, Cesar doesn't know enough to be valuable as a government witness, and it's going to be a tough task prevailing in court with nothing except Cesar's testimony that he didn't know anything about the drugs. That's one reason to take a chance on something coming out from the fingerprint analysis."

"What's the status of that?"

"The DA and the FBI are going to require a sample from both you and Cesar's wife. Otherwise, they won't perform the test."

Jon snorted. "That makes no sense."

"I agree, but it's nonnegotiable."

Jon was silent for a moment. Kelli held her breath.

"I guess so," he said with a scowl on his face.

Kelli exhaled with relief. She hadn't known when and how to bring up the issue.

"Sometimes law enforcement personnel like to throw around their power," she said.

"Yeah," Jon replied.

While they continued to wait for Lois, Kelli remembered Carly's comment about Jon's wife.

"Oh, my aunt says she knows your wife from the battered women's shelter," she said.

"Your aunt?"

"Carly Withers. She did some volunteer work at the shelter. My children and I are staying with her temporarily until we find a place of our own."

"Her name sounds vaguely familiar."

Lois Gautier returned with a sheet of paper in her hand.

"That went smoothly," she said. "One of the girls who does this all the time helped me."

She handed the sheet to Kelli. It was a standard property bond document with Jon's and Cesar's personal information and the case number filled in.

"Looks good to me," Kelli said, sliding the paper over to Jon.

Jon spent more time reading it than Kelli did. After a few minutes passed, he took a pen from his pocket and signed it.

"Will you keep the copies of the documents I brought in?" he asked Lois.

"Yes, they will become part of the file."

"With my name in the public record?"

"Yes."

"Okay."

"I'll scan a copy of the bond approval and send it to the jail," Lois said. "It should be entered into the system by the time you get there."

"We'll head over there now," Kelli said.

After a light lunch of fresh fruit, Carly felt better. One of the verses she held on to during tough times with her disease was Proverbs 18:14:

The human spirit can endure in sickness, but a crushed spirit who can bear?

As demonstrated during her time of prayer for Sarah, no sickness lived in Carly's spirit, and she looked there for strength. After a severe bout of pain subsided, gratitude often rose up in her heart. Being grateful in difficult circumstances had proven to be a helpful antidote to the trauma of pain. Carly didn't want to carry an open wound in her mind and emotions, or to live in fear and dread of the next flare-up. As the verse said, she didn't want her spirit to be crushed. Some days her strategy worked well; other days not so much. But entering into God's rest at any level was better than the alternative of despair.

Carly went into the backyard and sat in a padded lounge chair she'd bought from a pool supply company. The chair gave her body support in just the right places. It was an unseasonably cool day in Brunswick, and Carly inhaled the refreshing air. Resting her hands in her lap, she closed her eyes and let her ears amplify the sounds around her. She heard two different kinds of birds chirping in the vicinity of the feeder she'd hung up outside the kitchen window.

That was followed by rustling in the dry leaves beneath a nearby red maple tree. Carly didn't open her eyes but suspected the sound came from one of the chipmunks that would dash across the stone pavers of the patio. Then from high up in the air came the cry of a seagull that had wandered inland from the ocean. The chipmunk scurrying across the ground, the gull soaring in the sky—earth and heaven coming together. That's what Carly desired.

CHAPTER 24

Jon wasn't sure he should have been so open with Kelli when she asked what he thought about the two men interested in Cesar. But he was tired of holding back. Glad they were going to get Cesar out of jail, Jon remained deeply upset that the father of two little boys had been dragged into such a horrible situation. This needed to end.

A nagging worry in Jon's mind as he followed Kelli's SUV to the jail was about the danger Cesar would face as soon as he was free. The lengths to which the cartel might go to recover the one hundred thousand dollars also troubled Jon. There was no guaranteed way to protect an ordinary person from a determined criminal who didn't care what he did or who he hurt. Surveillance cameras and bigger locks on doors were minor bandages. They pulled into the jail parking lot. Jon got out of his truck and quickly glanced around. No brown pickup. He approached Kelli.

"What do I need to do?" he asked her.

"Come inside in case there's more paperwork to sign. Before Cesar leaves, I need to talk privately with him about the questions the DA gave me."

Jon sat in the waiting area while Kelli talked to a female deputy who looked over the documents from the clerk's office, then picked up a phone.

Kelli returned to Jon with an update: "Cesar will be brought up in a few minutes. They have to process him out of the cellblock. While we were driving over here, I called my office and asked Lauren to conduct a data search on Bartlett Construction and Southside Plumbing. She couldn't find a company with that name operating in either Savannah or Brunswick. If the companies don't exist, your theory about the purpose of the hats is even more possible."

Bold and blunt earlier, Jon didn't want to revisit the topic.

"My immediate concern is Cesar's safety now that he's released," he said, and then he told her what had gone through his mind during the drive to the jail.

"Cesar's bond requires him to remain in Brantley or Glynn County," she said. "Even so, maybe he and Maria should go someplace different and not tell anyone except us where they'll be."

Cesar entered the waiting area. He was wearing a shirt and a pair of pants that Jon recognized. As soon as he saw Jon, Cesar started to rub his eyes. Jon quickly walked over to Cesar and embraced him. Cesar buried his face in Jon's shoulder and wept. Jon held him. After a minute passed, Cesar pulled away and rubbed his eyes with the sleeve of his shirt. He was still sniffling.

"Thank you," he managed.

Kelli hung back while the two men hugged. She knew that Jon cared deeply for Cesar. Otherwise, the tree farm manager wouldn't have paid her fee or agreed to put his home at risk to get Cesar out of jail. The raw emotion between them was powerful.

"Cesar," she said softly. "I'd like to talk to you for a few minutes before Jon takes you home."

Cesar nodded. "Okay."

"Let's go outside."

The three of them left the building and stood beside Kelli's vehicle. She opened the passenger door and retrieved the folder containing the questions. She explained to Cesar what the DA had asked her to do.

"But before we go over this, I'd like to see the photos of the shipments of chocolate on your phone."

Cesar took his cell phone from the plastic bag of personal items returned to him when he left the jail.

"I'm not sure it's charged," he said, pressing the button on the side of the phone.

The phone turned on. Cesar showed Kelli and Jon the file containing pictures of the different shipments. It turned out the shipments weren't as uniform in appearance as Cesar had initially indicated.

"I'm not sure this is going to help," Kelli said doubtfully. "What do you think, Jon?"

"I'm with you," he said. "The last pallet is definitely different, but it's going to take more than that to prove it was tampered with."

Kelli started going through the questions. She jotted down Cesar's answers on the sheet of paper. All his answers to the background questions were consistent with what he'd already told her.

"They want to know if you knew anyone at the dock on the day the shipment of chocolate arrived," she said.

"Only the guy who works for the boat company," Cesar said and turned to Jon. "You know, the one who helped with the paperwork. I don't know his name."

Jon shook his head.

Cesar continued, "He was a clerk with the shipping company. He always gave me a paper to sign that the chocolate arrived in good condition."

"Did you always deal with the same man?" Kelli asked.

"Yes."

"Did he give you paperwork for the shipment that led to your arrest?"

"No, the police arrested me before I went to his office."

Kelli continued down the list. At the first question that implied Cesar knew something about the operations of the cartel, he gave her a puzzled look. "All I did was ask my relatives in the village to send me chocolate to sell in America."

"Would it be okay to tell the police the names of your relatives? Isn't it an uncle, a cousin, and a man in the village who processes the raw beans?"

Cesar opened his mouth and then closed it.

"Will they get into trouble?" he asked after a moment.

"Possibly," Kelli replied. "Someone from the government might want to question them."

"I can't let that happen," Cesar said, shaking his head. "Look what's happened to me."

Kelli continued to the next question, which asked for more information about Cesar's contacts involved in importing the chocolate.

"There's no one else," Cesar said.

Kelli decided to combine multiple questions into one.

"Do you know anything at all about the people who were smuggling in the drugs?" she asked.

"They are dangerous men," Cesar said.

"What can you tell me about the man who hit you?"

Cesar looked at Jon for a moment before answering. "I'm not sure about his real name, but they called him Buck. He was a white guy who said he hated anyone with brown or black skin. At first that's why I thought he hit me, but then I saw him hanging out with a group of Latinos. Some of them were in jail because of selling drugs. Before I went to court the second time, Buck told me I'd better hope I got out on bond because there were Mexican people in the jail who wanted to beat me up."

"Why?"

"Because they worked with people who wanted to buy some of the drugs on my pallet."

Kelli turned to Jon and spoke: "That makes it seem like a local group smuggling in the drugs, not an organization planning to ship them to another part of the country."

"Possibly," Jon said. "Or it was just a racist guy running his mouth to scare Cesar."

Kelli looked at Cesar. "The only way these questions could help you get out of trouble would be if you know something valuable about the people smuggling the drugs and are willing to tell the police about it."

Cesar held up his hands.

"I don't know anything!" he said in frustration.

"Okay, okay," Kelli said. "That's all. Make sure I know how to get in touch with you. Jon, I'll see you and Maria here Monday morning at ten."

"Maria?" Cesar asked in alarm. "Why does she have to come to the jail?"

With Jon's help, Kelli explained about the fingerprint testing.

"Hopefully, this will help show that you weren't involved with the drugs," she said.

"But is there a chance they'll put Maria in jail?" Cesar asked.

"No," Kelli assured him. "Zero chance."

Shortly after going back inside the house, Carly heard the front doorbell chime. Through the sidelight, she could see it was Jan Baldwin from the prayer group. Carly opened the door.

"Sorry to show up unannounced," Jan said, tucking a strand of short hair that was more silver than gray behind one ear. "But I couldn't get the thought out of my mind that you might be having a rough day."

"It has been both rough and wonderful," Carly said.

They went into the den. Carly moved the heating pads and cooling packs out of the way.

"These were my companions this morning," she said.

"Is there anything I can do to help?" Jan asked.

"Stopping by to check on me means a lot."

"Thanks, but I'd like to do something practical. Could I bring over a meal?"

Carly's love of cooking caused a no to form on her lips, but she hesitated.

"Maybe," she said. "I hate to put you out—"

"No, I'd love to do it. Are the kids picky eaters?"

"Emma can be, but Max isn't. He especially loves Southern cooking, which is different from most boys his age."

"I'll give it some thought and let you know what I come up with."

"That would be great."

Jan shifted on the couch. "How is Max doing at school?" she asked. "Any improvement with the bullying situation?"

"I was going to give an update when the group meets, but I can tell you now."

Carly told Jan what had happened.

"Coach Matthews is filling some of the gap left by Max's father abandoning the family," she said.

"I've been praying for Max."

"Thanks."

"And for Kelli," Jan continued. "I even had a dream about her last night. That's another reason I wanted to see you. I don't have a lot of dreams that I remember or think might mean something, but this one stayed with me after I woke up. I wrote it down in the journal I keep on my phone."

Jan had Carly's full attention. Her friend tapped the screen of her cell phone.

"Here you go," Jan said, clearing her throat. "In the dream I was at the beach sitting in a chair under an umbrella. I think it was down at Jekyll but can't be sure about that. I was watching the waves roll in. Anyway, a lifeguard called out that there was a shark in the water. People started running out of the ocean. I knew a few of them. The last person in the water was Kelli, your niece. I recognized her face from social media. She ignored the lifeguard and started walking deeper into the surf. I opened my mouth to call out to her but woke up. I wanted to go back to sleep and warn her, but then I was wide awake."

"That's terrible!"

"I know. I hated to tell you but felt I had to. Whether you say anything to her is up to you."

Carly thought for a moment. "It could relate to the past and Brad, her ex-husband. Brad was having a secret affair, and the split between them caught Kelli completely off guard. He was definitely like a shark."

"That would make sense," Jan said and nodded. "I hope that's the case instead of being about something now or in the future."

Carly remembered her conversation with Sarah. If she and her husband were in danger, that might also be the case for Kelli. Carly involuntarily shivered.

"I know it was hard to share that with me," she said. "But I'm glad you did. It certainly gives me something else to pray about."

Jan left, and Carly immediately turned on her laptop.

Jon and Cesar walked side by side to Jon's truck.

"I don't feel good about Maria coming to the jail," Cesar said.

"I'll be with her," Jon replied. "Do you want to call and let her know you're on the way home?"

"No, I'll surprise her."

When they got in the truck, Cesar fastened his seat belt and stared out the window at the jail as Jon backed out of a parking space.

"I hope I never have to go back there," he said in Spanish. "It was a nightmare. Worse than I told the lawyer."

"Do you want to tell me about it?"

"No." Cesar shook his head before continuing in Spanish: "Except if it looks like I have to go back, I'm going to take Maria and the boys and return to Mexico. I know my chances of getting a fair trial as a Latino man aren't good."

Jon stopped the truck before turning onto the street. He turned toward Cesar. "Cesar, if you skip town, the government will make me pay fifty thousand dollars or they'll come take my house. That was a requirement of the bond I posted to get you out of jail. They'll also track you down, arrest you, and send you back."

"Oh!" Cesar hit himself in the forehead with the palm of his right hand. "I forgot. I'm sorry."

Jon slowly proceeded into the street. They rode in silence for a few minutes before Cesar spoke again: "There were several men in my hometown who were put in jail in the States and then returned to Mexico after they were released on bond. They live like normal people. One of them even works for the local police department. But I'd never run out on you. I want to stay in America. I believe that's best for Sancho and Emmanuel."

Jon didn't respond. It was obvious Cesar had considered fleeing to Mexico. Jon's shoulder was still damp from Cesar's tears, and he wanted to believe he was telling him the truth about not jumping bond. When Jon was released from jail and waiting to testify, he considered skipping out but had no place to go. He decided to change the subject.

"Did Maria tell you about the man who tried to break into your truck?" he asked.

"Yes, and that you and Diego put up some security cameras and were going to install better locks on the doors."

"Right, but that won't guarantee your safety."

"I know. Maria talked to a family at our church. They're going to let her and the boys stay with them. I'm going to live at the trailer."

"Are you sure that's a good idea?"

"It's safer for my family if I'm not with them."

They reached the trailer park. There was no sign of Maria.

"Maria may be with Diego and Catalina," Jon said. "Check there first."

"Stay so Maria can thank you for what you've done."

"She can do that later, when—"

"No, now."

"All right," Jon relented.

Cesar walked up the steps to the front door of Diego's trailer and knocked on the door. Jon lowered the window of the truck. A few moments later, Maria opened the door, screamed, and fell into Cesar's embrace. The boys appeared and wrapped their arms around their father's legs. Cesar picked up both boys and hugged

Maria again. Jon could understand why Cesar would consider leaving the country if he thought it would give him a chance to remain with his family. Holding the boys, Cesar and Maria walked toward the truck. Before saying anything, Maria stuck her tear-streaked face through the open truck window and gave Jon a kiss on the cheek.

"Thank you," she said in a voice that trembled.

"You're welcome," Jon replied in Spanish. "I'll leave now and let you spend time together."

Driving away, Jon looked in the rearview mirror and saw Cesar and Maria returning with the boys to their trailer.

CHAPTER 25

Kelli left the jail. At the office, she pushed Cesar's case to the side and worked on other matters. Late in the afternoon, Ann came in to see her.

"No one can accuse me of not making house calls," Ann said, plopping down in the chair across from Kelli's desk. "I've gone from one client meeting to another. But it was worth it. I have six wills to write and two estates to probate."

"Good."

"Oh," Ann continued. "And we never talked yesterday about the hospitality company. Were you able to make sense of their financial records?"

Kelli turned toward her computer and hit a few keys. "Not yet, but I'm sending you questions for the client."

"Great. How was your day?"

"Most of it was taken up with the Mendez case."

Kelli gave Ann a summary of what had taken place. At the mention of Jon running after two men walking down the street, Ann's eyes widened.

"That's wild," she said. "Did he catch up with them?"

"Yes, and there's a lot more," Kelli said, going into a lengthy explanation of what happened in court and at the clerk's office.

Ann's face became more serious.

"I've never thought about how scary a criminal case could be," she said. "I mean, it could obviously be that way, but I've never been this close to one."

"Jon and I are concerned about Cesar. If Jon is right about a connection between the two men who were interested in what happened in court and the man who attempted to break into the trailer, Cesar is in danger whether he's in the jail or on the outside."

"I'm glad you refused to let Jon Tremaine leave that cash with you," Ann said, standing. "Did anything else come up about the fingerprint evidence?"

"Yes, we're going to turn over the envelope and the cash to the detective who interrogated Cesar at the jail. That happens Monday morning at ten."

Kelli was the last one to leave the office. She locked the back door and started walking toward her car. As she did, she saw a man in an orange-and-green cap walking away from her on the next street. Kelli did a double take and realized the hat was mostly green, not orange.

Driving home, she saw a "House for Rent" sign in front of a cute two-story cottage with a flat front yard and a fenced-in backyard. Kelli made a mental note of the address. Carly likely knew about the house.

Kelli parked beside an unfamiliar car in the driveway. A slender older woman stepped off the front porch as Kelli got out of her car.

"You must be Kelli," the woman said with a bright smile as she approached. "I'm Jan Baldwin, a friend of your aunt Carly. When I found out she was having a rough day with her arthritis, I offered to bring by supper. I hope you enjoy it."

"Thanks, I'm sure we will."

"You have cute kids," Jan continued. "Emma communicates like an adult."

"With the emotions of a seven-year-old," Kelli replied. "She keeps me entertained and challenged."

"My youngest daughter was like that. Now she's in medical school at Augusta and wants to be a pediatrician."

The woman continued to her car.

"Hope to see you around," she said. "I'm praying for you."

Kelli went into the house. Carly and Emma were in the kitchen.

"Did you meet Jan?" asked Carly.

"Yes. I didn't know you were having a flare with your arthritis," Kelli answered. "I would have picked up something for supper."

"I felt better by this afternoon, but Jan had already offered to fix a meal, and I let her bless us."

"Mom, I'm not sure about this white stuff," said Emma, who was standing in front of the stove. "It looks like broccoli with all the color taken out of it. Did she put it in bleach? That's what happened to my green shirt; only a little bit of the green was left. Do you remember doing that?"

Kelli and Carly joined the little girl at the stove.

"That's a cauliflower pie," Carly said. "You'll want to try it."

"I'm not sure I want to."

"But you will," Kelli corrected with emphasis. "Where's Max?"

"Doing exercises in his room," Carly replied.

"Exercises?" Kelli asked.

"That's what he said when we finished our card game half an hour ago."

Kelli left the kitchen. The door to Max's bedroom was shut. Kelli knocked.

"It's Mom!" she announced.

"Come in," the boy replied.

Kelli opened the door. Max had his tablet propped up in a chair and was watching a video. He picked up his left foot and started hopping up and down on his right leg.

"I have to concentrate," he said before Kelli could say anything.

Kelli watched as he spent a full sixty seconds going up and down before lowering his foot. Max touched the tablet screen.

"Okay, I can talk. These are exercises Coach Matthews told me to do. They're going to strengthen my legs, but I also need some weights."

"Are boys your age supposed to lift weights?"

"Sure," Max replied. "I need a pair of ten-pound, twenty-pound, and thirty-pound dumbbells."

"Ask Coach Matthews to send home a note recommending some."

They went into the kitchen. In addition to cauliflower pie, the menu included baked chicken and yams cooked in brown sugar and butter. Emma immediately focused on the yams.

"Everything, not just one dish," Kelli said to the little girl as she watched Emma fix her plate.

As soon as they were seated and after Carly said the blessing, Kelli turned to her aunt.

"I saw a house for rent on Luckie Street," she said. "Someone was putting a sign in front when I passed by on the way home. It's a two-story painted light yellow with a nicely manicured yard in front on a flat lot. The backyard is fenced in."

"I like it here," Emma piped up. "I'm not ready to move yet."

"And I like having you here," Carly said. "That's the Blackmore house, or at least that's what I call it. Bob and Sue Blackmore haven't lived there for years, but they're the ones who restored it. I'm not sure who owns it now."

"Have you been inside?" Kelli asked.

"Not in at least ten years. I recall the bedrooms being small, but the living room is large."

"What about the kitchen?" Emma asked. "That's important for us."

"I can't remember the kitchen," Carly said. "In most of those houses, it's at the rear and faces the backyard."

"I may take a look at it tomorrow," Kelli said. "Would you like to come with me?"

"Sure."

Kelli enjoyed eating everything Jan Baldwin brought. Emma grudgingly ate a tiny bite of cauliflower and immediately turned up her nose.

"Any homework for Monday?" Kelli asked the children after they finished the meal.

"Yes," they both said.

When she was alone in the kitchen with Carly, Kelli ordered her aunt to sit down.

"I'm not an invalid," Carly protested.

"But you need to take it easy after a flare-up."

While she rinsed the dishes and put them in the dishwasher, Kelli thought about her day.

"Did I mention that I'm handling a criminal case?" she asked.

"Yes."

"I spent most of the day in court followed by a trip to the jail. I'm pretty sure my client isn't guilty, which increases the pressure. Also, there are some potentially very bad men interested in what's going on."

"Are you in danger?" Carly asked.

"No, but my client is at significant risk. He was released from the jail on bond and may have to go into hiding with his family."

Carly was silent for a moment.

"You be careful too," she said. "There can be sharks in the water."

"Sharks?" Kelli glanced at her aunt. "Lawyers are usually the ones called sharks."

Later that evening in her bedroom on the second floor, Carly sat in a chair next to a window that looked out onto the street. Her laptop was open on a small round table with a white lace covering. It was dark outside. An occasional car passed by. Carly had considered moving downstairs as her health deteriorated, but that would have to wait until Kelli and the children were out of the house. Besides, Carly loved her bedroom. It had been her refuge since childhood and had undergone multiple transformations during both her teen and college years, as well as when she returned to the house as an adult. It was uniquely her space. She kept clothes in an antique walnut dresser that came from her grandmother's house. The walk-in closet, though not large, was a well-organized space for clothes and shoes. For many years, the nightstand sat beside her parents' bed. On the stand was a windup clock with hands and numbers illuminated in green. Carly rarely had to set the alarm, but she didn't mind the rapid bell signaling that it was time to wake up. The petite twin bed with twisting spindles that had served Carly for many years had been replaced by an electric model that enabled her to change positions at the touch of the controls. The new bed was ugly, but at this point in her life, function was more important than aesthetics.

Carly didn't mention to Kelli the phone call from Sarah. There was nothing to share. At least not yet. Remembering the conversation with Kelli at dinner, Carly now regretted letting the shark comment escape her lips. It was premature. So much information had been deposited on her plate that it was going to take time to digest. Most could wait for tomorrow, but she felt well enough to begin tonight.

As Jon and Sarah were finishing dinner, he told her about the day's events in Brunswick and the successful outcome of the request to lower Cesar's bond. Sarah smiled broadly when Jon described Cesar's reunion with Maria and his boys.

"That makes all the time and money you've put into this worth it, doesn't it?" Sarah said. "If only we could be sure the charges are going to be dropped."

"Yeah, but I've had second thoughts about hiring Kelli Quinn. While I was waiting all morning at the courthouse, I did some background checking. I knew she worked for the U.S. Attorney's Office in Atlanta, but all of her experience has been as a prosecutor. It's not uncommon for prosecutors to switch sides, but it takes a different mindset to serve as a defense lawyer. Sometimes Kelli is sloppy and unprepared. It makes me nervous."

"How hard would it be to switch lawyers?"

"Not very difficult this early in the case. I think Kelli would return most of the fee. I'm just not sure what another lawyer would charge."

"Does Cesar like her?"

"He seems okay, but he doesn't have any experience with attorneys." Jon paused. "Oh, and she mentioned that she's living with her aunt, a woman named Withers who has volunteered at the shelter."

"Carly Withers," Sarah said casually. "I talk to her every so often. She's the one who taught a Bible study for the women at the shelter a few years ago. I sat in to observe and got more out of it than anyone else. I knew she had a niece that's a lawyer."

Jon remembered some of Sarah's comments at the time. He hadn't had a problem with her increased interest in religion. He just hadn't joined it.

After the meal, Jon looked outside. There was a full harvest moon. He invited Sarah to join him on the deck to look at the enormous orange orb. They held hands and enjoyed the view for a few minutes.

"I'm going to take Betsy for a walk," Jon said after they returned to the house.

"It's a great night."

It wasn't unusual for Jon to go for walks on moonlit nights. He and Sarah lived so far from other houses or businesses that the moon and stars didn't face serious competition in the night sky. He snapped a leash on Betsy.

Jon was carrying a small flashlight in his pocket, but one of the main reasons for the walk was to enjoy the natural light from the moon. His eyes quickly adjusted, and he had no trouble making his way down the gravel-and-dirt driveway. Betsy pattered alongside him. The dog alternated between putting her nose to the ground and raising it in the air. Jon wished he had the senses of the animal and could absorb the vast information she gleaned through her black nostrils. He reached the entrance to a trail that veered off to the right and into the woods. The trail led to a clearing caused by a lightning strike fire that occurred two summers earlier. The three-acre area had been replanted, but the seedlings were still small. Jon liked standing in the middle of the clearing surrounded by tall trees that framed the sky overhead.

Tonight, though, he ignored the trail and continued down the access road for the house. He approached the intersection of the driveway for the house and the main road that bisected the tree farm. To the left, the road snaked through the woods for several miles before ending up at the employee housing area. To the right, it connected to the main highway. Betsy suddenly perked up her ears. Jon stopped. He didn't hear anything. In summer, cricket calls would surround him. Now they were in hibernation.

"What do you hear?" he asked the dog, kneeling beside her.

The night absorbed the sound of Jon's voice. They continued toward the intersection. Betsy let out a low woof. Jon stopped again. The tree farm was home to hundreds of deer and scores of wild turkeys. Seeing a male turkey strutting through the forest was one of the noblest things in Jon's world. Betsy pulled on the leash. Jon stepped off the driveway into the edge of the trees. On the far side of the road was a brown pickup pointed in the direction of employee housing. The interior lights of the truck were on. Jon could see the middle-aged Latino man he'd encountered earlier in the driver's seat. There was another man beside him and two more in the rear seat. None of them were wearing orange-and-green ball caps. Betsy let out a sharp bark. The driver spun his head in their direction.

CHAPTER 26

After the kids were tucked into bed, Kelli checked out the house on Luckie Street by accessing the real estate records. The house had been sold three times in the past ten years, always for quite a bit more than the previous purchase price. The current owner was a real estate investor with multiple properties spread across Brunswick. The more she thought about the house, the more she wanted to see it.

Preparing to turn off her laptop, Kelli debated whether to check her office emails. Reading work emails at night wasn't always a good idea. Over the years, she'd received questions from a client that forced her to drive to the office and make sure she hadn't made a mistake in a case. Curiosity prevailed, however, and she opened the screen. At the top was an email from Matt Davis sent at 8:38 p.m.:

> Working late and wondered if you'd had a chance to go over the questions with Mendez? I know he's been released from the jail because he's no longer listed as an inmate.

Kelli decided to reply.

Yes, and as I suspected, he doesn't have any knowledge about the people or organization trafficking the drugs.

She sent the email and continued down her new communications. A reply from Matt appeared. Kelli returned to the top of her queue and opened it.

That's not the end of the matter. After learning about the money in Mendez's truck, Gretchen Smith says the FBI is interested in using Mendez to gain information. Cooperation would have a significant impact on the state and potential federal charges against him.

Kelli pursed her lips. That was an angle of the case she'd not anticipated.

Would need more details. I'm not sure my client would be willing or able to do something like that.

Within seconds another reply came:

Do you still believe he's totally innocent? He's already at risk. The threat associated with the money in his truck isn't going to go away.

Kelli remembered how concerned she and Jon were for the safety of Cesar and his family.

Willing to discuss?

She waited a full minute for a reply. None came. Kelli then wondered if the email actually came from the DA. She hurriedly verified the sender address. It checked out as correct. Kelli shut down her computer. Lying in bed, she tried to figure out what the government had in mind. Did they want to put a wire on Cesar so they could record a conversation? Did they want him to contact someone about the money while the FBI monitored what happened? Various scenarios played through Kelli's mind. She turned onto her other side and shut her eyes but still couldn't go to sleep. Did the government know about the orange-and-green caps that now seemed significant? How much of that information, if any, should she pass along to the DA? The weight of responsibility for Cesar, which was already substantial, felt heavier.

Jon stepped deeper into the trees and knelt beside Betsy. He stroked her neck in an effort to keep her quiet. The man behind the steering wheel shone a bright flashlight through the open window. The beam moved slowly and methodically through the woods and down the driveway. It came closer to Jon and Betsy. Jon placed his arm around Betsy's neck. He could feel the rumble of a growl coming up from the dog's chest. If she barked, he knew he'd have to run directly into the woods. It would be hard for anyone to follow. His greater fear was that the truck would turn onto the driveway for his house. Jon felt his phone with the hand that wasn't encircling Betsy. He could call Sarah. Hopefully she would answer and get out of the house before anyone arrived.

The light beam came closer. Jon lowered his head and shielded Betsy's face so there would be no reflection from their eyes. The beam landed on them. Out of the corner of his eye, he could see it bounce off adjacent tree trunks. Jon held his breath. The light continued on. He heard one of the men speak in Spanish.

"It must be a wild dog. Let's go."

Jon kept his face lowered. The light passed over them more quickly on a return journey. The engine of the truck started. The truck moved forward toward the employee housing area. Jon confirmed the license plate was the same. He quickly pulled his phone from the pocket of his pants and called Cesar. The call was about to go to voicemail when Cesar answered.

"Hello," he said.

"I believe men from the drug cartel are coming to your trailer!" Jon said rapidly. "They should be there in about ten minutes. You and Maria and the kids need to—"

"We're not there," Cesar said. "I took them to the place where they're going to stay. The boys are in bed, and I was going to leave in a few minutes and go home."

"Don't! Stay there, at least for the night."

"How do you know men are coming to my house?"

Jon told him where he was and what he'd seen.

"Okay, I'll stay here," Cesar said.

"Good. I need to call Diego and let him know what's going on."

To Jon's relief, Diego answered, and Jon relayed the information to him.

"I have a gun," Diego said.

Jon didn't know that Diego owned a firearm.

"Stay inside with the doors locked and the outside lights on. Notify the others to do the same."

"Nobody here but Catalina and I know about the money that was in Cesar's truck."

"Just text everyone and let them know an unauthorized vehicle is coming your way. I'm going to call the sheriff's department and report a trespasser. Make sure nobody comes outside to confront them. They're dangerous men."

"Okay, okay."

Unless a patrol car happened to be in the area, it would take the sheriff's department at least thirty to forty minutes to arrive. Nevertheless, Jon dialed 911 and reported the truck, including the license plate number.

"Mr. Tremaine, how can you be sure someone didn't invite the individuals onto the property?" the woman who took the call asked.

Not wanting to give out too much information, Jon responded succinctly: "It's my job to keep track of everything that happens here."

"I don't have a deputy in the area and can't send someone for a simple trespassing complaint. Is the property marked 'Posted'?"

"Yes, signs are everywhere, along with 'No Hunting' and 'Violators Will Be Prosecuted.'"

"Some people view those signs as an invitation to see what they can get away with."

Jon shook his head. "I can't read the minds of the men in the truck," he said.

"When was the last time you filed a complaint about trespassers?" the woman continued.

"At least a year and a half ago for illegal hunters. The game warden came out and gave them citations."

"Okay. Is there anything else I can do for you?"

"No, that's all."

Jon ran up the driveway. He was panting and out of breath when he reached the house. He released Betsy into the backyard. He paused to catch his breath before going inside the house. Sarah was sitting up in bed reading a book.

"Did you have a good walk? It's a beautiful night!"

"It was fine," he said, avoiding eye contact. "I'm going to hang out in the kitchen for a while."

"I bought you some chocolate chip ice cream today."

Jon went into the kitchen and slumped down in a chair at the table. He hadn't heard back from Diego, so he texted him. Seconds later, Diego called.

"Did the men in the brown truck show up?" Jon quickly asked.

"Yes, but they're gone. You can see the truck on the surveillance cameras."

"I'll check in a minute. Did they stop at Cesar's house?"

"Yes. It was the only place without the lights on. One man got out for less than a minute and checked the door. I opened my door and shined a flashlight at them."

"Diego!"

"After that, they drove off."

"They could come back later. I'm going to come and keep watch."

"No, we'll do it. All the men are going to take turns staying awake."

"Okay," Jon said, relaxing slightly. "I called the sheriff's department and reported the trespassers, but I doubt that a deputy will show up. If he does, go outside and tell him what happened. Maybe show him the surveillance video."

"Will do." Diego was silent for a moment before adding, "Thanks for caring so much for Cesar and the rest of us."

After the call ended, Jon pulled up the surveillance videos on his phone. Everything confirmed what Diego had told him. None of the angles captured clear facial images of the men in the truck, and he couldn't see much of the man who got out. Jon closed the app. He walked over to the refrigerator and took out the ice cream. He wasn't in the mood for a bowl of ice cream but didn't want to explain to Sarah why he didn't eat any.

Kelli yawned when she came into the kitchen Monday morning. The weekend had been blessedly uneventful and had given her a chance to catch up on some rest. She'd slept through her usual time to take a walk.

"I need caffeine," she said to Carly, who was preparing oatmeal on the stove.

"I saw your light on last night when I came downstairs to take a pill," Carly replied.

"Yeah, I started thinking about the criminal case right before falling asleep. I slept for a couple of hours, woke up, and couldn't keep my mind from getting in gear. Finally, I turned on my laptop and made some notes."

"Coffee will be ready in a minute."

Kelli made sure Max and Emma were awake before pouring herself a cup of coffee. She took a long sip and sighed as she sat at the kitchen table. Her phone pinged, signaling a new text message. It was from Jon Tremaine. Kelli opened a long message from Jon about the events Friday night on the Granger property. The Mendez case had poked a hornets' nest. Thus far, the hornets had only swarmed, but Kelli sensed an attack was coming.

"Ugh," she said.

"What is it, Mom?" Emma asked as she brought her bowl of oatmeal to the table.

"Law office stuff," Kelli replied. "What are you up to today?"

"I'm going to school unless you let me stay home and work on my art project."

"You're going to school," Kelli said.

"I need a break," Emma said with a pout. "There are times during the day when I'm bored."

"Boring isn't necessarily bad," Kelli replied as she thought about the text she'd just received. "At least your life isn't in danger."

"What?" Emma asked.

"Never mind. You're going to school."

Max dragged in a minute later and came directly over to Kelli.

"I'm tired. Do I have to go to school today?" he asked.

"Do you have a fever?" Kelli asked, raising her hand and placing it against the boy's forehead.

"Mom won't let us stay home unless our life is in danger," Emma added.

"That's not what I meant," Kelli said, lowering her hand. "You don't feel hot. Maybe the reason you're tired is that you've worked out too much."

Max moved his right arm in a small circle.

"Yeah, I guess that's why my arm is sore. I couldn't remember hitting it or running into something."

They finished breakfast, and the kids left the kitchen to brush their teeth. Kelli and Carly remained at the table. Both women took another drink of coffee.

"Should you stop representing the man in the criminal case?" Carly asked.

"Once I commit to something, I don't like to quit," Kelli said, then paused. "That even applied to my marriage, until Brad made it one hundred percent clear that we were done."

"You've been a determined person since you were a little girl."

"Was I as determined as Emma?" Kelli asked with a smile.

"I'm not sure about that, but like you, her verbal development is off the charts."

"Yeah, that's what her teacher last year in Atlanta said. Not that I needed someone to tell me what I live with every day."

"She's a special girl."

"Yes, she is." Kelli stood. "And I'd better finish putting on my battle armor."

After she dopped off the kids at school, Kelli drove past the rental house on Luckie Street. The sign was gone. Surprised, Kelli pulled to the side of the road and called the number she'd saved the previous evening. A woman answered the phone.

"Hey, this is Kelli Quinn. I'm interested in the rental house on Luckie Street. I saw the sign last night, but it's not there this morning. Is it still available?"

"No, it's been rented. A cute house like that won't last long. We have other properties if you want to check out our website."

"I may do that."

Miffed, Kelli continued to the office. She needed to talk to a person with local knowledge and contacts. Entering the office through the back door, she went to the reception area. Lauren was playing a game of solitaire on her computer but quickly downsized the screen.

"Busted," Kelli said.

"Yeah," Lauren said, blushing. "Ann doesn't care so long as I get everything done."

"I'll leave that between the two of you. Do you know of any rental houses on the market that might be a good fit for my children and me? I'd prefer to stay in the downtown area so my commute to the office isn't longer than ten minutes. We're staying with my aunt temporarily. She's a great hostess, but her health isn't good, and I don't want to put more strain on her."

"Hmm," Lauren said as she brought one finger to her lips. "Let me think about it. Curt's uncle works for a real estate company. I'm sure he'll have an idea. I'll check with him."

CHAPTER 27

Jon woke from a fitful sleep. One of the windows in their bedroom faced east, and the sun was still below the tree line. Jon reached for his phone. There were no new messages from Cesar or Diego. He lay on his back, staring at the ceiling. Sarah was sound asleep, her breathing regular and peaceful. He looked over at her and saw the outline of her abdomen and their unborn son beneath the sheet. Jon was deeply grateful for the new life of his son. To be a first-time father at forty-two wasn't the typical timeline for parenthood. Another wave of appreciation washed over him. Their baby wasn't the only person in the bedroom who had been given the opportunity to experience newness. Jon had received a second opportunity to begin life from the U.S. government. He quietly left the bed.

After feeding Betsy, he squeezed an extra-large glass of orange juice. Sitting at the table, he sent a text to Cesar.

> Where should I pick up Maria to take her to the sheriff's department for the 10:00 a.m. meeting?

There was no immediate reply. Jon started a pot of coffee for Sarah. He had sent a long text message to Kelli Quinn about the events of Friday night, but the lawyer hadn't responded. Jon knew they could talk when they met at the sheriff's department.

He prepared a cheese-and-mushroom omelet. He was about to flip his omelet in the pan when Sarah appeared.

"How many hours did you sleep last night?" she asked.

"What do you mean? I slept all night."

"Jon, you tossed and turned and talked. At first I tried to make sense of it, but that was impossible. I even thought about recording what you said on my phone so you could interpret it for me, but it would have been a waste of time."

"I'm not sure how much sleep I got," Jon replied as he turned over the omelet. "Would you like an omelet? I can give you this one and make another one for me."

"Very clever attempt to divert my attention. What has you so upset?"

Jon could tell from Sarah's tone of voice that she wasn't going to give up.

"The situation with Cesar. I'm concerned for his safety, whether he's in jail or out of jail."

Without elaborating or mentioning what had happened Friday night, Jon told Sarah about the two men tracking Cesar's status at the courthouse.

"It's about the one hundred thousand dollars, isn't it?" Sarah replied. "There's no other reason that I can think of. And these men can't imagine Cesar turning the money over to someone else and not trying to keep it for himself."

"Correct."

Jon slid the omelet from the pan onto a plate and placed it on the table.

"Eat your omelet while it's hot," he said.

Sarah didn't touch the food. "Is there a way to let the bad guys know Cesar doesn't have the money? You know, something that will convince them to leave him alone."

"I have no idea how to do that. They're not going to believe a notice from the sheriff's department or the DA's office stating that the money is in the possession of the FBI."

Jon poured the rest of the omelet mix into the pan and sprinkled sea salt on top.

"Does my omelet have salt in it?" Sarah asked.

"Yes, I was making it for myself before you showed up."

"Okay, that's good. I like the salt on the inside."

Sarah took a bite of the egg dish.

"This is perfect," she said. "The mushrooms are fresh."

"I try to make the things I can control in life as good as possible," Jon replied with a smile.

Jon watched as the second omelet began to bubble. When it was time to fold it, Sarah spoke: "Maybe the police can use the lure of the money as bait to set up a sting operation and catch the criminals. Whoever is arrested might be willing to testify against others higher up the chain of command in return for leniency, kind of like you did."

"That's not a terrible idea. But in real life it's harder to control what takes place than it is on TV. That sort of operation would have a lot of moving parts."

"Who said anything about TV?"

"I did," Jon said as he jiggled the omelet in the pan. "Don't let me discourage you. Keep thinking."

Jon's phone vibrated as a text message came through. It was from Cesar:

> Maria and I will meet you and the lawyer at the jail at 10:00.

Jon sent an affirmative reply, then slipped the second omelet onto a plate. He joined Sarah at the table and told her what Cesar texted.

"On Friday he didn't want to see the jail ever again." Jon shrugged. "Today he's willing to take Maria there."

"That's easy," Sarah said. "Now that they're together, Cesar doesn't want to let her out of his sight. You'd be the same way if it was me."

Jon nodded and ate a bite of egg.

Kelli arrived at the jail a few minutes early. Any doubt she harbored about the threats to Cesar vanished after she received the text from Jon Tremaine. Her client was at risk twenty-four hours a day. The question was what, if anything, could be done about it. Neither Jon nor Maria had arrived, so she stayed in her vehicle to wait. Kelli scanned the parking lot for a brown truck, but unless the criminal gang had an informant within the DA's office or sheriff's department, there was no way they could know what was going to happen at 10:00 a.m.

Kelli didn't want to say anything yet about the DA's overture that Cesar become a government informant until she had a better idea of exactly what the FBI and the U.S. attorney had in mind. She scrolled through the work emails on her phone. There were several matters that demanded her attention as soon as she returned to the office.

A somewhat battered red pickup entered the parking lot with Cesar Mendez behind the wheel. Kelli got out as Cesar pulled into a nearby parking space. Cesar and Maria joined her. Kelli greeted the petite Latino woman with gorgeous dark hair in Spanish.

"Nice to meet you," Kelli said, extending her hand.

Maria replied in the same language. Kelli continued in Spanish, only slower.

"It's good to have Cesar home, isn't it?" she asked.

Maria glanced at Cesar and nodded.

"Only we're not at home," Cesar said in English. "Did Jon tell you what happened Friday night at the tree farm?"

"Yes."

"I've moved Maria and my boys to a safer place."

"Aren't you staying there too?"

"No, I'm going to stay at our house."

Before Kelli could ask for an explanation, Jon pulled into the parking lot. He got out with a white plastic grocery bag in his right hand.

"Not a very fancy way to carry that much money," Kelli said.

"Who wants to advertise? Have you been inside?"

"No, we were waiting for you."

Jon turned to Cesar. "Do you want to stay in the truck? I'll go in with Maria."

"No, I'm coming."

Kelli led the way into the building and approached a young male officer on duty at the front desk.

"We're here to see Detective Briscoe and FBI Agent Perez," she said.

"I'll let them know," the man replied in a thick Southern drawl.

Cesar and Maria held hands while they waited. In less than a minute, Detective Briscoe entered thc room.

"Follow me," he said without waiting for introductions.

Jon followed at the rear. Briscoe, a thin manila folder in his hand, led the way down a short hallway. Jon hated hearing the sound of the heavy metal door closing behind them. Once again, the click of the electric lock was chilling. They entered a spartan room probably used for both conferences and interviews. A tall, muscular Latino man in his early forties and wearing a dark suit, white shirt, and dark tie was waiting for them. Jon placed the bag on a plastic table. There was a small machine at one end.

"I'm Agent Angel Perez," the man said. "I'm one of the agents in charge of this investigation."

Perez didn't shake anyone's hand. To Jon, he looked like a typical FBI operative.

"Here's the envelope and the money," Jon said.

"Detective Briscoe, count the money," Perez said.

The detective took white vinyl gloves from the front pocket of his pants.

"We have a bill counter," he said. "That will be a lot faster and more accurate than counting by hand and removes the risk of contaminating any fingerprint evidence on the money."

"Okay," Jon said quickly, then clamped his mouth shut.

"Fine with me," Kelli added.

Briscoe removed the envelope from the plastic bag. He opened it by unwinding the red string. The pile of hundred-dollar bills was an impressive sight. Jon had seen that amount of cash and much more scores of times. He glanced over at Kelli, whose eyes were wide.

"That's a lot of money," she muttered.

"There are more hundred-dollar bills in circulation worldwide than any other denomination," Perez said, looking at Cesar. "A lot of them have a similar history to these."

Briscoe turned on the counting machine. He motioned to Kelli and Jon to join him.

"Stand beside me so you can see the total as it registers. The counter can recognize denominations as well as spot counterfeits using UV light sensors."

Briscoe inserted the first stack that rapidly ran through the machine. Jon had regularly operated a bill counter. The version at the sheriff's office was more sophisticated than the ones he'd used in the past. The total amount increased quickly. Brisco leaned over the machine as the last stack cycled through.

"I'm seeing one hundred one thousand, five hundred dollars," he said. "Correct?"

"Yes," Kelli and Jon replied.

Briscoe took a sheet of paper from the folder and entered the amount. He scribbled in a description of the envelope as "brown flat envelope with red string closure."

"Is that accurate?" he asked.

This time Jon kept his mouth shut.

"Yes," Kelli replied.

"We'll all sign, including the defendant," Briscoe said.

"Why do you want Mr. Mendez to sign?" Kelli asked.

"So he won't have a reason to complain later."

Briscoe, Kelli, Jon, and Agent Perez signed. Briscoe handed the pen to Cesar, who signed beneath Jon's name. Briscoe returned the money to the envelope and picked it up with a still-gloved hand.

"Put it in the evidence locker and bring in the fingerprint cards," Perez said to the detective.

Briscoe left. Maria asked the FBI agent in Spanish why Cesar had to sign the piece of paper. Perez answered in Spanish.

"Because there is still a question in our minds whether the money belongs to your husband," he said. "We don't want him saying later that the money was his and we didn't correctly count it."

Maria and Cesar started whispering to each other. Jon and Kelli stood in silence until Briscoe returned. There was no reason to discuss anything in front of an FBI agent in the middle of a sheriff's department. Jon glanced down at his fingers and steeled himself for the next phase of what they were going to do. Blurry images of the first time he'd been processed into a jail flashed through his mind. He'd been both terrified and numb with shock when his mug shot was taken and his inked fingers were forced onto a print pad.

Briscoe returned and led everyone into the hallway. As Jon walked behind the detective, he wondered if Agent Perez had talked to Chris Polter about Jon's history. Jon hoped everything Chris told him about the current status of Jon's fingerprint record was accurate. Otherwise, anonymity and safety were about to be destroyed. They entered the booking area.

Briscoe spoke to a deputy: "Bates, I'm going to handle the fingerprints myself. Did you pull the set we got from Mendez when he was arrested?"

"Yes, sir."

Deputy Bates retrieved the needed equipment from a nearby shelf.

"I'll go first," Jon said to Briscoe. "That way Maria can see what happens."

"Suit yourself."

Jon submitted to the process. He had a prominent scar on his right index finger where he'd sliced it with a knife when he was nine years old while trying to notch a homemade arrow. The cut went deep and left a narrow valley. If that print showed up on the envelope, it would instantly prove that Jon had touched it. Briscoe finished with him. Maria stepped ahead. Briscoe roughly grabbed her hand. Cesar leaped forward and reached for Briscoe's arm.

"Don't hurt her!" he said.

Briscoe struck Cesar in the upper chest just below his neck and knocked him backward. Jon jumped in between them. Briscoe leaned toward Jon, then stopped and took a step back.

"Does Mendez want assaulting an officer added to the charges against him?" Briscoe asked, pointing at Cesar.

"No, because it would make you look foolish," Kelli replied calmly. "I saw how roughly you handled Ms. Mendez. It wasn't necessary."

"Let's get this done without any unneeded drama," Perez said.

Briscoe grunted. Jon spoke to Maria in Spanish and reassured her. She approached the ink pad and extended her right hand, which trembled slightly. More gently, Briscoe pressed her fingers against the ink and onto the cards. Deputy Bates then gave Jon and Maria each a paper towel to wipe their hands.

"The results will be forwarded to the local DA's office," Perez said. "We're requesting that the analysis be expedited."

Briscoe turned to Bates.

"Escort them to the front," the detective said.

In the hallway, Bates turned to Jon and Kelli.

"Detective Briscoe has had a rough week. I probably shouldn't tell you this, but it's public record. His wife filed for divorce last week."

"That's not an excuse for mistreating an innocent woman," Kelli replied.

They reached the parking lot. Jon inhaled a deep breath of fresh air. The inside of the jail was stifling on multiple levels.

Kelli spoke to Cesar: "There's something I need to mention, even though I don't know the details. Should we discuss it here or later at my office?"

"Later," Cesar replied. "I want to take Maria home."

"Okay," Kelli said. "That will give me time to find out additional information."

CHAPTER 28

Carly was having a good Tuesday morning. There were very few days a month that didn't include the nagging ache of pain in several joints in her body. Today was one of those days, and she wanted to take advantage of the ability to move around. It was partly cloudy outside with a comfortable temperature. Putting on work clothes, Carly left the house and went into the backyard to clear her garden.

In the past, her father had prepared the soil every spring using a noisy rototiller that threatened to run away whenever Carly took the handles. Since his death and her illness, Carly had hired a local man to break up the ground. He was available to clean out the old plants in the fall, but Carly preferred to do it herself. She retained the desire for independence required of any woman who had journeyed through life without the cooperation and help of a mate. She never retreated before the advance of her physical limitations until absolutely necessary.

Carly put on gloves and began pulling up the dead or dying plants. She placed them in a small black plastic cart that was easy to pull around the yard. When the cart was full, she took the plants to the rear corner of the lot where her father had started a compost pile. The six-foot circular space was surrounded by chicken wire. Taking up the same patch of land for decades, Carly's pile produced compost without the need to flip barrels or use electricity. Buried beneath the new pile of plants and other organic material from the kitchen was a dark, loose mixture that was home to countless earthworms. Carly leaned over, grabbed a handful of soil with her gloved hand, and counted four red wigglers.

"These would also be good for fishing," she muttered.

It had been over two years since Carly had gone fishing, but today, while she felt better, she wondered if Max and Emma would like to go one Saturday. When Kelli was a child, Carly took her fishing, but the little girl was squeamish about putting a worm on a hook and shrieked when asked if she would remove a fish from a line. It would be interesting to see how Kelli's offspring reacted.

Carly returned to the garden for another load. After pulling up more plants, she stood and leaned back to stretch her muscles. When she did, she looked over the fence and saw an unknown vehicle parked along the street in front of her house. It was a black sedan with heavily tinted windows. Carly knew the cars owned by her close neighbors. She filled the cart and made another trip to the compost pile. When she returned, the car was still there. Curious, Carly took off her gloves and walked over to the gate in the fence. Opening the gate, she started toward the car. She couldn't tell how many people were inside. Even on a good day, Carly didn't move very fast. Halfway across the yard, she heard the car's engine start up, and the vehicle drove away. Carly got a glimpse of the license plate. She couldn't tell where it was from but knew it wasn't from Georgia. She put her hands on her hips for a moment before retracing her steps to the garden.

Carly was able to finish the job but knew if she pushed too hard, she'd regret it later. Shortly after she went inside to clean up, the door opened and the children arrived home from school. Emma burst into the kitchen and gave her a hug. It was the first time the little girl had done that spontaneously. It made Carly's heart glad.

"Hey, Aunt Carly. How was your day?" Emma asked before Carly could ask the same question.

Carly told her what she'd been doing and mentioned the compost pile.

"I'd like to see the earthworms," Emma said.

"Change clothes and we'll do it," Carly replied.

Max entered. Carly had given the boy a key to the house earlier that morning so that he and his sister wouldn't need her to unlock the front door.

"I see the key worked fine," Carly said.

"I'm not sure," Max replied. "The way it turned, I'm not sure the door was locked."

Kelli pushed her chair away from her computer and lifted her hands high above her shoulders to stretch. She'd had a productive day. It always felt good to complete projects successfully. That was one nice aspect of Ann's law practice. Unlike Kelli's work in Atlanta, which often stretched out over months or even years, issues at the office in Brunswick could usually be taken care of quickly. Kelli entered her time for the matter she'd just concluded. One suggestion she wanted to make to Ann involved switching to total electronic recordkeeping and solely utilizing her laptop. Her phone buzzed.

"Yes," she answered.

"Matt Davis is on the phone," Lauren said. "And I may have found a house for you. It's not that far from where you're living now with your aunt."

"I'll take the call and talk to you in a minute about the house."

Kelli retrieved the Mendez file from the corner of her desk. She'd been working on the case so frequently that she kept it close by.

"The sheriff's department confirmed that you and your client dropped off the money."

"Yes."

"Over one hundred thousand dollars in crisp one-hundred-dollar bills."

"That's right," Kelli said, puzzled by the way the DA was speaking. "And provided fingerprint cards from my client's wife and his employer."

"The fingerprint results, if any, probably won't be significant. We now have evidence that the cash is directly linked to the gang your client was working for. The fact that the money was recovered from his truck confirms the criminal connection."

Kelli was irritated by Matt's melodrama. "Are you going to tell me about this evidence or save it for trial?"

"I'm going to provide it to you because I think it will convince your client to cooperate with the FBI investigation. Did you meet Agent Perez?"

"Yes. And why are you talking to me? I'd expect to hear from someone at the U.S. Attorney's Office."

"Because they don't want to initiate federal charges unless it's necessary. Mendez is a small part of a much larger investigation. It makes sense to split up the work." Silence filled the line for a couple of beats. "And Gretchen Smith is going to be transferred to another office at the end of the year. There's going to be an opening for a new U.S. attorney, and I'm on the short list."

Generally, a U.S. attorney position was more prestigious than that of a local district attorney, and it could be a stepping stone to a higher appointment such as a federal judgeship. In light of his ambition, Matt Davis's conduct now made sense. He'd probably lobbied for more involvement in the Mendez case to build his résumé with the decision-makers in Washington.

"Okay, what sort of evidence do you have?" Kelli asked.

"A video of a man putting an envelope exactly like the one dropped off at the sheriff's department in your client's truck. Detective Briscoe sent me a photo of the envelope with the cash inside, and I compared it. When you zoom in, there's no question about it. The only logical conclusion is that it was payment to Mendez for his role with the organization. And we don't believe the pallet of Mexican chocolate was an isolated incident. One trademark of this gang is repeatedly using shipments of food to camouflage contraband. We saw this with a man in Savannah who was importing avocados."

"Unless my client is in the video, I'm not convinced there's a connection. If the money is linked to the cartel, I would contend it was stashed for retrieval in a hurry due to the bust on the docks."

"Do you really believe that's how a jury is going to interpret the facts?"

Kelli opened her mouth but then shut it. She could see herself making the argument in front of a jury but wasn't sure if she could sell it.

"Are you going to send me the video?" she asked.

"Yes, it will show up as an attachment in your inbox as soon as we end this call. Since you believe it will be exculpatory, I'll follow up with a formal notice of delivery and file it with the court. I believe it's a solid piece of incriminating evidence and should help you convince your client to cooperate with the investigation."

"Can you provide details about what he'd be expected to do?"

"The first step would be to initiate contact to return the money."

"My client doesn't have any contacts with the drug smugglers. How many times do I have to tell you that?"

"I believe he does, but we can facilitate that aspect," Matt said dismissively. "From there, he'd do what the FBI asks until it's time to pull him out. If they're satisfied with his work, both the state and the federal charges will result in probation and no jail time."

"That's a nebulous standard. What does *satisfied* mean?"

"That's all I can tell you at this point. If you want more information, it will require a meeting at which Mendez is at least prepared to cooperate with the return of the cash."

"How long will the FBI fingerprint lab have the money?"

"That's not important. If something opens up before it's returned, the money can be provided."

"One hundred thousand dollars?" Kelli asked in surprise.

"The government wastes that much every few seconds. And as I mentioned earlier, this is a large operation. I only have access to a small part of it."

Kelli was silent for a moment.

"I'll talk to him," she said.

"When?"

"Yet today if I can reach him."

"Is he still in Brantley or Glynn County? That's a condition of his release on bond."

"Yes. If I can't get him to respond, I should be able to reach him through Jon Tremaine."

"This Tremaine guy is unusually involved on behalf of one of his workers."

"Mr. Tremaine is like me. He doesn't believe Mendez has done anything illegal."

"Let me know as soon as possible. Otherwise, the feds will arrest him and lock him up on more serious charges than the ones currently pending against him."

Kelli knew the threat of a return to jail would motivate Cesar more than anything else. But threats couldn't create facts that didn't exist. After the call ended, Kelli went to Lauren's desk to find out more about the house for rent, but the receptionist had left for the day. It was later than Kelli realized. Returning to her office, Kelli checked to see if she'd received the video from Matt Davis. Nothing had appeared. She waited fifteen minutes and then sent the DA an email inquiring about the video. There was no reply.

Kelli wanted to look at a matter regarding a commercial lease before going home. As soon as she finished, a new email with an attachment from Matt Davis appeared. Kelli's heart began beating a bit faster. She opened the link and watched the eighty-seven-second video three times. She replied to Matt asking for a time to meet the following day. He replied immediately:

> 10:00 a.m. at your office.

Kelli tried to call Cesar. When he didn't answer, she left a message but also forwarded everything to Jon with a request that he bring Cesar to Brunswick at eleven in the morning.

Jon was covered in sawdust. He and a crew that included Diego and Cesar had been thinning a stand of trees with chain saws. The physical activity felt good, and Jon was glad to see Cesar smiling as he carried a large limb in his hand. Cesar needed to be working in the woods, not worrying about going to jail.

Jon remembered how impossible it had been for him after his arrest to think about anything except jail and danger and death. The mental toll during the nine months after he was originally processed into the jail until entering the witness protection program was devastating. One of the reasons it took so long for Jon to consider a relationship with a woman in Georgia was the depth of the scars left by those months. Guilt and worry about future danger constantly lurked at the edges of his conscience for years. Because of his past, Jon identified with Cesar's concern for Maria's safety and knew that she and Cesar were in more danger than they imagined.

Betsy came running over to him. The dog found the sound of the chain saws and the falling of the trees energizing. She ran in a tight circle around Jon before stopping in front of him and vigorously wagging her tail. Jon swiped away some sawdust from the dog's back.

"How did you get into that?" he asked. "Did one of the men throw sawdust on you?"

Jon filled a metal bowl with water for the dog. While Betsy lapped up the water, Jon took several swallows from a red-and-silver thermos that he'd been using for years. His phone was in the cab of the truck. Jon checked for messages. One was a text from Sarah reminding him of an appointment she had with her ob-gyn that morning. Jon had joined Sarah for the twenty-week ultrasound that revealed the baby's gender. When the tech announced that they were going to have a little boy, tears streamed down Sarah's cheeks. Jon didn't get emotional but stared intently at the remarkably detailed image to confirm for himself what they were being told. Since then, he hadn't taken Sarah to the doctor. At thirty-five weeks pregnant, she would soon be going for weekly visits. Switching to his emails, Jon found five new work-related emails and one unopened email from Kelli Quinn. He checked the work ones first and then clicked on the email from the lawyer.

Jon leaned against the truck while he watched the video. It was taken from a high vantage point, most likely a warehouse at the docks. Cesar's pickup was to the far right of the camera's field of view. Men who looked like dockworkers came into and out of the frame. Then two sheriff's deputies with their guns drawn ran past the truck and disappeared. A couple of seconds later, a short, muscular man in an orange-and-green cap appeared. He took a few steps over to Cesar's truck, opened the driver's-side door, and slipped an envelope inside the vehicle. Even from a distance it looked like the cash-filled envelope Maria had found beneath the seat of the truck. The man wasn't wearing gloves as he handled the envelope. When he closed the truck door, he suddenly ducked down. His head grazed the side mirror of the truck, and the cap fell from his head. He turned sideways to pick up the cap and looked directly into the camera. There was a clear view of the man's face.

Jon's heart dropped inside his chest. The man jammed the cap onto the top of his head and quickly moved away. The video ran for another fifteen or twenty seconds without any action until Cesar came into the frame. Before he could open the door of the truck, Cesar was surrounded by two deputies and Detective Briscoe. Briscoe forced Cesar to lean over the front of the truck and placed handcuffs on his wrists. The video ended. Jon rewound it to the moment at which the man in the cap appeared and enlarged the images. He stopped when the hatless man looked directly into the camera. Jon held the phone closer to his face. It was a face he recognized but hadn't seen in more than eighteen years. Jon, who had been cooling off from the day's physical exertion, felt new drops of sweat run down the inside of his shirt.

"Carlos Aguilar," he said softly.

Aguilar, also known as "Little C," was an enforcer for the cartel. Though small in stature, Aguilar was a fierce fighter. On one occasion, Jon had seen him knock a much larger man unconscious when the man refused to turn over a bank bag filled with cash. The larger man insisted on delivering the money in person to one of the bosses, but Aguilar had orders to do so himself. Holding the bag in his left hand, the man swung at Aguilar with his right hand. Little C avoided the blow and punched straight into the man's chin. The larger man staggered, then fell to the ground. Aguilar picked up the cash and spit in the man's face. Then he burst out laughing.

"That amigo's chin felt like a soft pillow," he said.

Jon's hands tightly gripped the steering wheel as he and Betsy left the jobsite.

CHAPTER 29

Carly and the kids were playing Battleship in the living room. Emma had beaten Carly. She and Max were playing for the championship. Carly checked both sides of the board. Max had scattered his pieces all over the grid. Emma had clustered all of hers except her tiny patrol boat in one area. It was a risky strategy, but so far Max hadn't scored a single hit. Emma had sunk his submarine and just discovered his aircraft carrier. Max furrowed his brow when Emma scored another hit on his carrier.

"You've put all your pieces in one place," he said. "Once I find them, I'll sink them right away."

"Don't say anything!" Emma quickly said to Carly, whose mouth was closed.

"That tells me what I need to know," Max said and nodded. "B-2."

"Maybe that's a hit," Emma replied morosely.

"It's either a hit or it isn't," Max said. "Aunt Carly?"

"Put a red peg in that hole," Carly said.

By the time Emma finished sinking Max's aircraft carrier and a nearby patrol boat, all of her vessels except the patrol boat had been sent to the bottom of the ocean. The front door opened and Kelli entered.

"Hey, Mom," Emma called out. "Can we eat now?"

Kelli entered the room.

"Why are you so hungry?" she asked.

"Because she's about to lose the game," Max replied.

Kelli sat down beside Carly.

"You still have your little boat," Kelli observed.

"And don't tell him where it is!" Emma exclaimed.

"It's someplace else on the board," Max said confidently. "J-9."

"Oh no!" Emma wailed.

"Hit?" Max asked.

"Yes."

"Emma beat me," Carly said, trying to remind the little girl of her recent success.

"You're easy," Emma replied. "You always put most of your ships along the outside edges of the board. They're never in the center."

Carly laughed. "I can be a creature of habit."

Once the game was over, Carly turned to Kelli. "Let's finish preparing supper," she said.

"We can play another game," Max said to Emma. "Maybe you will win."

"Okay," Emma replied, brightening up.

Carly and Kelli went into the kitchen.

"I have two different kinds of soup and thought we could eat grilled cheese sandwiches," Carly said.

"Perfect," Kelli replied. "I need something simple after the day I just had. I left complex litigation behind in Atlanta, but there are other kinds of complex problems."

"Can Ann help out?" Carly asked as she stirred a pot of split pea soup.

"No, it's regarding the criminal case. Ann doesn't have any experience."

Carly felt a surge of anxiety as she got out the bread for sandwiches.

"Do you think the kids will try split pea soup?" she asked. "If they don't like that, I also opened a big can of tomato soup."

"Max will try the split pea, but the tomato will definitely work for both of them."

Carly laid the pieces of bread on a cutting board while Kelli washed her hands at the sink.

"I'm fine here. You can change clothes," Carly said.

"Later."

"I thought we could mix Havarti with American."

Carly placed two pans on the stove and turned on the gas. Kelli retrieved the cheeses from the fridge.

"You find a way to make grilled cheese gourmet," she said.

"Not really," Carly said and smiled. "The girl I like at the deli suggested it and sliced both of them extra thin."

Carly and Kelli worked side by side.

"By complex, do you mean problems with people?" Carly asked.

"In part. It's hard to know the best thing to do. And there's the possibility of considerable danger for my client."

"Life-and-death danger?" Carly asked, frowning.

"Yeah. That's something I'm not used to facing when advising a client."

"My friend Jan had a dream in which you were in danger," Carly said, trying to keep her voice calm. "I didn't want to say anything about it earlier because it sounds crazy, but hearing you now, I had to mention it."

"Danger from what?" Kelli asked as she placed pieces of cheese on the bread slices.

"In the dream it was a shark attack. The sharks could represent other types of threats."

"Oh, that's what you meant the other day," Kelli replied. "I'm not in danger, but I can see how that would apply to my client."

Kelli was pleased that both children tried the split pea soup.

"It has a lot of depth of flavor," Max said.

"Where did you hear that?" Kelli asked.

"Aunt Carly had the TV set on a cooking show when I turned it on this afternoon, and I watched for a few minutes," Max said. "Did you know people eat steak that's raw? It's called steak tortured."

"Steak tartare," Kelli corrected. "And that's not going to be on our menu in the future."

After the meal, Kelli spent time alone with both children in their rooms. Emma's latest dramas within her increasing circle of friends were harmless. Max was integrating more and more into his new school. Participation as a future member of the track team and the support of Coach Matthews had made a big difference. When Kelli got ready to leave Max's room, he had a final request.

"Will you ask Aunt Carly to come in and pray with me? It makes it easier for me to fall asleep without worrying about stuff."

"Sure."

Kelli found Carly in the living room reading a book and delivered the message.

"I'd like to stop by Emma's room, too, if it's okay," Carly said.

"Go ahead. I gave you the green light the other day, and it's not turning yellow or red."

Kelli stayed occupied with her phone until Carly returned.

"How did it go?" Kelli asked as Carly resumed her seat.

"Good. Max prays too. Emma is still at the listening stage, which is unusual for her, but it lets me know she takes talking to God as serious business."

"I guess talking to God should be serious."

"But not in the way most people think. He wants us to pray even though our words aren't going to be perfect."

Kelli was quiet for a moment.

"You prayed with the kids; maybe I should ask you to pray for me," she said.

"What about?"

"Your friend Jan's dream, or anything else you want to bring up."

Carly bowed her head and closed her eyes. She didn't immediately say anything. Kelli closed her eyes but opened them after a few seconds because Carly remained silent. The silence continued. Kelli leaned forward in an attempt to make sure her aunt hadn't fallen asleep. Carly suddenly spoke, which startled Kelli and made her jump slightly in her chair.

"Lord, watch over Kelli by day and by night and keep her safe in every way, body, soul, and spirit. Give her wisdom in what to do with her cases, especially the criminal case that is taking much more time and attention than she thought it would. Keep her client and his family safe, and may justice be done. Also, we thank you for the precious children getting ready for sleep. May your hand upon them and your love for them become the greatest realities of their lives. Give all of them a deep sense of your peace and protection. In Jesus' name, amen."

"That was beautiful," Kelli said.

"I spoke what was in my heart."

Kelli started to say something but stayed quiet. She felt that whatever words came from her mouth, no matter how well-meaning, would have contaminated the atmosphere.

"Good night," she said as she got up from the couch.

"Sleep well."

Kelli put on her nightgown and sat propped up in bed with her back resting against a pillow. After a final check of her emails, she logged on to an AI program and entered:

> What is a good prayer to say before going to bed?

The answer appeared line by line on the screen. The generic prayer seemed decent enough, but it didn't come close to Carly's words that had brought peace to Kelli's soul. It was a wonderful break from the agitation that was her constant companion. For an analytical person like Kelli, the sense of settled calm was the closest thing to objective evidence of the existence of God and the legitimacy of prayer she'd experienced. She turned out the lights and laid her head on her pillow. Sleep came quickly.

Jon sent Cesar the email with the video and the lawyer's request that the two of them meet with her in the morning. Once inside the house, he called out to Sarah.

"First thing is a shower!" he said. "I'm nasty dirty!"

"Good!" she replied.

As Jon let the hot water flow over him, he thought about next steps. He needed to talk to Chris Polter, who should be informed of Aguilar's presence in the area. Jon also wondered if Carlos had been in the brown truck the night the men went to the trailer park. He wanted to go over the surveillance footage again. There was a knock on the bathroom door, and it cracked open.

"Are you okay?" Sarah asked. "Did you get into something that you can't clean off?"

"I'll be out in a minute. I was thinking."

"Think about supper getting cold."

Jon toweled off and put on clean clothes. Sarah's slight irritation about supper actually made him feel better. The ordinariness of her feelings brought him back to earth.

"Sorry for the delay," he said when he entered the kitchen.

"I made a ham-and-cheese soufflé," Sarah replied. "And it's about to collapse on itself."

The casserole dish was on the stove, and the soufflé was indeed starting to crater. Jon grabbed a plate and scooped out a generous portion from the area in danger.

"There," he said. "You get some from the edges."

Sarah had also sliced fresh tomatoes and cucumbers. They looked good for this late in the season.

"Where did these come from?" Jon asked as they sat down.

"Argentina, or at least that's what the label at the store said."

"You went to a grocery in Brunswick?" he asked.

"Yes, because I had an appointment with the doctor," Sarah said. "I expected a phone call from you asking how it went."

Jon was in trouble. Any excuse would only slightly mitigate the damage.

"We were in the middle of that patch of trees with spotty cell service," he said. "I couldn't get online or make a call until I was back to the truck and on the way home."

"Did you try to call or text?"

"No."

They ate in silence for a few moments.

"What did the doctor say?" Jon asked.

"Everything looks good. I'm on the schedule for weekly check-ups. Our son is big enough to be born and survive and will be bulking up from here on."

Jon reached out and touched Sarah's hand. To his relief, she didn't pull it away.

"Sorry that—"

"I know," she interrupted. "This thing with Cesar is dominating your time and thoughts."

"We have to meet with the lawyer again in the morning."

"Why?"

"The FBI wants him to cooperate with a bigger investigation. In return, the charges against Cesar may go away."

"How can he do that unless he knows something or someone on the inside?"

"That's what we'll find out tomorrow."

Jon told her about counting the money and the fingerprint cards but left out any mention of Little C.

"Cesar is scared for himself and Maria," he said.

"You can relate to that."

"Yes."

Sarah got up from the table.

"Do you want more soufflé?" she asked.

"Sure."

Sarah served him. Now that things had settled down between them, Jon didn't want to bring up anything else. When they finished eating, he offered to clean the kitchen.

"Deal," Sarah said. "My ankles are puffy from standing."

After she left the room, Jon quickly put away the leftovers and loaded the dishwasher. He sat at the kitchen table and pulled up the surveillance video from the night the men in the brown pickup trespassed on the property. He stopped it at the point when the man exited the truck and walked up to the door of Cesar's trailer. Jon couldn't see the man's face, but now that he'd seen the recent video of Carlos Aguilar, he decided the man at the trailer park looked and moved like Little C. Jon placed the phone, screen side down, on the table.

CHAPTER 30

Kelli woke up refreshed. She was out the door a few minutes earlier than usual. It was a foggy morning. As she walked, Kelli was able to think about Brad with less emotional chatter than usual. She was rational enough to accept the fact that when one side in a marriage wanted out, it was impossible for the other to make them remain. Perhaps on a personal level, she was moving forward down the path of healing. Kelli had already spent plenty of time castigating herself for her flaws and going over the list of Brad's faults. It was time to throw the lists in the trash. Or at least tear off a piece of the paper and discard it. As she made the turn back to Carly's house, Kelli identified several items in her life and aspects of Brad's conduct that no longer deserved her attention.

The impact of the divorce on the kids was a different issue. A huge rock of offense and unforgiveness remained in Kelli's heart. The damage to the children would be a lifelong burden to them. Brad's callous selfishness wouldn't evaporate like a morning fog. Kelli had considered taking Max and Emma to counseling in Atlanta, but her hectic schedule made it difficult. Perhaps there were resources in Brunswick that could help.

Slivers of sunlight shone through the lifting fog. They seemed like welcoming beacons. One shone directly onto the top of Carly's house. Inside, her aunt was in the kitchen brewing a pot of coffee.

"Good morning," Kelli said brightly to Carly.

"Good morning," Carly replied, still focused on the coffeepot. "How was your walk?"

"Better. And I slept great last night. More soundly than I have in a long time."

"That's wonderful."

"I think it had to do with your prayer for me in the living room. I felt so much peace when I went to bed." Kelli took a self-assuring breath. "And I'm starting to come to terms with myself over the divorce. At least for me, if not for the kids."

Carly faced her. "That sounds like a good start."

"I'll check on the children," Kelli said.

"Do you think they'll like eggs in a basket?"

A fried egg cooked in a hole in a piece of bread was a staple at Carly's house. As a youngster, Kelli liked hers covered in muscadine jelly.

"Do you have any muscadine jelly?"

"No, just homemade strawberry that's not too sweet and apricot."

"Sounds good. I'll be back in a minute to help."

Max was stirring, but Emma was fast asleep. Kelli gently rubbed the little girl's shoulder.

"Time to get up, sweetie," she said.

Emma put the pillow over her head.

"Don't threaten to pour water on me," she replied in a muffled voice.

The corners of Kelli's mouth turned up slightly. "I haven't said that in months."

"But you think it."

"Not today, but it's time to get up."

Emma's head appeared from its hiding place.

"Why are you in such a good mood this morning?" the little girl asked.

"I had a good night's sleep and a nice walk. Please get moving."

"Okay," Emma sighed. "What's for breakfast?"

"Eggs in a basket."

"What's that?"

"You'll find out in the kitchen."

Kelli helped Carly fix breakfast. Once the kids settled on their jelly preferences, things went well. Max and Emma selected strawberry. Kelli and Carly chose apricot.

"I like how you cooked the little piece of bread that you cut out of the center," Emma said. "It tastes good."

"That's the butter," Carly replied with a smile.

Kelli's upbeat attitude continued during the ride to school. Max wasn't very talkative, but Emma filled in the silence.

"I pray you have a good day," Kelli said when the car rolled to a stop and the kids unbuckled their seat belts.

Neither one of the children noticed or acknowledged her words, which felt a bit forced to Kelli. It might be better to leave praying to an expert like Carly.

Arriving at the office, Kelli stopped by Lauren's desk.

"Tell me about the rental house," Kelli said.

Lauren shook her head. "Sorry, I spoke too soon. It's only available for someone without children."

"No children?" Kelli responded in surprise.

"It comes furnished and is filled with antiques, the kind of things that can't be replaced at any price."

"Oh well." Kelli shrugged. "I'm really enjoying life at my aunt's house. Maybe I shouldn't try to push so hard to move out."

"Speaking of pushy, you've already received two phone calls from Matt Davis," Lauren said. "He refuses to leave a voice message and insists you call him as soon as you can."

Kelli went into her office. Taking out Cesar's file, she sat down and called the DA's office. A man answered.

"I'd like to speak to Mr. Davis. This is Kelli Quinn returning his call."

"Just a moment."

Kelli flipped open the folder and grabbed a pen to take notes.

"Kelli," Matt said, "is Mr. Mendez coming in at eleven this morning?"

"I was going to confirm with my client and let you know."

"Do it. I just finished a two-hour briefing with the FBI and would like to come over early and lay out in advance the proposal for your client's cooperation with the investigation."

According to the clock on Kelli's computer monitor, Matt's meeting with the FBI would have started around 6:30 a.m.

"I'm available now," she said.

"I'm on my way," Matt said. "Call your client."

The DA abruptly ended the call. Kelli resented Matt's demanding attitude, but there wasn't a way to let him know without sounding petty. She checked to see if Ann had arrived. Ann was in the kitchen pouring a cup of coffee. Kelli gave her an update on the case. She showed her the video from the dock and told her about the DA's phone call.

"Matt is ambitious," Ann replied. "If there's a way that can benefit our client, it might be a positive thing."

"The risk to Mr. Mendez from interacting with the criminal gang is what I'm struggling with."

"Of course," Ann agreed, then pointed at Kelli's phone. "But that video hurts. Most reasonable people will watch it and believe it's a payoff."

"Unless Cesar's fingerprints aren't on the envelope," Kelli said. "If they are, I have no defense."

"You're in a tough spot. It seems every time you try to cooperate with Matt, it backfires."

Kelli felt the blood rush to her face. She'd been so focused on pursuing what she believed was the best course to vindicate Cesar that she may have acted recklessly. She'd been playing chess without paying close attention to the other person's strategy. She took a deep breath and exhaled.

"It seemed like a reasonable approach when I started, but now I'm not sure. The video from the docks can be shown to a jury, but the prosecution wouldn't have known for sure what it contained if I hadn't told Matt about the envelope and requested the fingerprint tests. I may have made a huge mistake."

"I'm not criticizing you," Ann quickly replied. "I'm not a litigator—"

"I can see what I've done without someone having to point it out to me," Kelli said with a sigh. "The question is what to do now. How do I best represent Cesar?"

Ann shook her head. "I have no idea."

Kelli returned to her office. Making an unintentional blunder in the practice of law was always a possibility. But revealing the envelope and its contents so early in the investigation loomed before her as catastrophic. The inner peace she'd enjoyed since the previous evening evaporated. She checked her voicemail messages, which included a call from Jon Tremaine confirming that he and Cesar would be there at 11:00 a.m.

Before leaving the house, Jon texted Chris Polter and requested either a phone conversation or a meeting. There was no immediate response. When Jon approached his truck, he could see Betsy anxiously wagging her tail as she stood in front of the gate.

"Sorry, girl!" Jon called out. "Not today."

The place where Cesar and Maria were staying with their boys didn't have a street address and couldn't be found via GPS. Jon followed directions scribbled on a piece of paper given to him by Cesar. After two turns onto poorly maintained dirt roads, Jon pulled up to a run-down house that looked abandoned. The only clue to current habitation was the front of Cesar's truck peeking out from behind the residence. As instructed, Jon honked the horn three times. Cesar emerged.

"Who owns this place?" Jon asked when Cesar got into the truck.

"A woman in our church," Cesar said in Spanish. "She and her husband lived here before he died a few years ago. After that, she stopped the mail and electric service."

"Do you have running water?"

Cesar pointed to an outhouse. "We use that as a toilet and pump water from the well by hand. We're telling the boys this is how Maria and I grew up in Mexico. So far, they're treating it as an adventure. We heat water using a propane stove."

"What about school?"

"Maria told the school that she's going to homeschool them for the rest of the semester. They like that part. The boys miss their friends, but there are a lot of woods to explore and play in."

"It's probably safe here," Jon said.

"I hope so."

They followed the twisting route to the main highway. Once the roadway was smooth, Jon spoke.

"What did you think about the video from the docks?" he asked.

"It shows how the money ended up in my truck. I didn't know anything about it before they arrested me."

Jon knew Cesar was telling the truth but didn't have the heart to point out that it could be interpreted differently.

"What is the work crew going to be doing today?" Cesar asked. "Will we get back in time for me to get in some hours?"

"I hope so. They're putting down winter fertilizer for the seedlings we planted in the spring."

They arrived at Kelli's office. The young receptionist spoke before Jon and Cesar could sit down.

"Go on back. Ms. Quinn is in the conference room."

Jon led Cesar down the short hallway and to the left. Kelli was sitting at the head of the table with her laptop open in front of her. Earlier, she had spent an intense half hour with Matt Davis going over the details of the offer, dependent on Cesar's agreement to help, that could result in the dismissal of any charges against him.

"Have a seat," she said without getting up.

Jon and Cesar sat beside each other to Kelli's left.

"I'll try to do this without the need for translation," she said to Jon and Cesar. "But please let me know if something doesn't make sense."

Both men nodded. Kelli continued, "I had a conversation with Matt Davis, the DA. He wants Cesar to help with the investigation into the drug gang."

"Me, help?" Cesar quickly asked. "How?"

"In return for your cooperation, there's a chance the charges against you will be dismissed. Have you seen the video I sent to Jon?"

"Yes."

"That could make it much harder for me to convince a jury that you didn't have anything to do with smuggling the drugs."

"I didn't put the money in the truck!" Cesar protested. "Someone else did. It's on the tape!"

"It could be viewed as a payoff," Kelli replied.

Cesar's shoulders slumped.

"Did you ask if the police identified the man in the video?" Jon asked. "He's obviously a criminal. You saw the hat he was wearing."

"The DA says they're working on that. Nothing has turned up so far. But he wasn't wearing gloves, so hopefully his fingerprints will be on the envelope."

"You didn't mention the orange-and-green caps to the DA?" Jon asked.

"No, because I don't think he would take it seriously," Kelli said. "And I didn't want to tell him too much about what we think. At least not yet."

"You've already shared a lot of information," Jon replied.

Kelli winced but ignored Jon and turned to Cesar.

"The money hidden in your truck will be the bait to initiate communication," she said. "The FBI wants you to set up a meeting with a representative of the drug gang to turn over the money."

"Please explain," Cesar said anxiously. "I don't understand what you're saying."

Jon translated.

"How can I do that?" Cesar asked when he finished.

"You'll be put in jail with a man who has connections to the drug gang. He was arrested for DUI and other traffic violations. They've left him in the local jail and not charged him with any drug-related state or federal crimes. The police want you to tell him about the money. You'll offer to return it so that the cartel will leave you and your family alone."

Kelli watched Cesar's face while Jon translated. The client's eyes widened and he began to shake his head vigorously. He spoke to Kelli.

"I don't want to go back to jail," he said.

"It would just be for a short time," Kelli said. "You'll simply be providing information that we hope gets back to the cartel. The government would give you the one hundred thousand dollars to hand over. If everything goes well, the government will consider dismissing all charges against you. You could also ask the man how much it would cost for him to help you jump bail and flee to Mexico. He'll see a way to make money, too, even if he intends on ripping you off."

Kelli waited. Cesar sat silently as Jon talked.

"That plan has a lot of moving parts and places where it could go wrong," Jon said.

"I know, and there's more. Please tell Cesar there may be times when the FBI would ask him to wear a wire so conversation can be recorded. Once he's done everything he's asked to do, and if the information is useful to the government, the state indictment against Cesar would be dropped and he would receive a written guarantee from the U.S. Attorney's Office that no federal charges will be filed against him. Tell him and see if he has any questions."

Once again, Kelli listened. There was a rapid back-and-forth discussion between Jon and Cesar. Kelli could pick up some of the words, but the two men were speaking so rapidly that she couldn't follow the meaning of the conversation. Finally, they stopped.

"He's considering it," Jon said. "If Cesar does this, he wants to know how Maria and his boys are going to be protected. Once the cartel finds out that he helped the police, they may try to take revenge against him."

"I thought about a solution to that problem but didn't want to mention it to Matt Davis without Cesar's permission," Kelli answered. "If things go well, Cesar and his family may qualify for the witness protection program."

CHAPTER 31

Jon's jaw dropped open. He stared at the defense lawyer for a few seconds.

"There would need to be a guarantee of the level of cooperation required to trigger participation in the program," he managed.

"Tell him about it first."

Jon never thought he'd be doing this. It took several attempts for Cesar to grasp the concept. When he did, he spoke rapidly.

"You mean I'd never be able to see or talk to the rest of my family? Or Maria talk to her family? Our children wouldn't get to spend time with their grandparents? Or their aunts and uncles?"

"Any contact with your past would put you and them at risk."

"No way," Cesar replied emphatically.

"What about the government's plan?" Jon asked, continuing in Spanish. "I doubt it's going to work and would put you in greater danger than you already face."

"I'll do it," Cesar said with surprising conviction. "It seems like the best way to keep me from going to jail for a long time."

"Is he agreeing to do it?" Kelli asked.

"Maybe, maybe," Jon replied. "But how much success will it take to get every potential criminal charge dropped?"

"That's going to have to be ironed out. Cesar also has to realize that the DA, the U.S. attorney, and the FBI believe he's guilty, which convinces them that he's in a good position to accomplish what they're asking him to do."

Jon relayed the information. Cesar sighed.

"Do you and the lawyer believe that I'm innocent?" he asked Jon with an earnest expression on his face.

"Yes," Jon replied.

"I understood that question, and my answer is yes as well," Kelli said.

"Cesar still needs to think about it," Jon said. "And talk it over with Maria."

"Okay, but we're going to have to give an answer soon."

Jon looked at Cesar. There were so many ways this could go horribly wrong: either death while attempting to cooperate with the authorities or a federal criminal conviction resulting in decades in prison.

"Any questions?" he asked Cesar in English.

Cesar shook his head. "No."

Jon and Cesar rode in silence as they left Brunswick. It wasn't yet noon.

"Do you want to come into work?" Jon asked. "I'd understand if you'd rather have the rest of the day off."

"I need the money, and it keeps me from only thinking about my problems."

Jon dropped Cesar off at the ramshackle house. When Jon reached the main road that led to the tree farm, his burner phone vibrated. It was Chris Polter.

"Can we talk or do we have to meet in person?" Jon asked when he answered the call.

"In person."

"I just left Brunswick and am heading back to the tree farm."

"Then I'll wait here for you."

"You're in the area?" Jon asked in surprise.

"Yes. When I got your message, I decided to come to you instead of always making you come to me."

"That's nice of you."

"Don't thank me yet. Where can we meet in private? I don't want to go to your house."

"Uh, the crews are out in the woods. We can meet at the building where we store the large equipment. I'll text the address."

Jon pulled over and sent the information, then rerouted his course. When he arrived, he saw a black vehicle with government license plates parked near the door. Jon parked next to it. Chris got out. He was wearing a coat and tie.

"I didn't know it was a formal meeting," Jon said when he saw the inspector.

"It's not, but I have to appear in front of a magistrate in Savannah at five o'clock this afternoon."

Jon led the way inside to a small office in the corner of the large room designed to keep the equipment safe from thieves and out of the weather. The office contained only a table and a couple of chairs.

"Should I go first?" Jon asked when they were seated.

"I can save you time," Chris replied. "I know about an offer from the FBI asking Mendez to become an informant. Your name came up in the file, and the agent in charge wanted to talk to me."

"Is it Agent Perez? I met him the other day at the local jail."

"Yes."

"What did he want to know?"

"If I thought you were clean or had dipped your toe into the local drug trade by using Mendez as your front man. Investigative types are always suspicious. I told him I'd have to see hard evidence to believe you were anywhere near criminal activity."

"Did that satisfy him?"

"I can't say for sure. But you're on their radar."

Jon sat back in his chair. "What should I do?"

"Avoid potentially compromising situations."

"So long as I'm not linked to the fingerprints on the envelope I mentioned, I think I'm okay. But I saw a video yesterday from a security camera at the docks and recognized the man who put the envelope and money into Cesar Mendez's truck. The local DA sent it to Cesar's lawyer, and she forwarded it to me. It's on my phone if you want to see it."

Jon showed Chris the video. The inspector handed the phone back to Jon, who spoke: "I believe the orange-and-green hats are a quick and easy way for the men working in the cartel to identify one another. I've seen other men in the area wearing the hats."

Chris watched the video again.

"What's the man's name?" he asked.

"Carlos Aguilar. I knew him in Texas and Louisiana. I don't know if that's his real name or not. Aguilar was an enforcer at the time. He handled a lot of money for the cartel, which fits with him having the envelope full of cash."

"Would he recognize you?"

"Maybe, if he saw me up close. I knew more about him than he did about me. He went to prison for a while, but I didn't testify against him."

Chris returned the phone to Jon. "What you've shown me confirms why I'm here. The FBI believes the group operating out of the ports of Savannah and Brunswick is linked to the remnant of the Los Reyes cartel."

"The Los Reyes bosses are either dead or still in prison," Jon said. "I check every six to twelve months."

"What about the three Diaz brothers?" Chris asked.

"They're dead. Luis and Emiliano Diaz were killed in an ambush by the Sinaloa cartel to settle a grudge after everything went down with Los Reyes. That was all over the media at the time it occurred. My FBI handler at the time confirmed it. I testified at the trial of Pablo Diaz, the younger brother. Pablo was found guilty and sent to prison. Two years later he was murdered in jail, probably also by the Sinaloa cartel."

"You can't believe everything you read in a newspaper or that pops up online. Your handler was mistaken about Luis and Emiliano. Four people were assassinated and their bodies burned. The remains and ashes were kept in cold storage by the Mexican authorities, who refused to allow forensic analysis for over fifteen years. When they finally agreed, the FBI determined through DNA testing that the Diaz brothers weren't among the victims. We believe they struck a deal with an offshoot of the Sinaloa cartel to fake their deaths and create a new organization. There's evidence this new entity has opened a local branch utilizing the Georgia ports. Your identification of Aguilar as a link to the Diaz brothers makes that more likely."

Jon was stunned. Luis and Emiliano Diaz were fraternal twins. Jon had interacted occasionally with Luis, who was second in command over finances in the Los Reyes organization. Jon had met Emiliano Diaz only once at a restaurant in Houston. Emiliano had lifeless dark eyes that made Jon's skin crawl. Carlos Aguilar was one of Emiliano's lieutenants.

"Why didn't you tell me about this?" he managed after a few seconds passed.

"I didn't know anything about it until this week."

Jon felt sick to his stomach. "Have the Diaz brothers been seen in the area?"

"I can't answer that."

"What else can you tell me?"

"Nothing, but I'll give you some advice. Your connection to Cesar Mendez isn't a secret. From now on, interact with him as an employee but don't show up for any of his court appearances or be seen with him in a public place where he might be under surveillance by the cartel."

"It's too late for that," Jon replied, hanging his head.

He told Chris about the two men in the brown truck in the parking deck near the courthouse and the group that later drove to the company housing area.

"I'm ninety percent sure Aguilar was in the group that came that night onto the tree farm property," he said. "I didn't see Carlos's face, but the man's height, weight, and the way he walked looked similar."

"And you believe these colored hats with a company logo are an identifying sign?"

"Yes, it would be something they brought over from Los Reyes."

Chris rose to his feet. "If the FBI wants to talk to you, I can't prevent it."

Jon frowned. "I've told you everything, but I know that probably won't satisfy them."

After Jon and Cesar left, Kelli went into her office. Sitting behind her desk, she attempted to intellectually and emotionally process what she'd done so far in the case and where she stood in her representation of Cesar. Intellectually, she believed the chance of obtaining an acquittal at trial was slim even before she told Matt Davis about the envelope and the money. Linked with the video evidence of a man placing the cash-filled envelope in the truck, the possibility of a not guilty verdict was nonexistent. The only real chance Cesar had to walk away a free man was to cooperate with the FBI, even if the conditions needed to satisfy the government weren't crystal clear. Emotionally, the weight of responsibility for Cesar's future was huge. In her heart, Kelli believed Cesar was innocent. The stress of protecting the constitutional rights of a guilty person couldn't be compared to the pressure of representing an innocent one. Ann knocked on her doorframe.

"You've been huddled up with Matt Davis and then your client. How did it go?"

Before she could answer, tears appeared in Kelli's eyes.

"Uh-oh," Kelli said, grabbing a tissue. "There's a lot bottled up inside me right now that's going to force its way out one way or another."

Ann sat down. Kelli wiped her eyes with the tissue and took a few deep breaths.

"Don't be in a rush," Ann said. "I can wait or come back later."

"Don't leave," Kelli said and lifted her hand. "I need to vent."

Kelli didn't sob, but it took two tissues to stem the flow of tears.

"Okay," she said with a sniffle. "I'm even more concerned that I've not been very smart or professional in my representation of Cesar and put him in a worse position than when he first hired me."

Ann listened, only interrupting a few times for clarification.

"I'm sorry I encouraged you to take the case," Ann said when Kelli paused. "Did you feel any pressure from me to—"

"Absolutely not," Kelli said. "I made a voluntary choice. But it's going to be tough to watch this play out."

"Because you feel so out of control."

Kelli nodded. "Whatever Cesar decides to do, I can't really influence what takes place."

"And you think he's going to go along with the government's proposal?"

"Yes. I haven't met his children, but he's devoted to his wife. You should have seen how he jumped in when a detective at the sheriff's department didn't treat her with respect during the fingerprint process. He can't stand the thought of going to prison and being separated from his family. That's all he really cares about, and he'll take a big risk to have the chance to be with them."

"What are you going to do next?"

"Call Matt and tell him my client is seriously considering the opportunity to cooperate with the bigger investigation. I'm not sure how long he's going to give Cesar to make up his mind. That didn't come up."

"Is Jon Tremaine continuing to have a lot of input?"

Kelli paused for a moment. "I'd say yes in general but not so much on this decision. He knows it's up to Cesar. For a man who runs a tree farm, Jon is savvy about the criminal justice system. He challenged my judgment a bit at first but not so much recently when I've been questioning it myself."

Ann left. Kelli took a deep breath. There was no use putting off the call to Matt Davis, especially since Cesar needed to know when he had to give an answer.

CHAPTER 32

Carly had a good morning. Kelli's awareness of God's desire to be involved in her life was good news. Shortly before noon, Carly warmed up some soup for lunch. As she sat down at the table, her phone vibrated. It was Kelli.

"What are you doing?" Kelli asked.

"About to eat a bowl of split pea soup. Are you okay?"

"No. I can't give you the details, but there's a lot going on with the criminal case that's really upset me. Will you pray for me?"

Carly pushed her chair away from the table. "Of course. I can do it right now."

"Please."

Carly pressed her eyes tightly shut for a few seconds. "Lord, you know every detail about what Kelli is dealing with in this case. I ask you to intervene as only you can so that your will in heaven will be done on earth. Come alongside Kelli in such a way that she knows you are with her. Give her insight into what she should do, and don't let the enemy of her soul harass and attack her. In Jesus' name, amen."

"Thanks," Kelli replied in a subdued voice. "I hope that helps. See you later."

Her appetite gone, Carly poured the soup back into a container and returned it to the refrigerator. Taking out her laptop, she opened it and began a new session. Kelli was a grown woman, but her plea for help came from the child within, a little girl in need. It was the type of cry a heavenly Father hears. A militancy rose up in Carly's heart. Prayers for Kelli poured from her lips and appeared on the screen of her computer. One thought led to another and then another. It was similar to her prayer for Sarah Tremaine. On and on she went until the well of intercession was dry. Taking a sip of water from a glass on the table, Carly turned off the computer and slowly lowered the screen. Picking up her phone, she called Jan Baldwin.

"Are you busy?" Carly asked.

"Not really."

"Will you pray for Kelli? She's in a big battle."

Later in the week, Jon sent a large crew to plant seedlings in an area harvested two months earlier. The men stretched out in a long line with narrow spades and tiny pine trees piled in buckets. The process could be done with machines, but Jon had better success with the hand method. The goal was to plant around five hundred seedlings per acre. More than that and the trees could be stunted. Even then, the seedlings might need thinning as they matured. Bucket in hand, Jon walked in the middle of the group and stopped to plant. The men followed his lead.

Cesar was at the end of the line with Diego next to him. The men would occasionally sing a song in Spanish while they worked. Today they sang "De Colores" and several norteño folk songs. Jon knew the songs and joined in. It was a good distraction. When it was time to stop, the men gathered at Jon's truck for a drink of water from a large white container. Tired from running around all afternoon, Betsy lay in the shade close to the truck.

"Did you hear Mr. Jon singing?" one of the men asked in Spanish. "His heart was in it, but he sounded like one of the sick cows on the ranch where I worked in Chihuahua."

"It's what's in the heart that counts," Cesar replied. "And his heart is pure gold."

Several of the men nodded in agreement. The affection they expressed touched Jon and made him sorry that he was going to have to distance himself from Cesar.

"I'll keep practicing," he replied with a smile.

"It's not practice you need," Diego replied and pointed to his neck. "The doctor needs to put a new singing voice in your throat."

As the men moved toward the two trucks they'd take back to the staging area near the equipment shed, Jon motioned for Cesar to come over.

"Have you thought any more about what the lawyer talked to us about?" he asked.

"My answer is yes, but I want to speak more with Maria. We always try to agree on big decisions."

"That makes sense," Jon said, then added, "You'll be on your own if you do it. I won't be close by."

"I don't expect you to join me in the jail. You wouldn't know how to act."

Jon patted Cesar on the shoulder. "See you in the morning," he said.

"Yes, Boss."

Jon scratched Betsy's back during the drive home. Contact with the dog always had a calming effect on him. Jon's promise to be open with Sarah loomed large. But he'd made that commitment before he learned what was on the horizon. He parked beside her car. Betsy hopped out of the truck. Jon was opening the gate to the backyard when Sarah came out onto the porch with her hands on her abdomen.

"I'm glad you're home," she said. "I've been having contractions. I think they're Braxton-Hicks, but it still makes me nervous."

Jon climbed the steps and followed Sarah into the house.

"Do you need to lie down?" he asked.

"I've been drinking a lot of water and think I should take a warm bath."

"I'll fix supper. What would you like?"

"There are leftovers in the freezer. Pick what seems good to you and surprise me."

Jon washed his hands and arms in the kitchen sink, then used a wet washcloth on his neck. He could shower in the guest bedroom, but a proper cleaning would have to wait. He found leftover lasagna in the freezer and put it in the air fryer. Ingredients for a salad were in the fridge. Seeing Sarah on the front porch answered his question about what they should discuss over dinner. Jon's conversation with Chris Polter and Cesar's case wouldn't be on the menu. While he waited for the lasagna to warm up, he received a text message from Kelli:

> Talked with the DA. He wants an answer from Cesar by noon on Monday. The criteria for dropping charges is "material assistance." Couldn't get anything more specific. I sent Cesar a text, but he might want to discuss with you.

Jon replied:

> Will do.

Sarah emerged from the bedroom. She was wearing pajamas and wrapped in a bathrobe Jon had given her the previous Christmas.

"How do you feel?" Jon asked.

"Much better," she said. "The contractions are gone. What's for supper?"

"Lasagna and salad."

"Perfect. How did Cesar's meeting with the lawyer go?"

"There's the possibility of progress. We'll have to wait and see."

"Great. Let's eat. I'm starving."

The storm in Kelli's soul had subsided somewhat by Friday morning, especially after Carly prayed for her, but it had returned with full force when she'd spoken with Matt Davis late the day before. Everything the DA said threw Cesar's dilemma into her face. Matt didn't speak in an aggressive manner. On the contrary, the DA was congenial, but the situation carried inherent friction.

"If he does this, you have my word as a professional to deal favorably with the charges my office filed and advocate on his behalf with the U.S. Attorney's Office."

"I appreciate that, but it's hard to recommend that a client who's an ordinary citizen step into the role of a government informant."

"It happens all the time, whether the person is an ordinary citizen or an ancillary part of a criminal enterprise."

Kelli knew the DA was never going to agree with her about Cesar's ordinary citizen status. "When do you need an answer?"

"I'll give him a few days to make up his mind. Is noon on Monday long enough?"

"I'd like more time."

"And I deny that request."

"Okay. I'll notify you on Monday."

"Thanks. You'll have a proposed agreement in your inbox before you leave today. It won't be lengthy and will track what we discussed in your office. I'll look forward to hearing from you Monday."

The call ended. Kelli thought about talking to Ann, but she'd burdened her enough with the situation and didn't want to come across as weak as she felt. To distract herself, Kelli turned to other work. At 4:45 p.m. the email from Matt appeared. Kelli opened it and read the attachment. As promised, it was simple and straightforward, yet maddeningly vague in what was important. Everything would be kept under court seal and not be subject to public disclosure. There were signature lines for Cesar, Matt, Kelli, and Gretchen Smith. Kelli sent texts to Cesar and Jon Tremaine about the deadline to respond, but not a copy of the agreement. Just as Kelli was preparing to leave the office, Ann appeared.

"I know it's late notice, but Roy called and said tomorrow would be a good day for Emma to go to the stables. If you want to schedule next—"

"No, that would be wonderful. She'll be so excited. Can Max come?"

"Of course. There are several horses for beginners. Let's do ten o'clock in the morning. I'll text the address."

"Thanks."

Ann turned to leave. "Would you want to ride?"

Kelli shook her head. "No, I'll enjoy being a spectator."

Arriving home, Kelli went straight to Emma's room and delivered the news.

"What color is my horse?" she asked.

"Uh, I didn't ask and doubt Ann knows. Does that matter?"

"I'd like a white one with gray spots, but I'll be okay with another color."

Kelli hesitated.

"And you're sure you want to do this?" she asked.

"Yes! But I don't have any boots except the ones I wear when it snows. I think they're too small for my feet."

"You can wear sneakers."

"Are you sure? That doesn't sound right. Did you ask about shoes?"

"No, but I will right now and also the color of the horse."

Kelli sat on Emma's bed and sent a joint text to Ann and Roy, thanking them for the invitation and asking the questions. A response from Roy quickly appeared. Kelli handed the phone to Emma, who read the reply out loud:

"The horse I have in mind for you is a mare named Happy. She's thirteen years old with a brown coat and white socks to her hocks. She likes peppermints as a treat. You can wear sneakers. I'll give you a helmet."

"The horse is named Happy!" Emma exclaimed. "Just like the one on my lamp."

"Yep." Kelli smiled.

Emma read the text again. "What are socks and hocks?"

"Let's look it up."

Kelli showed Emma a photo of a horse with white markings that extended to the hocks.

"Okay," the little girl said, smiling and nodding. "I want you to take lots of pictures so I can show my friends at school, especially Larissa. She's horse-crazy."

Kelli confirmed that Max also wanted to go. In the kitchen, Carly was standing in front of the refrigerator.

"Am I too late to help fix supper?" Kelli asked.

"No, I was waiting on you."

"Let's do something simple that the kids will like. I'm not very hungry."

"Me either. Is it too soon for grilled cheese again?"

"No."

They stood side by side preparing the sandwiches.

"How was your day?" Carly asked.

"Challenging and stressful," Kelli replied. "I've been in tons of pressure-packed situations practicing law, but nothing compared to this."

"Maybe we can talk later."

"I'd like that."

Emma's excitement about riding the horse increased during dinner conversation.

"When do you think we can go back?" she asked. "One time isn't going to be enough."

"Let's enjoy the first visit and then see," Kelli replied.

"Will you come, Aunt Carly?" Emma asked.

"If your mom—"

"Yes," Kelli responded.

"I think it will be fun," Max added. "I rode horses at the day camp I went to the summer before Dad left."

"I forgot about that," Kelli said.

"Yeah, Dad dropped me off and picked me up every day. I enjoyed it, but the one time we were all going to talk about it, you and Dad got into a big argument."

Kelli remembered the blowup over whether they were going to take a family vacation. Now she understood why Brad showed so little interest in a family getaway.

"Sorry, buddy." Kelli winced. "I wish that hadn't happened."

Kelli lowered her spoon into the soup. Brad wasn't scheduled to see the kids until Thanksgiving. He would be flying into Atlanta to take them to his parents' house for a long weekend.

"Any homework?" Kelli asked the children when they finished supper.

"No," Max replied. "I did it as soon as I got home."

"I might," Emma replied slowly. "But I'd like to have Friday night off. It's been a long week, and I need a break."

Carly chuckled. Kelli rolled her eyes.

"As long as you get it done before Monday morning," Kelli said.

Kelli made Max and Emma do the dishes while she fixed a pot of decaf coffee. Kelli could handle caffeine in the evening. Carly couldn't.

"Good job," Carly said when the children finished.

"Can all four of us play a game?" Emma asked.

"Maybe later," Carly replied. "Your mom and I need to talk."

"About us?" Emma asked.

"Not this time," Kelli replied.

After the coffee finished dripping into the pot, Kelli filled two mugs. They sat at the kitchen table. Carly spoke first.

"You know that I'm available to pray for you anytime," she said.

"I was on the verge of a full-blown panic attack that day, which is something that's never happened before. And it was odd because a couple of hours earlier, I'd felt such a sweet inner peace. The contrast was huge."

"How are you now?"

Kelli took a sip of coffee. "Much better."

"That's good," Carly said, wrapping her fingers around her mug. "Have you ever thought about our minds as a battlefield?"

"Not specifically, but I can see how that's true."

"God wants us to experience peace. Once a person gets a taste of inner peace, it beats the best cup of coffee you could ever enjoy. Then some difficult circumstance in life steals it away. It's natural for a person to want peace to return. When you called, I hated what you were going through, but it let me know that you had been genuinely touched by the Lord."

Carly's comments were a bit esoteric. Kelli felt trapped in the practical demands of life.

"This case is more outside my area of expertise than I realized," she said. "The pressure is enormous."

"All the more reason to pray."

"I'm not on the same terms with the Almighty that you are."

"Just start. You don't expect Max and Emma to phrase everything perfectly when they speak to you."

Kelli sat silently for a few moments and took another drink of coffee.

"What game would you like to play with the kids?" she asked.

Carly rubbed the fingers on her right hand.

"Do you think Emma is ready for Life?" she asked. "She might need a little coaching."

"Let's try," Kelli said. "As for the real game of life, I'm the one who needs a coach."

CHAPTER 33

Jon made it through supper without revealing what was going on. The hardest part was once when he met Sarah's eyes. The innocent trust in her gaze caused him to waver, but the desire to protect her from fear kept his mouth shut. Toward the end of the meal, he was so full of feeling for her that he had to let it out. Sarah was about to take her plate to the sink.

"Just a sec," he said. "Don't get up."

"What is it?" Sarah asked, a puzzled look on her face.

"When was the last time I told you how glad I am that we're married?"

Sarah rewarded him by blowing a kiss across the table.

"I'll have to check the chart that I keep on the door to my closet," she replied.

"Add tonight to the list," Jon said. "And I'm so excited about meeting our son that I'm about to explode."

"I think about it all the time," Sarah said and smiled. "But I don't want to rush his arrival. I want him to be the perfect size. However, the width of your shoulders scares me a little bit."

"I wasn't born with this physique. I had to develop it."

Sarah rolled her eyes. "May I rinse my plate now?"

"Yes."

After dinner, they sat beside each other in rocking chairs on the rear deck. It was a cool evening, and Sarah wrapped a soft blanket around herself. Jon wore a jacket. Betsy lay near his feet. The sky was clear, and the stars began to appear like tiny lights.

"How often do you think about our son?" Sarah asked.

"I don't have a chart for that."

"That would be impossible for me. I'd fill it up in an afternoon."

They rocked in silence for a few minutes.

"Jon, is it okay to bring up something serious?" Sarah asked.

Jon stopped rocking.

"Sure," he said, holding his breath.

"Do you think we should tell our son about you working for the drug gang? Or would it be okay to let all of it disappear in the rear-view mirror?"

Jon didn't have to think about his answer.

"There's nothing I'd like better than to never think about or mention the past again," he said.

"You're not that man anymore."

Later, Jon rested his arms against the wall of the shower and let the water pour over him. He wanted to believe Sarah's final words, but they ran off his soul like drops of water. Once again, he was living a double life. The darkness of deceit had crept back in. His motivation to protect was noble. But in doing so he was building a bigger and bigger secret room and spending more and more time there. After drying off, he put on pajamas and went into the kitchen. Taking out his cell phone, he tried to call Cesar. It went to voicemail.

Jon lay awake in bed after Sarah went to sleep. She had started snoring softly during the final weeks of her pregnancy. It wasn't enough to keep him awake on a typical night, and he wasn't going to let her know about it. Sarah's breathing wasn't a major irritant. Jon couldn't sleep because his mind jumped back and forth between scenarios of what might unfold in the future. Some were good, others terrible. The logical side of his brain knew it was impossible to predict unknown events, but the emotional side refused to be squelched.

Finding it impossible to sleep, Jon quietly left the bedroom. He sat in his leather recliner and checked his phone. There were no messages from Cesar. He tried to distract himself by watching silly thirty-second videos on his cell phone. It didn't work. He stood and began pacing back and forth. It was five steps to the door into the kitchen and eight steps across the room to the hallway that led to their bedroom. Jon continued to walk until his mind surrendered its pointless pursuit of the future. He returned to the bedroom, lay down beside Sarah, and finally went to sleep.

Kelli forced herself out of bed on Saturday morning. During her walk, she unsuccessfully tried not to think about Cesar's case. When that didn't work, she took a stab at praying about it. That didn't feel right either, so she defaulted to asking God to answer Carly's prayers. During the last few blocks, she was finally able to enjoy the clear, cool air. It was going to be a perfect day to go to the horse stable.

Emma was waiting for Kelli in the kitchen. Carly wasn't there yet. The little girl had already poured a bowl of cereal.

"I was so excited I couldn't go back to sleep," Emma said. "It felt like Christmas morning."

"I'm glad you're excited. I'm sure Happy is looking forward to meeting you."

"Come on, Mom," Emma replied. "Don't talk to me like I'm a baby. I'm just going to be another girl who's climbed onto Happy's back."

"That's not what I've been told. Horses are smart and form opinions about people, maybe not on the first visit but over a period of time."

"Really?" Emma asked.

Kelli nodded.

"Do we have any peppermints?" Emma asked.

"We'll buy some on the way."

Carly entered the kitchen in time to hear the last exchange.

"Peppermints?" she asked. "I have a bag left over from last Christmas."

"Can we take some for Happy, the horse I'm going to ride?" Emma asked.

"Of course."

"But I'm the only one who should give her one," Emma added.

"Agreed," Kelli said.

Carly slowly lowered herself into a chair.

"I should probably pass on coming with you to the stables," she said. "I'd love to see Emma ride, but I'm in serious pain this morning."

"Mom can take plenty of videos," Emma said.

An hour later, they left the house. Emma had five peppermints in the front pocket of her jeans and Kelli had extras in her purse. Max found the boots he wore when he went to the summer day camp.

"I thought those would be in the storage unit," Kelli said when she saw what Max had on his feet.

"I pulled them out at the last minute. Maybe I'll wear them to school."

It was a thirty-minute drive to Cross Creek Stables. They entered beneath a large sign that announced the name of the farm and the year it was founded. The access road was fine gravel with rows of live oak trees on each side. Emma counted twelve horses in the lush green pasture.

"I don't think I saw Happy," she said. "There wasn't a horse with four white socks."

Kelli parked beside Roy's black pickup. He and Ann were standing inside the stables. Ann waved them over.

"Do you want to help me put a saddle on Happy?" Ann asked Emma. "She's in her stall waiting for you."

Emma and Ann left.

Roy spoke to Max: "You look ready to ride."

"Yes, sir."

"Tell me about your experience."

Kelli found out things she hadn't known. At the horse-riding camp, Max had learned how to make a horse walk, trot, canter, and gallop.

Roy nodded. "I'm going to put you on Chief. He's a very nice saddlebred."

"I'll watch Emma first," Kelli said.

"Go ahead. Max and I will be in the practice ring."

Emma was nervous, but once she was on Happy's back, she enjoyed Ann leading them out of the stable with the reins in her hand. They went into a nearby ring. Ann led horse and rider around in a circle several times and kept up a steady banter with Emma to reassure her.

"Do you want to hold the reins?" Ann asked. "I'll continue to guide her head."

Emma looked questioningly at Kelli.

"It's up to you," Kelli said.

"Okay," Emma said to Ann in a subdued voice. "She's not going to run, is she?"

"No."

Several more trips around the ring followed. Kelli took multiple videos. She could see the confidence rise in Emma with each circuit. For a child to be in control of such a large animal was a big deal. Emma's face exploded in a huge smile.

"This is so much fun!" she exclaimed.

When it was time for the ride to end, Ann and Emma returned to the stable to brush Happy and reward her with a few peppermints.

"I'm going to check on Max," Kelli said to Ann.

"The main practice ring is in that building," Ann said, pointing to a barnlike structure.

Kelli walked across the open space and into the building. There were three horses with riders. Wearing a helmet, Max was sitting up straight on a magnificent black animal. The other riders were teenage girls. Roy was standing by the gate. An older man called out directions to the riders. Kelli assumed he was a trainer. The horses trotted for a couple of rounds, then the trainer cupped his hands around his mouth.

"Canter!" he called out.

Kelli watched Max's horse respond and speed up. Her son moved easily back and forth in the English saddle. Kelli held her breath. A fall at that speed could be dangerous.

"Walk!" the trainer said after a couple of passes.

The horses slowed.

"Come over here," Roy said to Max, who turned the horse's head and came over to them.

The trainer joined them. He extended his hand to Kelli.

"Rick Whelan," he said. "Your son is a natural."

"I had no idea."

Max patted the horse on the neck. Roy held the animal's head while Max got off.

"That was fun," he said. "Chief is the best horse I've ever ridden."

"Except for that little problem when you first entered the ring, you did great," the trainer said.

"What sort of problem?" Kelli asked.

"I fell off," Max said. "But it didn't hurt."

Kelli followed Roy and Max out of the ring.

"Lessons aren't cheap," Roy said as they walked out of the building and toward the stables. "And things get expensive if you want to go to horse shows, but it's something to consider."

Kelli wasn't sure how to process what she was hearing. She turned to Max. "What do you think?"

"I like to ride, but I don't know about lessons."

While Max and Roy were tending to Chief, Kelli caught up with Ann and Emma. She told Ann about Max's performance.

"A trainer is always looking for more students, but if Rick said that about Max's ability, you can trust it."

Emma scampered ahead. Kelli and Ann followed behind.

"This was good for me," Kelli said. "I need to remember that there's more going on in my life than the Mendez case."

"I was worried about you."

"I was worried about myself," Kelli said, then paused. "Carly has come alongside me in a sweet way. She has things to offer that my mother never did."

"What sort of things?"

Kelli stopped, and the two women faced each other.

"You're going to like this," Kelli said. "It has to do with God."

CHAPTER 34

"Wake up, sleepyhead," Sarah said as she nudged Jon with her left foot beneath the covers. "Sometimes you pretend to be asleep, but not this morning."

Jon grunted and kept his eyes shut.

"Do you want me to bring you breakfast in bed?" Sarah asked. "Better speak now because that offer will expire soon."

"No," Jon mumbled.

"Then I'm going to squeeze a glass of orange juice."

Jon started to protest, but he was emotionally drained from worry and sleep deprivation. In what seemed like no time, Sarah touched him on the shoulder.

"You went back to sleep," she said, feeling his forehead. "Are you sick?"

"No, I'm fine." Jon forced himself to sit up enough to prop a pillow behind his head.

Sarah handed him orange juice in a frosted glass.

"I put the glass in the freezer last night," she said.

Jon took a refreshing drink. It was like a magic elixir. He opened his eyes wider.

"You're an angel," he said.

"No, I'm mortal, and when you see the to-do list on the kitchen table, you'll agree with me."

"I want to stay busy today."

"Then this is your lucky day in more ways than one."

Sarah wasn't exaggerating. She had written a long list of tasks on a legal pad.

"Is this your nesting instinct kicking in?" Jon asked as he glanced at the list of items.

"Probably."

They spent the morning assembling baby furniture in the nursery. Included was a crib that had arrived a few days earlier with instructions in French, German, and Japanese.

"Use the French you grew up speaking in your grandparents' home," Sarah said as she handed him the booklet.

"These weren't the words that came out of my grandfather's mouth."

They finished everything in the baby's room shortly before noon. Jon retrieved his phone from the bedroom. He had several texts.

"I'd better check these messages," he said.

"Go ahead," Sarah said, resting her hands on her hips. "I need to take a break."

Included was a text from Chris Polter asking Jon to call him on the burner phone. There was also a message from Cesar:

> Maria and I talked about it. I want to do what the lawyer said. It is the best way not to go to jail for a long time.

Jon wasn't surprised at Cesar's decision. But now that he knew more about the gang operating on the Georgia coast, the danger to

Cesar had many faces: Luis Diaz, Emiliano Diaz, and Carlos Aguilar. Going into his home office, Jon retrieved his burner phone, closed the door, and called Chris.

"What's the latest?" he asked. "Not more bad news, I hope."

"No bad news, if you believe avoiding an FBI interview is good news."

"Yeah, that's good news," Jon said. "I'd rather you be the go-between."

"The agent I'm dealing with didn't want to personally follow up with you. He's referencing you in the file as a 'reliable anonymous source.'"

"I'd like to keep it that way."

"Me too. Trying to relocate you and provide new identities for you and your wife would be a hassle."

Jon knew the agent intended the comment to be lighthearted, but he couldn't treat it that way. To watch what he'd built over the past eighteen years go up in flames faster than a dead pine tree after a lightning strike would be devastating.

"I'm going to follow your advice and steer clear of being in public with Cesar in Brunswick, either in court or at his lawyer's office," he said.

"And I promised the agent I'd ask you to pass along pertinent information if anything comes up. Can I count on you for that?"

"Is that how you convinced him to leave me alone?"

"Yes."

"Then I'll do it."

"Also, if you're in a tight spot like the other night when the cartel members showed up at the farm, I'm here for you. I'll be carrying the burner phone with me and suggest you do the same."

"Okay."

The call ended. Jon slipped the phone into the rear pocket of his jeans.

The excitement of the morning faded by the afternoon. The children were in their rooms, and Kelli was reading an ebook in the living room. Carly had gone upstairs to lie down. A text from Cesar popped up on Kelli's phone notifying her of his decision to cooperate with the government. Working out the timing and final details would be the first thing on Kelli's to-do list for Monday morning. She considered letting Matt Davis know but didn't want to move up Monday's work to Saturday. She returned to the book. Thirty minutes later, she received a text from Ann, raving about Roy's opinion of Max's riding. Ann included two more videos of Max on the black horse. Even to Kelli's untrained eye, the way Max handled the large animal was impressive. Kelli responded with a thumbs-up. Ann continued:

> Would you and the kids like to go to church with Roy and me tomorrow? No pressure, but after what you mentioned today???

Kelli wasn't surprised by the invitation. Actually, she would have been shocked if it hadn't been forthcoming. But this was quick. While she was thinking about how to respond, Carly appeared in the doorway.

"I'm functioning at fifty percent," her aunt announced. "Which is a lot better than the ten to twenty percent earlier today."

"Sorry it's been a rough day."

"Do you mind if I join you?"

Kelli swung her feet to the floor so Carly could sit on the couch. She showed her the text from Ann and told her about the brief conversation at the stables.

"I didn't tell her much, but she's following up."

"Because she's in the group of people who care about you."

"Those are some wonderful people."

"Are you going to go?"

Kelli thought for a moment. "I'm not sure. Max would like it, and Emma would get a chance to meet a different group of girls. Maybe it's nothing more complicated than the fact that I like to have Sundays to myself with no obligations."

"There's no rush," Carly said casually.

"I wouldn't expect you to say that."

Carly touched her chest. "What's going on in your heart is more important than anything else."

Kelli closed her reader and picked up her phone.

"I'm going to take the kids and go," she said.

Kelli's first church experience in a long time passed without any surprises. Ann's excitement at Kelli's presence was touching. The young minister's sermon about the importance of unity among Christians, even when they disagreed about some theological issues, wasn't applicable to Kelli, but it was well thought out. Max and Emma attended a separate meeting for children. Emma liked it because of the focused attention she received from a teenage girl who was one of the volunteers. Max didn't offer an opinion, which probably meant he found it boring.

The best part of the day was lunch afterward with Ann and Roy at a local restaurant. Roy and Max talked about running track and riding horses. Ann listened to Emma talk about several topics. Kelli enjoyed a seafood salad loaded with fresh crab and shrimp. Ann and Roy walked with them to Kelli's SUV.

"Thanks again for coming," Ann said, giving Kelli a hug.

"And thanks to you for asking us. We should come to this restaurant for lunch sometime. Several specials during the week looked delicious."

"It's not close to the office, but it could be worth the drive."

When Kelli and the children arrived home, Carly was sitting in a rocker on the front porch. She greeted them as they came up the walk.

"It warmed up so nicely, I wanted to spend some time outside," Carly said. "How was church?"

Emma launched into a report while Max continued into the house. Kelli followed Max.

"Was the meeting for children boring?" Kelli asked him when he reached his room.

"No," he replied. "A high school boy talked to me and asked about my relationship with Jesus. I wasn't sure what to say. That seemed to upset him."

Kelli felt herself get angry. It was exactly the sort of issue she'd wanted to avoid for herself and the kids.

"I'm sorry that—" she started.

"It's okay," Max interjected. "I gave him my email, and he's going to send me something to read."

"I'd like to look at it too."

Kelli returned to the porch where Emma was talking and rocking beside Carly. The little girl was rocking hard and threw her legs up in the air, causing the rocker to jump backward.

"It's not a toy," Kelli scolded.

"I know, Mom," Emma said as she jumped out of the chair. "I'm going inside to play on my tablet."

Kelli sat beside her aunt.

"You've heard from Emma; let me tell you about Max," she said.

The two women continued to rock while Kelli talked.

"Kids are hard to predict," Carly replied. "They'll surprise you."

"Max is at the top of the list."

"And you? What did you think?"

"It was okay. My favorite part was lunch at Randolph's Seafood Restaurant. It was kind of old-fashioned, but the seafood salad was top-notch."

"That's a good place. I've not been in years. I think they have a direct link to some local fishermen."

"Yes, they had photos of the fishermen and their boats on the wall near the hostess station."

After Kelli went into the house, Carly stayed on the porch. She wasn't totally surprised by Kelli's report. Max, not Kelli, had been the one on Carly's heart during services at her own church. For an eleven-year-old boy, Max had quite a depth. To see the Lord reach into that place was wonderful.

Carly heard a noise to her left and saw Lois closing the gate to her fence. Her neighbor began walking toward her.

"Beautiful afternoon, isn't it?" Lois asked when she reached the steps.

"Yes. Would you like to join me?"

"Actually, I wondered if Kelli is around."

"She's inside. I'll get her."

Carly found Kelli in the living room reading.

"Lois Gautier is here to see you," Carly said.

Kelli followed Carly onto the porch. Lois was leaning against one of the porch posts. Carly returned to her seat in one of the rockers.

"Sorry to bother you," Lois said. "But something came through the clerk's office late Friday afternoon that I believe you would be interested in. It could have waited until tomorrow, but it's such a nice day that I thought I would walk over."

"What is it?" Kelli asked.

"It was a request from a lawyer in Houston for a copy of the file on Mr. Mendez, the man you're representing in the criminal case. The criminal court files in Glynn County aren't available online yet, so someone had to submit a request via email or regular mail."

"Did you send him the information?"

"Yes, there wasn't a reason not to under the public records law. I have his name and address if you'd like to see it."

"Yes," Kelli said.

Lois showed her the information and Kelli entered it into her phone.

"Thanks for looking out for me," Kelli said. "Any idea why you'd receive a request like that from an out-of-state attorney?"

"It usually happens when someone is charged with an offense in another jurisdiction. Is your client in trouble in Texas?"

"Not that I know about."

Lois left, and Kelli sat in a rocker beside Carly's.

"Are you going back to your book?" Carly asked after a minute passed.

Kelli shook her head. "Not now. I appreciate Lois coming over, but it seems every time I'm getting a break from the criminal case, something comes up to remind me that it's out there waiting for me."

Kelli looked up the Houston attorney on her phone.

"The lawyer from Texas is with a big firm," she said to Carly. "His area of expertise is criminal law. He's also licensed in North Carolina."

They rocked in silence for a moment.

"I wonder if Jon Tremaine contacted him," Kelli said.

"Why would he do that?"

"If he and Cesar are thinking about firing me and hiring someone else."

CHAPTER 35

After dropping off the kids at school, Kelli arrived at the office. She stopped by Lauren's desk.

"How was your weekend?" Kelli asked.

"Dreamy," Lauren gushed. "Every time I think Curt has done all he could possibly do, he shows me there's no limit to his love."

"You don't have to tell me, but I have to ask," Kelli replied with a smile.

"Oh, I want to tell you. Good news is for sharing, right? Curt took me to dinner Saturday night at my favorite restaurant, and while we were eating a violinist came up and started playing at our table. Nobody in my life now except my mother knows how much I love violin music. My high school friends made fun of me for liking the violin, but I think the violin is such a soulful instrument. I mean, the emotion that comes from the strings is over the moon. Anyway, not only did the guy play the violin, but he also played two of my favorite songs. I almost fell out of my chair."

"That's very romantic. I guess your mother helped Curt plan all this."

"Yes, which is also awesome. She loves him and is totally in support of the relationship."

Kelli and Brad's mother had a cool but cordial relationship. Brad didn't like Kelli's mom. The phone light came on. Lauren answered, then put her hand over the receiver. "It's Matt Davis. Are you in yet?"

"Yeah, I'll take it in my office."

Kelli hurried into her office and picked up the receiver on the third ring. "Good morning, Matt."

"Good morning. I know it's not twelve o'clock, but I have a reason to ask if your client has made up his mind about cooperating with the government."

"What's the reason?"

"A man with possible links to the drug gang was arrested last night in Savannah and is going to be transferred to the local jail today. The FBI would like him and Mendez to be placed together in a holding cell. It will be a natural setup for a conversation. Can you give me an answer? This is the perfect scenario."

"Mr. Mendez will do it."

"Great. How soon can you get him into town?"

"I'll have to check with him."

"Do it and let me know. Once he arrives, keep him at your office."

Once again, Kelli didn't appreciate the DA's bossy manner but let it pass.

"Okay," she said.

"I don't have to be in court this morning. As soon as your client is there, I'll come over with Agent Perez and brief Mendez on first steps. We don't expect him to follow a complicated script."

"Will I be able to sit in on the meeting?"

"Of course. But no recordings by anyone."

As soon as the call ended, Kelli phoned Cesar and informed him.

"I'll be there as soon as I can," Cesar replied. "Jon isn't coming, so a friend named Diego will be with me. His English is better than mine, and he can explain things if I need him to."

"I'm not sure Diego will be able to sit in on the meeting. There shouldn't be a need for a translator because Agent Perez will be here. But it would be good for him to translate what's said in Spanish for me if it gets complicated."

"I'm not sure what you mean."

"I'll let Diego know when he arrives." Kelli hesitated before asking, "Did you or Jon contact a criminal defense lawyer in Houston? A lawyer from Texas requested a copy of your file from the clerk's office."

"I didn't, but maybe Jon did. What's his name?"

Kelli told him. "Let me know when you're on your way."

Kelli lowered the receiver and leaned back in her chair. She heard Ann's voice in the hallway and stepped out to tell her the news about Cesar going back to jail.

"An undercover informant," Ann said. "I've never been close to anything like this."

"I had occasional contact with government informants when I was with the U.S. Attorney's Office, but this is totally different."

"While you wait on Mr. Mendez, may I go over a few things with you?"

"Sure."

They went into Ann's office. Kelli was glad she'd spent time working on the other matters Ann had assigned to her.

"You're fast," Ann said when she reached the bottom of the list. "I've always heard that big-firm lawyers drag everything out so they can bill more hours."

"That never was my style."

Kelli's cell phone vibrated. It was a text from Cesar.

"Mr. Mendez and his translator will be here in forty-five minutes," Kelli said to Ann. "I need to let Matt Davis know."

Jon got off the phone with Cesar. Mention of the lawyer in Houston who was interested in Cesar's case got Jon's attention, and he looked him up. The attorney was with a big firm and, based on the list of representative clients, would be expensive. Lawyers didn't list drug cartel members as representative clients, but further research uncovered news articles confirming that the attorney had represented drug kingpins. This likely meant someone with the local group had asked the lawyer to obtain the information. Evidence of what was going on behind the scenes increased Jon's already heightened level of concern.

He dispatched two crews to opposite sides of the tree farm. Since they didn't need direct supervision, Jon was going to perform routine maintenance on one of the company's tractors. As a teenager, Jon worked two summers on a soybean farm in southern Louisiana. One of his jobs was to help the man who worked on the farm's equipment. Jon enjoyed working on big engines. He arrived at the shed. Betsy jumped out of the truck and walked over to the dog bed Jon kept for her in a corner of the building. Jon tossed her a long-lasting treat. One of the tractors needed repairs on the hydraulic system that raised and lowered a loader on the front of the machine. It was dirty work. Jon used the type of latex gloves common in a garage, but grease and hydraulic fluid found their way onto his arms.

He had his back to the large opening to the shed when he heard a vehicle approach. A large metal wrench in his hand, he went outside as a black car with tinted windows pulled in beside his truck. Chris

Polter and a medium-built man in his thirties with dark hair and sunglasses got out. The man was carrying a tablet. Chris raised his hand in greeting to Jon.

"You can put your weapon down," Chris said with a smile on his face. "This is Agent Peter Burroughs."

Burroughs looked like he'd come straight from the golf course. He was wearing a knit polo and white pants. He removed his dark glasses.

"How did you find me?" Jon asked Chris.

"Your wife told me when I called her."

"What did you tell her when you said you wanted to see me?" Jon asked sharply.

"Just that I was checking up on you. I described this as a surprise visit to make sure you were continuing to do well. Nothing else."

Jon pointed to the partially disassembled tractor inside the shed. "Well, there's nothing illegal about repairing a tractor."

"That's true," Chris replied. "Peter has a few questions he'd like to ask you."

"I thought you were going to serve as my go-between."

"That was with another agent. Something came up that required a quick turnaround. Is there a place where we can sit and talk?"

"Yeah. I'll wash up."

Jon went into the tiny bathroom and scrubbed his arms with industrial-strength soap. The window in the bathroom was propped open, and he wished he could turn into a bird and fly away. He returned to the work area. Chris and Burroughs were sitting at a makeshift table consisting of a piece of plywood laid on top of a pair of sawhorses. The agent was looking at his tablet.

"Thanks for meeting with us," Burroughs said. "First, I'm going to show you some photos and ask if you recognize any of these people."

Burroughs handed Jon the tablet. The image was of a Latino man who looked to be in his late forties or early fifties. Jon studied it for a few seconds.

"No," he said.

"Are you sure?"

"If it's somebody I knew almost twenty years ago, he's changed too much for me to identify him."

The agent repeated the process with five images of faces taken using surveillance, none of which were familiar to Jon. He began to relax a little bit. Burroughs pulled up another photo. This time it was a woman. Jon grunted.

"This could be a woman I knew as Margie," Jon said. "I don't remember her last name. She worked for about six months as an admin in the office with me before my arrest."

"Margaret Phillips is the name we have," Burroughs said.

"That may be right. I'm not sure."

"But you believe it could be the same person?"

The hair was a similar shade of blond, though likely the result of dye. Jon studied the photo more closely, then nodded. The distinctive green eyes were the proof.

"It's her. I remember the eyes."

Burroughs scrolled to another photo. Jon didn't need to look twice. "Yes, that's Carlos Aguilar, the guy I mentioned to Chris. He was an enforcer for Emiliano Diaz."

Burroughs pulled up a photo and handed the tablet to Jon. The photo was of two men taken from across a street. Jon enlarged the figures. His mouth suddenly became dry.

"That's the Diaz brothers," he said, licking his lips. "Luis is on the right in the yellow shirt and jeans. Emiliano is on the left in the white shirt and black pants."

The brothers were standing on a sidewalk. Jon returned the image to its original size and noticed something that was even more disturbing.

"That's Newcastle Street in Brunswick! How long ago was this taken? It looks like spring based on the flowers in the background."

Burroughs retrieved the tablet and didn't answer.

"What about this one?" he asked, returning the tablet to Jon.

"No."

Six more photos without an identification followed.

"How many more do you have for me?" Jon asked.

"One more," Burroughs replied, handing the tablet to him.

At first Jon was going to say no to recognizing the Latino face, but then he took a closer look. "This guy looks familiar, but I can't remember his name or place him in the organization."

Jon continued to study the face.

"May I tell him?" Chris asked Burroughs.

"I will," the agent replied. "This is the man who's going to be booked into the Glynn County Jail today with Mr. Mendez, your employee."

Jon enlarged the image and held the tablet closer to his face.

"I'm not sure," he said after a moment. "What can you tell me about him?"

"Nothing," Burroughs replied as he took the tablet from Jon's hand. "But if you remember anything, let Inspector Polter know."

Jon clenched his jaw for a moment.

"What's the second item on your agenda with me?" he asked.

"That can wait," Burroughs replied.

CHAPTER 36

Cesar and the man named Diego arrived before Matt Davis and Agent Perez. Kelli took the two Latino men to the conference room. Cesar sat at the table wringing his hands. Kelli explained that he was going to be processed into the jail with a man who had connections to the drug gang. They would be placed in a cell together for several hours.

"Agent Perez will tell you what you're supposed to do," she said. "Is that clear?"

"I understand."

Diego spoke: "Did Jon tell you about the man arrested in Savannah with drugs hidden in a shipment of avocados? I think it's the same thing that happened to Cesar."

"Yes, but it's not clear how that's going to help us."

The phone in the middle of the table buzzed. Kelli picked up the receiver.

"Mr. Davis and Agent Perez are here to see you," Lauren said.

Kelli lowered the receiver. Taking a deep breath, she left the conference room and made her way to the reception area. Matt and Perez stood.

"My client and a translator are in our conference room," Kelli said.

"No need for translation," Perez replied crisply. "I can explain everything to your client."

Kelli hesitated. The absence of Diego would remove her ability to verify what the FBI agent said to Cesar.

"I need to know what's being said," she countered.

Perez looked at Matt and shook his head. Matt shrugged his shoulders.

"Given that your client is going to be working for us, the fewer people who know what's going on, the better for everyone," Perez replied. "Otherwise, there's no use for a meeting, and we can leave now."

Kelli knew Cesar would want to proceed.

"Okay," she surrendered. "I'll ask Diego to step out."

"Is there a back door?" Perez asked. "I'd rather he not see my face."

Out the corner of her eye, Kelli saw Lauren's eyes widen. Returning to the conference room, she delivered the news to Cesar and Diego. Neither man protested.

"I'll wait for you in my truck," Diego said to Cesar.

Cesar and Diego hugged and quietly exchanged words in Spanish that Kelli couldn't hear. She took Diego out the rear door of the building before bringing Matt and Perez into the conference room. Perez smiled and greeted Cesar. The agent talked much longer than necessary for a basic greeting.

"What did you say to him?" Kelli asked.

"Just enough to set him at ease."

Cesar didn't look at ease. Kelli and Cesar sat on one side of the table with Matt and Perez facing them.

"I know you've been over this, but I'm going to explain to him why we're here without going into the details of what we want him to do," Perez said to Kelli.

The two men had a back-and-forth conversation for several minutes. Matt looked at Kelli and rolled his eyes. The DA leaned forward toward her.

"Makes me wish I'd paid attention in tenth-grade Spanish class," he said in a soft voice.

"It would take more than that to keep up."

"Do you understand?" Perez said to Cesar in English. "If so, please let your lawyer know."

Cesar looked at Kelli and nodded his head.

"I understand," he said.

Kelli spoke to Perez: "Before you go into the details about what you want Cesar to do, please explain it to me."

"It's simple. We want him to engage in conversation with a man named Alejandro Hernandez. That may not be his real name, but it's the name on his driver's license when he was arrested in Savannah two days ago for reckless driving, no proof of insurance, and assault on a police officer."

"The charge of assault on a police officer wasn't filed until this morning," Matt added. "It probably won't stick, but it's the best way to keep him in jail and stall his release on bond."

Perez continued: "As you know, Hernandez and Cesar will be booked into the jail and placed in a holding cell for several hours. During that time, Cesar is going to tell Hernandez what happened to him. Nothing fancy, just the basic facts and reason for his arrest. The cell will be bugged so we can hear everything they say. As part of that conversation, Cesar is going to mention that he's worried the police will find out about a large sum of money that ended up in his truck and claim it's linked to the drug charges. Cesar will tell

Hernandez that he wishes there was a way he could give the money back to the rightful owner before the police find out about it. If that takes place, Cesar hopes the owner will leave him and his family alone. He won't reveal how much it is but will say that if someone contacts him and tells him the exact amount of money, Cesar will turn it over so long as it can be done in a public place. He'll give Hernandez the number for a cell phone we're going to provide Cesar that can be tracked and everything sent to it or spoken through it captured. Our goal would be to document the transfer of the funds as part of the larger investigation."

"If this plan is successful, will you arrest whoever picks up the money?" Kelli asked.

"That's subject to operational priorities," Perez replied. "If the fish is big enough, we may haul him in quickly and try to turn him into a government witness in return for a plea agreement."

"But that's not likely to happen," Matt added. "Rather, the pickup will be handled by a lower-level worker who will then be placed under surveillance."

So far, everything Kelli was hearing seemed reasonable. The greatest danger would be the transfer of the money.

"Will you decide the location for the exchange?" she asked.

"We'll provide three options for Cesar to suggest. Otherwise, he's not going to agree to come."

"What are the options?"

"Edo Miller Park, Mary Ross Waterfront Park, and the Glynn County Recreational Complex. We have plans in place for each location."

Kelli wasn't familiar with any of the sites.

"If they turn him down, that will increase the danger to him," she replied.

"Come on, Kelli," Matt said impatiently. "The cartel already believes Mendez has the money. Danger exists no matter what."

It was the first time Kelli had heard someone in law enforcement describe the drug gang as a cartel.

"Is that all Cesar has to do in order to obtain dismissal of the charges against him?" she asked.

"He has to convince the cartel to reach out to him and set up a meeting to recover the money that is successful and reveals valuable intelligence," Perez replied. "Without that, he's not done anything to help us."

Kelli turned to Matt. "Cesar's willingness to cooperate has to be taken into consideration."

"No, I agree with Agent Perez. If this works, Cesar will also be expected to identify and fully testify against his contacts within the group who are eventually arrested and charged."

Kelli pressed her lips together tightly for a moment.

"And if those people don't exist?" she asked.

"We'll administer a nonadmissible polygraph test to confirm the truth," Perez answered.

Matt glanced quickly at Perez.

"I didn't know about that," the DA said. "Based on my experience, lie detector tests aren't one hundred percent accurate."

Perez shrugged. "With all due respect to the Georgia Bureau of Investigation, the test will be administered by an FBI examiner utilizing enhanced protocols not currently available outside the federal government."

Kelli shared Matt's skepticism of polygraphs and knew nothing about more sophisticated testing.

"And if he fails the test?" she asked.

"Then he lied to you about his involvement," Perez said. "We won't pursue federal charges if he successfully follows through with what I'm proposing. DA Davis will be free to move forward with the state prosecution."

Kelli looked at Cesar, who was listening and watching with a mixture of uncertainty and apprehension in his eyes.

"Cesar, how much of that did you understand?" she asked.

"Parts of it," he responded slowly. "But not everything."

"I'll go over it with him, and then the two of you can decide," Perez said.

Jon was anxious all morning. He wanted to be present to support Cesar but knew he couldn't be. Diego was sharp though unsophisticated in legal matters. Jon's only hope was that Kelli would advocate for Cesar in every way possible. He spent the morning driving his truck back and forth between two crews. At noon he stopped by the equipment shed to eat a sandwich he'd brought from home.

Sitting inside the building, Jon thought again about the photos Agent Burroughs had shown him. Time had dimmed his recollections, but seeing the images triggered memories. He recalled more about Margie, a woman about five years older than he was. Margie desperately needed a job because of some problems in her family. Jon couldn't remember exactly what those were. Given his high level of self-centeredness at the time, he would have been surprised if he could remember details. What did surprise him was that the woman had maintained and continued her involvement in a criminal enterprise for almost two decades. When the FBI raided the office, Margie began crying hysterically. She was taken to jail with everyone else, but the rumor Jon heard was that the feds talked to her once and released her as a nonparticipant in criminal activity.

Jon took a bite from the salami-and-cheese sandwich. He'd slathered on more spicy brown mustard than Sarah believed a sane person could tolerate. The mustard cleared up his sinuses. Jon took a long drink of water and tried to make the connection between his past and the man who was going to be put in the jail cell with Cesar.

Suddenly, Jon remembered. He'd seen the man in the rear holding area of the federal courthouse in Houston. They sat within ten feet of each other for an entire morning but weren't allowed to communicate. The man went into the courtroom before Jon, and an hour later he wasn't there when Jon was called in before the judge. That day, facing some of the leaders of the cartel, was one of the most terrifying times of Jon's life.

Glad to be sitting in an unair-conditioned shed in southeast Georgia, Jon finished the sandwich and took a bite from a homemade brownie that Sarah had prepared. The brownie was the perfect combination of crisp on the edges and chewy in the middle. He hoped there would be another one left in the pan when he got home so he could top it with a large scoop of ice cream. His phone vibrated. It was Kelli. Thoughts of a brownie with ice cream fled.

"How did it go?" he asked before she could say anything. "I've been thinking about Cesar all morning."

"I'm still in the conference room at my office. Cesar is on his way to the jail in a sheriff's department vehicle. They're booking him for a bond violation because he didn't provide a current address. The last thing Cesar said to me in private was that he wanted me to give you an update. The FBI wouldn't be happy with me sharing any of this with you, but I didn't have to sign a confidentiality agreement. For Cesar's safety, please don't repeat what I'm telling you."

"I'm not talking to anybody."

Jon listened to Kelli's summary of the plans for Cesar. The government tendency to make things sound so organized and predictable was obvious. Multiple times during Jon's time cooperating with the FBI, there had been a shift in direction and focus. Nothing was certain. Everything was fluid.

"They're going to want more from him than a polygraph," he said when Kelli finished.

"Why do you say that?" she asked.

"Uh, just a hunch."

"I forgot to tell you about the man who's going to share a cell with Cesar. They told me his name is Alejandro Hernandez, but that's likely an alias."

If he'd heard the name of the man at the Houston courthouse, Jon didn't remember it. Kelli continued, "If things go well, they're going to let Cesar out tomorrow so he can wait to be contacted about dropping off the money. For appearances, you'll come in to renew the property bond previously posted."

"I have to go to the jail?"

"Yes, but just for a few minutes. If the cartel reaches out to Cesar, the FBI will have the exact amount of money in the same kind of envelope for delivery at the designated location. Given the efforts the cartel has already made, the agent believes chances are good someone will text or make a call."

"How did Agent Perez treat Cesar?"

"Professionally. He didn't come across as accusatory or aggressive."

"Good. That's not always the case."

"Do you know any local FBI agents?"

Jon regretted his carelessness.

"I've met a couple but don't really know them," he said.

CHAPTER 37

Carly and Emma were playing pick-up sticks in the living room. With her diminished manual dexterity, Carly was no match for the little girl. After winning three straight games, Emma spoke up: "Aunt Carly, you're doing great, but let's see if Max wants to play. He's been in his room ever since we got home from school."

"Okay, ask him."

"It will be better coming from you."

Carly knocked on Max's closed door.

"Max, it's me," she said. "May I come in?"

"Yes."

When she opened the door, Carly saw that Max was getting up from his knees beside his bed.

Startled, she asked, "Were you—"

"Yeah, I was trying to pray," Max replied sheepishly. "I've never done it like that and wanted to see how it felt."

Carly never imagined she'd see an eleven-year-old boy praying on his knees at four o'clock in the afternoon in one of her guest bedrooms.

"Max, that's one of the most beautiful things in the world."

"It's not that big a deal. What do you want?"

"Emma and I are playing pick-up sticks. Would you like to join us?"

They returned to the living room. Carly's mind stayed in the moment when she'd opened the door. Emma's reign as pick-up sticks champion quickly ended.

"Do you have Jenga?" Max asked after a couple of games. "It's like pick-up sticks, only for adults. I think Emma is old enough to play."

"Yes, I think it's in this cabinet," Carly replied with a smile.

Carly made her way to a low wooden storage cabinet in a corner of the room. Close by was a used brass floor lamp she'd bought many years before. The drawer to the cabinet stuck, and when she pulled harder, Carly lost her balance and fell into the lamp, causing it to crash to the floor. She ended up on her rear end with her legs out in front of her and her back against the cabinet. Both children rushed over to her.

"Are you hurt?" Emma asked anxiously.

Carly managed to raise her right hand.

"Be careful of the broken glass from the lamp," she said.

"I'll get the broom and dustpan from the kitchen," Max said, springing into action.

Carly didn't think she had seriously hurt herself but didn't want to move for a few moments. Emma looked like she was about to cry.

"I think I'm okay," Carly said, trying to soothe the little girl. "Let Max clean up a bit before I try to move."

Max returned and began sweeping the glass into a yellow dustpan. He made a trip to the bin in the kitchen and returned. With the glass mostly out of the way, Carly tentatively attempted to get up. It was painful, but not wanting to upset Emma, she gritted her teeth and slowly moved to her knees. She used the top of the cabinet to get to her feet. Everything in her body seemed to be working. Max picked up the lamp pole and set it upright. He reached over and took hold of something hanging down and connected by a wire to the inside of the upper portion of the lamp.

"What's this?" he asked, showing it to Carly.

It was a small round object attached to the electric wire inside the pole near the light switch. When Max pulled on the wire, it came loose. Carly, whose left elbow was beginning to throb, glanced at it for a second.

"I don't know," she said. "I need to sit down."

"It looks like a microphone," Max continued. "You know, the kind police hide in rooms when they want to listen to what people are saying."

"There's no microphone in that old lamp," Carly replied as she took a few steps toward the couch. "I bought that over twenty years ago, and it hasn't moved a foot since."

All afternoon Kelli wondered what was happening in the cell occupied by Cesar and the man known as Alejandro Hernandez. There was no word from Matt Davis or the FBI by the time she left the office.

Arriving home, she found Carly in the kitchen sitting at the round table and drinking a glass of tea.

"How was your day?" Kelli asked.

"Different than I expected when I got up this morning," Carly replied. "I had a fall while getting out a game for the kids after they got home from school."

"Are you okay?" Kelli asked with concern in her voice.

"Sorer than usual, but I didn't break anything."

Carly picked up a tiny metal object from the table and held it out in the palm of her hand. "I knocked over the brass lamp in the corner of the living room. Max found this attached to a wire near the on-off switch."

Kelli took the object from Carly and inspected it.

"What is it?" Kelli asked.

"Max thinks it could be a listening device. It's shaped kind of like a hearing aid."

"Come on," Kelli scoffed. "That wouldn't make sense."

"It was wired into the lamp as a power source. There's no battery. Do you think we should have someone take a look at it?"

Kelli examined the item more closely.

"How old is the lamp?" she asked.

"At least twenty years. I bought it used."

"It could be something installed by the previous owner of the lamp in an effort to save electricity. There have been scams like that around for a long time."

Kelli handed the piece back to Carly.

"Why would anyone be interested in listening to you and the children playing games in the living room?" Kelli asked.

"I know it's far-fetched, but a strange car with heavily tinted windows was parked out front the other day while I was working in the garden. When I walked toward the car, the driver drove off. I wasn't in the house for at least an hour and a half."

"Did you see anyone else?" Kelli asked.

"No, but I've been sitting here thinking and praying about the criminal matter you're handling. Is it possible someone would want to be listening to what you're saying about the case?"

Kelli opened her mouth to say no but then reconsidered. In reality, she had no idea of the lengths to which a criminal enterprise like a drug cartel would go to protect its interests. Still, planting a listening device at Carly's house seemed beyond the realm of possibility.

"You can buy devices to scan a room for signals and impulses," Kelli said slowly. "I've always thought they were for paranoid people who take them into hotel rooms."

"Paranoid or not, I ordered one, and it will be here tomorrow afternoon with overnight shipping," Carly replied.

"You did?" Kelli's eyes widened.

"And it wasn't one of the cheap ones. It had a bunch of five-star reviews. Max helped me pick it out."

Kelli stared at Carly for a moment and then burst out laughing.

"Okay," she said, covering her mouth. "I'm sorry, but the idea of you and Max doing that is hilarious."

Carly gave her a wry grin. "I'm not offended by your laugh, and I'm not a scared old lady huddled behind triple-locked doors. If we don't find anything, it will be like a science experiment for the kids."

"We can take it to the office tomorrow evening after supper," Kelli said, still smiling. "If someone was going to plant a bug to listen to me, that would be a better place to do so."

Jon came home early from work and told Sarah what Cesar was doing.

"Are you sure it's worth the risk?" she asked doubtfully.

Jon shrugged. "Fighting the power of the government limits options. What do you think about taking dinner again to Maria and the kids? I think she'd appreciate some company."

"Absolutely."

With Sarah sitting beside him at the kitchen table, Jon called Maria and told her what they wanted to do.

"Thank you," she said in Spanish. "Anything you and your wife bring would be great. The boys are confused because their father was here for a few days and now he's gone again."

"I know it's been tough on everyone."

"I wish you could have been with Cesar today when he talked to the lawyer. You know so much more about how things work."

Jon shook his head before answering. "I'm sorry, but I'll go to the jail to pick him up tomorrow."

"Are you sure they're going to let him out? I don't trust them."

"I hope so. We'll see you in about an hour and a half."

"Thank you and your wife."

The call ended.

"Does she want us to come?" Sarah asked. "Her voice didn't sound positive."

"She said yes to supper, but she's worried they won't let Cesar out of jail tomorrow."

"I'm sure her mind is running out of control about what could happen."

Jon thought about how his thoughts had broken loose in the night and galloped away like a wild stallion.

"That's understandable," he replied.

Working together, Jon and Sarah prepared a chicken-and-rice dish with a white cheese sauce along with black beans.

"We can take the rest of the brownies for dessert," Sarah said.

"How about some peanut butter cookies?"

"But the brownies are already made."

Jon didn't reply. Sarah chuckled.

"Just admit you want the brownies for yourself," she said.

"I so admit. With ice cream on top."

"We can do some no-bake cookies in fifteen minutes."

Delivery of the meal at the new place where the Mendez family was staying was a success. Jon and Sarah ended up staying longer than they intended. While Sarah and Maria engaged in limited conversation, Jon played with the boys. It was dark when they left the house to drive home.

"I wonder if we should have brought Betsy," Jon said. "The boys are a perfect age to interact with a dog."

"They wanted to interact with you. Emmanuel was about to cry when you told him we had to leave."

"I know," Jon said, gripping the steering wheel tighter.

"You're going to be a great father," Sarah continued.

They rode in silence on the bumpy roads. Shortly before they reached the main highway that led back to the tree farm, Jon pulled into an open area beside the road and stopped.

"There are things I need to tell you about Cesar's case," he said.

"I knew you'd been keeping information from me," Sarah said before he could continue. "You think your face is a brick wall, but it's not. And there have been the times when you were awake in the night and unable to sleep."

"Why didn't you say something to me?"

"I started to a couple of times, but it never seemed like the right moment."

"There's a lot to tell."

"We're supposed to be in everything together. That's what marriage is all about."

Jon sighed. "At times the pressure and stress have overwhelmed me."

Sarah reached over and put her left arm on his right shoulder. "Jon, you're strong, but no one is strong enough to go through life on their own. I've struggled too. We need to pull together."

It took a while for Jon to tell Sarah everything he'd held back.

The interior light in the truck was on so that he could see her face. She held it together emotionally and asked a few questions when something wasn't clear.

"That's as much as I can remember," he said.

"It's a lot to take in."

Neither of them spoke for a moment.

"Do you think I've made any mistakes?" Jon asked.

"That's impossible to know right now. You've lived this, and I'm hearing it all at once. Let's go home. I'm feeling very, very tired."

Jon started the truck's engine and pulled out of the clearing. He felt both better and worse. He'd unburdened his soul. Sarah was right; it did help to share the load. She was strong. But now she was carrying more than their unborn son.

Carly was usually early for the Tuesday morning prayer meeting at the church. Today she was so caught up in her personal time with the Lord that she didn't check the clock. Having Kelli and the kids had created new challenges, opportunities, and concerns that popped up faster than daffodils in her yard at the beginning of spring. Normally, Carly didn't rely on her handicap sticker when parking, but because she was late, she parked in a reserved space near the entrance to the church. A woman who rarely came to the meeting was rapidly walking across the lot and joined her as they made their way to the entrance. Wanda, a jolly woman in her early sixties, spoke first.

"Thanks for being late," she said as she held the door open for Carly. "It makes me feel better not to be the only one walking in after the meeting has started."

"It's not a big deal," Carly replied. "There's always some chitchat at the beginning. How are you doing?"

Wanda's eyes suddenly filled with tears. She brushed them away with her right hand.

"Drat!" she exclaimed. "I promised myself not to do that, and here I am leaking like a faucet at a simple question before I walk into the meeting."

Carly stopped in the hallway. "Would you rather talk here and avoid the chitchat?"

Wanda nodded. "It's Darryl," she said, referring to her husband. "He was diagnosed with prostate cancer a few weeks ago. At first it looked treatable, but more testing shows that it's spread to his lymph nodes and may be in his bones. He was six months away from retirement, and we had such wonderful travel plans—"

Wanda's tears became a torrent. Carly guided the anguished woman into a nearby Sunday school classroom where they sat beside each other. Suffering had many faces, from Carly's chronic pain to sudden, catastrophic, life-threatening news. But the source of strength was always the same. Wanda talked; Carly listened.

"Darryl blames himself for taking so long to return to the doctor for an annual physical. He's been working hard getting financially ready to step away from the office. It's been three years since he had a PSA test. If they catch that sort of cancer soon enough, it can be stopped."

Wanda's husband was being hit with the brutal combination of guilt and a deadly disease. Wanda's tears returned. Carly put her arm around the woman's shoulders and silently prayed for supernatural comfort. One frequent suggestion Carly offered to an individual facing dire circumstances was to ask the Lord to send what she called burden-bearing angels to assist the person. She did so silently. Wanda took a tissue from her purse and wiped her eyes.

"Telling you seems to help," Wanda said. "Some of the load I've been under doesn't feel so heavy."

"I'm glad," Carly said, then shared verses about God being an ever-present help in times of trouble.

Wanda jotted down the references.

"I'm going to go home and print these out," she said. "Seeing you is what I needed."

Wanda left. Carly made it into the meeting as Jan was offering up a final prayer.

"Where did you come from?" Jan asked when she opened her eyes and saw Carly beside her.

"I was delayed on my way from the parking lot."

Jan gave her a puzzled look. Carly didn't want to repeat what Wanda said without permission. The women in the group began leaving. Carly and Jan walked out together. Carly gave her an update about Kelli and Max.

"I'd like to be excited," Jan said.

"You're not?" Carly asked. "God is on the move."

"I can't shake my concern for Kelli since I had the dream about her being in danger at the beach. It could be my imagination, but the thoughts won't go away and pop up every time I think about her."

"Kelli is stressed about a case at work. We've even prayed together about it. There's a good chance it has to do with that."

"Perhaps," Jan agreed. "And don't let me pour cold water on your enthusiasm about everything else that's going on."

They reached Carly's car and parted. Jan may not have intended to dampen Carly's hope, but that was exactly what she had done.

CHAPTER 38

Kelli took the little object Max had found in the lamp with her to work and placed it on Lauren's desk. The young woman was drinking a large cup of coffee from a local shop.

"What do you think this is?" Kelli asked. "Max found it in a lamp that fell over and broke at my aunt's."

"I'm not ready for questions," Lauren said, stifling a yawn. "Curt and I had a late night talking on a bench downtown."

"Is everything okay?"

"I think so. He found a list of things a couple needs to discuss before engagement and wanted to go through it with me. And he wasn't satisfied with short answers. We talked till I almost lost my voice. After I got home, I spent the rest of the night wondering if I'd said the wrong thing."

"Did you tell him the truth?"

"Mostly. I mean, there was some pretty personal stuff."

"Did Curt have to answer the questions?"

"Yeah, and some of his answers were hard to hear."

Kelli didn't want to begin her day with premarital counseling and didn't feel qualified to do so anyway. Her efforts at communicating with Brad to save the marriage had been immediately squelched. Lauren picked up the piece.

"This looks like those things they sell that supposedly make your light bulbs last for a hundred years," she said. "My granny bought a bunch of them a few years ago and made me help her put them in her lamps. It's a rip-off."

"I had the same thought."

Kelli continued to her office. A few minutes later Ann came in to see her.

"Any word on your client at the jail?" Ann asked. "I've been thinking about him."

"No, I'm waiting on a call or email from Matt Davis."

Kelli's phone buzzed and she hit the speaker button.

"It's Matt Davis from the DA's office on the phone," Lauren said.

"I'll take it," she said and looked up at Ann. "Do you want to stay and listen?"

Ann sat down across from Kelli as the call came through.

"How did it go?" Kelli asked.

"So far so good," Matt replied. "I watched the edited video and recording of their conversations early this morning. Hernandez was interested in what your client had to say. Mendez did a good job of acting both knowledgeable and scared."

Kelli wasn't exactly sure what that meant but let it go. She looked at Ann, who gave her a thumbs-up.

"The FBI wants to let things play out," Matt continued. "Tremaine can get Mendez out of the jail anytime he wants to. I wanted to let you know as soon as possible."

"Any additional instructions for Mr. Mendez?"

"If there are, we'll be in touch."

"Can I get a copy of the recording from the jail?"

"We didn't agree to do that."

"It could be considered exculpatory under *Brady v. Maryland*."

"No, it doesn't provide evidence of your client's innocence, just his cooperation."

"Which he could testify to at trial."

"I don't have time to debate with you what hasn't happened," Matt said. "Talk to you later."

The call ended.

"What are you thinking?" Ann asked.

"That there's something about Matt Davis that irritates me."

Jon's day started early. During breakfast, Sarah didn't say anything about the information he'd dumped on her the previous evening. He assumed she was still working through what she'd heard.

"If I get a call from Cesar's lawyer this morning, are you okay with me going by the jail to get him out?" Jon asked. "I'll make it as quick as possible."

"I don't see that you have a choice." Sarah took a deep breath and let it out before continuing. "If you have to be in town this morning anyway, would you be willing to go with me to my doctor's appointment? It was rescheduled because of something they saw the other day. I'd like you to hear what the doctor has to say. If we do have Cesar with us, he can wait in the truck."

Jon knew better than to suggest that Sarah simply relay the information to him from the doctor.

"Of course. Once I get the crews pointed in the right direction, I don't have to be on-site to make sure they follow through with the assignments."

A couple of hours later, Jon was leaving one location and heading toward another when he received a call from Kelli. He pulled to the side of the dirt road.

"They're going to let Cesar out of jail," she said.

"How did it go?"

Kelli told Jon what had happened the previous afternoon and evening. It sounded positive but was much different from Jon's experience with the government. His role was geared to what he'd already seen and learned, not collecting new information.

"Everything is set up for you to swing by the jail and renew his bond," Kelli said when she finished. "Will you be able to do that?"

"Yes."

"After you talk to Cesar, let me know if he tells you anything different from the summary I received from the DA. I'm not going to have access to any of the jailhouse surveillance."

"Wouldn't that be admissible in court to show he's cooperating?" Jon asked. "I assume they can monitor any conversations they want to at the jail for security reasons so long as a lawyer isn't present."

"Not necessarily, but in this case Cesar consented. Anyway, that's not an issue yet, and I hope it won't be."

"Okay. I'll call you after I talk to him. It will have to wait until we're back on the farm. My wife is going with me to Brunswick because she has an appointment with her ob-gyn. She's getting close to her due date."

"I'd forgotten your wife is pregnant."

"Yeah, we're going to have a boy in a few weeks."

The call ended. Jon texted Sarah, who immediately replied:

I'll be ready and waiting.

During the drive to the jail, Jon again waited for Sarah to bring up what he'd told her the previous evening. At the halfway point, she'd still not said anything about it.

"Okay," he said. "I'm going to ask how you're handling everything I said last night."

Sarah continued to stare straight ahead out the windshield.

"Right now, I'm trying not to think about it too much and to focus on the task at hand." Sarah touched her ever-expanding abdomen. "I can't do anything about Cesar's case and how it impacts us. You're worrying enough for both of us."

"Do I need to apologize?"

Sarah glanced over at him.

"A husband should never miss an opportunity to apologize," she said.

"I apologize," Jon quickly replied.

"No," Sarah said with a shake of her head. "An apology requires specific details."

Jon took a deep breath. "I apologize for withholding information from you after I'd promised to be honest with you. And I'm sorry if I've gotten so caught up in trying to help Cesar that I've put us in danger."

Jon stopped and waited.

"Is that all?" Sarah asked.

"For now, unless you can think of anything to add."

"Apology accepted about not being honest with me. None needed for your desire to help Cesar. If I were in Maria's shoes, I'd want my husband's boss to do the same thing."

Jon reached over with his right hand and squeezed Sarah's left hand.

"And it's been too long since I told you how much I love and respect and appreciate you," he said.

Sarah smiled slightly. "That apology is also accepted."

They arrived at the jail. Jon didn't see the brown pickup in the parking lot. He went inside and told the female deputy on duty why he was there. The woman opened a drawer and took out a piece of paper.

"The DA's office sent over the paperwork for you to sign," she said as she handed him the paper.

It was similar to what he'd previously received at the clerk's office. Jon took out a pen, signed it at the bottom, and returned it to her.

"May I have a copy?" he asked.

After the woman made a copy, she picked up the phone.

"Bring Mendez to the front for discharge," she said.

A few minutes later, Cesar appeared. He shook Jon's hand.

As they were leaving the building, Jon told Cesar about the detour to the doctor's office.

"That's fine. While your wife is seeing the doctor, I'll call Maria and talk to her."

Cesar sat in the rear seat during the short drive to the doctor's office. The entrance to the local emergency room was close to the medical office building. Jon parked the truck.

"We shouldn't be too long," he said to Cesar.

Jon and Sarah entered the cream-colored building and took the elevator to the second floor. The doctor's office was in suite 210. Sarah chatted with the receptionist as she checked in.

"Christine knows Lisa Roberts," Sarah said when she and Jon were seated. "They go to the same church."

A nurse called them back. With Jon's help, Sarah climbed onto the examination table.

"What would you do if I wasn't here?" he asked.

"I'd manage, just like I do when I'm at home and you're at the far end of the tree farm."

The doctor of the day was an older man whose name appeared at the front of the list on the door.

"Your blood pressure, which was elevated the other day, is good," the doctor said. "That's why we wanted you to come in."

The doctor listened as Sarah described her contractions from a few days earlier and performed a brief exam with Jon and a nurse present.

"No dilation yet, which is good," the doctor said. "Any questions?"

Sarah looked at Jon, who shook his head.

"No," she said.

"See you next week."

On the way down the hallway, Sarah spoke: "I like Dr. Crawford. He's like an old-fashioned doctor who would make house calls."

Jon hadn't picked up on any old-fashioned vibe. They left the building and walked toward the emergency room to reach the parking lot for Jon's truck. A woman and a man with his right hand wrapped approached the ER entrance. When they drew closer to Jon and Sarah, the woman looked at them and stopped.

"Jason Favreau?" she asked. "Is that you?"

While eating a salad for lunch, Carly opened the box that contained the electronic device designed to locate audio and video surveillance bugs. The instructions were extensive. As she studied the information, she decided it was written to shift blame to the user in case the apparatus didn't work. Any mistakes would be attributed to operator error. She returned everything to the box.

When the children arrived home, the first words from Max's mouth had to do with the detection device.

"Did it come?" he asked when she met them in the foyer.

"Yes, it's in the kitchen. I opened it but couldn't figure out how to use it."

Max dropped off his backpack in his room and met her in the kitchen. They sat beside each other at the table. Carly enjoyed watching the intensity on Max's face as he read the instructions and fiddled with the unit.

"Okay," he said. "This is the setting to use when you're looking for an audio device. They put out a different signal than a camera. I wish the piece we took from the lamp was still attached."

"Your mom took it to work."

Max stood. "Let's check all the lamps in the house and see what we find."

Carly followed Max as he moved through the rooms. He opened the door to Emma's room.

"Knock before you come in here!" his little sister shouted. "That's the rule!"

Max raised his fingers to his lips and whispered, "We're looking for another audio bug."

"There aren't any bugs in here," Emma replied. "And if I see a roach or spider, you'll hear me scream."

Max held the device close to Happy on the lamp beside Emma's bed. "Nothing," he said. "Let's move on."

"Good," Emma said. "And remember to knock next time."

"How was your day at school?" Carly asked the little girl.

"Okay, I guess."

Carly turned to Max. "Go on without me while I talk to Emma for a minute."

It turned out Emma had a spat with Larissa, who tried to convince Polly to side with her. Emma then enlisted Jenny to counter the move.

"And I'm not sure what to do," Emma said. "I really like Larissa, maybe more than Jenny."

"What makes Larissa feel special?" Carly asked.

"Sharing snacks," Emma replied immediately.

"What are her favorite snacks?"

Emma looked at Carly and smiled. "She likes anything with M&M's."

"We could bake cookies with M&M candy pieces on top, and you can give her one tomorrow."

"Or two."

While Carly and Emma made the cookies, Max completed his scan of the house for both audio and video bugs.

"Nothing," he announced when he returned to the kitchen. "I thought I picked up a video signal in your bathroom, but it was what they call a false positive in the instructions."

"My bathroom?" Carly asked in alarm.

"There's nothing there," Max reassured her. "Do you think we could go to Mom's office before supper?"

"You can ask her," Carly replied. "We're almost done here."

"Will you ask her?" Max persisted. "She'd never tell you no."

CHAPTER 39

Ann was leaving the office early when Kelli caught her in time to tell her about the kids coming to sweep the office for hidden surveillance devices.

"I talked to Carly, and Max is excited to try it out."

"And why did your aunt order this thing?"

Kelli showed her what they'd found in the living room lamp.

"It doesn't look like anything to me," Ann said, returning it to her.

"Lauren thinks it's supposed to make light bulbs last longer. I had a similar idea."

"Why would anyone want to plant a bug at your aunt's house?"

Kelli knew Ann was in a hurry to leave and didn't go into the story about the car with heavily tinted windows.

Kelli was in her office when Lauren let her know that Carly and the children had arrived. In the reception area, Emma was looking at photos on Lauren's phone.

"Here we are at this milkshake bar on wheels," Lauren said. "Curt ate all of his and part of mine."

"That looks amazing," Emma said. "And I like your shirt. Purple and pink are my two favorite colors."

Max had a walkie-talkie-shaped device in his hands.

"Where should we begin?" Kelli asked.

"Her desk?" Max pointed at Lauren.

"What?" Lauren asked, startled.

Kelli explained what Max was doing. Lauren laughed. "Emma and I will sit on the couch and keep looking at pictures."

Kelli watched as Max moved the locator over the receptionist's work area.

"How will you know if you find something?" she asked.

"A red light will come on," he replied. "Right now, I'm only looking for listening devices."

Kelli glanced over at Carly, who shrugged and shook her head. Max finished.

"Where next?" Kelli asked.

"Your office," Max replied.

Kelli and Max went into her office. Carly stayed in the reception area with Emma and Lauren. Kelli sat in the chair across from her desk.

"Where do you think a listening bug would most likely be?" she asked.

"Near your phone or next to it," Max said.

Max slowly moved the locator over and around Kelli's phone. No light came on. He moved to the credenza behind her desk.

"There!" he exclaimed. "A red light!"

"What do you mean?" Kelli sat up with a start.

"Somewhere around here!" Max continued.

Kelli quickly joined him and confirmed the presence of a red light. Max opened the top drawer of the credenza. It only contained blank paper for the printer that sat on the cabinet. He moved the locator farther along the top and the light went out.

"It's somewhere around here," he said.

Kelli pulled out the drawer and emptied it of paper. Max stuck his hand into the space and felt along the top of the vacated area. He then moved to the four-inch lip on the top of the credenza.

"There's something here!" he said. "You can feel it!"

Kelli put her hand where Max directed and felt a bump of metal or plastic stuck to the wood. She got on her knees and looked. There was a small round disc. She pried it loose with her fingernail so that it fell into the palm of her other hand. There wasn't a wire attached to it. She laid it on her desk.

"See if it triggers the locator," she said.

Max passed the detector over the object, and the red light came on.

"Now check the credenza again," Kelli said.

Max did so. No light appeared.

"I can't believe it," Kelli said.

"I'm going to tell Aunt Carly," Max said excitedly, running out of the room.

Kelli plopped down in her office chair and stared at the electronic bug, which was apparently powered by some kind of tiny battery. Thoughts of the conversations she'd had in her office with Ann and on the phone since arriving in Brunswick tumbled through her mind. Carly, Lauren, Emma, and Max appeared. Max pointed to the object on the desk.

"There it is!" he said triumphantly. "It's different from what we found in the lamp. I guess it runs off a battery."

Kelli raised her index finger to her lips.

"Quiet!" she commanded. "No talking in here! Go to the conference room."

They left the office and gathered in the conference room.

"Silence until Max checks this space," Kelli ordered.

They sat around the table while Max worked.

"Why can't we talk?" Emma asked after a few seconds passed.

"Carly, please take Emma down the street to the little convenience store on the corner and buy her a treat."

"We haven't had supper yet," Emma replied.

"Come on," Carly said, getting up from the table. "Text me when you want us to come back."

Carly and Emma left. Kelli and Lauren watched Max. Several minutes passed.

"I'm not picking up on anything," he said.

"I hope you're right," Kelli said. "There have been some very sensitive conversations in this room over the past few weeks."

"What's going on?" Lauren asked in alarm. "Why would someone plant a bug in your office?"

"The criminal case I'm handling for Mr. Mendez is my best guess," Kelli replied. "There may be people who want to know what I know and what I've heard."

Lauren wrapped her arms around her body and shivered. "That's terrifying! It's like your house being burglarized."

Kelli checked the time on her phone. It was past time for Lauren to leave for the day.

"Go home and don't say anything about this to anybody," she said to the receptionist. "I'll call Ann and let her know."

At the sound of his birth name, Jon's defense reflex kicked in.

"Excuse me," he managed. "My name is Jon, not Jason."

The woman, who was standing about three feet away, looked at

Jon, then Sarah. The man beside her had his right hand covered with a white T-shirt. The shirt was stained with blood.

"You look exactly like a man I used to know in Louisiana named Jason Favreau," she said. "You even sound like him."

"Looks like you need to get to the ER," Jon said.

Jon grabbed Sarah's hand and pulled her away. She didn't need any encouragement as they walked rapidly down the sidewalk.

"Is she following us?" Sarah whispered after they'd gone twenty or thirty feet.

"Keep going! I'm not looking back."

"Did you know that man? Was he in the cartel?"

"No idea."

Jon's heart was pounding as they crossed the street toward the parking lot.

"Who was that?" Sarah asked.

"A woman I knew who worked for a short time in the office with me. She didn't know much about what was really going on and was arrested and released. The FBI agent I told you about showed me her picture the other day. I was surprised that she was still involved with a cartel."

"What was her name?"

"Margie is what I called her."

They reached Jon's truck.

"And now she knows you're here," Sarah said grimly.

"Unless she writes it off to mistaken identity. If she really thought it was me, I think she would have followed us. Don't say anything in front of Cesar."

"Of course not."

Inside the truck, Cesar was on the phone with Maria, talking to her in Spanish about the boys.

"I'll spend extra time with Sancho when I get home," he said. "Jon and Sarah are here, so I have to go now."

Jon buckled his seat belt. Cesar spoke to them in English.

"Is everything good?" he asked. "It was hard waiting for our first son to be born."

"The baby and I are fine," Sarah replied.

They rode in silence until they were outside the city limits. Jon turned to Sarah.

"Is it okay if I talk with Cesar in Spanish about what happened at the jail? I need to verify events for the lawyer."

"Go ahead."

Jon quizzed Cesar about his interaction with Alejandro Hernandez. They talked for several minutes.

"How interested did he seem when you brought up the subject of the money you found in his truck?" Jon asked.

"He said he wished someone would put a bunch of money in his truck. If they did, he wouldn't tell anyone about it. I told him it's too late for that, and I was worried about the drug gang coming after me, and I was willing to do whatever it took to return the money. He nodded his head and said he might be able to help. I asked how he could help, and he told me he knew someone who knew someone else who might be connected with the right people. I told him I would really appreciate it. He also liked talking about football. He's a big Cruz Azul supporter. I like Guadalajara but pretended to be a Cruz Azul fan."

"Did you give him the phone number for the phone the FBI gave you?"

"Yes, and I told him that I only use it for business purposes."

"Do you think he will pass along the information?"

"Who knows? If he doesn't, I'm not sure what else I can do. I'm very scared about meeting someone dangerous with the money in my hand, but I don't see another way."

Jon hadn't heard anything beyond what he'd learned from Kelli Quinn. They reached Cesar and Maria's house.

"Thank you for everything you're doing for me," Cesar said in English. "You didn't have to help me."

They watched Cesar trudge across the yard to the house. "What are you thinking about?" Sarah asked as Jon put the truck in reverse and turned it around.

"Whether I should report what happened outside the hospital to Chris Polter or not. If Margie is still connected to the Diaz brothers, she'll tell them."

"Who are the Diaz brothers?"

"Leaders of the cartel. I thought they were dead, but they're alive." Jon paused. "And I testified against their little brother, who was sent to prison and murdered."

"Oh no!" Sarah replied.

Jon shook his head and didn't look in Sarah's direction.

"That's one reason I need to talk to Chris," he said soberly.

Neither of them spoke for a couple of minutes. Sarah shifted so that she was more directly facing the driver's seat. When she spoke, her voice shook: "Jon, I don't want to have our lives turned upside down. I don't want to flee someplace halfway across the country where we have to live a lie with a baby who will never know his family or the truth about who he is."

"I don't want that either."

Jon waited for Sarah to say something else, but they rode in silence. As a single man, Jon had needed a lot of time to adjust his thinking about entering the witness protection program. And even though Sarah knew his background and had been married to him for years, it was a completely different scenario considering what a new identity might mean for her. Sarah had multiple relatives, including her parents, in the Brunswick area. They reached the boundary of the tree farm property.

"Why did that woman call you Jason?" Sarah asked. "I thought you always went by Jay Favreau."

"I did except at work. My boss called me Jason when I first showed up, and I never tried to change it. I thought it sounded more businesslike."

Kelli called Ann and told her what they'd found.

"That's shocking! But I don't want to rely solely on Max. We should hire a professional to come in and sweep the entire office as soon as possible."

"Agreed. In the meantime, my question is, do we notify the sheriff's department, the DA's office, or the FBI?"

"FBI is my suggestion. They have the highest level of capability."

"Yeah, the FBI would be best. I'll try to reach Agent Perez and hope he's still available."

"Did Max check my office?" Ann asked.

"No, just Lauren's desk, my office, and the conference room. I'll take him in there as soon as we hang up and let you know if he finds anything."

"Okay."

Kelli unsuccessfully tried to connect with Agent Perez and left a message asking him to call about something important and urgent. She also provided her cell phone number. Carly and Emma returned from the store and were in the reception area with Max.

"I told Aunt Carly what to buy Max," Emma said when Kelli appeared. "Now he says he doesn't want it."

"You did that because you wanted two things," Max retorted.

Kelli ignored the sibling dispute.

"Max, I need you in Ann's office," she said. "Bring the locator."

Kelli watched her son repeat the process.

"I've been treating this like a game," the boy said as he ran the locator slowly over the area near Ann's desk. "But I know it's serious."

"I'm just glad you're here."

Max finished and shook his head.

"Nothing that I can find," he said.

Kelli sent Ann a text, then told Max what she was going to do. His eyes widened.

"Do you think I could be here? I'd like to see it. When they do a sweep for bugs in the movies, they find something so fast it's over before you can really tell what's going on."

"I doubt you can come," Kelli said. "They may not let me watch, but I'll let you know the results."

"What are you going to do with the bug we found in your office?"

"Leave it where it is until the FBI comes."

Kelli made sure she locked the office doors. The two portions of candy Emma ate on an empty stomach made her hyper.

"Let's go out to eat," Kelli suggested. "Something quick that you kids will like."

They settled on Max's suggestion of fast-food chicken. Kelli didn't have an appetite and nibbled a drumstick as she sat across the table from Carly, who seemed equally disinterested in food. Max and Emma left the table to refill their drinks.

"What are your thoughts on all of this?" Kelli asked her aunt.

"I'm doing more praying than thinking."

When they reached home, Kelli supervised Emma's bedtime preparations. Carly sat alone in the living room. After a few minutes, Max, wearing pajamas, joined her. He sat on the edge of the couch.

"How do you feel?" the boy asked her. "Are you okay?"

Max's brown eyes held a look of genuine concern. Carly patted him on the arm.

"Max, having you in the house and getting to know you better makes me feel wonderful," she said. "Next time you ride a horse, I hope I feel well enough to come and watch. And it was so special that you prayed in your bedroom yesterday afternoon."

Max rewarded her with a smile and settled back into the couch.

"That was pretty cool finding that bug at Mom's office, wasn't it?" he asked.

"Yes, and there's no way I could have figured out how to operate that locator thing."

Kelli joined them. Before she said anything, she received a phone call. Kelli remained standing while she answered.

"Agent Perez," she said. "Thank you for getting back to me."

Carly listened as Kelli explained what they'd found at the house and the office. It was clear the FBI agent was skeptical. Kelli listened for a long time.

"Would you at least have someone look at the device found at my office and determine what it is?" she asked with obvious frustration.

Another period of silence on her end of the call followed.

"I guess we'll need to hire a private company to identify what we found," Kelli said on the phone. "Do you have any recommendations?"

Kelli tilted her head to the side and frowned. "Bye."

Kelli placed the phone on the coffee table in front of the couch and sat down.

"That was a waste," she said. "The FBI isn't interested, and he wouldn't recommend a private company."

"Did he think it was a waste of time to check because I'm a kid?" Max asked.

"He didn't put much weight on what any of us did."

Carly shifted in her seat. "I was telling Max how proud I am of him," she said. "In many ways."

CHAPTER 40

Jon knew he shouldn't simply drop off Sarah at the house and continue on to work, but she showed no interest in talking further about the encounter with Margie and its implications. She spent half an hour on the phone with her mother discussing baby matters, immediately followed by fifteen minutes with her older sister who lived in Macon. Jon stayed out of sight but not out of earshot and sent several texts to the work crews. Cesar had decided to join the crew working on the east side of the property. Jon sent Chris Polter a text requesting a conversation about an urgent matter. Five minutes later, Chris called on the burner phone.

"What's up?" Chris asked. "Did you remember something else to tell Agent Burroughs?"

"No, it's more serious than that."

Jon told him what had happened. When he mentioned Margie Phillips calling him by his real name, Chris interrupted: "And your wife was present?"

"We were all within three or four feet of one another."

"Did Phillips ask more questions?"

"No, we ignored her and left as fast as we could. As far as I know, she didn't attempt to follow us, but you know she'll report it to her boss or bosses."

"Yeah."

Jon waited for Chris to continue, but he didn't.

"What should I do?" Jon asked.

"That's a tough one," the inspector replied after a moment of silence. "Because you played a big role in sending Pablo Diaz to prison, they may be motivated to come after you. You didn't testify against Carlos Aguilar, and the Diaz brothers faked their deaths. Did you testify against Phillips?"

"No. As far as I know, she was arrested and released without being charged."

"The more immediate impact of this will be to increase the risk to Mendez. He'll be under greater suspicion if he's linked to a person who previously cooperated with the FBI in an investigation."

This was something Jon hadn't considered.

"Oh no," he said dejectedly.

"Let me think about this and talk it over with my supervisor in DC. I haven't wanted to bother him up to now, but I need to cover myself."

"Cover yourself?" Jon asked.

The line was quiet for a moment.

"Don't make me say it," Chris said.

Jon realized the inspector meant revealing a blown cover that resulted in harm or death to a person like Jon while under the inspector's oversight.

"Are you going to talk to Burroughs or someone else with the local FBI office?" Jon asked.

"I have to say something to Burroughs because of the impact on Mendez. A Latino agent has been brought in to be in charge."

"I've met him. His name is Perez."

Jon told Chris the latest about Cesar and Alejandro Hernandez.

"They're moving fast and hard on this case," Chris said. "It sounds like they want to wrap it up soon."

"It won't be soon enough for me. Getting back to my original question, have you decided what I should do?"

"No, but I'll see what they say in Washington. The supervisors in charge of the witness protection program don't like to initiate reassignment and incur the additional expense without a clear and present danger. That's not the case yet, and I hope it won't get to that."

The call ended. Jon lowered the phone. He sensed a presence behind him and quickly looked over his shoulder. Sarah was leaning against the doorframe with her hands folded across her chest.

"That was Chris—" he started.

"I know. I heard what you said. Will you tell me his side of the conversation? And please don't leave anything out."

When Kelli arrived at the office the following morning, Lauren had emptied her desk. The receptionist was on her knees looking beneath her workstation.

"What are you doing?" Kelli asked.

"I wanted to finish this before you and Ann arrived," the receptionist replied. "I'm looking for a bug like the one your son found in your credenza. I figure they'd put the same kind of device at my desk. The thought of a criminal listening to what I say freaks me out. So far, the only bug I've seen is a roach that didn't survive the last visit from the pest control guy."

"We're going to hire a company to come in and do a professional sweep."

"Okay. I'll put everything back together. I asked Curt about it—" Lauren said as she stood, then clamped her hand over her mouth. "You told me not to say anything."

"That's true," Kelli said with a frown.

Lauren spoke rapidly: "I just blurted it out when he asked me about my day, and I started to cry. I didn't want to lie to him."

"I understand, but confidentiality has to be the rule around here all the time."

"I know, I know. I never talk about clients, or at least I don't mention their names."

"Cut back on any information."

"Yes, ma'am."

Kelli continued to her office. Total secrecy at a law firm was impossible to expect, but the confidentiality rules remained the standard. In her office, Kelli came face-to-face with the audio device in the middle of her desk. She picked it up and tried to decide what to do with it. She took it to the tiny storage room where they kept office supplies and placed it behind a box of copy paper. From that spot, the only thing it might hear would be the sounds of a mouse coming out after dark. Ann arrived and came in to see her.

"Where's the bug?" she asked in a whisper.

Kelli told her.

"Roy knows a company that can do a sweep of the office," Ann said in a normal tone of voice. "I've already left a message with the owner to set up an appointment."

"I'm sorry for all the drama I've brought into your life," Kelli said. "I'm sure things were calm around here before I arrived."

"No apology needed."

Kelli told her about the conversation with Lauren.

"Good reminder," Ann said. "Lauren's personality is a plus in interacting with clients, but she can be overly chatty."

The phone on Kelli's desk buzzed, and she pressed the speaker button.

"Would you like to talk to Matt Davis?" Lauren asked.

Ann moved toward the door and waved bye.

"Yes," Kelli responded to the receptionist.

"Good morning," Matt said in a cheery tone.

"Good morning," Kelli replied without matching his mood. "Did you talk to Agent Perez?"

"Not since the initial briefing about your client's interaction with Hernandez at the jail. I'm calling to let you know we received the results of the fingerprint analysis from the envelope and cash sent to the FBI. I'll send the official results via email but wanted to give you the courtesy of a call."

"Okay," Kelli said, drawing out the word. "Any surprises?"

"Good news for you is that Mr. Mendez's prints weren't on anything, although it's not probative of innocence because I would expect him to wear gloves."

Matt never seemed to miss an opportunity to spin information in an adverse way toward Cesar.

"His wife's prints showed up along with those of a man who's probably the person who appears in the surveillance video."

"What's his name?"

"I don't know. The FBI office lists him as 'CA.' There were also prints of another individual whose identity is known but whose name is redacted."

"That would be Jon Tremaine. He provided sample prints at the sheriff's department and admitted to handling the envelope."

"I know, which makes the absence of identification puzzling. Why didn't the examiner simply make that clear?"

Kelli thought for a moment. "I have no idea, but I guess it isn't important so long as the fingerprints don't belong to somebody linked to the drug gang."

"Yeah, but I'm going to ask Agent Perez about it. I'm still learning the federal procedures and protocols for an investigation. It's interesting to see how they build a case. I can see why their conviction rates are so high."

Kelli didn't share the DA's enthusiasm for his educational opportunity. However, it was true that when she was in the U.S. Attorney's Office, they rarely lost a case that went to trial.

"Any fingerprints on the bills?" she asked.

"Just the wife's. Whoever else handled the money didn't touch it without gloves. The money is being returned by the FBI, along with a substitute envelope for Mendez to use if he's contacted by the cartel and told where and when to return the money. Also, the bills have been marked with a dot only visible via ultraviolet light." Matt paused. "I shouldn't have mentioned that to you. Don't repeat it."

Lauren wasn't the only person in Brunswick with difficulty controlling her tongue. "I won't."

"One more thing," Matt said. "Are you interested in a follow-up lunch at the oyster bar where we ate the other day?"

Kelli started to abruptly turn him down but pivoted. "Yes, but only when we celebrate the dismissal of all charges against my client."

"That's good," Matt laughed. "But there's no way I'll go easy on your client just so I can eat oysters."

After all the turmoil of the previous two days, Carly was looking forward to peace and quiet. As soon as Kelli and the kids left the house, she positioned herself in front of her computer in the kitchen. The only sound in the house was the ticking of the antique grandfather clock in the corner of the room. The foyer would be the natural place for the clock, but for reasons lost to memory, it had been in the kitchen for as long as Carly could remember. The clock chimed the hour: a deep, deliberate sound that reinforced the seriousness of the passage of time. Carly's grandmother was fond of saying, "Once an hour passes, there's no way to get it back." Carly wanted the next hour she spent with the Lord to count.

She powered up her laptop. Her phone, which was on the table beside the computer, vibrated. It was Jan Baldwin. With anyone else, Carly would let the call go to voicemail.

"Good morning," Carly said to her friend.

"I know you're probably in the middle of your morning time with the Lord, but I had to call you. In the middle of the night, I got up to read my Bible and a verse jumped out at me for you or your niece. It's from Psalms in this different translation I've been using."

Psalms was a book in which Carly often meditated. Jan continued, "Psalm 56:2 says, 'All day long my enemies spy on me. They harass me. There are so many fighting against me.' It made me think of the dream I had of Kelli being in danger and how—"

"You have no idea how true that is," Carly interjected.

She told Jan what they'd found in her house and at the law office.

"I'm not sure what to say," Jan replied after a moment of silence.

"That sort of thing has never happened to me before. I'm sitting over here without a clue as to what's going on."

"Revelation has a reason," Carly said, shifting her shoulders and sitting up straighter in her chair. "And in this situation, I believe it's so we can pray specifically for Kelli."

"Agreed."

Before Carly said anything else, Jan launched into a prayer that lasted for several minutes. Carly held the phone close to the microphone for her computer and pressed the button so it would transcribe the words. It was amazing to see the prayer that included Psalm 56:2 and other Scriptures appear before her eyes.

"Amen," Jan said before adding, "Wow. That poured out of me."

"I love when that happens," Carly said.

The call ended. Carly lowered her cell phone to the table and prayed again the words on the screen before her.

CHAPTER 41

Sarah remained surprisingly stoic while Jon told her about the conversation with the U.S. marshal.

"Do you think this will convince the local FBI office not to drag you deeper into Cesar's case?" she asked.

"Why?"

"So they don't need to spend money creating a new identity for you," Sarah said. "And us."

Jon shook his head. "I don't know how they evaluate things like that. For now, I'm going to maintain a low profile and hope no one cares about me after all these years."

Sarah came over to the kitchen table and sat across from him.

"I wish I hadn't insisted that you come to the doctor's appointment," she said morosely. "There really wasn't a good reason for you to be there."

"No, no," Jon said as he held up his hand. "Don't let your mind beat you up."

Jon's phone vibrated. It was Kelli.

"It's Cesar's lawyer. Do you want to listen?"

"No and yes," Sarah said, then faltered. "Go ahead and put it on speaker so I don't have to quiz you later."

Jon accepted the call.

"Did you find out any additional information from Cesar that I should know about?" Kelli asked.

"No. He's scared but determined to see it through if that's the way it unfolds."

"Okay. I talked to the DA earlier today. The results of the fingerprint analysis came back."

Jon and Sarah listened to the results.

"It's odd that they didn't identify your prints since you provided a fingerprint card."

"My prints aren't relevant."

"That's what Matt Davis and I decided."

Jon looked at Sarah, whose face registered relief.

"Of course, Davis refused to agree that the absence of Cesar's prints is evidence of innocence. And the man identified as 'CA' is most likely the man in the surveillance video from the docks who wasn't wearing gloves when he put the envelope in Cesar's car. I'm guessing his identity is known to the FBI."

"Yeah, that's reasonable," Jon said.

"One other thing you should know," Kelli said. "I believe my office has been bugged. Cesar's case is the only matter I'm handling that would be the basis for that sort of action."

Jon furrowed his brow.

"I think I've had several conversations with you when you were probably sitting in your office," he said.

"Yeah, it's hard to remember where I was. We always met in the conference room."

While Kelli talked, Jon racked his brain for details of previous conversations with the lawyer that might be a problem.

"We talked about the money and the envelope."

"Which isn't a secret."

"And the search you did on my background in Louisiana."

"Nobody cares about that."

When Jon looked at Sarah again, he saw that her face had gone pale.

"Yeah, I guess you're right," he said.

Kelli continued, "Let's hope Cesar is contacted about the money and that it works out for the best so he can put this behind him."

"Right."

The call ended. Jon turned worried eyes on Sarah, who spoke.

"That worries me," she said.

"Yeah, me too."

Lou McGraw, the man who'd agreed to sweep the office for listening devices, arrived and inspected what Kelli and Max had found under the lip of Kelli's credenza. The short, chunky man with a ponytail took out a sharp pointed instrument the size of a tiny screwdriver and pushed it against the back of the bug.

"This is a standard-issue unit," he said, then spouted off some technical data. "I turned it off."

"Based on the type of battery, how long would it have remained active?" she asked.

"Six months or more if it was fresh when installed."

"I've been working here for days, not months."

"Let me turn it back on and test one other thing before I see if it has any friends in the neighborhood."

McGraw took out his tiny screwdriver and opened the bug. He touched it with a probe from another piece of equipment.

"That's interesting," he said. "It wasn't transmitting. Maybe you damaged it when you dislodged it from the credenza."

Using a much larger locater than the one Carly had ordered, McGraw finished his sweep of the office.

"Nothing here," he reported to Kelli and Ann, who were waiting in the conference room.

"That's good," Ann said. "It was weird feeling like we weren't in a private place."

"Oh, let me show you what we found at my aunt's house," Kelli said.

She retrieved the device from a drawer in her office and handed it to him.

"That's old-school," he said immediately. "I haven't seen one like it in years. Can you tell me where you found it?"

"In a floor lamp that was knocked over by accident. One of my kids noticed it."

"That's pre–lithium battery, which is why it was wired to an electrical source. They connect it to the wire before it reaches the on-off switch so that it's constantly on. No telling when that was put there."

"You don't think it was recent?"

McGraw pointed to the bug from Kelli's office. "That's recent. The other one is ancient. It's possible, but I doubt it was a recent install."

The two women stood.

"Thanks for coming on short notice," Ann said.

"I had no option. Roy met me at the clinic on his day off when Rocky, my English bulldog, was ailing."

McGraw left.

"That's mostly a relief," Kelli said. "The unknown factors are whether the bug here at the office worked until Max and I removed it and whether the one at my aunt's house is related."

"Yeah, it's a very creepy vibe."

They went into the reception area and gave Lauren the news.

"Great," she replied. "That means I don't have to look for another job."

"Are you serious?" Ann asked.

"No, and the expression on your face lets me know that you'd care if I did."

"Get to work," Ann said with a forced smile. "You have to save up for the fancy honeymoon you're dreaming about. What are the latest options?"

Kelli wasn't interested in joining the inner circle of Lauren's honeymoon plans. She went into her office and placed the disabled listening device in a desk drawer. After a few seconds, she took it out and returned it to the storage closet. Kelli wasn't comfortable having even a dead bug in her office.

She spent the rest of the afternoon working on new projects. Toward the end of the day, her phone buzzed.

"It's your favorite DA," Lauren said. "He sounds upbeat."

"He came across that way this morning. I'll talk to him."

The call came through.

"I just got off the phone with Agent Perez. Someone contacted Mendez on the phone the FBI gave him."

This was news Kelli wanted to hear, but it still gave her a queasy feeling in the pit of her stomach.

"I've not heard from Cesar."

"Agent Perez asked him not to communicate with you at your office."

"That doesn't shock me," Kelli replied. "Are you aware that my office has been bugged?"

"What?" Matt exclaimed.

Kelli told him what they'd found and her request to Agent Perez to conduct a sweep.

"I've worked cases in which there was illegal surveillance but never involving a lawyer's office. I'm sorry that happened."

The DA seemed sincere.

"To call it unnerving is an understatement."

"But the fact that Perez refused to authorize his office to conduct a sweep isn't a surprise. The feds prefer to focus only on what they come up with." The line was silent for a moment before Matt continued. "If this bug is linked to the drug gang, what could they have overheard?"

"I've gone over that several times in my mind and think most significant conversations took place in our conference room. But I know you and I talked a couple of times while I was in my office."

"Yeah."

"And I don't even know if it was working. A private company came in earlier today, and the owner didn't find anything else during a sweep of the office. He wasn't even sure the device my son and I found was working."

"I'm going to order a search of our office suite," Matt replied. "Send me the name of the company you used."

Jon left the house. It took fifteen minutes to reach the area of the farm where Diego and two other men were working. Jon had to park the truck and walk another ten minutes through the woods before he heard sounds of the crew working in an area where they'd had drainage problems. It was a difficult region to access, and they were having to dig the trenches by hand. The men weren't aware of Jon's presence, and he watched them for a minute. He told Betsy to be quiet, and the dog sat on her haunches beside him. It was hard work, and the men were singing as they swung the mattocks and used shovels.

"Brothers, need another helper?" Jon called out in Spanish.

The men gathered around him. Jon told them about Cesar's release from the jail.

"That's good," Diego said.

"I'm serious about helping you out," Jon offered.

Diego shook his head doubtfully. "Boss, you start out good, but you get tired quicker than the rest of us."

Jon chuckled. "Then squeeze as much out of me as you can before I sit down and pat my dog."

One of the other men handed Jon a shovel. As they walked to the trench they were digging, Jon spoke to Diego: "Do you have an update on Mateo?"

"They let him out of jail yesterday. He posted a cash bond. Mateo always seems to have money. He claims he's figured out how to play one of those lottery games—you know, where you scratch off numbers—but he won't let anyone in on the secret."

"What about the man who was arrested when drugs were found in the shipment of avocados?"

"Mateo didn't mention him, and I didn't ask."

CHAPTER 42

Carly was upstairs in bed suffering from a late-afternoon flare of arthritis when she received a phone call from Sarah Tremaine. Even in pain, Carly wasn't going to postpone a conversation with Sarah.

"Is this a good time to talk?" Sarah asked.

"Always. What's on your mind?"

"The situation with Jon and the man Kelli represents is getting more serious. I don't know what she's told you, but we're all in danger."

"I had a sense of that," Carly replied. "And I've been praying."

"Something happened yesterday when we were leaving my doctor's office that I can't tell you about. But our whole lives could be turned upside down. Jon and I might even have to move away from the area."

"What?" Carly asked in shock.

"That's more than I should probably say, but it's that serious."

"But you love it here, and most of your family lives in Brunswick."

"Yes," Sarah replied, her voice shaky. "That's why I'm calling you for help. I can't mention any of this to them. But because of your relationship to Kelli, I feel safe talking to you."

"I'm glad for that," Carly managed. "And I want to support you."

"That's all I can say for now."

Carly heard the front door open downstairs as the children arrived home from school.

"The kids are home from school, so I'd better go," she said. "Call me anytime. Day or night. I mean it."

"Thanks."

Carly heard Emma calling for her downstairs, followed by the sound of the little girl's footsteps on the stairs. She burst into Carly's room.

"Are you having a heart attack?" Emma asked, her eyes big.

"No, just a lot of pain, and I needed to lie down. How was your day at school?"

"Okay, I guess. My teacher keeps going over stuff that I learned at my school in Atlanta. I know all the answers, but I don't want to raise my hand because the other kids will think I'm showing off."

"It's okay to answer some questions."

"Yeah, but I'm not sure which ones. How can I know?"

"Sit on the edge of the bed and give me some examples."

Listening to Emma rattle off information reinforced Carly's hunch that the little girl would qualify for placement in a gifted program.

"Maybe your mom can talk to your teacher about finding challenging things for you to do when you already know the material."

"Ms. Turner might put me in time-out with a book to read," Emma replied. "I don't want that!"

"There are other ways to do it without making a fuss about it."

"I'm not sure that's a good idea," Emma said. "Sasha gets special treatment, and the other kids make fun of her. She speaks like ten languages."

"Ten languages?" Carly asked in surprise.

"Maybe not ten, but I know she understands English, Russian, Spanish, and German. She told us the names of the food in her lunch box in different languages. I thought it was cool, but Jenny and Larissa said she was showing off and believes she's better than the rest of us. I don't want them to say that about me."

Peer pressure was a powerful force of nature. Emma touched Carly on the hand. "Do you want me to bring you a glass of milk and a snack? We still have some cookies left over from the other day."

"Is that what you'd like to eat?" Carly asked.

"Yeah, we could have a picnic in your room."

"That sounds wonderful."

Emma left. There was no sign of or sound from Max.

"Where's Max?" Carly asked when Emma returned with milk and cookies for both of them.

"In his room."

"When we finish our snack, will you ask him to come up to see me?"

"You're not in a hurry, are you?"

"No."

Emma liked to barely dip her cookie into the milk and nibble it. She was very systematic in her approach. Emma ate the last bite of cookie and finished her milk.

"That was delicious," she said with a satisfied look on her face. "We should do this every afternoon when I get home."

"Then it wouldn't be as special."

"It would be for me. Do you want me to get Max?"

Carly had taken a second round of meds before the children arrived home, and the pain began to diminish.

"No," Carly said, slowly swinging her legs off the bed. "I feel better. I'm going downstairs."

"Milk and cookies always help me feel better," Emma stated.

Carly made her way slowly down the steps. She knocked on Max's door.

"Not now, Emma!" he responded.

"It's me," Carly answered.

After a moment of silence, the door opened. Max looked somber.

"Is everything okay?" Carly asked.

"I got in a fight at school," he said. "Well, not exactly a fight. There was just some pushing until Coach Matthews came up. It was about Mom. A boy whose father works for the sheriff's department says she represents drug dealers and ought to be sent to jail."

"Did you have to go to the principal's office?"

"No," Max said and shook his head. "But Coach Matthews told me I couldn't act that way if I wanted to be on the track team. Don't say anything to Mom. I'll talk to her myself."

"Okay, you can tell her. But I want to show you a Bible verse my friend sent me this morning. Come to the kitchen, and I'll turn on my laptop."

Max followed her.

"My friend Jan didn't know anything about the listening device you located at the law office. She called this morning and told me the Lord put a specific verse on her heart for us."

Carly showed Max the wording of Psalm 56:2. His eyes widened.

"That's in the Bible?" he asked.

"Yes."

"That's amazing," he replied before worriedly asking, "How is Mom in danger? Are the police going to put her in jail?"

"No, no," Carly quickly responded. "I'm not sure exactly how she's in danger, but we're going to pray and ask the Lord to take care of her."

Carly could see that her words didn't remove the concern from Max's face. She offered up a quick prayer that didn't seem to have any effect. She started to suggest that Max not mention their conversation to Kelli, but she knew that wouldn't be right.

"What would you like for supper?" she asked, changing the subject. "I'll let you decide tonight."

Max thought for a moment. "Do you ever cook cheeseburgers in your cast-iron skillet?"

"I haven't in a while, but I can."

"That's what I'd like. I ate them at a friend's house in Atlanta. They were kind of crispy on the outside. His mom said that was because of the skillet."

"I can make that happen."

Before leaving the office, Kelli received a text from Carly asking her to stop by the grocery store and buy ground beef. While she was waiting for the butcher to weigh and wrap the meat in brown paper, Kelli's phone vibrated. It was Agent Perez. Kelli answered.

"Can I call you back in a few minutes?" she said.

"Yes. Cesar Mendez received a text message about the money."

Kelli turned away from the meat counter as she told the agent she would call him back in private from her car.

"Ma'am, don't forget your beef," the clerk said.

"Sorry."

Kelli went through the self-serve checkout line. As soon as she was behind the wheel of her car, she called Agent Perez.

"Are you in your office?" the agent asked.

"No, my car. We hired a private company to sweep the law office. They didn't locate any other bugs, either audio or video."

"I hope they knew what they were doing."

"What about Cesar?"

"He received a text message at 3:15 this afternoon asking him to reply if he's interested in handing over the money."

"Why did you wait several hours to let me know?"

"I had other matters to look into."

"Who sent the text?"

"We're working on that. It wasn't from a number we've linked to known members of the cartel."

"Is it connected to the man who was in jail with Cesar?"

"Possibly, which concerns us."

"Why?"

"Hernandez was released on bail a few hours after Mendez left. There's a chance he's trying to collect the money himself without notifying his bosses and is using the phone of a friend or accomplice to do so."

"You knew this was a possibility, didn't you?" Kelli asked with frustration.

"That's why we're tracking down the number. As was the case in the jail cell, we're going to tell Mendez to ask the person who sent the text to provide the amount of money and details about the envelope. That's it for now."

"Keep me informed," she said.

At home, Carly was in the kitchen patting dry potatoes that had been cut into French fries.

"Max asked for cheeseburgers, so I thought we'd make homemade fries," Carly said. "I'm going to double-fry them."

"Here's the meat," Kelli said, placing the package on the counter. "What are the kids doing?"

"Not sure."

Kelli went to check on Emma. The little girl was lying on her bed reading a slender chapter book. This was a new development, and Kelli asked her about it.

"I checked it out of the school library. I talked to the librarian. It's about a horse."

"Sounds good," Kelli said with a nod. "It is a happy or a sad book?"

"I don't know yet. Molly just got sold to a new owner, and I don't know if he's going to be nice to her or not. Do you think Molly is a good name for a horse? I think I would call her something else."

"When you write a book about a horse, you can name it whatever you want. We're having hamburgers for supper."

"I know, but I want to eat the French fries. Aunt Carly is going to cook them twice."

"She's about to start if you want to watch."

Emma jumped off the bed and headed toward the kitchen. Kelli continued to Max's room. He was sitting at his LEGO table. He glanced over his shoulder when she entered.

"Did Aunt Carly tell you what happened today at school?" he asked.

"No."

Kelli listened as Max described his encounter with the boy whose father worked at the sheriff's department. She frowned when he reached the part about her deserving to go to jail for representing drug dealers.

"Are you mad at me?" Max asked when he finished.

"Coach Matthews didn't send you to the principal's office?"

"No."

"Did he hear what the other boy said?"

"No, but I told him."

Kelli sat on the edge of Max's bed. "I appreciate you standing up for me, but I don't want you to get in trouble. If something like that happens again, do you think you could just walk away?"

"Maybe," Max replied hesitantly.

"That's what I'd like you to do."

"Is it true what he said about you?"

"No. Even people who are guilty deserve to have a lawyer look out for them. That's the way it works in this country."

Max grunted but didn't respond. Kelli decided it wasn't time to explain to him the value of legal representation in a society that recognized the rights of every individual.

"Ready for a cheeseburger?" she asked.

Max didn't move. "Did Aunt Carly tell you about her friend who read a verse in the Bible about spying on people?"

"No."

"You should ask her about it, because her friend also believes you're in danger. Is that true?"

"No," Kelli quickly replied. "I feel safe."

Max came over and gave her a hug. It had been a while since she'd felt the boy's arms around her. Kelli held him close and kissed him on the top of the head before she released him.

"Thanks," she said. "I always love a hug from you."

Jon was driving home from the equipment shed when he received a call from Cesar and learned about the message on the phone the FBI gave him. Jon wanted to cut the conversation short but couldn't find a way to do so without coming across as uncaring.

"The Latino FBI agent told me exactly how to respond," Cesar said in Spanish. "Do you think the drug gang will answer the question proving they know about the money?"

"I have no idea. What you do is up to the FBI. It's out of my hands."

Jon prepared to end the call.

"I also got a call from Diego's cousin Mateo. He was asking questions about you. He said he talked to you about using him to order stuff we need for the farm."

"Yes, but we're not going to use him. What did he want to know?"

"He was interested in trying to find out where you grew up and what you did before you started working for Granger. I told him you're from Louisiana but that I didn't know about your family or anything like that."

Jon gritted his teeth.

"Are your dad and mom still alive?" Cesar continued.

"My father is dead, and I've not had contact with my mother in years. If Mateo asks you any more questions about me, tell him you don't know about my past."

"That's pretty much what I said. He'd already called Diego." Cesar paused. "I'm sorry about your parents. Do you have any brothers or sisters?"

"It's best I don't go into that," Jon replied. "Bye."

Jon returned the phone to the cradle on the dash of the truck. All he could think about was the photo of Mateo wearing the orange-and-green hat provided to members of the cartel. There was no doubt Mateo had been ordered by someone to ask the questions. Fear rose up inside him. He reached over and put his right hand on Betsy's head. The rest of the drive was a blur of swirling thoughts.

When Jon reached the house, he didn't get out of the truck. The inescapable conclusion was that whoever was tracking him down needed to be behind bars or dead. Jon had to contact Chris Polter with the latest news but hated the thought of what it might trigger. Even worse was the prospect of breaking the news to the woman who waited for him inside the house. Jon laid his forehead against the steering wheel.

CHAPTER 43

Kelli smiled as she watched Max eat a second serving of French fries. He'd already devoured a cheeseburger and was treating the fried potatoes like dessert.

"I didn't know French fries could taste like this," he said as he dipped another one into ketchup. "I'll never be able to enjoy them at a fast-food restaurant again."

"It will be okay," Kelli replied. "Hunger masks food preferences."

"What does that mean?" Emma asked.

The little girl had eaten a few bites of a burger but preferred fresh strawberries to the fries.

"When a person is hungry enough, they'll eat food that isn't necessarily what they want," Carly said.

"I wouldn't," Emma replied. "I'd starve to death if all I had to eat was broccoli."

"You ate the broccoli casserole Aunt Carly fixed," Kelli said.

"That was so covered in cheese and a bunch of stuff I like that I could pretend it wasn't there."

After supper, Kelli insisted on cleaning the kitchen while Carly and the kids went into the living room to play a game. Regular game nights might not continue once they left her aunt's house, but she hoped they would remain an addition to their family routine. She heard Emma exclaim in excitement. As Kelli was wiping off the counter near the stove, her phone vibrated. It was Cesar Mendez. She picked up the phone. Cesar spoke rapidly.

"I got a text with the right amount of money. They want me to meet with someone tonight at eleven o'clock. I tried to call Agent Perez, but he didn't answer his phone. What do I do?"

"Slow down. Tell me exactly what you received."

"Wait. I'll read it from the phone the FBI gave me."

Kelli glanced toward the living room. She could hear the children talking.

"I got a text at 6:35," Cesar said more calmly. "It said, 'Bring $101,500 in a white grocery bag to Edo Miller Park at eleven o'clock tonight. Put it in the back of the brown pickup truck and walk away. Reply 1 if you will be there.'"

"Okay. Did you reply?"

"No. And Agent Perez told me not to call you, but you're my lawyer."

"You did the right thing. Did you leave Agent Perez a message on his phone?"

"Yes."

"I'll try to reach him. I suspect the FBI will reschedule so they can get everything ready."

"What do I do if the FBI agent calls me?"

"Tell him to call me."

Kelli phoned the agent, who didn't answer. She hesitated for a moment, then called Matt Davis. The DA answered on the first ring.

"What's going on?" he asked.

Kelli told him.

"Did Mendez send you a copy of the text?" Matt asked.

"No, but I remember the gist of it. Whoever contacted him wants him to come to Edo Miller Park tonight at eleven o'clock and put the money in the back of a brown pickup. Jon Tremaine mentioned that he'd seen members of the cartel driving a brown truck."

"That's the old baseball field. It's been around for decades," Matt said, then stopped before asking, "No personal delivery?"

"Doesn't sound like it, which makes sense. They can watch him without being seen. It also seems safer for Cesar not to have direct interaction with someone from the cartel. He can drop off the money and leave."

"Yeah," Matt grunted.

As she talked, Kelli realized this approach was good for Cesar. It might be better if the FBI didn't try to reschedule.

"This is so time-sensitive," she said. "Can you contact Gretchen Smith or someone else at the FBI and let them know what has happened? Maybe expedite approval?"

"That was going through my mind. Gretchen will know the chain of command at the FBI. I don't know why Perez has been out of pocket. I talked to him a few hours ago."

"He's ignored me."

"Stay available," Matt said in the tone of voice he used to order Kelli around. "Let's make this happen."

Kelli joined Carly and the kids in the living room. They were playing Rapid Rumble, a category game Kelli wasn't familiar with. Everyone was shouting at once. Kelli watched for a minute.

"Mom, you have to play," Emma said. "Except you're so smart you'll win every time."

"I'm not sure about that," Kelli replied. "All of you are quick thinkers."

"Even Aunt Carly," Emma said. "Her tongue works fast even if her arms and legs don't."

"Emma—" Kelli started.

"It's the truth and a compliment," Carly interjected with a laugh.

Distracted by constantly checking her phone, Kelli didn't win either one of the next two games. Her phone vibrated. It was Cesar. She headed to the foyer.

"Yes," she said.

"Agent Perez called," he said. "He told me to reply 1 to the text message and meet him across the street from your office at ten o'clock. He said he'd have the money with him and tell me what to do. Should I agree to the meeting?"

Even though she'd thought a few minutes ago that Cesar should move forward, Kelli reconsidered for a moment. "Only if you want to go through with this."

"I do. For Maria and the boys."

"Okay."

Kelli returned to the living room but remained unable to focus on the game.

"You're not trying," Emma said. "Is it because I said you'd always win and you want to show that I'm wrong?"

Kelli adjusted herself on the couch. "No, no. I'm going to do my best."

Before the game started, her phone vibrated again. It was Agent Perez.

"I have to take this call," she said and left the room.

"Mendez received a second text after agreeing to the meeting," Perez said. "They want his boss to drive him to the ball field."

"Jon Tremaine?"

"They didn't give a name, just described him as Mendez's boss."

"Why do you think they'd ask that?"

"Maybe to make sure no law enforcement officer is behind the wheel. Regardless, we'll have the place surrounded and be ready to lock it down in a few seconds. Will you call Tremaine and set it up?"

"I'll ask him," Kelli replied. "But I can't make him do anything."

"He'll be more open to the idea coming from you than us."

"Possibly."

"The clock is ticking. Do it now."

Kelli went upstairs to her bedroom and entered the number for Jon's cell phone.

Jon and Sarah didn't speak while they put the dishes in the dishwasher. Neither of them had eaten much supper. Food wasn't a high priority. With Sarah's permission, Jon sent Chris a text message requesting a call back as soon as possible.

"I'm going to take a warm bath and see if it helps to calm me down," Sarah said. "I think you should bring Betsy into the house. She'd bark if anyone came close."

"Okay."

Sarah stopped by the door. "And I'll pray."

Jon didn't respond for a few seconds.

"I'll get out my guns," he said.

Jon owned two hunting rifles, a shotgun, and a handgun. He was a hunter, not a soldier, and he didn't know how to strategically protect the residence. He pulled the guns from the safe where he kept them in the garage and loaded them with ammunition. Going onto the rear deck, he whistled for Betsy, who came running. It was close to a full moon on a cloudless evening. Jon heard one of the pair of owls who lived near the house calling out.

"Want to spend the night inside?" he asked the dog as he patted her head.

At the word "inside," Betsy headed for the door. Jon let her into the kitchen. He then walked through the house, making sure all the windows and doors were locked. But ordinary doors and windows provided barely more protection against a determined intruder than a canvas tent in the middle of the woods. The security lights on the corners of the house automatically came on at sunset and cast a semicircle of light that extended about twenty-five feet. There weren't any lights farther away in the yard.

Jon's cell phone vibrated. It was Kelli Quinn.

"Yes," he said, returning to the kitchen.

"Someone with knowledge of the money contacted Cesar and set up a meeting," she said. "It's going to be a drop-off, which will be much safer for Cesar."

"Possibly," Jon replied.

He listened silently until Kelli said, "They sent a second text asking you to drive Cesar to the meeting at Edo Miller Park."

"No!" Jon exploded. "No way!"

"Excuse me?" Kelli responded.

"You heard me! I'm not going anywhere near Edo Miller Park!"

"All the FBI wants you to do is drive. You'd stay in your truck and wait for Cesar. The feds will have the entire place surrounded and under surveillance."

"No," Jon said in a more normal tone of voice. "I won't do it."

"There is a certain level of risk, but it's—"

"You have no idea of the level of risk to Cesar or me," Jon said, cutting her off. "Tell Agent Perez he'll need to find another driver."

Kelli was silent for a moment. "Could the FBI use your truck? Maybe one of the agents could drive it."

"No." Jon paused. "Why don't you drive him to the drop-off?"

"Uh, I'm just a lawyer."

"And I'm just a tree farmer!"

Jon abruptly ended the call. Taking out his burner phone, he called Chris. There was no answer. Sarah came out of the bedroom wearing a nightgown and wrapped in a bathrobe.

"I heard you yell," she said. "Was that Chris?"

"No, he hasn't contacted me yet. It was Cesar's lawyer."

"What did she want?"

Sarah sat across from Jon at the kitchen table while he told her about the call from Kelli and the request that he drive Cesar to the old ball field to drop off the money.

"That's when you heard me yell," Jon said. "I told her I wouldn't do it. She then suggested I let the FBI use my truck, but I nixed that too."

Sarah lowered her head, closed her eyes, and stretched her hands out in front of her on the tabletop for several moments. She raised her head and opened her eyes.

"Do you think they want to kill you?" she asked in a soft voice.

"Why else would they want me there?"

Sarah buried her face in her hands. "What are we going to do?"

Jon stood.

"Get dressed," he said. "We can't stay here. We need to leave the house."

"And go where?"

"Drive a hundred miles in any direction and check into a motel."

Jon's phone vibrated. He looked at the caller ID.

"It's Cesar," he said. "I'm not going to talk to him."

Jon let the call go to voicemail.

Each time Kelli returned to the living room after taking a phone call, Carly could feel increased tension oozing from her niece. Thinking about her conversation with Sarah and the danger Sarah had mentioned made her feel twisted on the inside.

"Can you tell me what's going on?" she asked.

"No, but I need to go to the office. A client is going to meet me there later this evening."

"Is it the criminal case?"

"Yes, but I can't give you any details. I should be home around midnight," Kelli said, then added, "Or whenever everything wraps up."

"You're not putting yourself in danger, are you? Remember Jan Baldwin's dream."

"No, no."

"Why not stay here and play a game?" Max asked. "It will take your mind off your problems. That's what it's done for me."

Kelli turned to Emma. "Both of you go to bed at your usual time. Don't argue with Aunt Carly."

"I never argue with Aunt Carly," Emma sniffed.

"Don't start."

Kelli moved toward the foyer.

"Text me how you're doing," Carly said. "I won't go to sleep until you're home."

"That's not necessary," Kelli started. "There's nothing you can—"

"Yes, there is, and I'm going to do it."

Kelli knew Carly was talking about prayer.

"Okay, but don't expect any news from me until after eleven o'clock."

CHAPTER 44

As soon as she was in her car, Kelli called Agent Perez.

"I'm on my way to the office," she said.

"Mendez should be there within the hour. Bring him to the parking lot at the dry-cleaning business down the street."

"Still don't trust security at my office?"

"The dry cleaner is my choice."

Kelli stopped at a red light.

"Did you instruct Cesar to respond via text that his boss would drive him to Edo Miller Park?" she asked.

The FBI agent was clearly in a no-negotiation mood. "I did. I don't want any excuse to delay what's in place. We're ready to go."

"But you know that Jon Tremaine isn't going to do it."

"I'm going to contact Tremaine through different channels and see if someone can convince him to cooperate."

"That's not going to work."

"Leave it to us."

"What sort of channels?"

"I said leave it to us."

Kelli hated being stonewalled.

"Why would the drug cartel care who drives Cesar to the drop-off?" she persisted.

"I'm not sure. All I'm asking you to do is be present to reassure Mendez that you're on board with the plan. We don't want him to back out at the last minute."

"That would be up to him."

"And you can reiterate the consequences if he does."

"Anything else?"

"No."

Kelli drove through mostly deserted streets to the office. She parked and went inside. She turned on all the lights in an effort to banish her fear based on concern for Cesar. Sitting behind her desk, she thought about Jon and the vehemency with which he'd refused to help Cesar. Jon and Agent Perez seemed to be drinking from the same fountain. Jon's reaction especially didn't make sense given all the time and money he'd invested in his employee's defense. Now, when they were close to a path for freedom, Jon abandoned Cesar. Maybe it was Jon's pregnant wife, but whatever the reason, the tree farm manager harbored secrets. Kelli just didn't know what they might be.

She logged on to her computer and once again opened the database that the law firm used to investigate and locate people. Instead of typing in Jon's name, she launched an inquiry about his wife, Sarah. The estate planning file listed her legal name as Sarah Constance Tremaine, formerly Huggins. Everything about Sarah Tremaine was vanilla. Born and raised in the Brunswick area, she had lived with her parents in three separate houses, graduated from a local high school, and worked for a number of years in the human resources department of a company that owned a car dealership. Sarah's marriage to Jon Tremaine was duly recorded with the local probate court. Kelli pulled up the marriage application and certificate of marriage. Jon was ten years older than his wife. Neither of them was previously married. Jon's legal name didn't include the first name Harold. That wasn't a big defect. Sarah included all three names.

Kelli logged out of the program. Her phone vibrated. It was Matt Davis.

"I saw the lights on at your office and your car parked out front when I was driving home," the DA said. "Did you finally hear from Agent Perez?"

Kelli assumed Matt was in the information loop. "Yes, but it would be up to the FBI or U.S. Attorney's Office to clue you in about what's going on."

"They should have," Matt replied curtly. "What are you doing?"

"I'm at the office waiting for next steps."

"Don't be coy with me. I'm still in charge of prosecuting your client."

Kelli hesitated. Matt, Agent Perez, and Jon needed to be in the same room and forced to work out their aggression.

"I can't stop you from waiting here with me if you'd like to," she said with a sigh. "Whether Agent Perez wants to fill you in is up to him."

"I'm turning around now," Matt replied.

Jon went into the bedroom to pack a suitcase. Still wearing her bathrobe, Sarah already had a suitcase on the bed.

"I'm not sure what to take," she said. "How long are we going to be gone?"

Jon immediately thought "forever" but didn't say it. "A couple of days while we sort things out."

They worked side by side in silence until Sarah spoke: "Do you think Cesar will be in danger if he shows up at the ball field?"

Jon threw a pair of clean socks into the suitcase. "There's always an element of danger in cooperating with an FBI investigation."

"But it's more dangerous than he realizes, isn't it?"

Jon was about to fold a shirt but stopped. "Yes, much more dangerous."

"Maybe you should call Cesar and tell him not to go. If something happens to him and you didn't warn him, it would be on your conscience."

"The FBI will be there to protect him."

"But do they care more about protecting Cesar or advancing their investigation?"

Jon stood up straight.

"What are you getting at?" he asked.

"I can't wipe the thought of Maria and the boys out of my head. I'm scared for us but also for them."

Jon sat on the bed and put his head in his hands for a moment before lifting it. "What can I tell Cesar to convince him to back away? He sees this as his best chance to avoid going to prison."

Sarah grabbed a tissue from a box on the nightstand next to her side of the bed. Jon continued: "If I tell Cesar about my history and connection with the drug cartel, my security—our security—is compromised, and we'll have to ask for relocation."

"I don't want that," Sarah said and sniffled.

"But relocation may be necessary anyway because Margie identified me at the hospital."

Jon picked up his cell phone and stared at it for a moment. "All right. I'll call Cesar. Do you want to listen?"

Sarah nodded her head. Jon pressed the call button.

"Thanks for getting back to me," Cesar said when he answered. "The lawyer said you don't want to drive me to the place where I'm supposed to deliver the money. That's okay with me. I don't want you to be in any danger."

Cesar started out in English but switched to Spanish. Jon pressed his lips together tightly for a moment. He then spoke to Cesar in Spanish. "Cesar, the danger to you is much greater than you realize. I recommend you call it off and try to set up something during the day. If all the drug gang wants is the money, they'll work with you. Edo Miller Park isn't a safe place at night."

"I believe it's too late for that. I'm on my way to the lawyer's office to meet with her and Agent Perez."

"Is Agent Perez going to take you to the ball field?"

"I don't know. I think I'll drive myself. I've thought about it. All I'm going to do is put the money in the back of the brown pickup and then run back to my truck. It will only take a few seconds."

Jon could imagine Cesar rehearsing everything in his mind with a successful outcome.

"Promise me you'll tell Agent Perez you want to set up a daytime meeting like I recommend."

"Are you sure?"

"Yes, and insist on it. Refuse to go to the ball field."

"Refuse?"

"Yes."

Cesar made a noncommittal sound that caused Jon's heart to sink.

"This could be a matter of life and death," Jon continued.

"I'll try my best."

The call ended. Jon returned the phone to the bed.

"Let's hope he does what you told him to do," Sarah said.

Jon put his burner phone in the front pocket of his shirt. "The only person I want to hear from tonight is Chris Polter."

Sarah closed her suitcase.

"Do you want to take the truck or my car?" she asked.

"Your car. It's more comfortable and cleaner than the truck. Betsy can ride in the rear seat."

Jon took the suitcases to Sarah's vehicle, which was parked beneath an attached carport at the rear of the house. He grabbed his handgun and put it beneath the front seat. At his command, Betsy jumped into the car. Jon put a bag of dry food and the dog's water bowl on the floor mat. He returned to the house.

"Ready to go?" he asked Sarah.

"Not really, but I guess we have to."

In Jon's mind there was no time for sentimentality. He held the door open for Sarah, who descended the three steps to the carport.

"Oh, I forgot my daily meds," Sarah said. "They're on the counter in our bathroom in a little blue bag."

Jon left her in the car and walked rapidly through the house to the bathroom. It took him a minute to find the bag that turned out to be on the nightstand. He returned to the car and found Sarah in the driver's seat.

"No, no," he said. "I'll drive."

Sarah held up the pistol. "I found this and want you to be able to focus on everything around us, at least until we're ten miles down the road."

"Okay."

Jon sat in the passenger seat. As Sarah reached to press the button to start the car, Jon saw a bright flash of headlights from a vehicle approaching the house.

"Wait!" he said, leaning forward. "Somebody is driving up! Get out of the car and into the house! Hide in the closet in our bedroom! Take Betsy with you!"

Kelli kept an eye out for Matt Davis's vehicle. When she saw him pull into the law office parking lot, she went into the reception area and unlocked the front door. The DA was wearing a dark suit, white shirt, and red tie.

"Long day in court?" Kelli asked when he entered.

"Jury trial in a manslaughter case. Judge Godfrey made everyone wait to see if the jury would reach a verdict this evening."

"Did they?"

"Guilty. That makes fourteen victories in a row." Matt looked at his watch. "What time is everyone going to arrive?"

"About forty-five minutes. Agent Perez wants to rendezvous at the dry cleaner down the street. He still doesn't trust the security of my office."

"Should we be talking here?" Matt asked.

"It's been double-checked and found clean."

Kelli and Matt sat at angles across from each other.

"Will you tell me the plan?" Matt asked. "It will save time later."

Kelli hesitated. As much as she might get momentary pleasure from denying the DA's request, it didn't make sense to play games. She told him the details, including the drop-off of the money at Edo Miller Park.

"Whoever is texting with Cesar wanted Jon Tremaine to bring him, but that's not going to happen. I'm not sure what Agent Perez has in mind. I assume he'll ask Cesar to drive himself."

"That's a strange request about his boss," Matt said.

"Yeah, and Tremaine was adamant that he wouldn't do it."

They sat in silence for a moment.

"Would you like a cup of coffee?" Kelli asked. "I could use one."

"Sure. Black with cream and one white sugar. I don't like raw sugar or substitutes."

Kelli went to the break room to perform her barista duties. Matt Davis was a mixed bag of ability, ego, and ambition. In some ways he'd not matured since law school. She returned with the coffee. The DA was texting furiously on his phone.

"Everything okay?" she asked.

"It has to do with a case set for trial in the morning. I didn't plan on handling it, but one of my assistants has come down with norovirus."

Kelli returned to the break room and fixed her coffee. She knew the jolt of caffeine would keep her going for at least a couple of hours. Returning to the reception area, she took one sip before her phone vibrated. It was Agent Perez.

"The cartel has moved up the drop-off time," he said rapidly. "Where are you?"

"At the office."

"Go to the lot at the dry-cleaning business and wait for me."

"Matt Davis, the DA, is here too."

At the mention of his name, Matt looked up. Kelli pressed the speaker button for the phone so Matt could listen.

"He wants to be in the loop of what's going on," she continued.

"His effort to act like a federal agent is comical," Perez replied. "Bring him, and I'll tell him to stay in his car."

"Okay."

The call ended. Matt's face was flushed.

"I'll remember that comment when I'm the U.S. attorney," he

said. "Agent Perez is on special assignment for this case, but our paths may cross in the future."

Kelli stood.

"Let's go," she said. "We should take both vehicles."

Kelli drove down the street and pulled into the parking lot of Veteran Cleaners. Matt followed her. Two minutes later Agent Perez showed up in a black sedan with heavily tinted windows. He and another man got out. They were wearing SWAT gear with vests, helmets, and other protective equipment. It was an impressive sight. Kelli and Matt joined them.

"I just got off the phone with Mendez," Perez said. "He should be here shortly."

"Were you able to convince Jon Tremaine to come?" Kelli asked.

"No, they couldn't reach him. He's probably screening our calls. We'll send Mendez in on his own."

They stood awkwardly in silence for a few moments before Perez and the other agent stepped away and began to talk in low voices. They returned. Perez spoke: "Mr. Davis, this is now an operational zone, and we're asking you to leave."

"I'm going to stay and observe."

"No," Perez said emphatically. "I'm going to insist that you go. It's in the best interest of everyone's safety and security."

Kelli couldn't see Matt's face in the dim light, but she suspected he was glowing red.

"I'll report this to Gretchen Smith," Matt sputtered.

"Be my guest. She told me to make sure you didn't overstep your role."

"She did?" Matt exploded. "When?"

"Yesterday during a briefing. She knew you might be interested in joining the operation. If you have concerns about the decision, take it up with her."

Matt pointed his finger at Kelli. "What about her?"

"She's representing her client." Perez shrugged and then looked down the street. "And here he comes."

An older-model red pickup came slowly down the street and pulled into the parking lot. It was Cesar. The door to the truck creaked when Cesar got out. Kelli could see the fear etched on his face.

"Ms. Kelli, I want to talk to you alone," he said.

Kelli led the way to the edge of the property as Matt Davis drove away.

"What is it?" Kelli asked.

"Five minutes!" Perez called out before Cesar could say anything. "We need to get moving!"

"Jon says I should refuse to go and ask the FBI to set up something during the day in a place with a lot of people around."

Kelli thought for a moment. Everything about the past few minutes made the FBI's plan seem even riskier.

"I think that would be better too," she replied with a nod of her head. "Do you want me to inform Agent Perez?"

Cesar glanced over at the two agents.

"They don't look like they want to wait for another day," he said.

"They can't do anything without you."

"Okay," Cesar agreed. "Tell them."

The kids were fast asleep. Carly remained downstairs, slowly pacing back and forth from the kitchen into the foyer and to the living room before retracing her steps. She was the only person on the planet entrusted with knowledge from both Kelli and Sarah. Normally, Carly wouldn't walk so much at the end of the day because it would translate into a painful night, but she couldn't make herself sit still if she tried. It was a march of faith. With each step she advanced against the enemy. Even a frail warrior wields great power when correctly positioned in the right army. Carly leaned against the doorframe at the entrance to the foyer and closed her eyes. She wasn't sure how much longer she could keep this up, but without a sense of release from the Spirit, she had to continue. She made five more circuits before collapsing into her chair at the kitchen table. Turning on her laptop, she waited for the prayer of her heart to find its voice so it could appear on the screen. Her phone vibrated. It was Sarah.

"Sorry to call so late," Sarah said in a hushed voice that trembled. "I'm afraid someone is coming to kill Jon."

"What?!" Carly exclaimed.

A dog barked.

"Quiet!" Sarah said.

"Do you want me to call the police?" Carly asked.

"There's no time for that! Please, pray that we'll be safe!"

There was a sound in the background that Carly couldn't distinguish. The call ended. Stunned, Carly didn't move for several seconds. Taking a deep breath, she tried to calm her racing thoughts enough to do what Sarah had asked her to do.

CHAPTER 45

Pistol in hand, Jon was inside the house in seconds and headed straight to the living room, where he'd put his shotgun behind the couch. The shotgun was a fully loaded semiautomatic that could hold five shells. Jon grabbed the gun as a fancy black pickup came into view through one of the front windows of the house.

Jon positioned himself beneath the window with the best view of the yard. The driver of the truck turned off the lights. Jon's hands were trembling. Both doors to the truck opened. The driver got out. The security lights were dim, so Jon couldn't make out much about him except that he was short, stocky, and wearing an orange-and-green hat. Jon raised the gun so that the end of the barrel rested on the windowsill, and he pressed the stock firmly against his shoulder in an effort to hold it steady. Even with a case of nerves, Jon's chance of hitting the man with the shotgun was good. Jon looked down the barrel of the gun and sighted in on the man's chest. A second man got out of the truck on the passenger side. When Jon recognized who it was, he gasped. It was Diego. The two men walked deliberately side by side toward the house.

Not sure what to do, Jon froze. As the men came closer, he saw no indication that either of them was armed with a weapon. They reached the porch and climbed the steps. Diego stepped forward and rang the door chime. Holding the shotgun firmly in his right hand, Jon went to the door and cracked it open so he could peek out.

"I'm sorry to bother you," Diego said. "But it's an emergency. This is my cousin Mateo. He needs to talk to you."

Shotgun still in his hand, Jon opened the door wider so he could see Mateo, a muscular Latino man in his late thirties. Mateo took off his hat and held up both hands in the air.

"Mr. Tremaine, you don't need that gun," he said in clear English. "I'm not here to harm you."

"What's going on?" Jon asked.

"Can you come outside so we can talk?" Mateo asked.

Thinking about Sarah huddled in the closet, Jon shook his head.

"Go back to the truck and wait for me there," he said.

Jon closed and locked the door as the men retreated. He hurried into the bedroom.

"Sarah!" he called out.

The closet door slowly opened. Betsy bounded out and began jumping around Jon. Her face pale, Sarah slowly followed. Jon told her who was there and what happened at the front door.

"Stay in the bedroom with the door locked until I come back," he said.

"Okay," Sarah said shakily. "I've been praying. I hope we can trust Diego."

Jon returned to the living room. Outside, Diego and Mateo were standing in front of the black truck with their hands in their pockets. Still carrying the shotgun, Jon left the house and approached them.

"Don't start your car," Mateo said as soon as Jon was within ten feet of them. "There is a bomb set to go off as soon as someone presses the start button."

"How do you know that?" Jon asked.

Mateo held up his hands again. "I didn't do it, but I know who did. The goal was to kill your wife after you went to town with Cesar."

Jon pointed the gun at Mateo. Diego stepped between the gun and his cousin and held up his hands.

"Mateo came to me," Diego said. "He said he wanted to warn you, so we came straight here."

Jon's eyes narrowed. He didn't lower the gun. "My wife was a second away from starting the car when you drove up."

Diego turned and spoke to Mateo. "I told you we should have called him."

Mateo didn't answer but stepped to the side so he could face Jon.

"You know some of the men I work for," Mateo said. "When I found out that they were going to kill you and your wife, I came to see Diego."

"Why warn me?" Jon asked without relaxing his grip on the shotgun.

"I want to get out, and I'm willing to tell what I know to get protection."

"Protection?"

Mateo motioned for Diego to step away. He waited for a few seconds while he did so.

"You're in the witness protection program, aren't you?" Mateo asked in a soft voice.

"My protection isn't much good right now."

Mateo ignored Jon's statement.

"I have solid evidence on the Diaz brothers, Little C, and a bunch of others," Mateo said. "I've been planning this for a while, and now is the time to act. Can you connect me with your handler at the U.S. Marshal's Office or someone in the FBI? I'm sure they'll want to talk to me."

Everything Mateo said about the government's interest in someone like him was true, but that didn't make him trustworthy.

"Do you have evidence on Margie Phillips?" Jon asked.

"Yeah, she's in charge of local finances. Someone who works for her will provide evidence against her if pressured."

That was surprising news about Margie's rise within the revamped cartel. Jon still had the burner phone in his pocket. He checked, and he hadn't received a call from Chris Polter.

"I'm waiting to hear from my handler," he said to Mateo.

"Can I stay here until that happens? At this point, I'm a dead man if I'm caught out."

That part Jon suspected to be true.

"When was the bomb wired into the car?" he asked.

"This afternoon after the request went out for you to drive Cesar to the Edo Miller ball field for the handoff of a hundred thousand dollars."

"Is Cesar in danger?"

Mateo glanced at Diego, who was still out of earshot. "I'm not sure exactly what their plans are for him. They want to recover the money, especially Little C, because he put it in Cesar's truck and then didn't get it back. It was going to be taken from his pay. But the Diaz brothers are more interested in settling the score with you because of their brother and the money you cost them. No one from the cartel will be anywhere near the ball field since they know it's a trap. They planted a bug at the lawyer's office and know what's going down. There is to be a truck at the ball field as a decoy, but before Cesar gets there, he'll receive a text changing plans and telling him to go someplace else. The plan was that when he got there, you and probably Cesar were going to be taken out and the money recovered."

"Where is the new drop-off location?"

"Someplace near the Mayor's Point Terminal. I have the address in my phone."

Of the three port facilities in the Brunswick area, Mayor's Point was the one most familiar to Jon because of its focus on the shipment of forestry products.

"I know the area well."

Mateo took out his phone and told Jon the address. Jon could picture the access road. It was a secondary route to reach the port area. There were a lot of run-down and abandoned buildings along the route. It was likely deserted this time of night.

"This is bad for Cesar," Jon said. "What was your job tonight?"

Mateo looked down at the ground for a second before answering.

"To make sure you were dead if you didn't go to town with Cesar. And to confirm your wife's death either in a car bomb blast or—" Mateo stopped.

Jon involuntarily shivered. The man who stood before him was a killer. Jon didn't know what the FBI might offer a man with blood on his hands. At least some time in prison was likely. Jon again tightened his grip on the shotgun.

"Who did you report to?" Jon asked.

"Emiliano. But only for the past couple of months. Before that Little C told me what to do."

Diego rejoined them.

"We need to get in touch with Cesar," Jon said. "I told him not to go forward with any drop-off plan tonight."

"We tried to phone him on the way here," Diego said with a scowl directed at Mateo. "He didn't answer the call."

"Where are you supposed to go after leaving here?" Jon asked Mateo.

"A condo where the operation is being staged."

"Who's there?"

"Everyone. They're going to video the hit and watch it remotely."

Jon's stomach felt queasy.

"Can I stay here until you hear from the U.S. marshal?" Mateo asked again.

"Yeah," Jon said grudgingly before turning to Diego. "But we need to figure out how to warn Cesar."

Kelli walked over to Agent Perez, who was checking the assault rifle in his hands. She was determined not to be intimidated by the weapon.

"Cesar isn't going," Kelli said in a firm voice.

"Yes, he is," Perez said without looking up. "If he backs out now, he's going to face so many federal charges that he'll never see daylight as a free man again."

"He wants to set up a time during the day for the drop-off in a public—"

Perez looked up. "It's your duty as an attorney to communicate to him what I told you. I'll wait here."

Kelli returned to Cesar and repeated the agent's threat. Her client's eyes widened.

"He's saying that to force you to cooperate tonight," she said, trying to keep her voice calm. "I think we should tell him no. They want you to work for them, whether it's tonight or another day. You're no good to them in prison."

Cesar rubbed one hand across the top of his head. "I want to get this over with."

"Cesar, don't let fear make your decision!"

"There's fear everywhere I turn," Cesar said, glancing around. "Going forward tonight is the shortest way home."

"Are you sure?"

"Yes."

Kelli turned toward Agent Perez, who was watching the conversation, and nodded. Perez motioned for Cesar to approach. Kelli joined him.

"English, so I can hear everything," she said to the agent.

"Give me your cell phone," Perez said to Cesar. "Only keep the phone we gave you so that we can monitor all messages or calls."

Kelli realized the agent still didn't believe Cesar was innocent of involvement with the drug gang and was concerned he might notify them about what was going on. Cesar handed him the phone. The agent with Perez frisked Cesar. The only thing he removed was Cesar's wallet, which he checked and returned to him.

"Keep it," the agent said with a slight smile. "We don't want you driving without a license."

Perez opened the rear door of their sedan and took out a white plastic grocery bag. He gave it to Cesar.

"Here's the money. Don't look in the bag or touch anything in it. Is that clear?"

"Yes."

Perez checked his watch. "Let's go. We'll be behind you but keeping you in view until we get close to the ball field. Then other officers you can't see will take over to protect you. Everything is going to be okay."

"Call me as soon as it's over," Kelli said to Cesar.

Holding the plastic bag in his right hand, Cesar got in his truck. Kelli watched as he left the parking lot with the agents behind him. With a heavy heart, she returned to the office to wait. Trying to pass the time would be brutal, but nothing compared to the pressure Cesar must be feeling. She went into the conference room. Her phone vibrated. It was Jon Tremaine. She resented the way he'd abandoned Cesar. Jon's unwillingness to help disqualified him from receiving real-time updates about what was taking place. But she pushed aside her resentment and accepted the call.

"Yes," she said tersely.

"Where's Cesar?" Jon asked frantically. "Has he left for the ball field?"

"Maybe five minutes ago, probably less."

"He can't go! It's a trap!"

"What?" Kelli sat bolt upright.

"Diego's cousin Mateo is here. He works for the cartel but is wanting to make a deal with the FBI and get out."

"Why did he come to you?"

"Not now," Jon replied. "Cesar is going to get a text message telling him not to go to the ball field but to a location near Mayor's Point Terminal off Ellis Street. I believe they're going to kill him."

Kelli swallowed.

"I need to call Agent Perez," she said.

"Tell him there's going to be an ambush somewhere along the new route, most likely a section of the road with a lot of old rundown buildings."

Kelli's hand trembled as she entered the numbers for the agent's phone. Her heart sank when it went to voicemail. She left an urgent message.

"He's not answering," she said to Jon.

"Okay, here's what you need to do. There's an intersection Cesar will have to go through to access the area. All traffic funnels through there. Go to that spot and stop him."

"What? I can't do that!"

"Who else can get there in time?" Jon asked, raising his voice. "You're closer to the Mayor's Point Terminal at your office than someone would be from the ball field."

"No, I'm not able—"

"We don't have time to debate this! I'll send you the address in the next ten seconds."

"Why didn't you drive Cesar to town?" Kelli asked desperately.

"If you don't do this, Cesar doesn't have a chance!"

Kelli felt every muscle in her body contract. It was unlike any sensation she'd ever experienced. "Okay, I'll try."

"Leave now. You'll have the address for the intersection on your phone as soon as we hang up."

Trying not to think about the danger, Kelli got in her vehicle. She put her phone in the cradle attached to one of the air-conditioning vents and then opened the text from Jon with the address. She gripped the steering wheel as the calm GPS voice told her where and when to turn. Kelli came to a stoplight that changed to red. She slowed, but since there was no traffic crossing in front of her, she ran the light and continued. Within a few minutes she reached the area Jon had described to her. The GPS guide informed her that she would reach her destination in two minutes. Instead, Kelli stopped in the middle of the road and put the transmission in park.

"What am I doing?" she asked, pounding the steering wheel with both hands. "This is insane!"

Kelli stared at the image of the streets on her phone. Her destination was identified by a blinking light. Jerking the transmission back into drive, Kelli continued. She slowed and stopped about three or four car lengths from the intersection. She could see several hundred feet up the road in the direction Jon said Cesar would be coming from. A box truck with the name of a seafood company on the side approached and rolled through. There was no sign of Cesar or his truck. A minute passed. Then two minutes. Two cars came through. Kelli pulled closer to the curb. A car came up behind her. When she saw the car's lights in the rearview mirror, Kelli panicked and considered stomping on the gas pedal to get away. She resisted, and the car passed by on the left. She could see a woman driving the vehicle. The driver didn't even glance at her. Kelli lowered her head and rested her forehead against the top of the steering wheel. And in that moment, she suddenly remembered that Carly was praying for her.

When Kelli raised her head, she saw Cesar's truck approaching the intersection. She pressed on the gas and moved forward. She inched toward the intersection and started honking her horn and flashing her lights. Exactly how she intended to stop and warn Cesar hadn't yet taken form in her thinking. Cesar continued forward. When he was in the middle of the intersection, Kelli stepped down hard on the gas. Her SUV shot into the crossway and struck the rear panel of Cesar's truck, spinning him around. The speed and force of impact was enough that Kelli's airbag inflated. Startled, she needed to take a few seconds to collect herself. She opened the door and stumbled into the street. Seconds later, someone grabbed her from behind and threw her against the side of her vehicle.

CHAPTER 46

Jon refused to let Diego and Mateo wait inside the house. They remained standing in front of Mateo's truck. Jon tried to reach Cesar, but the call went to voicemail. The burner phone vibrated. Jon quickly pressed the receive button and answered.

"Sorry it's taken me a while to get back to you," Chris said in a friendly tone of voice. "I'm in Biloxi. My daughter had a baby boy about three hours ago. Travis is my first grandson. He's a good-looking—"

"Chris, there's an emergency. My cover is blown, and the cartel is planning on killing me and Sarah."

"Where are you now?" Chris asked in alarm.

"At home. The hit man sent to kill us decided not to go through with it. He wants to turn himself in and cooperate. Cesar Mendez is in serious danger and needs to be warned immediately."

As quickly as he could, Jon told Chris what he knew.

"I'll call someone I know who is connected to the operation as soon as we hang up. Also, text the address of the condo where the group is meeting tonight."

"Okay. What about the man who wants to cooperate?"

"I'll call you back as soon as I can and talk to him. I have a safe house in Savannah where he can go. Where is he now?"

Listening to Chris brought back memories to Jon. "Outside. I didn't want him in the house."

"Understood. Are you armed?"

"Yes. My shotgun is three feet away from me."

The call ended. Shotgun in hand, Jon went outside and told Mateo he'd spoken to his handler with the U.S. Marshal's Office.

"Agent Polter will arrange a safe place for you to go."

"Tonight?"

"Probably. He's going to call back as soon as he can."

"I need to get some things from the truck," Mateo said.

"Not now," Jon said with a firm shake of his head. "I want to keep things status quo."

Mateo continued toward the driver's-side door of the truck.

"I mean it," Jon said. "Stay where I can watch you."

Mateo stopped and returned to his place beside Diego. "Okay, although you should know there's no turning back for me."

They stood in silence for a moment. Jon turned to Diego. "Will you step over to the front porch so Mateo and I can talk?"

Diego nodded and left them. Jon turned to Mateo.

"What do you know about me?" he asked.

"Only that you worked for the old Los Reyes cartel years ago and testified against some of the big shots who went to prison. The Diaz brothers hate you because they blame you for their little brother's death."

"What about Little C?"

Mateo shrugged. "I don't think he cared either way. He said you were a flea on the dog."

"And Margie?" Jon asked.

"I don't know anything except she saw you at the hospital when she took a man who works for us in to be treated for an injured hand." Mateo thought for a moment. "When Margie claimed she saw you, Luis didn't say much. Emiliano went off in a rage, and he ordered the hit on you and your wife. Emiliano is very paranoid."

What Mateo said about Emiliano was accurate. He wouldn't hesitate to order a killing based solely on suspicion. Jon checked his watch. Ample time had passed for Cesar to be on the way to the docks. It was eerie talking calmly in his front yard without knowing what was going on in Brunswick. The burner phone buzzed. Jon answered.

"I made my calls," Chris said. "Not sure what's going on, but I passed on what you said and vouched for it. I hope you're right. Let me talk to the guy who wants to turn himself in."

"Okay." Jon held out the phone to Mateo. "It's my handler. He wants to talk to you."

Mateo didn't immediately take the phone. Jon knew what a big step the man was about to take. Mateo accepted the phone and held it to his ear.

"Yes," he said. "This is Mateo Torres."

Jon stepped away and joined Diego on the porch.

"Stay here while I talk to Sarah," Jon said. "The man who called works for the government and is trying to help Cesar."

"Okay."

Inside the house, Jon gently knocked on the bedroom door.

"It's me," he said.

Sarah opened the door. Betsy darted out and ran into the living room. Jon and Sarah stayed where they were. Jon spoke: "The guy with Diego is talking to Chris Polter about becoming a government witness. If it works out, Chris may send him to a safe house."

"Are we safe?" Sarah asked, emphasizing the last word.

"I hope so. I desperately hope so." Jon opened his arms, and Sarah fell into them. Sarah didn't cry. Neither did he. Never had Jon held her with greater relief. Nothing in his life was more important than loving and protecting her and their unborn son.

Kelli turned her head to the side and managed to see who'd grabbed her. It was Agent Perez.

"What are you doing!?" the agent yelled in her ear without releasing his hold on her.

"It's a trap," Kelli said, gasping for breath. "I got a call from Jon Tremaine."

Perez didn't respond. Instead, he called out over his shoulder, "Is Mendez okay?"

"Yeah," a voice replied.

"Can the truck be driven?" Perez asked.

"Not sure."

Perez released Kelli. She faced him. The agent pointed his finger directly at her nose. "Ms. Quinn, you are in serious trouble. You've intervened in a federal investigation."

Kelli was shaking. She rubbed her arms with her hands. She was both scared and angry.

"Don't touch me again," she warned in an unsteady voice.

Perez placed his index finger on his ear where Kelli could see a communication device. He listened for a moment before stepping away. Kelli got a better look at Cesar's truck. She'd struck one of the rear tires so hard that it popped the tire and bent the rim. The truck wasn't going anywhere. Kelli leaned back against her SUV and closed her eyes for a moment. She heard the door of Cesar's truck open. He got out slowly.

"Are you okay?" she called out to him.

Cesar gave her a puzzled look and didn't respond. The agent with Cesar guided him away from the truck. Kelli heard sirens in the distance. They quickly grew louder. Four cars from the sheriff's department and two unmarked cars came racing down the street. One patrol car peeled off and stopped. The others slowed only long enough to make their way around the vehicles in the intersection and then sped up. A deputy approached Agent Perez and the two men talked. Perez motioned for the other FBI agent to join him. They got in their car and left.

A young sheriff's deputy came over to Kelli. His name tag identified him as Deputy Carmady.

"Do you need medical attention?" the deputy asked.

"I don't think so," Kelli replied. "Please check with Mr. Mendez."

Glad to be steady on her feet, Kelli followed the deputy to Cesar, who was leaning against the front of his truck. The deputy repeated his question.

"No." Cesar shook his head, then turned to Kelli. "Why did you hit my truck?"

"To save your life. You were driving into a trap."

"I'll transport both of you to the sheriff's department," the deputy said.

Cesar didn't move.

"I don't want to go back to jail!" he protested. "I was willing to cooperate!"

Kelli spoke: "Are you going to put him in jail?"

"My orders are to take both of you to the sheriff's department."

"It's going to be fine," Kelli reassured Cesar. "Jon Tremaine called me. That's why I had to stop you."

Cesar eyed her doubtfully. As they were about to get into the patrol car, Kelli stopped. "May I get my phone? It's in my SUV."

The deputy nodded. Kelli walked rapidly to her vehicle. Her phone had been knocked from its holder by the airbag and into the passenger seat. She knew the first person she had to call.

Carly's eyelids were heavy, but she refused to surrender to sleep. Nothing was going to force her to step down from her place on the wall of intercession. Her phone vibrated. It was Sarah.

"Yes," Carly said.

"We're safe," Sarah said. "The FBI is on their way. The man who was going to kill us is going to turn himself in."

Tears appeared in Carly's eyes and ran down her cheeks. It was impossible for her to speak.

"Are you there?" Sarah asked.

"Yes," Carly managed. "I'm so, so thankful—"

More tears washed away her words.

"Have you heard from your niece?" Sarah asked.

"No." Carly's lips drew together for a moment. "I've got to keep praying for her."

"Let me know, please."

"I will."

Carly went upstairs to the chair in her bedroom. Jan Baldwin's dream of danger followed her. Carly read and prayed through a passage about David's early exploits and how the Lord faithfully preserved and protected the future king's life. Her phone vibrated. It was Kelli. Carly grabbed the phone but dropped it when her fingers didn't cooperate in grasping it. She managed to retrieve the phone and answer before the call went to voicemail.

"Hello," she said anxiously.

"I'm okay but on my way to the jail," Kelli said. "My car isn't drivable, so a deputy is taking me there."

"You wrecked your car?"

"On purpose. I'm sure the kids are asleep, right?"

"Yes."

"If a deputy can't give me a ride home, I'll get an Uber or a Lyft. I don't want you leaving the kids alone at the house."

"What happened?"

"I'll explain later, but Cesar and I are safe. Now that all the adrenaline is draining out of my body, I'm exhausted. All I want to do is collapse into bed."

"Were you in danger?"

"Yes," Kelli said. "Real danger, but I'm okay and unharmed. I'll let you know as soon as I leave the jail."

Carly was finally able to exhale with relief.

"Thank you," she said.

"Are you kidding? If you hadn't been praying for me, I might be dead."

"Don't say that."

"Who knows? But a thousand thanks."

The call ended. Carly returned the phone to the small table. There were no more tears to shed at the moment. She turned to Psalm 107, one of her favorite psalms of thanksgiving to God and a declaration of the Lord's ability to rescue people from a multitude of different kinds of troubles. Standing up, she declared the verses to earth and heaven in a loud voice.

Jon and Sarah were sitting in the living room waiting for Agent Burroughs to arrive. The agent had called to let them know he was on his way to pick up Mateo. Jon put the phone on speaker so Sarah could listen.

"Is Cesar Mendez safe?" Jon asked. "And Kelli Quinn, his lawyer?"

"They're in custody and on their way to the jail."

"Why are they in custody?"

"Their vehicles are inoperable."

"Shouldn't they be going to the hospital?"

"My understanding is that they weren't injured."

Whatever awaited Cesar and Kelli at the jail could be sorted out as more facts came to light.

"What about the members of the cartel?" Jon asked. "Should I be concerned about someone coming after me or Mateo Torres?"

"I can't answer that, but we'll formulate a plan once I arrive."

"What's your ETA?"

"My GPS says twenty-two minutes."

Jon hoped the agent would be receiving input from his superiors while in transit to the house. Giving people options wasn't typical for the FBI.

"Thank the Lord," Sarah said when the call ended. "That's wonderful about Cesar and Kelli. It sounds like she may have saved him. I hope she's been able to call her aunt."

"Yeah." Jon glanced outside. "I'll let Mateo know."

"You're on a first-name basis with this guy."

"I talked to him a few weeks ago. He claimed he could save us money with chemicals we need to manage pests. He had a supplier in Mexico. But it was probably the first step to using our orders as a way to smuggle drugs into the U.S. Then he was arrested—"

"That's enough, please," Sarah said, holding up one hand. "Go ahead. I'm going to text Carly Withers."

Jon went outside to Mateo and Diego. He told Diego that Cesar was safe. Diego covered his face with his hands. Jon turned to Mateo.

"An FBI agent is on the way to get you," he said. "No word yet on what happened in town."

"How long will it take him to get here?" Mateo asked anxiously.

"About twenty minutes."

They stood in silence for a few moments.

"What was it like for you when you agreed to cooperate?" Mateo asked. "How did they treat you?"

Jon turned to Diego, who was wiping away tears. "Sorry, but can you give us privacy again?"

Diego moved away. Jon waited.

"You do what they tell you to do," he said matter-of-factly. "The feds call the shots. They keep you in protective custody, which is lonely but better than the alternative. Do you have any close family? Wife? Kids? Parents or siblings?"

"My wife divorced me a few years ago. My kids are teenagers and stay with her. My parents live in west Texas. That's where most of my brothers and sisters are with their families."

"Your family connections are a lot more extensive than mine. I'm not sure how all that will be handled, but I doubt you'll see anyone for a while."

Mateo glanced down for a second before looking up.

"Is it worth it?" he asked.

Jon pointed to the house. "I love what I've built here, but I'm not sure what's going to happen to my wife and me. We're going to have a little boy in a few weeks."

"Diego told me your wife was pregnant. That's another thing that made me know this was my time to get out. I didn't want that on my plate."

It was a callous way for Mateo to describe killing Sarah, but Jon let it pass.

"Ending this is a relief but also scary," Mateo continued.

"I understand." Jon looked past him at the black truck. "Do you have a weapon in your vehicle?"

Mateo glanced up. "Yeah, several."

"But none on your person?"

"No," Mateo said, raising his hands again.

"The agent who's coming will want to inventory everything. Any contraband?"

"No, I haven't used drugs in years and stay away from liquor."

Jon started to ask Mateo some questions about his life but stopped. He didn't need to know and probably didn't want to know. Jon hoped they'd never meet again after tonight.

"The agent will put you in handcuffs for security reasons," Jon said.

"I'd expect that. Did they rough you up?"

"No. Like I said, they were professional but detached."

Mateo nodded. "Did you have to face any of the big bosses when you went to court?"

"Yes, but I don't want to go into that," Jon said, then stepped back a couple of feet. "I'm going to wait in the house."

Inside, Sarah was sitting on the sofa in the living room. She took a sip from a glass of water.

"What were you talking about with that guy?" she asked.

"Just telling him what to expect."

"Is he the one who put the bomb in my car?"

"He denies it. He knew you were pregnant, and that's one reason he decided to warn us and get out of the cartel. Once the FBI agent arrives, he'll take him away."

Jon saw Sarah shiver.

"A bomb," she said in disbelief.

"I know," Jon said. "We were close to death. You're probably in shock."

Sarah shivered again.

"Have you ever been close to death?" she asked.

Jon nodded. "Yes. But it's how close it was for you that's going to torment me. If I'd done something differently, maybe this wouldn't have happened."

"No, no," Sarah said softly as she shook her head. "That's not what I think."

Jon and Sarah sat together in the living room until the lights of a white sedan appeared. Jon tensed for a moment until he saw Agent Burroughs emerge. Mateo immediately held out his hands, and the agent placed him in handcuffs.

"That's it for now," Jon sighed. "I'll talk to Agent Burroughs once he has Mateo in the car."

CHAPTER 47

Kelli and Cesar sat beside each other in the waiting area for the jail. No one was paying attention to them. There was a lot of scurrying around with people coming and going and talking on their phones. Whatever was happening in Brunswick that night was a big deal. Several times multiple flashing lights appeared at the front of the building as cars made their way to what she guessed was the entrance for people under arrest. Cesar finished a second long conversation with Maria in Spanish on his cell phone.

"Is Maria okay?" she asked.

Cesar shrugged. "She's scared and worried until I'm home with her and the boys."

Kelli left Cesar and went to the window where a young female officer was on duty.

"Any update on when Mr. Mendez and I can leave?" she asked.

The woman was about to answer when a phone call came in. She held up her index finger to Kelli, who stepped back. It was a couple of minutes before the woman finished the call. Kelli repeated the question.

"Let me check with Detective Briscoe," she said.

Kelli returned to her place beside Cesar and gave him the news about Briscoe.

"Uh-oh," Cesar replied.

"Yeah," Kelli said in agreement. "He won't be in a hurry to do anything for us."

Five minutes passed, and the door to the lockup area opened. Detective Briscoe came over to them. Kelli started to stand, but he motioned for her to remain seated.

"First, thank you for what you did tonight," he said to Kelli. "It was very courageous. Lives could have been lost. It's the sort of thing that should receive recognition from the city and county, but I suspect you want to keep a low profile."

"Yes, including any notices given to the press. No mention of my name or Mr. Mendez would be much appreciated."

"I understand and will make sure that's the case."

"What about the charges against Mr. Mendez?"

"He's free to leave based on his bond. I'm sure the DA's office will be in touch with you about dismissal of the accusation. If you like, I can ask Mr. Davis to come out to see you. He's in the back where we're processing the people arrested."

"Don't bother him," Kelli replied. "We can talk later. I'd just like to go home and get to sleep."

"Understood. I'm here if you need me."

The detective left.

"Did you understand all that?" she asked Cesar.

"I think so."

Kelli explained the implications of the conversation. Her phone buzzed. It was Jon Tremaine.

"Where are you?" he asked when she answered.

"About to leave the jail."

"Is Cesar with you?"

"Yes."

"Tell him Mateo told an FBI agent that Cesar was being used as an unknowing accomplice for smuggling drugs. There were several other shipments involved."

"You give him the news," Kelli said and handed the phone to Cesar.

The conversation went back and forth in Spanish and obviously covered other topics. Cesar kept nodding. At one point, he raised his free hand to wipe away a tear. The call ended, and he returned the phone to Kelli.

"Diego is on his way to pick me up and take me home," he said.

Kelli knew that for her, getting a ride home at this time of night in Brunswick would take some time.

Diego got out of his truck and embraced Cesar. The two men stepped back, looked at each other, and hugged a second time.

"Jon said you were very brave tonight," Diego said to Kelli. "Not many lawyers would do what you did to help a client."

"It wasn't in my contract," she replied with a wry smile. "I'm thankful it worked out."

"Thankful" wasn't in Kelli's normal vocabulary, but she knew it fit. Her ride arrived. It was a compact electric vehicle. The driver, an older Latino man wearing a suit and tie, got out and with a flourish opened the door for her to get in. Kelli was silent during the ride home.

Inside the house, there was no sign of Carly downstairs, so Kelli tiptoed up the stairs. She hadn't realized how loudly a couple of the treads squeaked. A light was on in Carly's room. Fully dressed, her aunt was lying on her back in bed, her lips slightly apart. Kelli could hear the faintest sound of snoring. She spread a blanket over Carly, turned off the light, and left the room.

Carly woke up with a start. It took a couple of seconds for her to realize that Kelli must have come in and covered her up. She looked at the clock. It was 5:55 a.m. Even before she tried to move, Carly knew she was stiff and sore. She managed to get out of bed and take some medication. The night was too far gone to change into pajamas. Holding on to the wall for support, she made her way down the hallway to Kelli's room. In the dim predawn light, she could make out her niece's form in the bed. She looked unharmed and at peace. Carly slowly raised her right arm as high as she could in thankful acknowledgment of God's protection.

Carly took a warm shower and changed into different clothes. It was light outside, and the children would be waking up soon. She carefully closed the door to Kelli's room. Downstairs, Carly brewed a pot of coffee. As it finished, Max poked his head into the kitchen.

"I didn't see Mom's car out front," he said. "What time did she come home?"

"I don't know. I was asleep."

"Did everything go okay?"

"I think so. Don't wake her up. I can take you and Emma to school this morning. What would you like for breakfast?"

"Oatmeal, please. With all the stuff you can add."

Carly was stirring the pot on the stove when Emma appeared.

"Max told me not to bother Mom," she said. "But I need to pick out my outfit. I have three things on my bed. Can you help?"

Carly turned down the heat on the stove and followed Emma into the bedroom. The little girl had three options, all including pants with different shirts and multicolored socks. Nothing stood out to Carly.

"Can you tell me why you like each one?" she asked.

Emma happily chattered about the pros and cons of each ensemble. If the little girl chose not to follow in her mother's footsteps as an attorney, she could be a fashion consultant or designer. Carly pointed to the outfit in the middle.

"I like all of them, but I would select that today," she said. "It's going to be warm this afternoon, and you won't get hot in that."

Emma nodded. "That's my first choice."

"We're having oatmeal in a few minutes, and I'm going to drive you to school if your mother doesn't wake up. She got home late last night."

"Okay. If you're driving, we need to leave early. You don't go as fast as Mom."

"Yes, we should definitely leave a few minutes earlier."

They ate a quiet breakfast. There was still no sign of Kelli when they left the house. After Carly dropped the kids off at school, her phone vibrated.

"Are you taking the kids to school?" Kelli asked in a sleepy voice.

"Leaving the school now. I wanted you to get extra sleep."

"I needed it. Did you listen to the morning news on the radio?"

Carly would often tune in to a local station for news and weather.

"No."

"I'm curious if there was a news report about the arrests last night."

"I was busy cooking breakfast and helping Emma decide on her wardrobe."

"Thanks so much," Kelli said.

Carly called Jan Baldwin on the way home.

"I don't know any details," Carly said, "but Kelli was in danger. She wrecked her car and ended up at the jail. Not because she was in trouble, but because of everything that happened."

"Oh my. They mentioned on the news this morning about the arrest of some members of a drug ring. Was that it?"

"I think so. All I care about is that Kelli and everyone else is okay."

When Carly saw Kelli sitting in the kitchen drinking a cup of coffee, she burst into tears. All the pent-up emotion of the past twelve hours overflowed like a dam break. Kelli hurried over and embraced her. Carly leaned against Kelli's shoulder and sobbed.

"Sorry," Carly said, her voice shaking. "I'm so relieved that you're safe."

Kelli gently rubbed her back.

"Thank you, thank you," Kelli repeated.

Carly took a deep breath, and they parted. Kelli's eyes were dry.

"I'll probably cry later," Kelli said. "But for now I'm just relieved. Sit down. What can I get you?"

"Nothing," Carly replied as she sat at the table. "All I want to do is let my eyes celebrate seeing you."

Jon woke up before Sarah. He lay quietly in bed listening to her soft, steady breathing. It was a beautiful sound. Before going to sleep, he'd received a call from Agent Burroughs, who let him know that all the major members of the cartel had been arrested. The FBI arrived at the condo identified by Mateo moments before the group was about to scatter. Carlos Aguilar pulled a gun from a holster behind his back but was knocked to the ground by an officer and placed in handcuffs. Both of the Diaz brothers were apprehended without a problem. Margie Phillips was arrested as she fled the luxury apartment complex where she'd been living. Mateo was now in an undisclosed location. An agent was coming later in the day to remove the bomb from Sarah's vehicle. It had been a hugely successful operation.

But all the good news didn't answer the main question that remained for Jon and Sarah. What about their future? Lying on his back and staring at the ceiling, Jon knew it wasn't a decision that could be made easily. The people who might want him dead were now behind bars facing much bigger problems than revenge against someone who'd caused difficulty almost twenty years earlier. But the fact that Jon had helped send Pablo Diaz to prison remained. For that, Jon doubted there was a statute of limitations.

Sarah turned over on her side so that she faced him and opened her eyes. If listening to her breathe was the most beautiful sound in the world, seeing her eyes filled with soft morning love was the most beautiful sight in the world. Jon leaned over and kissed her.

"I guess you want your orange juice and breakfast," Sarah said, stretching out in the bed.

"Yes, my love."

Sarah closed her eyes for a moment and then opened them.

"What are you waiting for?" she asked. "Get to it. I'd like a mushroom-and-cheese omelet."

Jon slipped out of bed. He fed Betsy, who showed no sign of realizing how stressful the past twenty-four hours had been.

"I know the ancient wolf in you eats in a hurry," Jon said as he watched the dog gobble down her food. "But I wish you could savor your breakfast."

Betsy ignored him and stuck her mouth in her water bowl for a drink. While he brewed a pot of decaf for Sarah, Jon squeezed three oranges. Usually he only used two, but he felt like rewarding himself. He was carefully flipping Sarah's omelet in the skillet when she came into the kitchen.

"You know I like it a little crispy on at least one side," she said.

"Yes."

"Did you add salt?" she asked when he let it slip out of the skillet onto a plate.

"Yes, but not too much."

Sarah poured her coffee and sat at the table while Jon made an omelet for himself.

"This is perfect," she said after she took a bite. "Just like you."

Jon glanced over his shoulder. "Let me get my phone so I can record that for future use."

"No need. I mean you're perfect for me."

Jon finished preparing his omelet. He joined Sarah at the table. She was almost finished and ate the last bite.

"I want to tell you something before you ask," she said.

"What?" Jon asked as he focused on his food.

"Look at me," Sarah said.

Jon lowered his fork and met her gaze. Sarah spoke: "Never ask me whether I believe you did the right thing helping Cesar, even though it's turned our lives upside down. If you hadn't gotten involved, many people could have been terribly hurt or worse."

Jon hadn't eaten a bite of food, but he swallowed, his eyes moist.

"It was incredibly unselfish," Sarah continued. "And no matter what happens in the future, I'm going to do my best to remember that."

A muscle twitched in Jon's jaw as Sarah went on: "Remember what I'm saying now when the male protector part of yourself tries to blame you for compromising our security. That woman from your past who recognized you outside the hospital could have shown up even if you'd done nothing to help Cesar. It was always a risk."

"What do you want to do?" Jon asked, finding his voice. "Should I talk to Chris—"

"All I want to do is have a healthy baby boy and not name him Harold."

"I agree with that," Jon chuckled.

Later, as he was driving from one jobsite to another, Jon received a call on his regular cell phone. It was Chris Polter.

"I'm flying back to Savannah this afternoon," Chris said. "I received a briefing on the operation last night. Burroughs said he kept you in the loop."

"Yes."

"It was a home run. And this guy who's going to testify is the real deal. Burroughs believes he wouldn't have come forward when he did without knowing about you."

"That's good, but people knowing about me is a problem."

"I agree. If it's okay with you, let's get together and talk after I return."

"Sure. Sarah doesn't want to think about anything except having the baby."

"Having just been with my daughter, I couldn't agree more."

CHAPTER 48

Kelli drove Carly's car to the office. When she entered the reception area, Lauren greeted her with a wide-eyed expression on her face.

"What happened last night?" the receptionist asked. "Curt heard from a friend at the sheriff's department that you ended up at the jail."

"I did, but not because I was in trouble. And I'm not ready to talk about how I got there. I'm just thankful I'm okay, and it looks like all criminal charges are going to be dropped against Cesar Mendez."

"What can you tell me?" Lauren asked. "I'm about to explode with curiosity!"

Kelli hesitated. It wasn't fair to totally shut out the receptionist.

"Do you want something totally confidential or the version you can tell other people?" Kelli asked.

"When you put it that way, I guess something I can share."

"God was with me," Kelli said, then closed her mouth.

"That's it?"

"Yes."

Ann spoke from the entrance to the hallway that led to the offices.

"Which is the greatest gift someone could ask for," she said.

Kelli turned toward her friend, and the tears that failed to appear with Carly suddenly started to flow.

"Let's go to your office," Kelli managed.

Ann closed the door behind them.

"I'm not going to pry if you're not ready," she began.

"No, I think you're the one who is supposed to get the full download."

Sharing what happened brought back some of the anxiety and fear but also relief and gratitude for the outcome.

"Wow," Ann said when Kelli finished. "If you need to borrow a car, we can loan you one. Roy's mother in Miami gave it to him to sell for her, but there's no rush. She's already bought another one."

"What kind is it?"

"It's a big white Cadillac."

"I'm not sure the kids will want me to drive it to the school."

"It's available if you want it," Ann said. "Also, are you one hundred percent sure Matt Davis is going to drop all charges?"

"Maybe I should have talked to him last night when I was at the jail, but that's what the detective told us. I was so tired that all I wanted to do was go home and crawl into bed."

"Let me know if there's anything I can do to help, although I can't imagine what that might be."

Kelli was quiet for a second.

"I want to be more like you and my aunt Carly," she said.

An hour later, Kelli was sitting at her desk when Lauren buzzed her.

"Matt Davis is on the phone," she said. "Was he involved in what happened last night? A friend told me she saw the two of you sitting in the reception area of our office last night when she was driving home from a movie."

"Only briefly, and you don't need to ask me questions. It seems your friends are a treasure trove of information. Yes, put him through."

"Good morning," Matt said in a normal tone of voice. "I understand you walked the line between being a hero and facing a felony charge for obstructing a federal officer in the performance of his duties."

"I'm trying to keep everything quiet."

"I understand and will honor that request. I called to confirm that we'll be dismissing all state charges against Mr. Mendez. His bond will be canceled. I believe a property bond was posted by his boss."

"That's true. I'll notify Mr. Tremaine."

"Mr. Tremaine is an interesting man."

"Yes, he's done a lot more than a typical employer would do for an employee in trouble."

"Much more," Matt added.

"I'm not aware of anything else."

"He's a brave man. Take my word for it."

"Okay," Kelli responded slowly.

"And since I'm protecting your actions from public disclosure, I'd appreciate you keeping my interaction with Agent Perez confidential."

"I barely remember it already."

Kelli was prepared for the call to end, but Matt continued: "Oh, and I'm not going to forget about our oyster lunch. I'll call to set it up."

"I look forward to it."

A couple of weeks later, Jon sat in his truck with the door propped open and watched the work crew make their way across an open field. Betsy lay outside on the ground. The men were culling and fertilizing young seedlings. On the end of the line closest to Jon was Cesar. Someone said something to Cesar, and Jon could see a big smile on the recently exonerated man's face. There was nothing like the departure of guilt. Cesar could now appreciate freedom at a level impossible for someone who'd not faced a long prison sentence and gut-wrenching separation from family. Earlier that morning, he told Jon that he'd spoken at his church on Sunday morning.

"Talking in front of a crowd of people scares me more than a nest of rattlesnakes," Cesar said. "But when the first words came out of my mouth, it seemed like nothing could stop them."

"We're going to start calling him Cesar the Preacher," piped up Diego, who was standing nearby.

The events of the recent weeks brought back something for Jon that he'd not considered in a long time. Unlike Cesar, he was guilty of criminal conduct that damaged untold lives. But there was nothing Jon could do about it. It wasn't possible to erase the past. A reboot like the witness protection program offered a new beginning but not a clean slate. The best he could do was focus on loving Sarah, being a good boss to the men working in the field, and becoming a new father.

Jon and Sarah continued to put off the formal decision of whether to request new identities and relocation. But he knew what both of them wanted to do—stay on the tree farm and hope no one hated him enough to risk the consequences of seeking to harm them. That didn't mean they would talk openly about their status. Diego, who didn't fully understand what Mateo and Jon discussed, had already agreed not to mention anything, not even to Cesar. Chris confirmed that Jon's true identity would not appear in the FBI reports of the operations against the drug cartel. That left only the criminals in jail awaiting trial and sentencing as the people with any knowledge of Jason Favreau.

Jon's phone vibrated.

"I think it's time," Sarah said. "These contractions are nothing like what I've felt before. They're for real."

"I'm on my way."

Jon whistled for Betsy, who jumped into the truck. They sped off toward the house.

Eight hours later, Nathan Jon Tremaine uttered his first cry. At nine pounds, one ounce, he stood out in the nursery. Never had Jon respected a human being more than he did Sarah during labor and delivery. Both of them cried when the delivery nurse held up their son. Jon squeezed Sarah's hand for the hundredth time since their arrival at the hospital.

"You're amazing," he whispered in her ear. "And he's a big boy."

"You don't have to tell me he's big," Sarah managed. "I was planning on calling him 'Little Jon,' but now I'm not sure it fits."

"No," Jon replied. "He's going to be Nate and have his own name."

"That he never has to change."

Jon squeezed Sarah's hand for the one hundred and first time.

CHAPTER 49

SIX MONTHS LATER

Carly was humming as she worked in the kitchen. Her phone on the counter vibrated. It was Sarah Tremaine.

"What time do you want us to be there?" Sarah asked.

"Depends on the baby, doesn't it?"

"Yeah, he dictates the schedule. He's been taking a good nap in the afternoon this week and then stays awake until around eight o'clock."

"Is he sleeping through the night?"

"No," Sarah laughed. "But Jon is good about changing him and bringing him to me in bed."

"Will five o'clock work for you?" Carly asked. "Kelli's kids don't mind eating an early supper."

"Sounds great."

It was a Saturday in April, and the flowers that wintered beneath the sandy soil in Carly's yard had blossomed over the past few weeks into multicolored splendor. One of Emma's favorite pastimes was collecting flowers and bringing them into the house. With Carly's guidance, the little girl was an increasingly accomplished floral arranger. Her most recent creation stood in the center of the dining room table. Kelli joined Carly in the kitchen. Carly told her about the dinner schedule.

"Make sure we send the flowers home with Sarah," Kelli said. "I transferred them to a vase I bought for her. And are you sure they like shrimp and crab? That's in almost everything we're serving except dessert."

"That's what Sarah told me. She also said Jon likes crawfish, but I don't think we can convince the kids to eat them."

"Or me," Kelli replied.

Shortly before 5:00 p.m., Max entered the kitchen. To Kelli, it seemed her son had grown two inches since they'd arrived in Brunswick. But the growth inside was even more spectacular. There were times when Kelli was around him and felt inspired. Max was one of the best listeners she knew, and when he heard something wise, he recognized it. He'd spent an extra week with his father over Christmas break, and Brad commented how mature Max seemed. Kelli didn't point out that Coach Matthews and Roy Carter were investing time with Max. However, Max also gave hints of teenage independence that wasn't far over the horizon.

"They'll be here soon," Kelli said to her son.

"You're not going to ask me to babysit, are you?" he asked.

Emma entered the room and heard Max's last comment.

"I will," Emma volunteered. "I'm not afraid of babies. How old is he?"

"Nate is about six or seven months."

"That's a good age," Emma noted. "They can mostly sit up and don't flop all over the place."

Kelli was impressed.

"Your mom was talking at six months," Carly interjected. "Or at least she thought she was. We couldn't understand a word she said."

"Is that true?" Emma asked skeptically.

"Aunt Carly isn't usually a liar," Kelli replied.

The kids went into the living room. Kelli and Carly finished preparing a Mediterranean shrimp salad and a shrimp-and-crab étouffée. They had a generous amount of shrimp to boil in water seasoned with Old Bay. They knew the kids would eat boiled shrimp even if they had to peel them.

Jon and Sarah pulled onto Union Street. Jon was familiar with the older neighborhood but had never been in one of the houses. Nate was buckled into his infant seat in the back seat of the truck with a pacifier in his mouth. When Jon stopped for a red light, he could hear Nate sucking on the pacifier. Everything about the little fellow was strong.

"When was the last time you talked to Kelli?" Sarah asked.

"About two weeks ago. She and Ann are handling our domestic and international contracts with purchasers. It's saving us quite a bit from what we were paying the law firm in Atlanta."

The light turned green.

"You need to invite Max back to the farm," Sarah said.

"Yeah, he had a blast on the four-wheeler."

They reached the house. Sarah held Nate in her arms. The baby was wearing a sea-creature-inspired outfit in honor of the meal. Jon was tasked with transporting everything else.

"I still believe we should have let him handle some shrimp so he would be ready for the meal," Jon said.

"After what he's been putting in his mouth the past week, he would have thought it was sushi," Sarah said.

"You're going to have to ring the doorbell," Jon said, his hands full.

Max opened the door.

"Hey, Mr. and Mrs. Tremaine," he said in a pleasant voice. "Come in."

"Nice manners," Sarah said over her shoulder as they followed Max into the house.

They went into a large, open kitchen. Jon knew Sarah had visited Carly several times over the past few months, but this was the first time he'd been to the house. He winced when he saw the older woman's misshapen fingers. Sarah had mentioned the presence of rheumatoid arthritis, but seeing the devastating impact made it real. He delivered a bowl of freshly cut fruit to Kelli. Emma stepped close to Nate.

"He's a healthy-looking baby," the little girl observed. "Are you giving him formula or breast milk?"

"Emma!" Kelli said from where she was working at one of the kitchen counters.

"It's fine," Sarah replied. "He gets breast milk, but we've given him a few tastes of solid food this week. He likes to hold the spoon."

"Are you going to give him any solid food tonight? I could help."

"Okay." Sarah smiled.

Max spoke up: "Mr. Tremaine, would you like to see my LEGO collection?"

"Sure. I used to build sets when I was your age."

Max led Jon across the foyer and down the hallway into a bedroom. There were at least twenty to twenty-five completed LEGO sets and a couple more under construction. Max had an eclectic collection, from movie themes to vehicles and buildings. There was one Star Wars kit that Jon remembered building when he was a boy.

"Here's a four-wheeler," Max said, picking up the plastic ATV. "I got it after coming to the tree farm."

"Would you like to come back and ride?" Jon asked. "I bought a new one a few weeks ago. It's fast."

"Yes!" Max responded enthusiastically.

"We'll make that happen."

They returned to the kitchen.

Dinner was served in a small dining room that was filled up by a table with seating for ten. Jon sat between Sarah and Max. Nate was in an ancient high chair retrieved from a remote cranny of the house.

"It's been a while since we had a meal in here," Carly said as everyone settled into a chair.

"I want some of the kiwi in that bowl," Emma said, reaching for the spoon in the fruit.

"You'll get first chance to pick," Kelli replied. "As soon as Aunt Carly says a prayer."

Carly bowed her head. Jon did the same. The older woman thanked God for the food and added a request that the Lord especially bless baby Nate.

"Thank you," Sarah said. "I've been praying for him every night since he was born."

Jon knew Sarah prayed but not that consistently. He absorbed this bit of news as the food bowls made their way around the table. The salad and the étouffée were exceptional and occupied his attention for several minutes.

With prompting from Sarah, Carly proceeded to talk about her life. Jon couldn't deny that the older woman exuded refreshing honesty. To her, God was like a good friend.

"Carly has been an inspiration to me and helped me come out of the shadows of the past," Kelli added.

"It's been a wonderful journey to watch," Carly said with a smile.

"That's beautiful," Sarah replied, rubbing her arms. "It gives me goose bumps."

The last time Jon had goose bumps was when he was caught out in twenty-degree weather with only a windbreaker to keep him warm. Dinner concluded with a peach cobbler made with fruit Carly had canned the previous summer.

"Canned fruit makes the best pies," Carly said when Sarah complimented her.

Jon checked his watch. They were trying to keep Nate on a schedule. It was time to leave for home, but he could tell Sarah wasn't ready to go. Thirty minutes later, they were finally in the truck with Nate securely fastened in his seat.

"That was different than I expected," Jon said as they backed out of the driveway.

"How?"

"The conversation around the table. Listening to Kelli's aunt, I can understand why you've been drawn to her."

"What did you think about what she and Kelli said?"

"Which part?"

"About knowing the Lord and coming out of the shadows of the past."

Jon chuckled. "I see where you're going with this."

"Is that okay with you?"

They rode in silence for a couple of minutes. Jon had to admit that he'd been intrigued when Carly Withers described her relationship with God. She was a woman in pain who nevertheless exuded a sense of joy that defied her circumstances.

"Yes," he said.

"What?" Sarah asked.

"I'm willing to consider what Carly and Kelli said about coming out of the shadows of the past. But only if I can do it with you."

Sarah leaned over and kissed him on the cheek.

"Always," she replied.

ACKNOWLEDGMENTS

Working with Becky Monds, Deborah Wiseman, Jacob Whitlow, and Chris Pfohl greatly improved this story. Your insights and suggestions are much appreciated! Special thanks to my wife, Kathy, who knows like no one else how to come alongside me in the creative process.

DISCUSSION QUESTIONS

1. Jon Tremaine lives with the burden of a hidden past and is part of the witness protection program. How does secrecy shape his character, relationships, and decisions? Do you think he ever truly escapes his past?
2. Kelli Quinn faces major life changes—divorce, a new job, and relocating her family. How does her struggle with identity and purpose parallel Jon's?
3. How does faith influence the choices of characters like Carly, Kelli, and Jon? Did any moment of faith feel especially moving or thought-provoking to you?
4. Jon's marriage is built on trust, while Kelli is trying to rebuild after betrayal. How does the book contrast different kinds of marriages and families under stress?
5. Jon is very involved in the case against Cesar, even to the point of putting his own protection at risk. Why do you think he risked so much for Cesar?
6. Carly anoints her home with oil and prays over Kelli and the children. How does this act of faith represent

protection in contrast to Jon's government-assigned protection?

7. The author often uses the rural Georgia setting, especially the tree farm, as a backdrop. What does this setting symbolize for the characters? How does it contrast with the urban dangers and pasts they are trying to escape?
8. Think about the supporting characters like Cesar, Maria, and even the children, Max and Emma. Which secondary character's journey did you find most compelling, and what did they add to the main story?
9. Suspense is a key element of the plot. Was there a specific moment or plot twist that caught you by surprise? How did the author build tension throughout the book?
10. The ending leaves the characters in new phases of their lives. Do you believe true redemption and a completely fresh start are possible for someone with Jon's history? What do you think happens next for these families?

ABOUT THE AUTHOR

Photo by David Whitlow, Two Cents Photography

Robert Whitlow is the bestselling author of legal novels set in the South and winner of the Christy Award for Contemporary Fiction for *The Trial*. He received his JD with honors from the University of Georgia School of Law, where he served on the staff of the *Georgia Law Review*.

Website: robertwhitlow.com
X: @whitlowwriter
Facebook: @robertwhitlowbooks

ALSO AVAILABLE FROM ROBERT WHITLOW

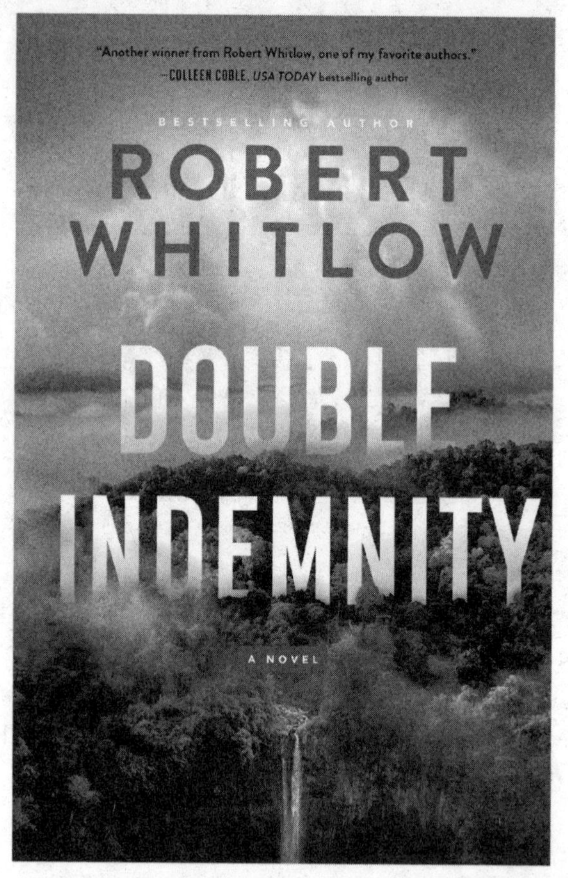

"*Double Indemnity* is another winner from Robert Whitlow, one of my favorite authors. The taut suspense builds until the likable pastor is falsely accused of murder, and his new girlfriend, an attorney, has to solve the case. Highly recommended!"

—Colleen Coble, *USA TODAY* bestselling author of *The View from Rainshadow Bay* and the Annie Pederson series

AVAILABLE IN PRINT, E-BOOK, AND AUDIO DOWNLOAD